THE BROTHERS LUNA

Madmen or Geniuses

Jules Delgallego

JDR Publishing
San Diego, CA

Printed by CreateSpace, Charleston, SC
www.createspace.com/1767883

ISBN-10: 1494791269
ISBN-13: 978-1494791261

To my wife and children,
for their support during this process.

HOLA MELISSA Y RAFFY!
HOPE YOU ENJOY THIS FIRST
EDITION OF MY BOOK. MUCHAS
GRACIAS AMIGOS FOR YOUR
SUPPORT ~~AND~~ COOPERATION IN
THE COMPLETION OF THE BROTHERS
LUNA. WARMEST REGARDS.
3/20/2014

Author's Note

The Brothers Luna is a novel that is based heavily on historical facts about the lives of two brothers: Juan and Antonio Luna. These young men—who experienced and achieved so much for their country—were only in their twenties for most of the time they were in Europe. Thus, the attempt to penetrate their inner souls and bring context to the specifics of their lives by focusing on their years abroad and return to their motherland, their romantic love interests, personal glory and tragedy, incarceration, sea voyage, friendship with the national hero of the Philippines, and their role in the Spanish-American War and the Philippine American War. Consequently, no one can say for sure what motivated them to make the personal and political decisions that shaped who they were, and in the end, created the legacy they left.

Their accomplishments deserve a greater audience beyond their own borders, which was the motivation to write a semi-fictional account of their lives and of the major historical events in which they were directly involved.

The author wishes to emphasize that this is, above all, a novel. Conversations with the fictional characters, and many of the internal motivations laid out in the novel that drive historically known decisions are the product of the author's imagination. All characters other than the well-known historical figures that inhabit these pages are fictional. Any resemblance to any other person, either living or dead, is entirely coincidental. But when facts are in dispute, the author also makes up his own mind based on the evidence, as he understands it. When there is a gap in the historical record, he invents, as a novelist should, a fiction that accounts for the known facts.

Historical facts intertwined with a compelling story based on his Filipino heritage, years of tedious research, and his travels to all the many locations the brothers Luna visited guarantee you will enjoy this novel.

INTRODUCTION

Spain ruled the Philippines—which was the farthest and what became their last frontier—almost continuously from 1521 until the end of the Spanish-American War in 1898. Prior to the 16th century, the Spanish East Indies ruled as part of the Viceroyalty of New Spain and administered from Mexico City, their most important territorial possession due to its proximity to the islands and success of the Galleon Trade.

In its heyday, Spanish merchant ships sailed once or twice yearly across the Pacific Ocean between Manila and Acapulco and continued until the Mexican War of Independence against Spain ended the alliance. The trade route allowed for the easy access of Spanish friars into the Philippines, which included the small island of Guam for the purposes of bringing Christianity to their only Asian colony.

In the middle part of the nineteenth century, the Philippines, and Manila in particular, experienced a cultural revolution. A critical issue was education for the poor masses known as Indios—a name given to Filipinos by the ruling Spaniards.

While the push for Christianity presented its own set of problems for the Filipinos regarding culture and traditions, the Spanish missionaries believed in education. Thus, upon reaching the islands, and wherever they penetrated, church and school went together. As a result, in1863, the Spanish authorities implemented an Educational Royal Decree that provided a normal school for men, as well as elementary public school systems throughout the islands for the purpose of educating all Indios. The drive to improve academics extended to the construction of schools, universities, and even hospitals throughout the archipelago.

The Royal Decree marked the end of one era and the beginning of another in the history of education in the Philippines. Whereas in the past, only students with pure Spanish blood and in some cases "*mestizos*" from the elite were being fully educated, the native Filipino children were now also going to school. By the time the United States became the colonial power, the Filipinos were the most educated subjects in all of Asia.

This one piece of legislation led to an important class of learned Filipinos who at times were still being referred to as Indios by the Spaniards. Apolinario Mabini, a leader in the Philippine quest for freedom wrote regarding the state of education:

"If the Spanish were to maintain their domination they had to perpetuate the ignorance and weakness of the Indio. Since science and wealth signify strength it is the poor and ignorant who is weak. However, it was deemed indispensable to give the Indio some religious education in order prevent him from reverting to his ancient superstitions. It was the kind of education that was meant to accustom him to keep his eyes fixed on heaven so that he would neglect the things of this world. The Indio was to know how to read his prayers and the lives of the saints which were translated into their native dialects; but it was deemed necessary that he should not know any Spanish, for if and when he would come to understand the laws and orders of the authorities, he would cease to consult the friar curate. He was not supposed to read dangerous books, and thus these books coming from abroad or published locally had to pass a rigorous censorship controlled by ecclesiastical authorities ... in

brief, the Spanish government, in collusion with the friars, succeeded in isolating the Filipinos, both intellectually and physically, to prevent the Filipinos from receiving any impression except that thought expedient for them to have."

If Mabini was on target in his assessment of education for Filipinos before 1863, did the Spanish authorities blunder in implementing the royal decree? Were the Spanish friars right after all, that "*friarcracia*," their influence and power to control the Indios, would cease to exist once the native Filipinos became educated?

One way to understand the consequences of the educational revolution of 1863 is to examine the lives and short careers of three men who were products of their time: the brothers Juan and Antonio Luna and their good friend José Rizal. Their propaganda movement incited patriotism and exacted reforms that culminated in a rebellion against Spain, and eventually led to a revolution against a new foreign invader, the United States. As freedom fighters, the story behind these beloved sons of the Philippines will be of interest to any global community in which human rights is a core value.

PROLOGUE

Rue Pergolese, Paris
September 1892

In a traditional Hausemann-style terrace home popular in Paris during the nineteenth century, lived Juan Luna—a well-known painter in Spain. Villa Dupont, as the Luna home was called, was close to a number of bistros, cafes, and shops along the rue where he entertained friends and family. Although he had a lucrative career as an artist, the money he made did not cover the cost of residing in such a prestigious neighborhood with his five-year-old son Andres and the glamorous and extravagant existence of his wife, Maria Paz.

Not wanting to compromise his lifestyle, Juan Luna humbled himself and bade his rich mother-in-law, Juliana Pardo, to move in with his family and share the expenses. She accepted his invitation. However, from the onset of her arrival into the household, she caused disorder and exacerbated the tension between her daughter and Juan Luna.

Juan Luna realized rather quickly the dreadful mistake he had made. Now with her mother to help care for Andres, Maria Paz spent even more time away from home shopping and lunching out with her friends. Juliana Pardo was unkind to Juan Luna, thinking he was a failure for not supporting Maria Paz in the manner she desired.

Such were the circumstances on Thursday, September 22, when Juan Luna rose from bed already with thoughts of telling his mother-in-law she had to leave. Whatever he had on his mind, outwardly the day seemed to start no differently from any typical day along the Rue Pergolese. Children played the latest craze in Paris—Boules, a game that originated in Italy and was known to Italians as Bocce balls. Café owners opened their businesses for breakfast, and served freshly baked croissants and a variety of crepes. The aroma of freshly brewed French coffee attracted the early rising clientele on their way to work.

A skinny neighbor with a trimmed mustache tended to his bed of roses along the short steps leading to the entry of his house on Rue Pergolese. With casual curiosity, he surveyed three men who were having breakfast at a café facing the townhouses and wondered why he had never seen them before.

And then suddenly, the serenity and peaceful environment ceased, and everyone stopped what they were doing when screams for help were heard from the upstairs bathroom window of Villa Dupont.

Stunned, the neighbor dropped his shears and watched as the three men ran across the street and rushed inside the unlocked entry of the villa. Their attempt to abort a tragedy was futile. They were barely up the stairs when they heard a single gunshot. There was a loud ruckus of angry voices followed by three more shots fired in rapid succession.

Finally getting his wits about him, the neighbor summoned the police as a mob of curious onlookers assembled. But no one approached the man on the floor of the front porch leaning against the wall. Blood seeped through his shirt below his heart.

The police pushed their way through the crowd.

"I heard a number of pistol shots from inside the unit," the neighbor said to the police. "Be careful."

Although weak, the man on the porch identified himself as Felix Pardo. "My brother-in-law Juan Luna shot me in the chest." He began to sob. "He may have harmed my sister and mother."

"Who else is up there?" The police inspector asked.

Through his tears, Felix said, "Our family lawyer and my brother, Trinidad."

"Stay calm. The doctor will be here shortly," the police inspector said and then instructed one of his men to press a cloth against the man's wound.

The inspector motioned for his other officers to accompany him to the second floor where they heard voices raging in Spanish.

"Police! We're coming in," the inspector announced loud and clear.

Upon entering, the police spotted two women lying in their own blood, both with gunshots to the head. After checking their pulses, the police inspector discovered the older woman was dead. The younger one was unconscious, but still alive.

"Get a stretcher up here as soon as the doctor arrives." The inspector signaled for the officer nearest him to stay with the young woman.

A tall, bearded man, his eyes wet from crying, moved closer to the woman. He spoke softly to her in Spanish.

Another man isolated himself on the opposite end of the room. He knelt on the floor and cried out. "I am sorry. Please forgive me."

Beside him was a young boy also crying for his mama and grandma.

"I am Inspector Legrand, *certains d'entre vous parlent Français*?"

"We all get by in French." A man dressed in a white suit of fine fabric responded in that same language.

"I am French," the maid said. She held the revolver by the trigger with two fingers and let it dangle upside down as she extended it gingerly to the inspector.

"What is your name," Inspector Legrand asked.

"Brigitte Blanc."

Legrand recognized the revolver to be an 11 mm, Chamelot Deluigne model 1873. "Where did you get this from, Mademoiselle Blanc?"

"Monsieur Luna gave it to me after he shot Madame Juliana and Madam Maria Paz," Brigitte said.

At this point, a policeman called the attention of the inspector to the bathroom and indicated blood on the bathroom floor, the walls, and the vanity sink. "The crime may have been committed in this room and the bodies moved to the bed."

"Can someone tell me who did this and what happened here?" The inspector asked.

"I can," the man in the white suit said. "My name is Antonio Regidor. I am the family lawyer for the victims. I came here early this morning to settle the impending separation of Mr. Juan Luna—" Regidor pointed to the man on the floor—"and his wife, Maria Paz Luna" He motioned to the almost lifeless body of the young woman on the bed. "During the discussions, Juan Luna became suddenly violent and kicked us out of the house so we went across the street to the café."

"What happened next?" The inspector asked.

"We were discussing what to do about the situation when we heard screams coming from the house. That's when we ran back. We only started up the stairs when Juan Luna shot his brother-in-law. The little boy crying is their only son, Andres Luna. The man leaning toward his younger sister is Trinidad Pardo."

Inspector Legrand walked towards the man on the floor. "What is your name?"

"My name is Juan Luna."

"Monsieur Luna, I want you to answer truthfully. As accused, you do not deny that you are responsible for shooting all three victims with this revolver?"

"Yes, it is true," he said and kept his head lowered. "I went crazy. My wife was going to leave and take away my son. I was going to lose everyone, my precious ones."

Juan Luna pulled himself up, looking quite frail as the inspector ordered two policemen to apprehend him. The taller man on the other side of the room sporting a full beard shouted back, "That is a big lie. He shot my sister out of jealousy. He thought she was having an affair with another man. But it is not true. My sister was always true to him. This man is crazy and a murderer."

The doctor arrived finally. While walking down the stairs to be taken to the nearest police station, Juan Luna stopped when he saw his good friend and brother-in-law in the entry foyer.

"I am sorry Felix," Juan Luna moaned. "I did not mean to harm anyone and don't know what came over me. I completely went out of my mind! Please forgive me," he begged as the police dragged Juan Luna out into the street. They had to push through the much larger crowd that milled along Rue Pergolese in the hopes of hearing the newest information about the murders.

From the onset, Antonio Luna made it a point to visit his older brother in jail. At the close of the first week, Antonio brought along a columnist from one of Spain's liberal periodicals, interested in writing an article on the life of Juan Luna and his family.

"*Hola* Juan, how are you doing this morning?" Antonio greeted his brother, who still seemed dazed by his imprisonment.

"I am not well and don't know how I am going to get through my time here," Juan said.

"I have great news that will cheer you up," Antonio announced."

"Maria Paz is still in the hospital in critical care but is under the watchful eye of her doctors. Although still in a coma, everyone is praying for her recovery."

Juan Luna looked at his brother and nodded. "I am praying, too."

"Juan, I brought someone with me today. He is Don Adriano Gomez, a freelance writer from Madrid's *Diario Imparcial*. He believes he can help with your case. "Señor Gomez, this is my brother, Juan."

Juan studied the handsome young gentleman in front of him. He was tall, and dressed in a light suit, clothing that seemed to authenticate the writer's confidence and energy.

"It is a great honor and pleasure to finally meet you, Señor Luna. I had a chance to view two of your famous works: the majestic *La Spoliarium* on display at the Diputacion Provincial de Barcelona and the *Battle of Lepanto* now hanging side by side with Spanish artist, Pradilla's painting, the *Surrender at Granada* on a center wall of the Spanish Cortez."

Juan Luna remained stoic and silent as his brother Antonio prodded the columnist to continue talking.

"Señor Luna, I hope you don't mind if I call you Juan? I heard from friends inside the Palacio Real that the Queen Regent Maria Cristina is very much concerned for your well-being. She is very influential among the politicians and judges here in France. There is a slight chance she might be able to obtain your freedom."

Juan Luna began to blink nervously at hearing this latest revelation. He remained unspeaking, but the way he cocked his head toward Don Adriano showed his acute interest.

Señor Gomez spoke in the first person plural, an indication of his support. "We need public opinion on our side. In order to achieve our goal, we need to demonstrate to the French and all of Europe that you are not the monstrous killer the prosecution will portray you to be. We need to show you as the loving father to your only son, Andres. But also, and perhaps more importantly, we need to stress your talent as a great artist who has so much more to contribute to society."

"What do you want of me?" Juan Luna asked.

"Very simply, tell me the story of your life and the accomplishments of your family." Señor Gomez looked at Antonio. "I would also like to hear from you, Antonio, please feel free to interject."

"Of course, anything," Antonio said. He sat on the single bed in jail, a hanging hammock that was attached to opposite walls in the cell.

"Señor Gomez, if you want you may sit on the table," Antonio answered.

"Oh, thank you," Don Adriano said.

Juan Luna's desire to hug his only son one more time, and to tell him how sorry he was, filled his head. Thus, in a very sad tone he said, "Ah, my life story and accomplishments—the last time someone asked me to relate anything personal seemed ages ago when I was a student in a Jesuit school in Manila."

PART I

CHAPTER 1

In 1859, within the Walled City of Intramuros in Calle Arzobispo, the *Escuela Municipal de Manila* became the *Ateneo Municipal de Manila* when it was elevated to an institution of secondary education. The city of Manila handed control of the institution over to the Jesuit priests who were members of the Society of Jesus and respected for their roles as educators compared to the powerful and politically influential Dominican friars.

The priests and lay instructors occupied the third floor of the school for their dormitory, and allotted the first and second floors for classrooms. Consequently, there was a lot of interaction between the priests and students after school hours. Oftentimes, Juan Luna could be seen in conversation with one or more of his instructors. He was bright and studied hard.

So it was in the summer of 1873 that a young Father José Vilaclara sat behind a high standing desk that had the appearance of a judge's seat inside a courtroom. He called Juan Luna's graduating class to attention. "Today, I would like you to get to know more about each other before you leave this school and cease to hear from each other. I would like you to recite in front of the class…"

Father Vilaclara was interrupted by murmurs of objection from students.

A Spanish student stood up. "Padre Vilaclara, why, it's the last day of school and we are graduating this week. What is this all about?"

The pure blooded Spaniards seemed to protest regularly as compared to their Filipino counterparts whenever a priest instructed them to accomplish a task that was not in keeping with the curriculum.

"What is this all about?" The priest repeated his question to make a point. "This has to do with the reaffirmation of our undying friendships as *Ateneans*. It is about a renewal of who we are and who we will be." He paused as if letting the students absorb what he was saying.

The priest continued. "I want to hear what you have learned and accomplished in your years here at *Ateneo*. This is about sharing each of your individual life experiences. In this way, I hope you can teach, refresh, and reinvigorate each other…" he pointed to the door of the classroom, "… as you step over the threshold for the last time this afternoon."

Several of the students rolled their eyes at the priest.

"I expect your full cooperation. Remember, I have not submitted your final grades in Philosophy yet, and your participation with this project might very well change your average for the better or for the worse."

This time when Father Vilaclara looked around the classroom, he was met with expressions of approval. "All right, let us begin. As I call your name, I want you to tell us about your family, and your ambitions for the future."

Father Vilaclara summoned one student at a time in alphabetical order according to their surnames.

Juan Luna sighed in relief as his started with the letter "L," which meant he had more time to prepare for his presentation. He wanted to make himself respectable in front of his peers. Growing up in his Binondo neighborhood and having inherited heavy Malaysian features from his father made him reserved when dealing with the public, especially with the elite Spaniards. At times, he wished he looked more like his older brother, Manuel, who had the appearance of a mestizo. On the other hand, Juan's reclusive personality made him spend more time studying the arts, and in particular, painting. Even at his young age, he already displayed amazing talent.

"Luna, Juan it's your turn. Please come forward," Father Vilaclara called out.

Juan Luna walked slowly toward the front of the class knowing all eyes were on him. Like his peers, he wore the school uniform, which consisted of light grey cotton pants, a black coat and tie, and a starched white shirt.

Normally shy, Juan's posture stiffened. His face seemed utterly blank at first, mouth drawn, cutting a thin line across his face. He took a deep breath and began. "My father, Don Joaquin Luna is a respectable businessman from Badoc, Ilocos Norte and my mother is a Spanish *mestiza*, Doña Laureana Novicio from the northern province of La Union. They met, fell in love, and married, and my mother gave birth to seven children. My siblings are Manuel, José, Joaquin, Antonio, Numeriana, and Remedios."

There was a soft, but unmistakable slight local accent in the way Juan Luna spoke perfect Spanish. He cleared his throat and continued. "I was born on October 23, 1857 and was named Juan in honor of Saint John the Baptist. In 1861, my father, Don Joaquin, decided to move the family into the highly populated Binondo commercial district in order to expand his business."

He tilted his head and peered at Father Vilaclara from an odd angle, apparently trying to see if he approved of his presentation, and to direct his message of appreciation. "I am thankful to *Ateneo* for making me understand the importance of learning and mastering the Spanish language or I wouldn't have been able to express myself well today. I also learned and excel at the art of fencing. But my most important accomplishment and what I take most pride in, is the acknowledgment and inspiration I received from my instructors regarding my skill in the creative forms of painting and sculpture."

"My plan for the future is to further my artistic studies and to be very famous some day." A wide smile crossed Juan Luna's face when he said, "I plan to attend the prestigious university in Madrid."

Father Vilaclara began to applaud and encouraged the students to join in. "Well done, Juan. You have great fortitude, and I believe that you will achieve whatever you set you mind to, including being preeminent in the arts."

Several days later, Juan Luna graduated from Ateneo Municipal de Manila. Knowing that his father could not afford to pay for his studies in Spain, but determined not to abandon his dream of becoming a famous painter, Juan Luna devised a plan to earn the tuition himself. He and his brother, Manuel enrolled at Escuela Nautica, where they obtained certificates as pilots of the high seas, third class. As mariners, they traveled to many ports including Hong Kong, Amoy, Singapore, Colombo, and Batavia.

Juan Luna maintained his position as a seaman for five years. In the interim, he took drawing lessons in Manila from the illustrious painter and teacher, Lorenzo Guerrero. He later enrolled in Academia de Dibujo y Pintura (The Academy of Fine Arts), and in Manila where he became the student of Spanish artist Agustin Saez.

CHAPTER 2

During the years that Juan Luna traveled the high seas, his younger brother Antonio stayed at home. Being the last child—and nine years younger than Juan—their mother had time to tutor her son. By the age of five, Antonio was already learning how to read, write, and master *basi*c arithmetic.

The Luna family lived in a stone house on Calle Urbiztondo near the corner of Elcano and not far from the Binondo Church. The structure rose from the ground with gables to carry the weight of the expansive second floor. The entire frontage of the upper landing had wooden window coverings made of small-squared capiz shells, which were protected from the sun and the rain by cantilevered eaves.

During the long, humid summers, the windows remained open to cool the interior of the house. The exposure also allowed an unobstructed view of the street below, a feature that kept family and friends entertained watching the passing religious processions and town fiestas. Like most children in the neighborhood, Antonio spent most of his time after school in the commercial streets of Binondo.

"Antonio, Antonio my love," his mother called from her bedroom window. "It's time to learn your catechism." Doña Laureana heard children playing outside on the street below but did not see her son until she scanned the area and found him engaged in a make-believe sword fight with several neighborhood boys.

"Antonio, come on, it is getting late. You can come out again after your lessons."

"Mother dear, I've been reciting the catechism from memory for almost a year now," Antonio said.

"I know, but it's crucial not to forget the importance of such a little book. Besides, you still have other homework to complete."

"Yes," Antonio said to his mother and then ran toward his house looking over his shoulder at his friends, "Don't go home yet and you will see, I'll be back in a blink of an eye."

Antonio finished his assignments as quickly as he had predicted. He was about to dash outside when his mother stopped him.

"Where are you going so fast? There is more you need to do," she said and with her hand on his shoulder, she pushed him down on the seat.

"No Mother, here is my Spanish vocabulary and my math problems all complete," he said and slid his school folder toward her to inspect.

Doña Laureana smiled at her son. "There are lessons about life that only a mother can teach you. You are my youngest child and very special to me. So don't think my extra attention is out of meanness."

Antonio nodded. "What do you want me to know?"

"As you grow older, you will have to face many different kinds of challenges—physical, financial, emotional, spiritual…others as well, all of which manifest in various forms. What I want you to understand is not to let your problems overcome you. You have to be brave and forceful when your adversaries confront you." Doña Laureana made a swashbuckling gesture with her arms. "If someone challenges you with a sword or pistol, so be it, as long as you are on the side of justice. And if you believe that you have to attack so as not to be on the defensive, that's fine too."

"I am very tough at school, and in the neighborhood. My friends even say that I am a bully."

"Son, being tough, as you call it, is not about domineering your friends. A bully is someone who hurts another person intentionally. Rather, you need to be strong like your Papa. And resilient so that you do you do not break apart under strain."

"Papa is never weak," Antonio said with pride.

"That's right, my dear son, because being strong means that you stand up for yourself, but also, that you take risks and are man enough to admit your mistakes. And in everything you do, remember always to be sensitive, especially with family and friends."

"What do you mean, mother?" Antonio asked.

"You are sensitive already, Son. You have a kind heart and love comes easy for you. See how much you love me and Papa, your sisters and brothers."

"So I can be both tough and kind? Sounds strange to say together," Antonio said, and wrinkled his nose in puzzlement.

Doña Laureana was about to explain further when she heard Antonio's friends yelling for him.

"Antonio, Antonio! It is getting dark and there will be no more time for us to play."

Antonio jumped up from his chair and shouted back, "Hey, wait for me guys. I am on my way out." He grabbed his wooden sword, and as he started to bolt out of the room, his mother grabbed him.

"Wait, give your dear mother a big hug."

Antonio squeezed her tightly. "I love you very much, Mother." And then he ran to join his friends.

Antonio matured in the manner his mother had coached him. He was advanced for his age and very dedicated to his studies at the Ateneo Municipal de Manila where he received his Bachelor of Arts degree in 1881 at the age of fifteen. Like his older brothers, Antonio excelled at fencing and marksmanship, to the point that his reputation for toughness and bravery captured the attention of people who knew him with a mixture of admiration and fear.

CHAPTER 3

While Antonio forged ahead successfully with his studies, Juan Luna did not perform well at The Academy of Fine Arts. His instructors criticized his use of vigorous brush strokes and encouraged Juan to forego his art, and instead sharpen his skills as a sailor. He was so distressed that he sought the advice of his former mentor, Lorenzo Guerrero.

"I am being released from the academy," Juan Luna said. "They believe I am not good enough. But I love to paint. What shall I do?"

"I can make time to teach you again," Guerrero said. "But you need more than what I can offer. I think it is time that you go back to your original plan and study in Europe where you will be exposed to many various styles, forms, and techniques from the finest artists in the world.

"But am I ready?" Juan Luna asked, unsure of his own talent. "Am I good enough?"

"Juan, I believe you have the talent or I would not waste my time on you. You deserve to get the best education that you can at the Academia de *Bellas Artes* de San Fernando in Madrid."

Juan Luna felt a sudden surge of confidence and cried out, "You are right! Who cares what anyone thinks of me here. What count the most are the opinions of the instructors at *Bellas Artes*."

"Come, my son, let's go and break the news to your parents. I am pretty good at convincing people to agree with me."

Señor Guerrero was good to his word, and by the end of 1877 the whole Luna clan—with the exception of the energetic and playful Antonio—gathered at the Port of Manila on the mouth of the Pasig River bid goodbye to Juan Luna and his older brother Manuel, who decided to travel with his brother and pursue his studies in music.

"What's keeping Antonio away? Juan asked. "I will need to board soon."

"I told him specifically to go home straight after school so as not to be late for your departure," his father Don Joaquin said.

"I also told him because I know how distracted Antonio gets by his friends," his mother said. "I even suggested that he not go to school since he thinks he already knows better than his teachers."

Just as Doña Laureana predicted about her eleven-year-old son, Antonio's friends waylaid him.

"Antonio, you don't know how glad we are to see you," one of his buddies said. "We have been challenged to a kite fight by the neighborhood boys in Muelle."

"I am sorry, but you know very well my family is expecting me to be at the harbor pier to see my brothers off."

"But, it's early. We'll have plenty of time to fly our kites," another boy said.

"Yes, in fact, and I swear to God..." the boy turned around to face the church of Binondo as he swore..."that I saw your whole family leave for the harbor just before you arrived."

"I did not even bring my kite with me," Antonio said, but stared with longing at his friend who tied string onto his kite.

"Use mine," his friend said. "I even sharpened the string with candle wax like yours to make it easier to cut down your opponent."

"Oh, no, here they come! We need you, Antonio. There is no telling what will happen if they lose," pleaded the boy who knew Antonio the longest.

Antonio took the kite from his buddy and raised it in the air. "All right, let's go and show our challengers how the boys from Binondo win. To victory!"

"To victory," his friends chanted in unison.

The leader walked directly up to Antonio. "I am Roberto." He was about two years older than Antonio, taller, and skinnier. "Are you and your guys ready for multiple combat?"

"Sorry to disappoint you, but I need to be at the Manila harbor soon and would be glad to cut down your kite in an aerial duel." Antonio paused, "Just you and I."

"And not give me the honor to bring down all your kites, one at a time?"

Antonio stood tall, face to face with Roberto. "You must be dreaming because your kite will be in the hands of a kite runner in no time at all."

"Oh, yeah, if that is the case, I accept your challenge," Roberto said.

Antonio was well aware that most of the times the aerial combats ended in fistfights. Even the kite runners, those not involved in the competition, fought one another in order to claim a kite that had been cut down.

The mild sea breeze that blew towards Binondo that afternoon was enough to lift both kites up in the air with a degree of stability and pressure for fighting. It was all now in the hands and control of both combatants on land. At that point, Antonio begun to walk into the wind, and thus, reduced the tension on the line of his kite, making it spin dive.

"Antonio, what are you doing? Pull before your kite crashes to the ground," his friend yelled in warning.

"Nothing to worry about," Antonio pulled back his line and at the same time walked against the wind toward Roberto. Antonio's maneuver resulted in his kite shooting straight for Roberto's kite.

Sensing defeat, Roberto crashed into Antonio with his full body weight, causing Antonio to fall hard on the cobblestone plaza.

From the ground Antonio heard the kite runners as they sprinted towards one of the many creeks in Binondo. "*Al agua! Al agua!*" They screamed for joy that a kite was loose and free to be taken. He also listened as the boys from Muelle alternated between jeering at his friends and rejoicing for Roberto whose kite was still up in the air.

Antonio became angry, knowing he had been wronged. He bounced up and with his right fist clenched, delivered an upper-cut to Roberto's groin, who dropped like a log on the ground shrieking in pain.

"No one cheats on a Luna," Antonio said. "And to make sure that you remember…" With that, he lifted Roberto in the air, whirled him around and then dropped him at the entrance of the church.

Antonio addressed the group who circled him and Roberto. "Let it be known to all here and with God as my witness that you don't mess with a Luna or any of the boys from Binondo or you will end up like him."

Antonio turned his back on Roberto, and after bidding farewell to his friends, he ran as fast as he could to the harbor. He headed west along the banks of the *esteros* of Binondo, where small native boats called *cascos* floated along the Pasig River transporting people and goods.

"Antonio is here!" Juan Luna called to his parents in excitement. "Thank God he made it on time."

"Where have you been?" Doña Laureana asked. "And look at you, so dirty and bruised. Did you get into another fight?"

"All the carriages heading this way were taken and then I tripped…and I had to run all the way here," Antonio lied to his mother.

"Tripped while running…who are you kidding?" Doña Laureana cuffed her son on the ear. "Go quickly now, and give your brothers a farewell hug. They are the only ones who have not boarded the ship waiting for you" She hit Antonio lightly on the head with her open palm.

Antonio hurried to his oldest brother's side and buried his face in Manuel's chest. "I will miss you, Manuel."

"I will miss you too, Antonio, and you better take care of yourself. No more fighting." Manuel squeezed Antonio's chin in a brotherly fashion.

Antonio turned to Juan and he began suddenly to cry. "I will miss you so very much. Please write to me often. I cannot wait until I am old enough to follow you to Madrid. Take care of yourself," he said and hugged his brother tightly around his waist.

"I will think of you often, *mi hermanito*, and promise to send many letters. And before you know it, I will convince mother to send you to be with me. But you must promise not to be mischievous, and instead, to concentrate on your studies."

"I vow to do everything as you instruct and no more fights," Antonio said, and did not admit that he enjoyed the admiration of his friends who all looked up to him as their leader, especially with their pranks.

Manuel and Juan were about to board when Joaquin Luna hugged his sons once more. "Manuel and Juan, you are leaving us for Europe in order to pursue your education and individual goals. You are in our hearts and have our utmost support. We hope for nothing but great success for each of you. By the same token, remember there is no shame in failure. If you become despondent when fortune might not go your way, then come back to your family. We will love you always, miss you, and be proud of whatever you achieve."

"I will Papa," Juan Luna said, and looked at his father with a sad heart.

But then halfway up the boarding plank, the teary-eyed Juan was bidding a final farewell to his family, when Don Lorenzo shouted. "You are a good painter, Juan, and don't ever doubt that." He waved good bye to his young protégé, "Vaya con Dios, my son."

CHAPTER 4

Success came early to Manuel Luna. After his graduation from the Conservatory of Madrid, he held concerts as a violinist throughout France and Italy. But then tragically, while getting ready to travel back to Europe, he fell ill and died at the age of twenty-six. Fortunately, Juan had painted a portrait of his brother before Manuel had returned to Manila in 1879.

In the meantime, Juan enrolled at the Real Academia de *Bellas Artes* de San Fernando, which was established by royal decree in 1744. Twenty years later, the enlightened monarch, Charles III purchased a palace located just a short walking distance from Puerta del Sol on the Calle de Alcalá in the heart of Madrid as the academy's new home. The king commissioned the dean of architecture, Diego de Villanueca, to renovate the building for academic use. In keeping with Charles III's concept, de Villanueca decided on a neoclassical style in place of the original baroque design. The upper towers were added later for the purpose of covering the party walls of the adjacent building.

On Juan Luna's first day, while browsing the hallways and classrooms of the academy, he came upon three large openings, about five feet wide and twelve feet high, and each secured by a pair of wooden doors. He entered through the center portal and immediately noticed two portraits hanging side by side. They were of the same woman lying on a chaise bed, with the exception that in one, she was naked and in the other painting, she wore clothes.

Juan Luna liked the paintings very much and he wondered who the artist was when suddenly from behind him someone spoke.

"Both paintings were done by Francisco Goya and they are known as the *Clothed Maja* and the *Naked Maja*."

Juan Luna spun around.

"*Hola*, my name is Oliva, like the olive," the young man said and smiled.

He was somewhat taller than Juan and apparently a Spaniard with his dark handsome looks.

"Eugenio Oliva Rodrigo and this is my first day in school. These are fantastic, right?" He pointed to the portraits.

"My first day also, and I get introduced to Goya," Juan said. "But why are they hidden in this room and not hanging at the museum, the Museo de Prado?"

Before Oliva responded, Juan Luna extended his hand and introduced himself. "By the way, my name is Luna like the moon," he said, and grinned. "Juan Luna y Novicio and I come from Manila in the Philippines."

"A pleasure to meet you Señor Luna, like the moon," Oliva said. "The paintings were never publicly exhibited during Goya's lifetime. They were confiscated and banned as indecent during the Spanish Inquisition. Several years ago, when the inquisition ended the authorities returned them to the academy because Goya himself had taught here."

Although Juan Luna and Eugenio Oliva got along very well, they never went out socially as a pair. Regarding their academics, they relied on each other's specific skills and believed that they could learn more by painting and studying as a team.

In fact, soon after they met, Oliva said to Juan. "There is a method for stretching canvas linen and cotton canvas over stretcher bars. Larger canvases require the help of two or four people and are best stretched on a clean floor. New canvas can be soaked for half an hour and dried before stretching to reduce the likelihood of future sagging."

Oliva was patient in teaching Juan Luna the process, and soon enough, the Filipino student mastered the art of stretching canvas and securing them properly on the stretch bars.

In return, Juan Luna demonstrated for Oliva the various approaches to form and color. He helped his friend how to explore different themes and the *basi*c compositions—still life, landscape, and portraiture. One thing they both had in common was their love for the Roman classical art.

By the end of the year, Juan Luna came upon a crossroad. He felt that he had learned all he could as a student of the academy. He had won a major award for outstanding color, composition, and antique studies for his painting, *Las Damas Romanas* (The Roman Maidens) and was no longer satisfied with the school's traditional teaching style in the classroom.

Juan Luna was deciding how to expand his studies when Professor Alejo Blasco de Vera, the celebrated painter of two masterpieces, *Entierro de San Lorenzo*, and *Los Ultimos Momentos de Numancia,* invited the young painter to apprentice for him, in completing some of his commissioned paintings in Rome.

De Vera put his arm around Juan Luna. "I am very impressed with your talent. Your painting of the Roman Maidens is well done. But you can become even better, a thousand times better, under my tutelage."

Juan Luna bowed his head to the professor. "You are a real master of the pictorial arts. I am humbled by your invitation and I accept."

As soon as Juan Luna left the professor's studio, he ran throughout the academy looking for Eugenio to share his good news. He climbed up and down flights of stairs, taking two at a time and including six landings of the wide marble stairways. And with no sign of Eugenio.

He traversed the same corridors multiple times and it wasn't until bounding up the stairs to the second floor for about the fifth time that he bumped right into Eugenio.

"My friend, I've got great news for you!" Luna said.

After Juan explained about de Vera's offer, Eugenio said, "I am so happy for you, Juan. So when do you leave for Rome? Now both of us can travel together."

"What do you mean by both of us?" Juan asked.

"Yes, I am going to Rome as well! Professor Hernandez asked if I would apprentice for him," Eugenio said. "I cannot believe our great fortune!"

"Neither can I," Juan Luna said, and the young artists hugged each other and laughed until tears of happiness and excitement rolled down their cheeks.

CHAPTER 5

Although of Spanish heritage, Don Alejo Vera was born in Vinuelas, Guadalajara, Mexico. He and Juan Luna became friends immediately. Being twenty-three years older, Don Alejo eventually became a father figure. As his protégé, Vera was gratified to have chosen Juan.

In Rome, Juan was exposed to the art of contemporary Renaissance painters Michelangelo and Raphael and in particular, the Roman classical arts. To further inspire Juan Luna, maestro Alejo Vera took him throughout Italy, where he had the opportunity to study and absorb the beautiful sights and structures offered, especially where Roman and Greek arts and objects were excavated from classical sites such as Florence, Pompeii, and Naples.

Motivated by the opening in 1878 of the first art exposition in Madrid, known as the *Exposición Nacional de Bellas Artes* (National Exposition of Fine Arts), Juan Luna's artistic talents began to bloom. From then on, the thought of someday exhibiting and competing in

Spain's grandest court of artistic tournaments motivated Juan Luna. He produced a collection of art works that included a self-portrait at age twenty-two and *Daphne and Chloe*, which was awarded a silver palette from the Central Literary Artist of Manila.

After maestro Alejo Vera completed his commissions, he made plans to return to Spain. Juan Luna advised his maestro that he was so attracted by all of the amazing art and the classical environment of the City of the Seven Hills that he wanted to stay and further educate himself.

Maestro Alejo Vera bid his protégé farewell with the final words: "You have it inside of you, but you have not found it yet."

Juan Luna was puzzled by Alejo Vera's advice. In addition, soon after the maestro's departure, he felt so alone without a teacher to instruct him or a father to counsel him. And so he heeded his maestro's recommendation. He worked and studied diligently with the goal of seeking a beautiful subject to paint using his own artistic style and development.

Juan Luna was in and out of museums and examined the majestic works of arts that he most admired. In the Vatican, he sought solitude and absorbed in silence the brilliant beauty of his surroundings.

After Alejo Vera left, Juan Luna lived with the Benlliure brothers: José, Juan Antonio, and Mariano. José was a great public figure and leader of the art colony in Rome. He painted many historic sites, while the youngest of the trio, Mariano, became famous for his sculptures of bull fighting scenes. Juan Antonio, who was two years younger than Juan Luna, developed a loyal friendship with Juan. The brothers were among only a few artists pensioned by the Spanish government for residence in Italy to learn the Italian arts for consideration to decorate future public buildings in their home country.

In June 1882, Guiseppe Garibaldi—a hero of Italy known as the man of the common people—died. When the public learned of the funeral services, José Benlliure invited Juan Luna to attend a meeting of the art colony as they planned the best way to pay their respects to such an honorable man. Although they were Spanish, Benlliure and his group felt a close association with the Italians through their artistic connection as well as the fact that they recognized a great political leader. On that night, the decision was made to join the funeral procession that was scheduled in two days.

Juan Luna was anxious to be part of the ceremony that celebrated the man who had neutralized the tremendous power of the Vatican See. When the Italian army captured Rome in 1870, Pope Pius IX was forced to evacuate behind the walls of the Vatican City never to venture out again.

Juan Luna confided to José. "I only wish we had our own Garibaldi in the Philippines who would put a stop to the abuses by the Spanish friars and unite us as one nation, free from foreign interventions."

"Don't lose hope my friend, you shall overcome someday," José replied. "Believe me, the Dominicans won't rule forever."

And then José turned to the gathering. He related his plan for marching in the procession, informed them of the exact place and time, and reminded them of the proper attire. "I want each one of us to wear a loose, red shirt, with a crimson rose pinned to the collar and one of the red Garibaldian caps that are available in many of the stores."

"Anything else we should do?" One of his friends asked.

"Yes," José said. "We will walk with pride carrying the flags of both Garibaldi's country and ours." He pointed to Paulo. "You carry the Italian flag, and I will carry the one for Spain."

On the day of the funeral procession, thousands of mourners were already in line at the Piazza del Popolo ready to walk behind the fallen hero. Eight white horses with black cloths on their backs and feathers on their heads were harnessed to the hearse carriage.

On top of the carriage was a large bust of Garibaldi decorated with a laurel wreath and held by a female statue of liberty standing just behind—the same honor given to the Caesars of ancient Rome.

José Benlliure did not want to be at the end of the line. He felt that the crowd watching the procession from the sidelines and from rooftops would disperse by the time he and his men marched by with their colors and placards. So José and his men shoved their way about four hundred meters ahead in the procession, much to the anger of the people who had lined up earlier.

As soon as the procession started, the cheers and laughter among the crowd turned into tears and lamentations. But then as people began waving hundreds of flags representing the cities of Italy and as widespread as different nations of Europe, a mood of joyous celebration returned. Mourners chanted in loud voices, "Viva Garibaldi, Viva Italia," to the delight of the crowd.

The flags of Spain and Italy were hoisted side by side, as the Spaniards and Juan Luna chanted, "Viva Garibaldi, Viva, Italia, Viva Garibaldi, Viva *España*, Viva Garibaldi, Viva Italia, Viva *España*," over and over again.

When the procession got halfway to its destination, the *Campidoglio*, the huge crowd of mourners thronged on each side of the main street, and then like a funnel, they merged intermittently into one of the narrow roadways found all over Rome. The pushing and shoving caused marchers to trip on the wooden placards and flags. They fell like domino pieces on top of each other.

José Benlliure lost sight of the Italian flag. As he searched for Paolo, José trampled on the Spanish flag and was about to fall when he called on his Filipino friend. "Juan, take the flag. It's all yours. Take over for all of us and for Spain!"

Juan Luna grabbed hold of the flag with speed and agility. "I've got it!" he yelled back to José as he freed himself from the entangled pyramid of human bodies, and then carried on to the end, holding the flag of Spain high and never letting go.

The following day, the newspaper *El Porvenir de Visayas* highlighted the incident in an article:

"In the civic procession held in Rome for the funeral of Garibaldi, Juan Luna, who was in the group of the international circle of artists, carried our flag. Suddenly, as a result of panic caused by some kind of incident, there was such a stampede that all the flags dropped on the ground. Not so happened to our glorious standard—the Spanish flag—which was the only one that remained aloft. We are not surprised,

therefore, that Juan Luna will use the same fearlessness and the same enthusiasm he had done with his painting that will raise him very high in Rome as part of the national art."

The tabloid was correct in the assessment of Juan Luna's future as a famous artist. After almost four years of continuous study and painting in Rome, Luna's name finally became known at the stadium of arts he had strived for. After all, his painting entitled *The Death of Cleopatra*—better known as *La Muerte de Cleopatra*—was exhibited in the National Exposition of Fine Arts in Madrid a year earlier.

This particular piece was a testament that Juan Luna was discovering who he was as an artist just as Alejo Vera had inferred. Luna displayed his confidence in the choice of colors, the vitality of his brush strokes, and the manner in which he had meticulously chosen the theme or subject to paint: in this case, the death of Cleopatra, which resonated with meaning of beauty and artistic value.

Juan Luna proved to the world that with time he would compete with the finest artists of Europe. *La Muerte de Cleopatra* won him the silver medal at the exposition and was bought by the State for 1,000 ducats and placed in Madrid's Museo Nacional de Pinturas in the hall of contemporary painters.

CHAPTER 6

As soon as Juan Luna learned that he had won the Medal of the Second Class in the latest *Exposiciones Nacionales de Bellas Artes* for his painting, *La Muerte de Cleopatra*, he freed himself from all of his obligations in Rome and traveled to Madrid to claim his award.

He spent the rest of his time socializing with friends in Madrid. There were only about forty students from the Philippines in all of Spain. Although small in number, the potential to have a strong influence in their homeland was a given. However, many of them were sons of the wealthiest families, leaders of Filipino society, and they did not have the motivation to succeed. They would sleep until noon after a night of gambling, socializing at cafes, or out with women of the night.

Pablo Ortiga, a one time resident in the Philippines, occasionally organized events for the members of the *Circulo Hispano-Filipino* in Madrid. Juan Luna was invited to attend one of these gatherings normally held in the house of Señor Ortiga.

"Gentlemen, let me have your attention, please," Señor Ortiga announced as a frail looking, very young man stood by his side. "I have the honor to introduce to you our guest poet for tonight's social gathering, a *mestizo of Filipino*—Spanish and Chinese descent—who displayed great intelligence at an early age as a promising poet, writer, and young sc*hola*r at Ateneo Municipal de Manila. He just arrived from the Philippines and is now a student of medicine at the Universidad Central de Madrid. Gentlemen, Señor José Rizal."

Rizal took a place at the podium to a round of applause from the gathering. When the room was quiet again, he recited a poem he had written especially for the occasion. There were rumors about the disintegration of the association, and he believed his sad poem about what it was like being a Filipino away from home might sway the dissenters.

The poem, *Me Piden Versos* ("Request Verses From Me") ended with these four lines:

My heart is weighted down, and in a thread;
I roam through this waste without peace;
The pangs in my soul never cease;
And all inspiration is dead.

After reciting his poem, Rizal could not help but notice the servers were starting to place a variety of sumptuous food dishes on top of the dining table. He had not been eating much lately and felt weak and disoriented. While reciting his poem, he almost fainted earlier.

Rizal was running out of money. His pension, which came from his family in the Philippines, has been delayed due to problems in his hometown of Calamba, between his family and the Spanish friars. The problem pertained to his older brother's involvement in the revolutionary movement and the eventual eviction from their farmland, which was the main source of livelihood.

Rizal looked around and spotted two young men who seemed different from the rest of the Filipinos he had met in Spain so far. Both displayed confidence and an aura of distinction, and the best part for the hungry Rizal was they were closest to the buffet table. He walked over and introduced himself.

"*Hola*, my name is José Rizal. I hope you enjoyed listening to my poetry," he said. "I wrote it when I was very depressed."

Juan Luna shook hands with Rizal. "I am Juan Luna, and I loved your poem because it reminded me so much of home." Luna turned to his friend. "This is Felix Resurreccion Hidalgo, a fellow artist like me, who is based in Paris while I am pensioned in Rome."

"Tell me," Rizal said and pointed to the servers carrying more savory dishes to the table. "When one is on a daily diet of bread and water, is he excused to partake on all this manna from heaven before the rest of the guests are formally called to eat?"

"Go for it, as Felix and I can cover for you," Juan Luna said and then smiled as Rizal grabbed a leg of chicken and devoured it in what seemed like a second.

Rizal patted his stomach. "Oh, I almost forgot the taste of real food. Thank you for making that possible. How do you like Rome? He asked Juan.

"Very inspiring, especially for artists," Juan said.

"Paris and Rome are two places I hope to visit and learn their language someday," Rizal said. "Maybe after I complete my medical training."

Although Rizal was only a few years younger than Juan Luna, and they only had just met, Juan took an instant liking to the younger man and acted like a concerned father when he asked about Rizal's future plans.

"I am taking two courses of study simultaneously. They are medicine, and philosophy and letters. And in my spare time I am pursuing the arts and fencing."

"That is a heavy load," Juan said.

"Yes, but my purpose in life is to set myself as an example to others on what a Filipino is capable of achieving."

"Hey Felix," Luna said. "We have an idealist in our midst, a visionary, the way we approach the subject of our paintings. We hear you, Rizal."

"Welcome to the club," Felix said to Rizal. "There are but a few Filipinos who believe we can excel better than the Europeans in any form of undertaking."

Rizal shook his head and sighed. "I just don't understand the mentality of Filipino students in Madrid who squander their intellect and money on alcohol, and gambling. They don't even have the guts to stand up for themselves when arguing with Spanish students."

"Felix and I agree," Juan said.

"With the chaos that is facing our country today, there is no better time to influence our fellow foreign students as to who we are and why we deserve to be on par with them," Rizal said in a fired-up voice. "All we want is racial equality."

"Equal rights for Filipinos can only be attained through the Spanish parliament, the *Cortes*, or through the intercession of the King of Spain," Felix said.

"That is precisely my point," Rizal responded. "As long as Europeans think of Filipinos as native Indios, we will never command the respect or have the representation we deserve in the *Cortes*. We don't have enough native Filipinos born of Spanish descent, as the Creoles in Cuba and Puerto Rico had to demand the right to parliamentary representation. In order to succeed, the educated Filipino youth, the *illustrado*, must bond together into one movement for reform in our native land."

Since Rizal was new in Europe and he and Juan Luna attended the same school in Manila and loved politics and the arts, they immediately became best friends.

As the days passed, Juan Luna and José Rizal spent many happy hours discussing politics, school life, and various perspectives of their individual art style and ways to improve their own painting technique.

But then the time came for Juan Luna's departure back to Rome. Inspiration for his great masterpiece still eluded him, and he hoped being amidst the great Italian artists again would spark his imagination.

CHAPTER 7

Juan Luna went back to Rome and stayed again with the Benlliure brothers, but this time with a growing reputation as a renowned artist for winning the Second Medal of Honor in the Exposition. Through the efforts of Pablo Ortiga, the Government of the City of Manila granted the Filipino painter an annual pension of 1,000 pesos for four years. The condition was that he was obliged to create a painting that captured the essence of Philippine history, which would then become the property of the Town Hall.

Juan Luna's primary goal, however, was to win the First Medal of Honor for the next National Exposition of Fine Arts after coming so close in winning the first medal in 1881.

The *Exposiciones Nacionales de Bellas Artes* started by means of a Royal Decree issued by Queen Isabella II on January 12, 1854 in the Gaceta de Madrid. It was to be held every two years during the month of May and was open to all national and international artists, each of whom was allowed to submit up to three works of art for each competition. In 1881, during the reign of King Alfonso XII, son of Queen Isabella II, the date of the competition was changed to every three years.

By the beginning of 1883, Juan Luna still had no idea what to paint for the 1884 Exposition. Even so, he was sure that the theme was to be a Roman classic so he began days of exhaustive research on the annals of ancient Rome with the hope of capturing a mental image and then reflecting on canvas even a fragment of its immense historical scenery and value.

He recalled his former mentor Alejo de Vera's most famous and immortal painting, *Los Ultimos Momentos de Numancia,* which depicted the *Numantinos* killing themselves rather than surrender to Rome. The images of the *Numantinos* were his first flashes of inspiration, until he found himself seated outside the ancient Roman Colosseum. At last, after the most extraordinary efforts, ideas floated across the landscape of his mind. And although the total picture lacked clarity, Juan Luna was invigorated that he had finally found the theme for his most ambitious work of art.

He saw himself as an artist, not just vaguely in his dreams, but in reality, walking inside the ruins of the Roman circus. The chamber, situated below the amphitheater was where the corpses of the gladiators—dragged by horses and stripped of their armor and weapons—were discarded and where the fighters who had been mortally wounded ended their lives. Family and friends in mourning cried as they claimed the mutilated bodies of loved ones and took them away into oblivion. Moved by the beauty he found in Numancia, he decided to paint what went on inside the *Spoliarium.*

Juan Luna woke up very early one morning and rushed to Mariano Benlliure who was still asleep in a bed next to him. "Mariano, wake up. I just had this wonderful and inspiring dream. Well, not really, I was awake while dreaming."

"Come on, so early in the morning? What's up with this dream?

Is it of a wonderful and inspiring *signorina*? If you are horny, go fuck yourself and let me go back to sleep, *coño*."

"Hey, I was not dreaming of a woman. I finally discovered the subject to paint for my masterpiece."

Mariano tried to stand up, but he flopped back down and sat on the edge of his bed, rubbing his face and trying to wake up. After a huge yawn, he said, "Alright, so what is your masterpiece this time around? It better be good. I have heard so many of them in the past."

Juan Luna proceeded to describe in detail his vision of the *Spoliarium* as he stretched his arms as wide as he could. "It has to be the largest painting ever done on one whole piece of canvas like a wall fresco."

"Oh yeah, a wall fresco on canvas, it's like me finding the largest wooden block to sculpture Noah's ark in one piece, in its original dimensions." He laughed and snapped his fingers at Juan Luna. "Go back to sleep and continue dreaming. Where the hell will you ever find a canvas the size of a huge wall?

"I have an idea. But I need your assistance in getting there."

"Where? What are you talking about?" Mariano asked.

"I used to be a seaman, and where else does one go to find a large sailing canvas but along the coastline of the Mediterranean?"

"A sailing canvas!" Mariano almost choked on his own saliva. "You intend to paint your masterpiece on a sailing canvas, *amigo*? I'm sorry to say this, but you belong in a mental institution."

'Come on, it will work. I am an expert on canvas like you are on wood. In fact, we also may need to bring back some discarded wooden ship planks. I can use them for scaffolds and frames for my painting. I am so excited, Mariano! When can we leave for Ostia?"

"All right…all right, we'll go," Mariano conceded. "In this way, I can work on some sketches of the various Roman ruins in Ostia Antica."

The following day, Juan Luna and Mariano Benlliure rode on a borrowed cargo carriage on their way to the sandy beaches of Portus, the harbor in Lido di Ostia, which was a stretch along the southern delta cusp of the Tiber River not far from the center of Rome on the Tyrrhenian Sea.

The city of Ostia, which means mouth, was situated at the mouth of the river. Due to silting—sandy ground that caused the shoreline to move seaward—the city was now farther away from the sea.

Upon their arrival at the harbor, the two artists proceeded straight for the well-preserved old warehouses and docks lined along the various moorings. They were both excited to see a variety of newer ships as well as the old cannibalized discarded sailing vessels.

"I speak a bit of Italian, but do you understand Spanish?" Juan Luna asked an older Italian with a medium build and who looked like a retired seafarer.

"No, no Spanish, only Italian," the man said.

"*Bueno, Ti capita di avere una vela grande tela*?" Juan inquired in Italian if he had a large sailing canvas on stock. And then, he switched to Spanish. "*Por lo menos cuatro metros por ocho metros*."

"*Sí, quelli scartati, ma essi sono stati strappati in pezzi, Non ho qualsiasi tela vela grande, a meno che comprare un nuovo*," the old seafarer said.

"Darn it, he only sells them in cut up pieces," Juan Luna said.

"Let's check out the largest of the cut up pieces," Benlliure suggested.

"Yes, but it won't be much to my liking," Juan said as he focused his attention on a window that was partly covered by the face of the shopkeeper.

Juan Luna stared at something outside the window. "Do you see what I see?"

"Yes, a toothless old Italian," Mariano said.

"No," Juan said and he positioned Benlliure in front of him. "Look out through the window."

"Yes, an old Italian ship."

"Yes, but a two-mast square rigged vessel, a brigantine of Mediterranean origin," Juan said.

One of the two masts was cut in two with all its sailing canvas missing while the other mast was partially intact. Although the mainsail and topgallant sail were gone, the canvas on the topsail was still rolled along the horizontal yardarm.

"*Ti capita di sapere el dueno de quella barca antiqua*?" Juan asked the shopkeeper in mixed Spanish and Italian if he knew the owner, and pointed at the dilapidated vessel moored outside the shop.

"Abbiamo appena acquistato quella barca, ma abbiamo ancora a cannibalizzare per parti. Perché sei interessato a comprare la tela vela?"

"Thank God, they do own the old ship" Luna said excitedly, and confirmed his interest in wanting to buy the sailing canvas.

The old shopkeeper handed Juan Luna a sharp knife and told him to go out and cut down his sailing canvas since he was alone in the shop and was too old to climb the mast.

Juan grabbed the knife and prodded Mariano to assist him.

"You must be crazy, Juan. I'm not climbing up there," Mariano said.

"You don't have to. Just stand below and catch me when I fall," Juan Luna joked.

"Fuck you! I'm staying right here so I can better see you fall."

"Come on, let's go. You are not doing any climbing"

When Juan Luna boarded the old brig, the smell of the sea and the wooden deck planks brought back memories of his time as a seafarer in the Pacific. He began to climb the tall mast, which was about sixty feet off the deck. Attached to the riggings and supporting the mast was the ratline, a long slanting rope ladder made from a series of small Manila hemp rope used for sailors to climb and stay aloft.

Juan loved the sea and sailing and in order to better savor the moment, he climbed slowly. Once on top of the mast, he could not help but to look down the deck of the ship. Although about forty meters in length, he always thought the ship below him looked like a toy sailboat on a blue pond.

But then a slash of wind brought him back to reality as he figured the safest way to disengage the topsail canvas from its yardarms since they were mounted on the mast in such a fashion that they allowed free movement by the wind. It had been more than a decade when, as a young maritime student, since he had been aloft a yardarm. His plan was to hang on and move from one end of the yardarm to the other using a hand-over-hand technique.

There was neither a safety harness nor nets, so Juan Luna cut himself a makeshift harness with a piece of rope dangling from the topmast. He tied it around his waist and attached the other end to the rope ladder so there was no danger of him of falling out. Juan clung to the riggings, and on his first attempt to cross over one of the horizontal bars and halfway out, he lost his grip. He fell and struck full force onto the slanting network of rope ladders that climbed from the rail up to the mast.

"You are not only crazy but a very mad man, Juan. Get down here this very minute!" Mariano shouted nervously.

"I have done this before and just lost my touch, and as you can see I am safely tied to this rope."

The figure of Luna with his tanned complexion aloft the yardarms was a wonderful testimony to the marks of his arduous work on the high seas. Luna was confident as a sailor, and he ignored Mariano. On his second attempt, he managed to cut off all lines securing the topsails, and they dropped to the deck one by one. An hour later, they were on their way back to Rome.

CHAPTER 8

In the early part of 1883, Juan Luna attached his washed and stretched sailing canvas measuring 4.25 meters by 7.75 meters to the largest wall inside the house, and began working on what he believed to be his most important and prestigious work of art, *La Spoliarium*.

After assessing the situation, Luna took the narrow wooden planks taken from Portus and began building a scaffold with footings strong enough to support his weight, and wide enough for him to walk freely from one end to the other of the top horizontal plank. Mariano built a portable wooden ladder to climb safely up and down the scaffold while Juan Antonio assisted Juan Luna in its construction.

Luna completed a number of value sketches in charcoal for each of his main subjects and characters in the *Spoliarium*. He began sketching the small version of the whole portrait on a canvas pad, which he envisioned in his mind, and then painted his color study on the small design for his choices of colors. Luna decided not to draw directly on the large canvas. Instead, he utilized the age-old technique for enlarging a design or drawing by creating grid squares on his small design and a corresponding grid of squares on the large canvas with his charcoal stick.

"Don't you wish you had some kind of magic or power to project your small design directly onto your huge canvas so you can easily complete the outline?" Jose joked.

"I wish because by the time I'm done I'll be twenty pounds lighter," Luna responded.

"Maybe some day someone, like a future Da Vinci, might invent such a projector," Juan Antonio said.

For his outline on the large canvas, instead of paint Juan Luna used the same size of charcoal stick to prevent the paint from dripping down while he was on top of the foot plank. He consulted the Benlliure brothers, especially fellow painters, José and Juan Antonio, seeking their constructive criticism of his masterpiece as the painting progressed.

"*Hola, José y Juan Antonio.* Do you have a few minutes?" Juan Luna asked. "I am not so happy with my sketch work. In my mind, I can hear Professor Vera tell me he is also dissatisfied with what I have done."

"*Bale*, for you we have all the time," José said.

"How can we be of help?" Juan Antonio asked.

"I would minimize the Roman classic structure in the background, as it overcomes your iconographic model, the dead gladiator," José suggested.

Juan Luna turned to Juan Antonio and waited.

"Yes, I can see that you have been talking to Vera because I agree with José," Juan Antonio said. "This explains the classicism influence seen in the composition of your interior views, which I would darken a little. The same goes for some of the men in the crowd in the background, and then execute in a rich and soft technique on the dead gladiators."

"Ah, that would give my subject a magical and mysterious glow by concentrating the source of light focused over the bodies of the gladiators, especially their arms," Juan Luna said as he backed away from the canvas to take another studious look at the sketch. "And lightly done on the face and on the details in their clothes, the painting will come alive in the likeness of Rembrandt's powerful chiaroscuros."

"Don't forget to give it your finest technique to create the dynamism caused by your figures. Give it the precise combination of light and shades, and don't ever disregard the beauty and perfection of your vision," José said.

In return, Juan Luna critiqued the works of José, Juan Antonio and Mariano Benlliuere who were both planning to compete in the same 1884 Madrid competition. But then José decided to back out, and for this reason Juan asked him more often than the others to criticize his work.

"*Hola,* José. I believe I've done everything I could with this portrait," Juan said. "So, what do you think?"

"My pleasure to give my opinion. Let me see…hmmm…"

"Yes?"

"I love the way you express the earthy and bloody colors that blend perfectly with the expressions of your main characters, but I would lessen the ocher color a little bit."

"Is that all?" Luna asked.

"The haunting look of the old men staring at the cadavers dragged by very strong slaves hand on hand is truly explicit, and the Christian woman crying on the side completes the harmony and balance of the overall picture. You have created a masterpiece, my friend."

"Thank you, *amigo*."

CHAPTER 9

Eight months later in May 1884, Juan Luna rolled and shipped the large canvas signed LVNA ROMA MDCCCLXXXIV to Madrid for what had become one of the world's most prestigious art competitions—the *Exposiciónes Nacional de Bellas Artes*. With the assistance of the King and Royal family of Spain and the Spanish government, the competition was inaugurated on May 24 at the gallery of the Ministry of Fomento in what used to be the Convent of Trinidad located in Calle Atocha in the corner of calle De La Relatores.

Judges were selected from individuals who were members of the academy of San Fernando and were divided into three categories: painting, sculpture, and architecture. There were nine judges for the paintings.

Although rain started to drizzle on the opening day exposition, a huge crowd of festive supporters gathered outside the Ministry. On display were seventy-five paintings, fifty-six sculptures, and fifteen architectural designs.

Once inside the gallery, people studied and analyzed each painting. Moving from one to the next was like going through the history of Roman times. There were also hundreds of neo-classical paintings and sculptures representing captive faces and emotions of human behavior.

One painting seemed to resonate with everyone in attendance as they milled around the gigantic portrait that measured more than four meters in height and seven meters in width with solid and simple wooden frames about a foot in thickness mounted all around.

They were mesmerized and struck by the intense colors, especially the deep tones of red, which accentuated the poignancy of the work—the rendition of a tragic custom during the powerful Roman Empire, *La Spoliarium*. The depiction of near life-sized corpses of bloody gladiators being dragged out of the arena where they had entertained their Roman oppressors demonstrated a severe condition of an inhumane society as in the background of the painting, the crowd cheers for more blood while a loved one mourns for one of the victims.

Murmurs of awe and wonder buzzed around the room among the onlookers.

"Who is the author?"

"What genius composed this outstanding work so masterful in drawing and detail?"

"Amazing!"

"An artist of the first order," an appreciative onlooker pronounced.

And then from an unrehearsed and sympathizing audience, a group began to chant, "Luna! Luna! Luna!"

And even as the attendees moved on to other works of art, Juan Luna's *La Spoliarium* left them humbled with a lasting impression of having witnessed a true masterpiece.

When the day of reckoning arrived finally, Juan Luna waited nervously with the other 138 competitors, who included his dear friends: Felix Hidalgo, Eugenio Oliva, Mariano and Juan Antonio Benlliure. All five together with José Benlluire huddled together in one corner of the assembly hall awaiting the decision of the judges led by President Judge Aureliano Fernandez Guerra and the Secretary-General of events,

Benito Soriano Murillo.

The first awards announced were for Lithography and Engraving. Three awards for best architectural designs followed. The Medal for the First Class went jointly to Eduardo Adaro and Severino Sainz for their work, *Proyecto de Edificio para Banco de España*.

When it was time to announce the medalists for sculpture, Don Guerra surprised everyone when he declared, "*Desiertas*!" for the award of Medal of the First Class, which meant that none of the competitors deserved such an honor. For Medals of the Second Class, he announced five winners, the first being Mariano Gil Benlluire for his sculpture, *Accidenti*. Mariano entered his first competition at the age of six and was Luna's housemate in Rome. A loud roar of applause came from the audience as Mariano's name was called since he and his brothers were very popular in Spain with both the people and the critics.

After the fifth medalist was announced—Eduardo Barron for his bronze sculpture, *Viriato*—there was a loud enthusiastic stirring from inside the Ministry gallery. The excitement meant that the category for painting was the next to be announced.

Twenty winners were called for Medals of the Third Class. The last artist to be named was Cesar Alvarez Dummont for his painting, *La Defensa de la Torre de San Agustin* (The Defense of the Tower of San Augustine).

Juan Luna looked at Juan Antonio Benlluire, Eugenio Oliva, and Felix Hidalgo. "Thank God our names were not called, which means we are still in the running for the First Medal."

"Juan, they will have to open the upper extended doors of the gallery for your painting to go through," Felix said. "So, as long as they remain closed, you have nothing to worry about."

"What if it remains closed all the time?" Juan Luna asked nervously.

"Then it's time to cry and hit the bottle," Felix teased.

"Now you got me more anxious than ever," Juan Luna said.

"Just keep a steady eye on those doors," Eugenio said.

Out of fifteen awardees for Medal of the Second Class, Juan

Antonio Benlliure was first for his painting, *La Patria*. A deafening explosion of both woes and applause went through the hall for another member of Madrid's favorite family of art.

Juan Luna, José and Mariano Benlliure crowded around Juan Antonio, hugging him and lifting his hands in victory.

"Congratulations, Juan Antonio, for a well-deserved medal. I'm so proud of you, *mi amigo*!" Juan Luna said.

"*Bale*, a second medal is better than nothing, and now I have no other recourse other than to hope you win the big one," José Antonio responded.

"I've been praying in silence for that to happen. This is nerve wrecking…I hope the judges are not prejudiced to large paintings," Juan said.

The fifth name called was Juan's fellow Filipino, Felix Resurrection-Hidalgo, for his painting, *Las Virgenes Cristianas Expuestas al Populacho* (The Christian Virgins Exposed to the Populace), a depiction of the plight of Christian women enslaved and waiting to be sold in auction by the Romans.

Felix Resurrection-Hidalgo jumped excitedly up and down with joy. He turned to Juan Luna. "Are you sure they called my name?"

"Who else but you has the longest name is this completion?" Juan responded as he continued to stare at the door gallery, hoping the extended doors remained closed until the medals of the first class were announced.

Joaquin Sorolla won for his painting, *El Dos de Mayo*, who at age twenty-one was the youngest artist competing in the exposition. The last winner of the Medal of the Second Class was Luna's former peer at the academy, Eugenio Oliva for his work, *Cervantes en sus Ultimos Dias*.

All eyes were now upon Juan Luna. His friends were all medalists, so either Juan was going to win the first medal or he would return home empty-handed. Juan Luna prayed deep inside himself for the extenders on top of the twelve-foot gallery doors to open. Everyone in the room was waiting in anticipation to find out who would be the three recipients of the Gold Medal of the First Class and the distinguished sole Medal of Honor.

Juan Luna held his breath as the first recipient was named. Antonio Munoz Degrain won for his painting, *Los Amantes de Teruel.* José Moreno Carbonero was called second for his painting, *The Conversion of the Duke of Gandia.* The painting measured 315 x 500 cm and was the second largest painting and like Luna, Carbonero completed the work while he was in Rome.

"It does not look good. They have just awarded one of the gold medals to the second-largest painting," Juan Luna commented, his heart heavy, "The chance of giving the last gold to the largest painting is almost impossible."

After Carbonero's approbation had subsided, the president judge spoke to the eager audience. "So, needless to say, the final recipient of the Medal of First Class is not only the most discussed, but I would add, the most shockingly impressive work of art in the competition." The president judge paused to point at the gallery doors as the extensions opened slowly. "I give you *La Spoliarium* by Filipino artist, Juan Luna."

Four attendants were needed to roll out the immense work to the loudest applause of the day.

Juan Luna raised both his hands in victory and hooted with joy as his friends jumped all over him in praise. But the awards were not over yet and at once, there was silence again as everyone in the hall awaited the winner of the sole Medal of Honor, also known as the Medal of Excellence.

With his win, Juan Luna gained instant recognition among the art connoisseurs and critics that were in attendance. They surrounded him and called out questions, wanting to know who was this young genius coming from the far away colony of Spain, about to be honored with the grand prize. The critics noticed modesty about Juan Luna that was in contrast with the aureole of brilliance that was about to surround his head.

"Ladies and gentlemen, please, may I have your attention?" Secretary-General Soriano Murill cried out. "It is now time to announce the result of the Medal of Excellence for this year's competition."

There was a mixture of applause with a rumbling from the gallery floor as the audience and competing artists pushed each other to get closer to the podium.

"I would like to call forward President Judge Fernandez Guerra and his fellow judges for our most important announcement," Murillo said.

The president took his place at the podium. "First of all, an enormous thanks you to all of our participating artists. Without your worthwhile work we would not have anything to celebrate today. I also want to offer my appreciation to our judges, special guests and everyone present for your continual support of the exposition."

After a polite applause, the crowd settled down again when the president gestured for quiet.

"Before we close, I want to give a special word of thanks to all the wonderful artists who entered their works into this year's competition. And even if you did not win, please do not be discouraged. Many of you are wonderfully talented artists and a number of the works were truly outstanding. So I want you all to try again in three years time at the next exhibition. I also want to note the dedication of the judges in their selection of winners. Unfortunately…" and here the president sighed deeply. "The board has decided not to bestow the Medal of Honor to any of the three gold medalists."

The president and judges thought the people were going to riot so thunderous were the boos and disfavor. Fearful for their safety, they left the gallery as quickly as they could with the exception of the Secretary-General Murillo who had to make a final announcement at the podium.

"The 1884 National Exposition of Fine Arts is now officially closed. Thank you for attending, and we hope to see you again in 1887," Murillo announced hurriedly.

But the angry crowd hardly listened and could not be contained as they ranted on with disapproving cries of racism and unfairness to the Filipino painter, Juan Luna.

CHAPTER 10

The animosity against the biased judges continued all day in the streets of Madrid. The sheer size of Juan Luna's canvas captured the respect and awe of the public. Not only did they recognize Luna as a great artist, but the controversial subject of slavery and despotism also struck an emotional chord among the people. *La Spoliarium* was a painting that should have been dignified by the Medal of Excellence, and no one understood why Luna was not granted the honor deserving of his genius.

However, unknown to most of the public as they left the Ministry of Fomento was that the Medal of Honor had only been awarded twice in the history of the exposition. The first went to Vicente Palmaroli in 1862 for his painting, *Una Pascuccia*, and the other was awarded to Ignacio Suarez Llanos in 1864 for his work, *Sor Marcela de San Felix.*

Although disappointed for not receiving the top prize after all the hype *La Spoliarium* commanded from the public, and especially from the press and critics, Juan Luna was gratified to walk away with the first place medal around his neck. Weighing six ounces and strung with yellow and red ribbons, he proudly showed off the solid gold disc when he gleefully left the Ministry to celebrate together with his friends.

There were mixed emotions among the Spanish press and art critics regarding the results of the *Expocisiones Nacional de Bellas Artes*. One reviewer wrote: "The recently concluded Exposition introduced to us several new personalities, some of them mocking the 'grandiose' breadth, such as with Señor Luna who painted *La Spoliarium*."

Another critic pointed out the incorrectness of Luna's workmanship hidden in the enormity of the painted cloth and only after a second and third look, he discovered its missing breadth of life. Others would go as far as suggesting that Luna's work was a horrible theatrical line of broken bodies and fresh corpses, and that it was elevated to prominence prematurely during the exposition and that Munoz-Degrain's portrait, the *Loved Ones of Teruel*, should have been awarded the grand prize.

But the Philippine community ignored the negative criticism. Luna's compatriots were overcome with joy as two of their native sons had won medals. Juan Luna was an authentic genius and *La Spoliarium* was the colossal magnet that attracted the public to visit the 1884 Exposition.

In fact, the success of Luna and Hidalgo exploded among the European community as proof of Filipino ingenuity and creativity. As such, Filipinos gained the confidence and capability to compete with Europeans on any level, and opened doors for upcoming artists to succeed in their own field of expertise, which was not available to them in the past.

Emilio Castelar y Ripoll, a greatly admired Spanish literary figure and prominent politician wrote: *"In art there are two kinds of souls: the sublime souls and the beautiful souls. The sublime souls are like the ocean, immensity, surge of waves, tempests; the beautiful souls are like the Mediterranean Sea, grace, harmony, light, gentle contours, in a word, if what is defined can enter in a definition, beautiful."*

Critics and friends who knew Juan Luna concurred that his

soul was sublime because his inspiration and artistic sentiments had been greatly influenced by the mishaps, incidents, and hazards he went through during his brief life as a seaman.

He believed that life is nothing but a speck within the grandeur of Mother Nature. One must overcome each obstacle to survive, and that was the defining reason for his art as depicted in *La Spoliarium*.

On June 25, 1884 Filipino *illustrados* and Spanish nobles in Madrid organized a social event at the Hotel Ingles to commemorate the triumph of the two Filipino painters, especially Juan Luna who had won the first prize. Felix Hidalgo was not present, but the greatest accolade came from his close friend, José Rizal, who delivered a stunning speech in which he addressed two significant elements regarding Juan Luna's art—the glorification of Juan Luna's genius and the greatness of his artistic skills.

José Rizal stood in front of the audience and began.

"Spaniards and Filipinos were two peoples. Two peoples that sea and space separate in vain, two peoples in which the seeds of disunion, blindly sown by men and their tyranny, do not take root. Luna and Hidalgo are as much Spanish glories as they are Filipino. Just as they were born in the Philippines, they could have been born in Spain, because genius has no country, genius blossoms everywhere, genius is like the light, the air, it is the heritage of all."

The patriarchal age is coming to an end in the Philippines; the illustrious deeds of the sons, are no longer accomplished within its boundaries; the Oriental chrysalis is breaking out of its sheath; brilliant colors and rosy streaks herald the dawn of a long day for those regions, and that race, plunged in lethargy during the night of its history.

While the sun illuminates other continents, awakes anew shaken by the electric convulsion produced by contact with Western peoples, and demands light, life, the civilization that was once its heritage from time, thus confirming the eternal laws of constant evolution, periodic change and progress.

You know this well and you glory in it; the diamonds that shone in the town of the Philippines owe their beauty to you; she gave the uncut stones, Europe their polished facets.

And all of us behold with pride, you the finished work, and we the flame, the spirit, and the raw material we have furnished.

The paintings of Luna and Hidalgo embodied the essence of our social, moral, and political life: humanity in severe ordeal, humanity unredeemed, reason and idealism in open struggle with prejudice, fanaticism, and injustice.

Just as a mother teaches her child to speak so as to understand his joys, his needs, his sorrow, so also Spain, as a mother, teaches her language to the Philippines, despite the opposition of those who are so short-sighted and small-minded that, making sure of the present, they cannot foresee the future, and will not weigh the consequences; soured nurses, corrupt and corrupting, who habitually choke every legitimate sentiment and, perverting the hearts of the People, sow in them the seeds of discord whose fruit, a very wolf's bane, a very death, will be gathered by future generations.

Spain is wherever she makes her influence felt by doing good; even if her banner were to go, her memory would remain, eternal, imperishable. What can a red and yellow rag do, or guns and cannon, where love and affection do not spring, where there is no meeting of the minds, no agreement on principles, no harmony of opinion? "We have come here ... to give tangible form to the mutual embrace between two races who love and want each other, united morally, socially, and politically for four centuries, so as to constitute in the future a single nation in spirit, duties, aspirations, privileges.

I ask you then to drink a toast to our painters, Luna and Hidalgo, exclusive and legitimate glories of two peoples! A toast for those who have helped them on the arduous paths of art!

A toast for the youth of the Philippines, sacred hope of my country, that they may follow such excellent examples. And may Mother Spain, solicitous and ever mindful of the good of her provinces, soon put in effect the reforms that she has long planned; the furrow has been plowed and the soil is not barren.

A toast, finally, for the happiness of those fathers and mothers who deprived of the affection of their sons, follow their courses with moist eyes and beating hearts from that distant land, across the seas and space, sacrificing on the altar of the common good the sweet comforts which are so few in the twilight of life, solitary and prized winter flowers blooming on the brink of the grave.

José Rizal's speech was followed by prolonged applause and cheering. When he sat down, Juan Luna took his place. He raised his glass of wine and in appreciation offered a toast to Rizal. "On behalf of Hidalgo and myself, we cannot express how we feel in the beautiful way you did tonight. But thank you for such a wonderful and patriotic toast. Long live the Philippines!"

After dinner at about ten o'clock, a couple of friends and compatriots gathered at Juan Luna's place on Calle de la Gorguera 14 where the celebration, fun, and laughter triggered by the consumption of more wine continued until very late.

The next morning, Luna and his friends grabbed copies of the local newspapers to see if there was any commentary about José Rizal. Sure enough his speech inside the Hotel Ingles was well received by both the press and the general public.

Rizal successfully conveyed the message that the abused central figure mourned in Luna's painting signified the same kind of suffering and exploitation thrust upon the Filipinos at the hands of the Spanish authorities back home.

When news of Luna's triumphant feat, followed by Rizal's speech reached the shores of the Philippine Islands, José Rizal's parents worried about the negative repercussions his speech might create.

CHAPTER 11

The Prado Museum in Madrid was known to have a rich collection of paintings by famous European artists from the Romantic to the Baroque periods. Juan Luna and José Rizal were attracted especially to the paintings of Diego de Velasquez and Francisco de Goya. So one day they took a leisurely walk through the museum admiring the works on display.

As they got in front of Goya's work, *El Tres de Mayo de 1808* (The Third of May 1808), they stood mesmerized at the style and subject of the painting.

"What comes to your mind when you look at this painting? Rizal asked curiously.

"Very sad and dramatic," Luna responded. "Emotional and moving depictions of war and victims of executions, and no different from what gladiators had to face during the Roman times and what we may have to face if ever we have an armed rebellion against Spain."

"What I mean is how would you feel if you or I were facing

the firing squad?" Rizal asked. "You know, just like Fathers Gomez, Burgos, and Zamora felt when they were garroted to death." Rizal was remembering the martyred Filipino priests by the Spanish authorities for their alleged roles and involvement during the Cavite Mutiny in 1872.

"Well, one thing you and I should do is make sure we don't have to face such an execution," Luna said.

"But, if we do," Rizal said and pointed to the painting. "I would like to face my executioners the same way the angelic brown-skinned man is standing with his arms stretched wide open as he bravely challenges his executioners to go ahead and get it over with. Like he is saying to them, I am not afraid to die."

Luna looked at his friend with fondness in his heart as he realized the painting affected Rizal emotionally. "Come on," he said to Rizal. "We have more paintings to see and by the way, the execution occurred at the hills of Principe Pio and the reason the painting is also known as *El Fusilamentos de Principe Pio*."

Once outside of the Prado Museum Luna said, "I also need to take you to my former school, the *Academia de Bellas Artes*, so you can see my favorite paintings by Goya, *La Maja Desnuda* and *La Maja Vestida* (The Naked Maja and the Clothed Maja). Goya used the same model for both paintings who might have been the Duchess of Alba."

"If those two are the best paintings by Goya, then why are they not on display at the Prado Museum? Rizal asked.

"The paintings were never publicly exhibited during Goya's lifetime. They were confiscated as indecent just before the end of the Spanish Inquisition. After the inquisition, the authorities gave them to the Academy of Fine Arts of San Fernando," Luna explained. "You can just imagine how I felt on my first day at the Academy when I saw the *Naked Maja*. A sudden surge of inspiration flowed throughout my body."

"A naked Duchess, Oh! Yes, what you felt was more like a huge hard on." Rizal grinned and raised his arm with a clenched fist.

Juan Luna slapped Rizal on the back and then both of them hit and kicked and giggled as they climbed the hill toward Puerta del Sol for lunch.

"Are you really very hungry?" Juan asked when they got to the restaurant.

"Oh yes, I can eat a dog. I mean a horse," Rizal said, and they burst into laughter.

"Over here," Juan Luna pointed to a tavern on Calle Bola, a quiet backstreet laid with cobblestone. "This is a family owned *taberna* that serves a huge and hearty stew beloved by all Madrileños called the *cocido*."

As they entered the *taberna*, Luna said in an excited voice, louder than he thought. "See there is an earthenware pot of *cocido* cooking right this very minute in that wooden stove. I am telling you the *cocido* here is to die for. So Rizal, after lunch you can face any firing squad of your choosing."

A balding Spaniard in his late thirties had his hand on a half-empty bottle of wine ready to fill up his glass. "Why don't you two Indios shut-up and leave us at peace to enjoy our *cocido*? Better yet go back to where you came from," he said and smirked.

Juan Luna's immediate impulse was to slap the Spaniard in the face and then challenge him to a duel. But Rizal pulled him away toward the nearest empty table with two chairs. They sat down not to cause any trouble, but they both felt to be the object of scorn by a white man.

"Why did you stop me?" Juan Luna said to Rizal. "He would have been an easy target for the tip of my sword and wouldn't even have to aim my pistol."

"Luna, you are a celebrity now in Europe. You can ask for audience and see the King of Spain at any time. You have accomplished so much at a very young age. Why lower yourself to his status when you are already ahead in life?"

"Perhaps you are right," Luna said, miffed that he missed the opportunity to put the man in his place for his rudeness.

"Why don't we get back at him with words and if he comes to our table to accost us, then you can slap him."

Rizal lowered his voice but still spoke loud enough for the racist Spaniard and everyone close by to hear him. "You, Spaniard, fail to clothe the Filipinos, and then you poke fun at their nakedness. Apparently some people have not been to the Islands of the Philippines to know that some old colonial traditions no longer exist. Filipinos no longer take off their hats upon meeting a Spaniard. Upon meeting a Spanish friar on the street, Filipinos no longer have to kiss his sweaty hands. Nor do Filipinos want to be addressed as hey you—*tu*— or be called an Indio."

Another nearby patron who had been staring at Juan Luna as if he recognized him whispered to Rizal. "Go on, say more in defense of your countrymen."

Rizal spoke somewhat louder to allow more persons to hear him. "Filipinos no longer have to vote for the candidate of the Parish priest for *gobernadorcillos*. We are no longer limited to reading only the catechism and church-related literature, but are now subscribing and reading the latest Spanish and European periodicals and literature having to do with the arts. Filipinos are studying to be doctors, poets, and mastering all of the fine arts, like this famous man." Rizal placed his hand on Juan Luna's shoulder.

Juan Luna bowed his head to the people who were now all staring at him.

"This man," Rizal said, "who was just referred to as an Indio and who just happens to be a friend of the King and Queen of Spain, is also the recipient of the gold medal for *La Spoliarium*. This Filipino goes by the name of Don Juan Luna."

Rizal lifted his hands and began to applaud his good friend, Juan, and soon all the patrons in the *taberna* joined in.

A waitress approached their table and served them with a smile while the embarrassed Spaniard staggered quietly to the door and sneaked out.

"You saved that man's life and really have a way with words. I'm impressed," Juan said.

"I hope to remember all my words, experiences, and the people I meet for when I finally sit down to write my book."

After they ate, Juan Luna and Rizal left the *taberna* very pleased that they had defended their ideals against the nasty Spaniard and now headed for La Universidad Central de Madrid, where they found out the students were organizing a demonstration against the university.

"*Hola, amigo*!" Rizal called the attention of a student carrying a placard of protest. "What are you demonstrating about?"

"We are against the university and the Catholic bishops for castigating our history professor, Dr. Miguel Morayta." The young man walked faster to catch up with his fellow students.

Rizal kept pace with him. "What has he done that merits your call for action?"

"He did nothing wrong but to proclaim his belief that professors should have the freedom to teach the sciences the way they deem to be the truth."

Rizal and Juan watched the young man run off toward the destination of his meeting.

"Did you hear that, Luna? The Spanish friars are getting involved again with the freedom and rights of individuals here in Spain the same way they do in the Philippines. They still condemn liberal views and positive change for the society, as during the days of the Inquisition. Why can they not accept progress?"

Rizal was upset and invited Luna to join him in the demonstration. "Let us follow them. They have enough reason and deserve our support."

The protest was being staged in front of the main building of the Central Universidad de Madrid. A large crowd of students already occupied the plaza that faced the beautiful neoclassical nineteenth century building. Cries of protest for change and freedom intensified and grew even louder regarding their sole demand in support for the teachings of Dr. Morayta.

Rizal and Luna got caught up in the frenzy of the demonstration and joined in the chanting from their position at the right corner of the plaza.

"We want change! We want freedom and justice for Morayta! We want change! We want freedom. Justice for Morayta!"

A young man who seemed to be one of the student leaders rose up to the occasion and said, "Comrades, our time has come. We can no longer allow dictatorial Bishops with no perception of our rights and freedom to commit more injustices.

"Down with the Bishops. Down with the Bishops!" A circle of students yelled out over the speaker.

The young leader held up his hands to quiet the crowd. "Let us unite and demand freedom for our Professor Miguel Morayta…

"Justice for Morayta! Justice for Morayta!"

The speaker shouted over the rumbling. "Morayta has been one of the greatest defenders of science, freedom, and of self-determination. Now it's our turn to defend his ideals. Long live Morayta and down with the Bishops!"

A student carried a banner with their rallying cry: Down with Bishops. At the same time he shouted, "We will do anything to change this system of education!"

"Spanish students are so well informed of their role not only in trying to overhaul their educational system, but also in their desire for ways to attain freedom," Rizal said.

"Rizal, why cannot our fellow countrymen do the same back home?" Luna asked. "Why are they not more radical?"

Luna turned to a student standing right beside him and asked, "*Hola, amigo*. I know that you are here tonight demonstrating in support of Dr. Morayta. But I am curious as to why you would want to be labeled a radical?"

"Hey, as a student we can easily relate to anything radical because our politics are shaped by time and place, like what is occurring tonight." He looked to the far side of the building and his eyes opened wide. "But hey, see there—the police. I have to go."

The arrival of the Guardia Civil ended the demonstration, but it turned quickly into a riot between the police and students.

"We need to get out of here," Rizal advised Juan Luna.

Juan nodded, and they eluded the police by pretending to be bystanders. They made their way to the nearest street that crossed the plaza. A few blocks away, they came across a small *taberna* with three tables on the sidewalk under a red and yellow striped canopy.

"The night is early and I'm hungry. How about a *tapa*?" Juan suggested.

"Great idea!"

A perky young señorita showed them to their seats and took their order for two slices of *tortilla de patatas* and two cups of coffee.

"How true that politics are shaped by time and place the same way a student would experience a change from youth to adulthood while in the university," Rizal, remarked. "I don't know about you, but I've changed."

"I agree," Juan said.

"Juan, let me tell you a secret," Rizal continued. "My family back home sent me to study in Madrid not only for an education, but they also expect me to get involved in the politics of exposing the injustices of Spanish friars in the Philippines, especially the Dominicans. And with that, of course, are the abuses of the civil government. We are aliens in Europe, and without freedom, we become aliens in our own country. I know it is wrong and things have to change but my problem is how? Do we try, through armed rebellion or peaceful mediation and public relations?"

Luna raised his eyebrows at his friend. "Who is the most famous champion for freedom in history?"

Rizal looked at Luna and said, "Don't even ask me to guess since I have no idea."

"It was Moses. And he did his freedom work through words and deeds that might have seemed strange to his people, but were successful. He even confronted and managed to convince the very powerful and domineering Pharaoh to lead the enslaved Hebrews out of Egypt and into the Promised Land."

Luna then narrated an example of a failed armed rebellion in the Philippines. "Do you remember Hermano Pule? All he wanted was to be a priest, but he was denied because of his race. So he mastered the bible and listened to as many church sermons as were available to him. And when he felt ready, he organized his own Confraternity of St. Joséph for the purpose of propagating the Catholic virtues and faith among pure Filipinos only. When the confraternity memberships swelled to more than a thousand, the jealous and fanatic Spanish friars labeled the members as heretics and provoked the civil authorities to ban the group"

"What is the point between him and Moses?" Rizal asked.

"Patience, and let me finish my story," Luna said. "As soon as the authorities banned them, Hermano Pule and his followers, armed only with knifes and machetes, made a stand for their rights and religious freedom. But they had no chance against the heavily armed Spanish forces and were slaughtered. Hundreds of old men, women, and children were massacred on the day Hermano Pule was captured and executed." Luna paused and asked Rizal, "Now who do you want to be—Moses or Hermano Pule?"

"I agree with you and Moses that freedom is evolutionary and not revolutionary. We can inform and educate the people of Spain through peaceful means and then hope that they catch our spirit to influence the authorities and friars in the Philippines to change. What is so wrong in demanding equal rights in our own country?"

On the way to the nearest *taberna*s and shops in the Somosaguas neighborhood near the university where many students lived, a large group from the demonstration passed them in a jovial mood dancing in the middle of the street and singing patriotic hymns. Some of them still waved banners and chanted, "Down with the Bishops!"

Back in the studio, Luna and Rizal were getting ready to call it a night when Rizal smiled and tapped Luna on the shoulder. "The night is still young. Why don't we go out and search for two lovely señoritas with the pretense that the great Luna would like to paint them as the *Clothed and Naked Majas*? You take the clothed one and I take the naked one."

Luna laughed and threw a pillow at his friend. He flopped onto the bed and sighed. "Go to sleep and dream on." He sighed again, which transformed into a yawn. He closed his eyes and was soon fast asleep.

CHAPTER 12

In 1879, a strip of artist studios and workshops were built along Boulevard d'Arago—between numbers 61 to 67—in the southern part of Paris not far from Plaza d'Italie in the 13th district. Having used construction materials from the dismantled food pavilion at the Universal Exhibition of 1878, the area became known as Cite Fleurie (City Flower), a favorite haunt for many artists, sculptors and painters, including the French sculptor, Auguste Rodin.

Captivated by the art scene that Cite Fleurie offered, Juan Luna left Madrid in October 1884 and opened a studio at Boulevard d'Arago 65. Although he moved to Paris to study Impressionism, he felt compelled to continue with the realistic form in order to be accepted in the Salon de Paris, the members of which were against Impressionist art.

Consequently, Juan Luna traveled back and forth to Madrid whenever there was a demand for portraiture or when his compatriots needed his presence of stature in their pursuit for reform in the Philippine colony from the Madrid government.

In between, in accordance with the agreement Juan Luna had with the *Ayuntamiento* of Manila, he began a new piece, *El Pacto de Sangre* (The Blood Compact). The painting was a depiction of the blood compact ceremony between the Datu Sikatuna, one of the lords in Bohol Island and the Spanish conquistador Miguel López de Legazpi.

Desiring to apprentice for Dr. Louis de Weckert, a famous ophthalmologist, José Rizal also moved to Paris in July 1885. He stayed for a time with Juan in his studio, which had become a gathering place for Filipino students and artists. They would often take their meals there or pass the time in the company of the homeowners who were also Filipino, the Pardo family.

At one of the lunch gatherings, Juan approached Rizal. "You may be a great poet and a writer, but one thing you will never be is an actor," he said, referring to the time Rizal played the part of a Greek poet in Madrid.

"Are you making fun of me?" Rizal said.

"No, seriously, let me create a stage for you, a tableau to be called Pacto de Sangre. "Rizal, you can be the Rajah Sikatuna."

Rizal shook his head from left to right. "No way, I don't have the time. I have to start writing my novel, and still need to make a living. If you pay me to play the role…then maybe."

"*Basta*! Enough!" Juan interrupted Rizal. "What are friends for? Besides, not only that but with your sturdy physique and Malay features, you are perfect for the role."

"No problem, then. I will pose for you, especially since you promised to assist in financing the publication and art illustrations for my book when it's finished."

Juan turned around to TH Pardo. "And you can be my Miguel de Legaspi."

At first, TH was hesitant, but then he complied. "Imagine, someday I will bring my children and grandchildren to the Museo del Prado and point to Legaspi and tell them that it's really me, as painted by the great Filipino artist, Juan Luna."

"The rest of you," Luna said and positioned two boys behind

Rizal and three behind TH. "You be their followers."

He then moved swiftly around a wooden table and chair to the center of the room. He directed Rizal to stand on one end and TH to the other side.

"TH, pretend that you are preparing to drink cups of blood.

"*Hombre*, this is so beautiful. If I can only find a way to thank you all," Juan said.

"Yes, you can!" The boys responded in unison, knowing where to get the best rice dishes. "Take us out for Chinese food."

And so immediately, Juan set about preparing how he envisioned the background for the painting, and he watched with interest as well as with emotion as his friends Rizal and Felix and the other young men donned their costumes for the artistry of his brush. *El Pacto de Sangre* was one of the most beautiful episodes in the history of the Philippines, so the process of working on it with his best friends as his models was very special for Juan.

Afterwards, on their way to the Tuileries Quarter for Chinese dinner, the group walked along the Boulevard d'Arago past the famous La Santé Prison where inmates sentenced to death were executed publicly under the guillotine that had been erected at the corner of Rue de la Sante. Not far from there, the boys spotted two streetwalkers.

"Luna, I would not mind having one of them in exchange for what you will spend for my food tonight," Rizal joked.

"Sorry, Rizal. If I were to hire one of those ladies of the night, I would rather see them illustrated in one of my canvases," Juan said sarcastically. "You don't want to take a chance with a *Fantine*, such a lowly prostitute. I would pay more money at a brothel like the *Le Chabanais* near the Louvre, where the prostitutes are regulated and medically examine by doctors."

"And much safer," TH Pardo said. "And if you want the very best then grab yourself a French courtesan."

"Hey Luna, I remember you once telling me of having hired *chulas*, a number of times to pose for you. So did you paint them or lay them on the canvas?" Rizal said and laughed.

"Of course, on the canvas, but only the pretty ones, which was very rare," Juan teased.

"What do you know about women? I have bumped into a number of *chulas* in Madrid and I found them very attractive with their colorful mantillas wrapped around their shoulders and carrying fans as they graciously walked the streets," countered Rizal, who at the same time imitated the way *chulas* strutted.

"Rizal loves anything that moves and wears a skirt," Felix said as they arrived at the Chinese restaurant.

Chulas were the lower class of women in society who lived on the backstreets in the poor districts of Madrid. Juan Luna painted them mostly because they sold well and were well received by the public. One famous art critic wrote about Juan Luna's portraits: "From his palette emerged those *chulas* who should be seen to be admired."

Juan completed the painting early in 1886 and presented it to the Town Hall of Manila in return for his pension. *El Pacto de Sangre* was never exhibited in the last Philippine Exposition held in Madrid, which was a pity since many critics claimed that this work was the finest Juan Luna had ever produced.

CHAPTER 13

As Juan Luna's reputation grew as a great painter, his brother Antonio studied literature and chemistry at the University of Santo Tomas, where he won first prize for a paper in chemistry entitled, "Two Fundamental Bodies of Chemistry." He also studied pharmacy, swordsmanship, and became a sharpshooter.

At Juan's invitation and with his father's loving consent, Antonio joined Juan in Spain in 1886 to study and acquire a doctorate to become a licensed pharmacist.

And so it was that Antonio Luna bade farewell to his beloved Philippines for the first time when he traveled to Spain. The thought that his older brothers had taken the same route, sailing to and from Europe safely in the past, calmed his nerves as he stood on the deck of the three-year-old Spanish cargo steamer, *España*.

But the feeling that a storm could come up and yank the steam ship around like a little toy boat remained ever present in his mind even though the steamers built on the lines of sailing vessels were much better protected from incoming seas and the main deck was completely covered in. Instead of the bulwarks, there was a simple rail and netting, and any excess water flowed overboard.

As the steamer set sail, Antonio Luna had hopeful dreams for the future and imagined Madrid as a relentless and amazing city of excitement, bullfights, nobility, huge crowds, gambling, noise, and a faster pace of life. In the dazzle of his desire, he formed his impressions as what to expect, daydreams, which left him breathless. And even though Juan—his own brother—had achieved fame, the deep prejudice against a pure Filipino attaining recognition in Spain's society still very much existed, and fears of failure brought Antonio back to reality.

In sailing along the coastal line into the English colony of Singapore, Antonio had the opportunity to see for the first time the pristine beauty of the islands and mountains of the Philippines south of the city of Manila. This is when Antonio realized he was finally leaving his home and country, the land of his birth.

He thought about the assurance he gave to his father that although he intended to enjoy himself and travel around Europe, he would not be swayed from his real purpose, which was to study, learn, and attain a higher degree of education. But then he thought about his dearest mother in tears when she was told that her youngest son had left for Europe. Antonio had informed her ahead of time about his plans because he knew that she would go berserk at the idea of her favorite son leaving the country.

Thinking of his mother, alone, and gazing out at the endless horizon of the Pacific Ocean made him teary-eyed, and he spoke to her inside himself. "Forgive me, my dear mother, for going away without telling you. Don't be angry when you look for me and realize that I am gone. If I told you that I was leaving, you would have showered me with endless love and affection. As the son you love most, you might have changed my mind. Seeing you cry would have made my knees buckle and lose the courage to walk away from you.

"My dear mother, I leave you without malice in my heart, but rather, to broaden my horizon. I can only hope that you understand and give me your blessings. In return, I send all the love and affection that your favorite son has for you."

Later that evening, the weather suddenly changed. The sea became rough with white caps from the gale-force winds that crashed against the ship, rocking it like a cradle. Antonio was seasick for the entire time.

Six days later, the steamer reached the Port of Raffles along the banks of the Singapore River. The south bank made it possible for English and Chinese traders to establish warehouses on reclaimed land, not only making the British settlement an important coaling station for steam and sailing ships plying the Asian sea routes, but also increasing their maritime trade with the Chinese, Indonesians, and Europeans.

After a short visit in Singapore, the *España* prepared to set sail for its next destination, Pointe de Gales in the Indian Ocean. Antonio Luna stood on the deck, overlooking the boarding ramp where passengers were in cue to embark. His wandering eyes focused steadily on a petite and attractive girl in a red casual dress befitting her youthful looks. She must have been only in her teens. Antonio kept gazing at what he thought was the most beautiful of God's creations he had ever seen.

Realizing she was being watched from above, the girl looked up. Antonio blushed and immediately turned away as if interested in watching the sailors load fresh supplies onto the ship with high cranes. But then Antonio couldn't help himself and returned her gaze only to see her about to disappear from sight. He stretched his neck trying to spot her when a moment later she was at the end of the staircase and walking toward him.

Antonio stared at her long, slender legs and her light brown hair as it blew in the wind and brushed over her luscious red lips. Antonio smiled and as she passed him, he looked into her blue eyes. She reciprocated in the same manner, and Antonio knew that he was in love.

Later on, Antonio went out on deck to enjoy the sunset when he realized the same mortal beauty he saw earlier was standing by the deck railing gazing at the horizon at the point where the sun would dip into the ocean.

"What a beautiful sunset," he said and inched his way closer to her.

"*L'italiano, che capisce e parla un piccolo spagnolo*," she said

"An Italian who understands and speaks a little Spanish," he repeated. "Very well, my name is Antonio Luna."

She pointed to herself. "My name is Chiara Pagani," she responded in halting Spanish.

"I come from the Islands of the Philippines and am on my way to Barcelona for my doctorate in pharmacy," Antonio bragged.

"I know the Philippines, and I met a lot of people from there on the ship." Chiara paused and stared out at sea before continuing. "My father is a trader. He buys a lot of goods from Singapore to sell in Napoli. He is not done with his work and will come home next month, but my mother and I are returning early because I need to get back to school and graduate soon."

"Thank God for making Spanish sound a lot like Italian and for you to speak slowly or I would not have understood anything you just said." Antonio raised his eyebrows. "Graduating? So you must be around sixteen years old?"

"Yes, but turning seventeen next month. I'm behind in school because of my travels."

"I just turned twenty, so that still makes you close to my age," Antonio said.

"My mother married when she was fifteen while my father was ten years older. It was one of those arranged marriages, which I don't believe in," Chiara said.

"Yes, it is a very common custom in the Philippines as well. By the way, I want to apologize," Antonio said.

"For what? You've done nothing wrong." Chiara looked perplexed.

"For staring at you this morning. I could not help myself. You are so attractive, so very beautiful."

"Thank you, and don't worry because I enjoyed staring back at you, too." Chiara smiled and looked up at him under lowered eyelids.

"Would it be alright if we spent our time together until we arrive at Napoli?"

"Sure, I would love having someone to talk too besides my mother," Chiara said.

"Look, the sun is about to disappear on the horizon," he said.

"Yes, I see it as the end of a beautiful day and looking forward to the beginning of a new one tomorrow." Chiara turned to face Antonio. "Will I see you tomorrow?"

'It will be my great pleasure," he said.

The following night, Antonio stood alone on the wooden promenade deck. Thinking about his family and friends that he left made him depressed. He peered out onto the incessant waves, picked up his guitar, and began to play one of his favorite classical tunes, *Romanza Anonymous*. He hoped that the music would not only lift his spirits, but also if Chiara came around, she might be impressed with his skill.

"*Bravo, come bello, bravisimo*!" Chiara applauded and stepped into view. "You play the guitar like a virtuoso, music so beautiful and the sound of which I have never heard before."

"I did not even know you were there," Antonio said.

"Yes, the whole time I've been listening but did not want to interrupt. I am so impressed. Where did you learn to play like that?"

"Will you be more impressed if I tell you that I can also sing and play the Mandolin too?" Antonio laughed. "I am glad that you enjoyed my music."

Antonio and Chiara felt so at ease being together from the moment they met. They both had the perfect recipe for getting to know one another with endless conversations, sharing meals, singing, and gazing at the millions of stars that illuminated the night skies.

CHAPTER 14

Serenity filled Antonio's heart, but calm seas did not last long for Antonio. After only a week, a sudden tropical storm came up, common during the monsoon season. The heavy rocking woke Antonio from a sound sleep. Thunder and lightning followed. Antonio lifted himself from his cot, and steadying himself against the wall, saw from his portal window that the sea was pitch black. Strange, he thought, that at dawn, the rose pink light of daybreak was not lighting up the sky.

The constant rolling and swaying of the floor beneath his feet made him seasick, so he found the best alternative was to ride out the violent movement on the deck of the main lounge. The crew had secured all furnishings with cable on one end of the lounge. Antonio overheard a first-time traveler inquire from a crew member as to whether the ship was going to sink.

"Judging from the white caps, this is just a strong gale and there is nothing to worry about," he responded.

Antonio and the fellow passenger both jumped at what sounded like an explosion.

"What was that?" They yelled almost in unison.

"Yeah, what assurance can you give us that we are not going to sink?" Antonio held his arm above his face to keep the slanting sheets of rain from garbling his speech.

"The captain makes sure to point the bow of the ship towards the oncoming waves at a low speed, which is what causes the loud crashing noise you just heard," the crew hand explained. "And don't worry if she lists to starboard. That is a normal occurrence when riding out a bad squall."

Although Juan had told Antonio that the best place to be when riding the storm at sea was in the hull where there was no danger of flying objects as there was in the bedroom. Even so, he elected to remain in the lounge on the main deck where he was in constant view of the crew and would know immediately by their actions if the steamer were in danger of foundering.

But before he could even get comfortable, the environment changed for the worse when passengers in the cabins below the deck began pushing their way up the companionway, most of them still in their nightgowns and pajamas.

Apparently two windows blew out and caused the lower decks to fill with water. Both drenched, one woman was seriously injured with a concussion and her husband had suffered multiple lacerations.

Concerned for Chiara's safety, Antonio was relived to discover her and her mother among the passengers on deck.

"Chiara, Señora Pagani, over here," Antonio said. "How are you both doing?"

"Except for wet slippers and the hems of our gowns, we are fine," Señora Pagani said.

"*Il giovane, non posso mai essere usato di tempeste in mar*," Signora Pagani said frantically.

Chiara translated. "Young man, I can never get used to storms at sea."

"Sit with me here on the floor," Antonio suggested, and he

wrapped his blanket around them.

"*Ringraziarla molto*," Signora Pagani said and smiled at Antonio.

"Thank you very much," Chiara said, and my mother thanked you as well.

The three sat huddled together, and Chiara and her mother told Antonio about their past ocean travels. Both agreed that this trip was one of their worst experiences.

Although Antonio listened attentively to their stories, he could not help but notice how close he was to Chiara. His body was touching hers from his left shoulder to the tip of his smallest finger, and he felt as if he was in heaven.

As the hours passed, the trio dozed. And then as the second morning dawned, the torrential rain seemed to stop as suddenly as it had begun. They saw the sun trying to pierce through the dark clouds.

"The sun!" Chiara called out. "Look how bright it shines on the eastern horizon."

The strong gale winds ceased. The ocean swells subsided, and the *España* was now sailing calmly above the depths of the Indian Ocean.

Deck hands set out to work immediately. They went below into the passenger cabins to survey for damage. Others displaced salt water from the hulls and cabins as well as replace several broken windows.

The captain appeared on the main deck to personally assure everyone of their safety. "Unfortunately, the worse is yet to come."

"What do you mean?' A passenger called out. "Everything is calm."

"That's because we are in the eye of the storm and still have to come out on the other side. In the meanwhile, the stewards will serve coffee and pastries. And under no condition is anyone allowed back in their cabin until further notice."

"Accompany me to the outer deck," Chiara requested of Antonio.

"Of course," he said.

Halfway up the companionway, she looked back to insure that

her mother was out of sight and then asked Antonio to share the other half of the blanket.

He gathered her close within the woolen folds and they ventured as close to the bow as possible.

"I cannot believe how a few minutes can make such a big difference," Chiara said. "From a horrific loud storm to peace and tranquility, the sea is so beautiful and peaceful now."

"I remember my brother Juan called this phenomenon a dead calm, when the winds suddenly die, and a sailing vessel comes to halt, motionless except for a slight rocking."

"But we don't have to worry about that since we are on a steamship," Chiara said.

"Yes, but we cannot ignore the risk one takes voyaging on the open seas no matter the kind of boat whether made for sailing or steam," Antonio said. "No one can control the sea and fear makes me appreciate how powerful the ocean can be."

"Why do I have this feeling that there is nothing to fear when you are around me?" confided Chiara as she turned to face Antonio.

Antonio pulled Chiara close to his chest and they gazed into each other's eyes with neither of them uttering a single word. He stroked her face and brushed his fingers lightly over her eyelids. And then he kissed her on the cheek.

She touched her skin where she felt his lips and smiled at him in return.

"Chiara, dove lei è? La colazione è pronto?"

"That's my mother calling me for breakfast," Chiara said.

They headed back toward the main lounge to partake of a simple breakfast of coffee and cinnamon rolls. This time Antonio walked behind Chiara and her mother. Inside the main room, a number of passengers complained about not being able to get back into their cabins, but to no avail. The crew was adamant about getting the vessel ready for what lay ahead of them.

And sure enough, in less than an hour the *España* once again faced the full force of the storm. Higher swells, heavier rain, and short bursts of gale winds knocked the steamer from side to side. But every so often a mountainous wave rose out of the ocean like a huge sea serpent and lifted the *España* in an almost vertical position only to drop it like an anchor with a loud crash. Lesser whitecaps broke across the bow and sprayed water onto the large windows of the lounge in rapid succession.

Inside, a Dominican friar invited his fellow passengers to pray the holy rosary. Although the friar led the prayers in Latin, the responsorial came back in different languages.

Antonio and Chiara giggled at the cacophony of voices.

"The crashing of ocean waves is in tune with the strange murmur of prayers in Spanish, Italian, and French," Chiara said, "Like listening to a church choir with the volume increasing and lowering every time the vessel goes up and down upon the waves.

All of a sudden, the floor rose beneath Antonio and Chiara until they were almost vertical so that when the steamer came thundering down again, all hell broke loose. The reverberation cracked one of the large glass panes that opened onto the starboard deck from where a massive volume of ocean exploded into the room.

Passengers and furnishings got swept up in the surge of water. And the relentless howling of the gusting wind through the gaping hole made it impossible for anyone to hear Chiara crying for help. Suddenly, Antonio realized she was no longer beside him. In a panic he looked outside and saw her grabbing for her life on the deck railings along the starboard side.

Although the nettings saved her from completely going overboard, her right foot became entangled on the nettings and exposed her naked crotch to Antonio.

"Antonio, Antonio, please save me! I need help. Please help me!" Chiara cried hysterically as she tried to pull down her nightgown with one hand to cover herself.

"For the love of God, forget your modesty and hang on to those bars with both of your hands," Antonio ordered.

Antonio's first reaction was to lunge toward Chiara but on second thought, he figured he'd end up overboard or entwined with her and no chance of cutting loose. He saw a life float attached to the wall and as soon as the steamer climbed the next swell, Antonio sprinted for the floater.

"Where are you going? Don't leave me!" Chiara shouted.

"Trust me," Antonio said.

Antonio braced himself and then tied the end of the rope that was secured to the floater to one of the handrails attached to the open door. On the next swell, he dove for Chiara, but a horrendous howling gust of wind tossed him on the floor and flipped him onto his back.

"Look out!" Chiara screamed as a heavy wooden deck chair careened toward Antonio.

But her warning was too late and the chair socked him in the forehead. Momentarily dazed, he nonetheless struggled holding tight to the floater. He fought his way back to Chiara and this time secured her to the floater and then clutched onto the railings for the onslaught of the next wave.

By then, Signora Pagani got hold of two members of the crew who stood by and yanked Chiara and Antonio back to safety.

Chiara wrapped her arms around Antonio and would not let him go, even when her mother tried to set them apart.

Crying and in shock, she refused to surrender her hold on Antonio. "Chiara, you are safe now."

She still did not respond and only continued to shiver and sob. Finally after a few minutes, she asked for a blanket.

"*Chiara, il mio solo bambino, è venuto qui alla Mamma*," her mother begged.

"I am your only child, Mama, but I want to stay with Antonio," Chiara replied.

"Mrs. Pagani, I don't mind having Chiara in my arms until she calms down. Cover us both in blankets." Antonio seated himself with his back against the wall, Chiara's arms still around his neck.

"No, she is still my baby and I cannot allow her to be so close to a man," Mrs. Pagani said.

"Mama, this man saved my life. I am not well, so please just let me rest awhile," Chiara responded, her voice haggard.

Mrs. Pagani huffed. "Very well, Chiara. But as soon as you are strong enough to raise up, you will come with me."

Although the force of the storm subsided greatly, the rain continued. The steamer continued to rock, but now in a gentle motion so that before long, Antonio and Chiara were fast asleep in each other's arms.

Soon the rain stopped and the sun shone. The seas were calm and although most of the passengers still felt wobbly from being seasick, they headed for the outside to enjoy the calm weather.

Antonio sensed that Chiara was awake and back to her normal self. "Chiara, wake up and look at the beautiful day."

"I am so embarrassed to look at you," Chiara said.

"For what?"

"That you saw all of me," she said.

"Come on, it was an accident. You could not help yourself; otherwise, you would not have exposed yourself to me."

"Of course not. What do you think of me?" She pulled away from Antonio.

"Exactly, you would not because you are a nice girl, an angel—my angel."

"No, you are my guardian angel, my lifesaver, my hero!" She hugged Antonio once more.

With the steamer now out of danger, Antonio was amazed by how such a massive vessel withstood the deadly waves of Mother Nature and still managed to not only stay in one piece, but to be fully functioning afterwards with only minor damages. That evening, the *España* stopped at the port in Pointe de Galle, the pearl of the Indian Ocean, a paradise island located at the southern tip of India.

CHAPTER 15

The next morning, the *España* sailed to Colombo in Ceylon where they picked up three more passengers. Initially, the captain was going to set sail as soon as the passengers had boarded, but then he decided to stay to replenish the linen and furnishing that were rain-soaked in the storm.

Antonio and Chiara were joyful at the news of spending an extra day. On the other hand, Signora Pagani worried that Chiara was infatuated with Antonio and she'd now have to watch her every move. Signora Alessia Pagani was in her mid-thirties, a pretty woman with a voluptuous body and Chiara never minded having her around until Antonio had come along.

That evening as the *España* drew closer to the Port of Colombo, Antonio, Chiara, and their chaperone, Signora Pagani, stood together on starboard side near the same spot where Chiara almost went overboard.

"Do you see all those rows of tall trees near the port?" Chiara asked.

"Yes, they look like cinnamon," Antonio replied. "Why, what type of trees are they?"

"They are cinnamon trees inside the Cinnamon Gardens," Chiara said.

"Cinnamomum zeylanicum blume is the Latin term for cinnamon, and they can grow as high as thirty feet," Antonio said, trying to impress Chiara with his knowledge.

Speaking in Italian, Signora Pagani commented that she once heard that Emperor Nero ordered all of the cinnamon found in Rome to be taken to him so he could burn it on the funeral pyre of his wife, Poppea Sabina, who died because the emperor kicked her belly when he found out she was pregnant.

"Is that for real?" Chiara asked stunned.

"Yes," her mother said, "In fact, it took almost a year for the Romans to replenish their entire stock of cinnamon."

"Not that. Is it true that he killed his own wife?"

"*Si*, that is why you must be very careful you know the man you marry to make sure that he will always be kind to you," her mother said and gave Antonio a sideways glance.

"We should take a stroll inside the gardens once we disembark," Chiara suggested.

"I would love that and as a pharmacist, I have studied the uses and wonders of cinnamon," Antonio said.

"Wonderful, but first let's pack a bag of goodies and a bottle of wine, and then we will be all set for a picnic at Colombo's Victoria Park," Chiara said and then added excitedly, "You will see so many beautiful flowers, plants, and trees as well as water fountains and channels that we can tour. Or we can just sit and relax and enjoy the natural beauty surrounding us."

"I supposed the picnic will include me," Signora Pagani said.

"Of course, Mama," Chiara said while Antonio said nothing.

And so it was that Antonio escorted Chiara and her mother through the narrow cobblestone streets of the Port of Colombo bazaar district, also known as the Fort.

The Fort was busy with lots of vendors and shoppers as well as local Ceylonese trying to convince the tourists the need for a guide to take them around the city. Antonio steered the women away from the hawkers and headed them toward the Grand Oriental Hotel built in the nineteenth century. A second landmark was the clock tower lighthouse originally constructed as barracks for soldiers where they had a clear view of Slave Island. The Dutch kept slaves until the British abolished the practice in 1845.

After packing some fruits and meats from a nearby market place, they proceeded south towards Victoria Park and into the Cinnamon Plantation Gardens. Chiara was right about the beauty of the park, a landscape oasis recently developed by the British as a botanical garden and conservatory for tropical species and a large tract of wood plants.

"Chiara," Antonio said. "Thank you for suggesting that we come here. I wish Manila had something as majestic as these wonderful gardens."

"Maybe someday," Chiara said.

Later that evening as the ship sailed towards the African Coast, Antonio got a terrible case of seasickness. He blamed the spicy food he'd eaten in Colombo.

Feeling sympathetic, Senora Pagani kept Antonio on a plain diet until his stomach was back to normal, and Chiara sat on the deck chair next to him out in the open and kept him company.

Several mornings later, after being eight days at sea, Antonio spotted the magnificent South African coast and lands at Aden. For almost fifty years, the British East India Company occupied Aden as a precaution to safeguard British shipping liners from piracy at sea. When the Suez Canal opened in 1869, the area became an important location to stockpile coal utilized by vessels along the main shipping routes.

"There is news of pirates everywhere, but they are like phantoms. They appear in many places, whereas we find them in none." Chiara translated what her mother said.

A week later they reached the entrance to the Suez Canal, which was completed and opened a decade earlier. The steamship was quarantined for four days, after which it set sail for Port Said and then finally, the long voyage was coming to an end as the *España* pulled into the docks in Naples, Italy.

Antonio felt the air of the European continent he had only heard about previously. Now he walked along the shipping docks with Chiara and ate Neapolitan flatbread, called pizza, the authentic dish of the poor that Chiara bragged about. Everything was wonderful except for the lingering knowledge that he would soon have to say goodbye to the love of his life, a thought that made him very depressed.

The Pagani women were met at the Port of Naples by a large carriage upon their disembarkation from the *España*. Antonio vowed to keep in touch with Chiara.

"I promise you, my dear one, that after I visit my brother Juan and get settled in Barcelona, I will write to you every weekend. No—make that every day," Antonio said.

"That won't work," Chiara said.

"Why not?"

"Because I will still miss you so much," Chiara said sadly.

"I will miss you too," Antonio said.

"Chiara, è ora di andare alla casa." Signora Pagani told Chiara that it was time to go home.

"Wait, I will buy us food so we can have a few minutes to be alone," Chiara said. Once again, she ordered three larges slices of pizza for Antonio. While waiting for the flatbread to be served, she hid behind a pillar with Antonio, away from the wandering eyes of her mother, who watched over their suitcases.

"Three large pizzas to remind you that I will be seventeen in three days' time," Chiara said sweetly.

"Happy seventeenth birthday my love!" Antonio hugged Chiara.

"I've never been kissed before and for my seventeenth birthday, I want you to be the first." Chiara turned her face toward his. Her lips were an inch away from Antonio, who kissed her lightly at first and then a bit passionately. Chiara knew that she was madly in love with him.

"Why do I have this feeling that I have known you all my life?"

"Maybe it's because we were born for each other," Antonio said.

"Antonio, some people never fall in love their whole lives. And yet, in a month, I have fallen in love with you."

"I love you, Chiara!" Antonio's eyes misted with his tears.

"Antonio, as we go our separate ways, I want you to remember that where there is love, we can hear each other. Where there is love, we can see each other. Where there is love, we will find each other, all over again."

"Chiara, I hear your mother calling for you."

"I love you Antonio! You have my address, so don't forget to write every day as you promised." Chiara joined her mother who was already waiting and seated in their carriage. Chiara stopped, turned her back, and looked at Antonio one last time. "I will forever wait for you."

That evening the ship finally arrived in the prosperous port city of Marseilles, France. With colonies in northern Africa, the end of Barbary pirates, and the opening of the Suez Canal, the French made Marseilles the major port in the Mediterranean for their maritime trade.

Antonio dreamed of his beloved Chiara; he slept soundly on board the steamship for the first time since the start of a very long voyage. The knowledge that he would be traveling by land from now on made him sleep even longer. He disembarked from the *España* and checked in to a cheap hotel in the old Vieux Port area.

The next morning, he raced up the steps that led to the beautiful Gare de Marseille Saint-Charles, the main train station perched on top of a hill. When he took money from his pocket to pay for his ticket for Paris, Chiara's address must have fallen out. Because later, thinking that he wanted to write her, the paper was gone. He felt terrible. He had promised that he would keep in touch every day and all he thought about was Chiara waiting to hear from him.

Antonio's mood lifted when he arrived in Paris and was reunited with his brother, Juan. Also, while there, he met a young man five years older who he knew from the Ateneo school he attended. The Philippine youth was José Rizal, a rising star with whom he would become close friends.

Once in Spain, Antonio went on and obtained the degree of Licentiate in Pharmacy from the University of Barcelona. In recognition of his ability and with the connections of his brother, he was appointed commissioner by the Spanish government and given a grant to study tropical and communicable diseases.

CHAPTER 16

In January 1872, a bloody purge was perpetrated in the Philippines by newly appointed Spanish Governor General Rafael Isquierdo, who vowed to rule with the cross in one hand and with the sword in the other. What happened was that a group of Filipino soldiers of Spanish descent garrisoned in Cavite Province mutinied against the higher-ranking Spanish-born officers.

Don Joaquin Pardo, a former lawyer and member of the Spanish Governor-General's advisory council in the Philippines, was very lucky. Instead of getting executed by *garrote*, a form of strangulation, like his compatriot Fr. José Burgos, for their alleged participation in the mutiny, Don Joaquin was exiled to Guam, the southernmost and largest of the Mariana Islands.

Soon after Don Joaquin made Guam his home, he was pardoned. He immediately moved to Paris with his wife, Doña Tula de Gorricho—the Gorricho family were known in the Philippines as distinguished and wealthy landowners.

Don Joaquin chose Paris mainly because the persecuted Spanish *mestizos* from the Philippines found freedom for their kind of liberal politics and art. Dubbed the era of the Third Republic, late nineteenth century Paris flourished in all areas of business, academia, and especially art, and was home to many world-renowned artists.

The Pardo couple settled soon after their arrival in their new home at No. 47 Rue d'Maubeuge. They found relief immediately from the horror and sadness of having been deported. Here again, they resumed a cosmopolitan life where great coffee and good food were sprinkled with free thinking and economic activities, all of which made life more enjoyable and comfortable for them. The Pardos felt secure and at peace in their new surroundings.

Once established, Joaquin Pardo convinced his eldest nephew, Trinidad Hermenegildo, the son of his older brother Felix, to join him and his wife so that he could study at the University of Paris-Sorbonne.

His mother, Juliana Gorricho Pardo, agreed and Trinidad, nicknamed TH, left the University of Santo Tomas in Manila, where he was studying medicine, and moved in with his Uncle Joaquin and Aunt Tula. Sometime later, TH's mother, Doña Juliana, who also happened to be Tula's sister and her other children: Felix and Maria Paz also followed the family to the French capital.

When Don Joaquin died in March 1884, Doña Juliana and her family decided to stay in Paris at their family home on Avenue Wagram. TH and his brother Felix were already doctors. TH also became a published linguist and an expert in Malayan languages. At twenty-four years old, their sister Maria Paz had blossomed into a beautiful slim young lady.

Gradually, the Pardo house became a meeting place to a number of Filipino *ilustrado*s like Juan Luna, José Rizal, Maximino Paterno, Valentin Ventura, Mariano Ponce, Felix Hidalgo, and Antonio Luna. The Pardos enjoyed the company of Filipino intellectual expatriates and invited them into their drawing room to participate in spirited discussions about freedom, liberty, and reforms in their homeland. It was there that Maria Paz Pardo met Juan Luna for the first time.

Juan Luna was immediately attracted to this tall and vivacious redheaded woman. Her warm smile, blushing soft skin, and large penetrating brown eyes captivated him, and he dreamed of kissing her sensuous lips. Juan Luna was so excited to have found his own Mona Lisa, a muse to inspire him. He had truly fallen in love.

Perhaps, it was fate that drew Juan Luna, the victorious soldier of Filipino art, to Maria Paz, the lovely princess of the Pardos of Paris. Juan Luna belonged to a group of Filipino expatriates that the Pardos entertained in their home. Among this batch of Filipinos, Juan Luna was the most famous. Among the artists, he was the most talented. And this young man, although enormously shy and conscious of his accent and unpolished social etiquette, was drawn to the close circle.

One Parisian afternoon in September 1886, José Rizal got together with Antonio and Juan Luna at the home of Pardo. José had just returned from stays in Germany and in London. Upon his arrival, he gave Maria Paz a pair of Greek vases, which he had painted. One depicted a group of Filipinos engaged in cockfighting and the other showed the Filipinos at work as milkmen and as prisoners at hard labor.

Antonio Luna had just completed his doctorate at the University of Madrid and had found a job at the Institut Pasteur, where he did research in histology and bacteriology.

Although the opinionated Maria Paz Pardo would not join in the political discussions among the *illustrados*, she would socialize with them. She kept an album of all the guests who visited at their house as well as requested a piece of prose, a poem, or even a sketch as a reminder of them after they had gone.

When Maria Paz asked Rizal what his contribution was going to be, he decided on an illustrated story of a monkey and a tortoise, a moral lesson as it were, that had been recently published in a London newspaper. He remembered about it when he heard Felix Pardo and Juan discussing whether the fruit of the banana tree looked upward or downward. Both of them had been away from the Philippines for such a long time that they were no longer sure.

Rizal hesitated. "It's nothing more than a silly fable, and surely nothing compared to any of Aesop's. In fact, I am so amazed that it was ever published."

Maria Paz gently urged, "Come on. Rizal. I am curious now, so please recite it." She looped her arm in his and walked with him to the center of the room. "Here, full attention is on you."

Knowing that Juan Luna might react with displeasure to the consideration Maria Paz was giving him, Rizal glanced back at Juan with a look of assurance that suggested, "Don't worry, I know that she is off limits." Rizal adored women and had been known to have numerous love affairs. But he was also a very loyal friend. Otherwise, he would have been as infatuated with Paz as Juan was.

And so Rizal began his fable.

Once upon a time, a tortoise and a monkey found a banana tree floating amidst the waves of a river. It was a very fine tree with large green leaves and with roots just as if it had been pulled off by a storm. They took it ashore. "Let us divide it so we can each plant one half of it," said the tortoise. They cut it down the middle and the monkey, the stronger of the two, took the upper part of the tree, thinking that it would grow quicker because it already had leaves. The tortoise, the weaker one, took the lower part, which looked ugly but had roots.

After some days, they met. "Hello, Mr. Monkey," said the tortoise. "How are you getting on with your banana tree?"

"Alas," said the monkey, "it has been dead a long time! And yours, Miss Tortoise?"

"Very nice indeed, with leaves and fruits, but I cannot climb up to gather them."

"Never mind," said the malicious monkey, "I will climb up and pick them for you."

"Do, Mr. Monkey," replied the tortoise gratefully. And so they walked toward the tortoise's house.

As soon as the monkey saw the bright yellow fruits hanging between the large green leaves, he climbed up and began plundering, munching and gobbling as quickly as he could.

"But give me some, too," said the tortoise, seeing that the monkey did not take the slightest notice of her.

"Not even a bit of the skin if it is edible," the monkey replied, his cheeks crammed with bananas.

The tortoise meditated revenge. She went to the river, picked up some pointed shells, and then planted them around the banana tree. She hid and when the monkey came down, she saw him fall onto the points and began to bleed.

The monkey was angry and began searching for the tortoise. When he found her he said, "You must pay for your wickedness. You must die, but because I am generous, I will leave the choice of death up to you. Shall I pound you in a mortar, or shall I throw you into the water? Which do you prefer?"

"The mortar, the mortar," the tortoise said. "I am so afraid of getting drowned."

"Oh ho!" the monkey laughed. "Indeed! You are afraid of getting drowned, so that's how you will die!"

The monkey slung the tortoise into the water. The tortoise went underwater, but soon her body resurfaced, and she started swimming and laughing at how she had deceived the artful monkey.

Rizal bowed and everyone in the room applauded. "Now a kiss from me to anyone who can tell me the moral of my story." He looked around for Maria Paz and spotted her seated on a red velvet chair.

"No, who wants to be kissed by a monkey like you," one of his acquaintances called out.

"Come on, no one knows the moral of the story," Rizal said.

"I do," Maria Paz replied as she stood from her chair and mimicking a tiger; slowly approached Rizal. "Size does not matter and never under estimate the power of a woman, she can be as meek as a lamb and as bold as a crouching tiger," she hugged and thank Rizal and kissed him on both cheeks.

There was definitely an aura or sensuousness to her pause, her hand resting on her thigh after embellishing Rizal's cheeks. It did not reflect in Juan Luna that the woman he desired, believed in equality and freedom of thought. However, a wave of angry disdain transformed Luna's calm exterior. He blushed deep inside him with uncontrollable jealousy and decided to confront Rizal on their way back to his studio.

Juan Luna accosted Rizal. "I have known you for some time now and consider you one of my closest friends. You know how I feel about Maria Paz, and yet, you're flirting with her."

"Excuse me, although I do find her attractive and amiable, she is like a sister to me," Rizal said. "You have nothing to worry about my friend. She is all yours, and besides I will be leaving Paris soon to work on my book and the movement for a better Philippines."

"I'm sorry to see you go, but you will be back ... right? Juan Luna asked.

"Of course, and hopefully for your wedding" Rizal laughed.

"Darn it, she knows damn well how much I desire and love her. Why does she always make me jealous and mock me in front of everyone? And admit, you enjoyed every minute," Juan said. "I don't know what to do, or say, or feel anymore. How do I love her? Help me Don Casanova."

Since Juan's studio at d'Arago was only a short distance by tram from the Pardo's home, Juan Luna took the advice of Rizal. The next day, he began courting Maria Paz without the company of his friends, dressed nicely and smelling of fine cologne. He was deeply attracted to her beauty and vivacity, but lacked the confidence to court a girl from a higher class of society. Foremost in his mind was how to let his feelings be known to someone like Maria Paz since romancing her was not going to be easy.

Realizing that women like Maria Paz yearned to be wooed, Juan Luna decided from the start to make his intentions clear to her by showering her with flowers and show her how happy he was and how much he cared for her. He would impress her with tales of the important people he had met in the court of Spanish royalty; he even learned to be spontaneous when around her by taking her, on short notice, for a stroll and patronize the cozy cafes and bistros of Paris, the city of romance.

He would befriend her brothers, especially Felix. Their relationship gathered momentum.

CHAPTER 17

After spending the day at the Louvre located in the first district of Paris, Juan Luna and Maria Paz walked hand in hand along the Right Bank of the Seine. "Let's sit for a while," Juan said, indicating one of the many wooden benches along the river.

He wanted to announce his true intentions but found it difficult to find the right words. If only he was as articulate as his Antonio and Rizal, he thought.

"Maria Paz, do you ever dream of the future?" he finally asked.

"All the time, and do you?"

Juan considered her question and then said, "Yes, that the *Spoliarium* or any one of my paintings makes it to the Louvre someday."

"That is a very ambitious dream, but no doubt possible in your case," she said.

"But now tell me what dreams you have of the future," Juan said.

By the tenor of his voice, Maria Paz could sense Juan had difficulty in expressing his desire to propose marriage so she tried to help him along. Smiling indulgently, she took his hand, softly squeezed it and said, "Mine are much like any young girl with an ever-wandering mind. I imagine a knight in shining armor rushing towards me. He pulls me up on his grand white horse and we gallop off into the horizon together—forever."

They remained silent for a few seconds, but what felt more like minutes.

A cool, gentle breeze caressed her face. She tossed her hair and said, "By the way, I too may be an artist like you, for I paint my dreams in color," Maria Paz said.

"Good for you, we should find more time to be together. Then I can teach you how to paint."

Maria Paz smiled at Juan. "As a woman, I had the same fantasy as when I was a child because I know that dreams can become a reality. So I will find my knight someday soon."

Luna knelt down on one knee and looked straight into her eyes. "I believe love is forever, and you are definitely the love of my life. You are the only woman I ever want to know. Maria Paz, I want to be your knight. Please, will you marry me?"

Brainwashed by her mother to believe she was bred from a common pool of superior genes, Maria Paz suddenly felt her heart pound followed by a current of unease slither along her backbone.

"I would love to, but I cannot answer you this very minute," she replied. She paused and then blurted out, "I need the blessings of my family."

"I understand and am willing to ask for your hand in marriage when we get back tonight."

Maria Paz knew how her mother might respond so she said, "No, let me be the one to break the ice first, especially to my mother. As for Felix and TH, they like you and are proud of your accomplishments."

Juan cupped her cheek, stared at her face and said, "Yes, you are right. It may not be the right thing, but definitely the best way," Juan Luna said.

Juan also understood very well that Doña Juliana had every

reason not to want her only daughter to wed a man who was not of the same social status. She made herself abundantly clear from the moment he started courting Maria Paz. Doña Juliana believed that the rich begot the rich, and that landholdings equal money, and money is power. Consequently, a poor working class man would be a bad match for a beautiful, upper class woman. After all, the Gorricho family owned almost all of one of the most expensive blocks of properties in the Philippines, similar to Spain's Gran Via.

Later that evening, Maria Paz attempted to corner her mother into agreeing with the proposal. "Mamita, Juan asked me to marry him. What shall I say? What shall I do?"

"You would not want to hear my opinion of the man," Doña Juliana said flatly.

"But why? He is an artistic genius with so much prestige at an early age," Maria Paz said.

"Do you really want to know how I feel?" Doña Juliana said. "Listen to what I have to say. You are completely mismatched. We are of Spanish noble ancestry, and he is a native Indio who is short, has dark skin, and lacks manners. He is not in harmony with our family lineage. My dear daughter, you deserve more. Besides, I sense that you don't really love him that much. Do you?"

"I don't know. There are things about him that appeal to me very much, but then, there are some that I don't like. For instance, his physical characteristics are not to my best liking and clearly, he is not rich enough for my tastes. On the other hand, he is famous and a very talented artist, well connected in society. Imagine me, Doña Maria Paz, hobnobbing with royalty. I can grow to love him in time. Isn't that right?"

"Love—what do you know about love? You are just a child. Look at your brother who has already agreed to meet and get to know Doña Carmen's very wealthy granddaughter when they come to visit soon. Now that will be a match made in heaven!"

"There is something about Juan that I find intriguing. Maybe, it's his ingenuity and creativeness that I would like to be a part of."

Maria Paz paused, and then smiled. "I will marry him."

"Don't be stupid, my daughter. Mark my words, you will regret marrying a poor man," Doña Juliana responded. "Why don't you seek the advice of TH? He is the head of the family now that your father is no longer here."

The moment Maria Paz heard her brother came home from work, she broke the news of her proposed engagement.

"Now tell me, TH, is Mamita overreacting?"

TH went straight to their mother. "Mamita, rest assured, you have nothing to worry in having Juan as your son-in-law. The man is educated, civilized, talented, and a very well-known painter. We should be proud to have him in the family," TH said.

"Oh, thank you, dear brother, for giving me your blessings to marry." Maria Paz hugged her brother and then turned to her mother. "Now, Mamita, do I now have your blessings?"

"Oh, alright, I just hope my grandchildren all get to look like us and not the Indio side."

"Mamita, you have to stop being a racist," Maria Paz said. "Juan is going to be family now.

On December 7, 1886, Juan Luna married the beautiful señorita from the Pardo clan. For their honeymoon, the couple traveled to Rome and then to Venice, where he painted beautiful scenes from the city of gondolas. But most memorable to Juan Luna was seeing the love of his life wake every morning in bed. He was so much in love and still could not believe that a beautiful, wealthy woman from high society like Maria Paz, was his wife. He used to stare at her while she slept, and on that particular morning, he decided to immortalize her on canvas.

"My dearest love, what are you doing? How can you paint a portrait of me when I just woke up? Give me a chance to wash and powder my face," Maria Paz complained as she stretched her voluptuous body in bed.

"I love watching you sleep. You look so lovely that sometimes

I wish the night would never end so I can just continue to soak up your beauty with my eyes. You are so exquisite and will never be lovelier than you are right now, this very moment for my brush work. Stay still and pretend you are still sleeping, *mi amor*. I'm almost done with the underlay coat of paint."

Juan began to wake up early every morning during their honeymoon to complete his painting, *Ensuenos de Amor* (Daydreams of Love), which was oil on wood that depicted Maria Paz in a *contrapposto* pose underneath her bed sheets. The portrait was predominantly white with dashes of pink, green, and blue hues. Luna used the latest impressionist style of rapid brush strokes to capture the dreamy and sensual mood expressed on her face.

After their honeymoon, the couple settled in their new home located in a peaceful and tranquil vicinity of Paris, Villa Dupont, in Rue Pergolese. Doña Juliana Gorricho moved in with her daughter to financially assist the young couple with the cost of maintaining a home in the affluent section of Paris.

CHAPTER 18

The success of the *Spoliarium* did not stop Luna's brush. He produced hundreds of paintings, each one vying with the other for beauty. Among his works were *The Blind Slave, Roman Ladies, Lady at her Dresser, La Posada, and Excelsior.*

Meanwhile, Luna also started developing a friendly relationship with Alfonso XII, the very young king of Spain, who after learning of the publics negative reaction towards the biased judges in Madrid's recently held art competition, felt the need to personally meet and congratulate the young Filipino painter.

King Alfonso XII, who was a year younger than Luna, also received Juan Luna and the Benlliure brothers. The King was a personal friend of Mariano Benlliure and was a frequent visitor at his studio in Madrid. On this occasion, the King warmly congratulated Luna for his great painting, *La Spoliarium*, and expressed his sympathies for his not having been awarded the Prize of Honor by the Jury.

As a result of the alleged biased jury, and the friendship that developed between Juan Luna and the king, the Royal family influenced the Spanish Senate to commission Luna to paint *La Batalla de Lepanto* (*The Battle of Lepanto*). King Alfonso XII's plan was to hang Luna's Battle of Lepanto side by side with Francisco Pradilla Ortiz's 1878 winning masterpiece *La Rendicion de Granada* (The Surrender of Granada).

Barcelona proudly hailed the arrival of Luna's award winning *La Spoliarium* in their city to hang in their Town Hall. Juan Luna now had to travel back and forth from Paris to Madrid in order to meet the demands for portrait jobs, including the task of assisting Filipinos to push for reforms in the Philippines through the seat of the government of Spain in Madrid.

In the interim, Juan Luna found himself in a quagmire because even months after his success with the *Spoliarium*, some critics still did not accept that a Filipino native, rather than a Spaniard, was chosen to depict one of the most important naval victories in the history of Spain.

The Battle of Lepanto in the Gulf of Lepanto—which Luna had learned of the name changed to the Gulf of Corinth between the Peloponnese and mainland Greece—was a naval battle of paramount importance for Spain and the Christian world on October 5, 1571. A coalition of Christian states led by the Kingdom of Spain, and the Papal States, the Republic of Venice, the Order of Malta, the Republic Genoa, and the Duchy of Savoy joined forces in the Italian city of Messina to confront the growing menace of the Ottoman Empire.

Although King Alfonso XII announced his intention to have Luna paint *The Battle of Lepanto*, his decision had to be approved by the Spanish Senate. Even so, Luna fretted that the strong opinion of his critics might sway the sentiment of the senate. Moreover, he had personal fears of his skill to be able to create a work that would match in excellence Pradilla's masterpiece that already hung in the halls of the Senate, or that some critics would lambaste his work all over again.

And to make matters worse, Luna woke up on the morning of November 25 to the shocking news that his young benefactor, King Alfonso XII, had passed away of tuberculosis at the age of twenty-eight.

On his mind that day and all throughout the night was the question of whether they would they change their minds and give the project to a Spaniard or decide to leave the revered painting of Pradilla by itself and not to balance it with another painting.

When the news came that Queen Cristina was taking over the reign as Queen Regent of the Spanish Crown, and that the country was in peace, the economy was financially sound and regulated, and various administrative services were on, Juan Luna felt much better and decided not to think of any negative outcome, but instead to concentrate solely on *The Battle of Lepanto*.

Much to Juan's joy, he was informed that the Spanish Senate approved his commission. However, he was to insert a colossal and massive battle scene on a canvas smaller than the *Spoliarium*. Realizing it was futile for him to stay in Paris with no research materials on hand to assist him in finding the perfect theme and solution to his dilemma, Juan Luna, with the consent of his wife Maria Paz, who was about five months on the way with their first child, left for Madrid.

Upon arriving in Madrid, he socialized with his brother and fellow propagandists and also visited his old friend and fellow artist, Antonio Benlliure to discuss with him his latest project.

"*Amigo*, how are you doing? It's been a while since we last saw each other." Luna greeted Benlliure with enthusiasm.

"Yes, my old friend, more than two years, and congratulations! I heard the Senate finally approved the funding for your commission."

"Well, you know how the government works, but better late than never, and the timing could not have been much better," Juan said.

"What do you mean?"

"I got the confirmation and my initial fee a month before my wedding—you know that I got married last December."

"How would I know if you have not written me at all?" Antonio said.

"My apologies. Last year was such a crazy, busy and tremendously memorable year for me. I fell in love with the most beautiful girl in the most romantic city of the world. Oh, and by the way, I have since then dabbled a little in the world of impressionistic art."

"I'm gratified to hear that you are in love but not so thrilled about Impressionism," Antonio said.

"Come on, it's not at all that bad. It's easy, liberating, and most of all relaxing compared to painting an important historical event hanging alongside Pradilla's *Rendicion de Granada*, which happens to be the other reason I came over to see you."

"What do you know about *The Battle of Lepanto*?" Juan Luna asked.

"A little, but first let me offer you something to drink." Benlliure led Juan toward a small wooden circular dining table with four metal chairs. He poured two glasses of red wine, lifted his glass, and offered a toast, "Cheers to our days in Rome."

"Cheers" responded Juan Luna lifting his glass of wine and took a sip.

"Did you know that Miguel de Cervantes, yes, Don Quixote himself, was a veteran of the battle at Lepanto?" Antonio asked. "He was injured, and lost the mobility of his left hand, which earned the nickname of 'manco of Lepanto.'"

"Great, maybe I should include a soldier with a lamed left arm in the portrait." Juan Luna and Antonio Benlliure laughed.

"Another thing: do you know the significance of the first Sunday of October?" Benlliure asked.

"Of course, it's the Feast of the Virgin of the Rosary," Juan responded. "Don't tell me that, too, has something to do with the battle."

"It definitely did. The Pope held a prayer vigil of the rosary in the *Basi*lica Santa Maria Maggiore on the day of the battle. Thence, the victory was attributed to the Virgin and that's the reason it's celebrated on the first Sunday of October."

"Hey, that's good to know. I can place a priest, or even better, a bishop on board with a rosary on hand, raised for all to see," Juan Luna said.

"Don't forget a cross on his other hand. Bishops always carry a cross," Benlliure suggested.

"Listen, Benlliure … are you free tomorrow or anytime this week?" Juan asked.

"Hmmmm … not really, but why?"

"Nothing much, except to come with me to the library to research the battle further."

"I have to pass at this time, but I would be happy to get together again for *tapas* and wine, and to discuss the outcome of what you find."

And so on his own, the Filipino painter discovered valuable facts. He learned that the Ottoman Turks led by Ali Pacha had more men and ships than the Christian coalition, called Santo Liga, and under the command of Don Juan of Austria, who was appointed to the post by his illegitimate half-brother the King of Spain, Philip the Second. This was the same king for whom the Philippines was named by the Spanish explorer Villalobos. The Christian infantry choice of weapon was the harquebus, while the Turks preferred arrows.

At Messina, Don Juan of Austria had ordered to lower all spurs of the galleys to modify the bow trim, so that the guns had more shooting range. Juan Luna became excited to learn that Juan of Austria was aboard the command ship, La Real, and on a collision course with the Sultana, the command ship of Ali Pacha. The face off between the two command ships had begun as a duel at sea, which decided the fate of either the Christian cross or the Ottomans star.

At the critical moment, Juan of Austria out-maneuvered the Sultana and launched his latest attack with everything he had and brought his flagship, La Real close enough to ram the Sultana. A wave of infantrymen from La Real with the fury of a hurricane entered Ali Pasha's galley with fire and sword. A crack shot from a harquebus hit Ali Pasha's head and killed him on the spot. Only after the Ottomans saw the mutilated head of their leader stuck on a pike did they become demoralized. Soon after, the balance for victory tipped in favor of the Santo Liga.

Juan Luna traveled to Segovia to visit and study the sculptured sepulcher of Juan of Austria, who was buried in the Escorial when he died of tuberculosis. He also traveled to Venice to take a look at the other two renditions of *The Battle of Lepanto* by Paolo Veronese and Andrea Vicentino. Taking into consideration the magnitude of the epic battle, Juan Luna understood why the rendition of other artists on the subject was to capture the whole battle from a bird's eye view.

In contrast, and based on his research, Luna wanted to capture the passion of the whole battle by creating a close-up of the two main protagonists. Having worked as a seaman, he was able to clearly imagine how it felt to be on board either of the two vessels. Thus, his idea for the rendition of *The Battle of Lepanto* became a visual reality.

Luna saw Juan of Austria standing at La Real's bow stoically overlooking the nightmarish carnage going on when the Ottomans gave up the battle in defeat. He witnessed heads on tips of pikes, horned weapons, swords blazing, fires, thick clouds of smoke, and corpses floating side by side with the moving waves. He heard the roaring seas wrapped in blood, sounds of artillery, and he smelled burnt human remains. Death was all around him.

Luna saw a flag—a symbol of courage, and a bishop in a red cassock with a cross and rosary in his hand crying out prayers, amidst rage, fury, and anger. Ottomans who were afraid of drowning gripped their oars, with pitiful voices and cries for help and mercy as they tried to board and hang on to La Real while miserable Christian men, without souls, mercilessly ended their attempts with shots and cut off their hands or pushed them back into the sea with their oars.

Luna saw were a few good souls who saved some Turks. From this scenario emerged the true genius of Juan Luna in depicting with vivid colors the breathtaking portrait of the famous battle.

Juan Luna's *The Battle of Lepanto* provided proof of the Spanish victory against the Turks. For this reason, the widow of King Alfonso XII of Spain, Queen Regent Maria Christina of Austria unveiled Luna's masterpiece at the Senate Hall of Madrid in November 1887. Through the royal order of the Queen, Juan also received the Medal of Elizabeth the Catholic from the Ministry of the High Seas, for the Filipino's "outstanding service to Spain."

In a sense, by not winning the coveted Medal of Honor, Juan

Luna unexpectedly gained commissions for two additional paintings from the Spanish Senate, *The People and the King*, and *España y Filipinas*, thus giving further honor not only to himself, but to Spain and the Philippines.

About this time in Paris, Maria Paz gave birth to their son, Andres. Doña Juliana was thrilled that her new grandson inherited the European features of her side of the family, and she was not shy making comments to her friends even in front of her son-in-law.

Not long after his nephew's birth, TH was granted a royal commission to study medicinal problems of plants in the Philippines. He returned to Manila not only for the research, but also to comply with a marriage engagement to an heiress of a large fortune, Concha Cembrano.

The marriage had been prearranged by Doña Juliana, a close family friend and Concha's grandmother, Doña Carmen Barredo—widow of the founder of the Banco Espanol Filipino, the largest bank in the islands.

CHAPTER 19

In February 1888, Antonio Luna met with José Rizal, Graciano Lopez-Jaena, Marcelo del Pilar, and José Maria Panganiban in Madrid to further discuss the propaganda movement for reforms in the Philippine society. The Propaganda Movement was an organization established by them and supportive of the beliefs inspired by Rizal. The organization aimed to recognize the Philippines as one of Spain's provinces and for Filipinos to be treated no different from any other Spaniard.

"Gentlemen, before we begin brainstorming on the objectives of our movement, we will first like to recognize Don Jose Rizal for the success of his first novel," Antonio Luna announced.

The friends erupted in congratulations. "Bravo! *Bueno*!" They cheered in affirmation of the great accomplishment for their fellow propagandist.

"You all have been so supportive of my efforts in writing my book," Rizal said. "I could not have completed such a huge undertaking without your help."

"Of course, my good friend. We believe in you and are so proud that you took this upon yourself to finish so the world can see what is in our hearts," Panganiban said with much emotion.

Rizal looked at Antonio and said, "I want to especially thank your brother for the beautiful and relevant illustrations in my book."

This was a far cry from the time Jose Rizal tried to unite the Filipinos to coordinate their efforts in Spain when he first proposed writing the novel as a group to another set of Filipino expatriates.

Inspired by Harriet Beecher Stowe's book, *Uncle Tom's Cabin*, Rizal wrote *Noli Mi Tangere*, Latin for Touch Me not, to embody the words of Jesus to Mary Magdalene upon his Resurrection.

His novel exposed the abuse experienced by the Filipinos at the hands of the Spanish colonial authorities and friars. He wanted to describe the cultural status of Philippine society as being backward and not conducive to the ideas of the Enlightenment as understood by him.

Antonio opened the meeting by raising the cudgel. "Who would like to facilitate this discussion?"

"You can be the facilitator, Antonio," Rizal said, with the others all in agreement.

"We must aim at Filipino representation in the Spanish Cortes to disseminate information of the abuses to the motherland, and the separation of the church from the state to stop friars from controlling the colonial authorities," Antonio proposed adamantly.

"May I interject?" Marcelo requested.

"Let me finish with my other proposals for reform and then you can speak," Antonio said, interrupting Marcelo del Pilar, a reform-minded lawyer active in the anti-friar movement in the Philippines until obliged to flee to Spain.

"Yes, Marcelo, let him continue. What he has to say is important," Graciano said.

Antonio nodded and began. "Filipinos should be given equal rights in government positions and teachers to be given better pay. There must be a plan implemented to build more schools, and there should be freedom of the press and of religion. Finally, the colonial government must work for the people and not the other way around."

"After all, similar principals were adopted much earlier in the Philippines by Luis Rodriquez Varela, also known as El Conde Filipino," Marcelo said.

"Who was he?" Panganiban asked.

"He was an active mestizo nationalist in the beginning of the nineteenth century who was educated in France, and publicly supported and recommended the same reforms Antonio enumerated earlier. Sadly, the Spanish Governor eventually expelled Varela from the Philippines," Marcelo responded.

"It was the Age of Enlightenment, also referred to as the Age of Reason, a cultural movement that started in France in the eighteenth century. It was composed of people considered to be the best in a particular society that had the power, talent, or wealth to obtain, organize, and encourage reformation for any suffering society, which included the quest for a higher level of education for the populace. Reading about the era motivated me to complete my book and sparked me to write the sequel," Rizal explained.

The era of enlightenment promoted intellectual interchange and opposed intolerance and abuses in church and state, and not long after, their message through the Encyclopedia spread across the urban centers of Europe and all the way across the Atlantic into the European colonies, influencing the minds of the leaders of the American revolution in their writing of their Declaration of Independence and Bill of Rights.

The propaganda movement was distinctive, because each of the original organizers were destined to play an important part in the history of their country. With only their pens for weapons, and without any financial resources except the meager monthly allowances, which they received from their families in Manila, they obtained the ends they sought. While Antonio believed that actions spoke louder than words, Rizal believed that the pen was mightier than the sword, as evident that in any worthy campaign, brains count the most.

CHAPTER 20

In December 1888, the awarding for the Universal Fine Arts Exhibition was held in Barcelona inside the neo-classical pavilion Palace of Fine Arts, *The Battle of Lepanto* won the gold medal.

A few days later, in his speech at a banquet to honor Juan Luna's achievement of the painting, *La Batalla de Lepanto*, Graciano López-Jaena, Filipino orator and propagandist and equal rights advocate, praised the Filipino painter's artistic genius and compared the qualities of his work with that of other prominent European artists.

López-Jaena also used his speech as an opportunity to defend the abilities of the Filipinos and asked that the Philippines, which he called "a Spanish nation," be granted modern freedoms and representation in the Spanish Cortes.

When it was time for the thin and lanky López-Jaena to address the audience, he stood up in the center of the room, effortlessly and with elegance, and delivered the following speech:

"Gentlemen: My first salute is to Mother Spain. The second,

to her daughter the Philippines, and the third, to Luna whose genius astounds the world with his two works: Spoliarium and La Batalla de Lepanto.

Graciano prompted the assembled guests to remember the two great and influential citizens of the French Revolution, Voltaire and Mirabeau, who interacted well in the transition of their new society.

"Voltaire who upsets and Mirabeau who smashes, according to the beautiful expression of the great Victor Hugo; so in the great contemporary revolution in the art of painting are two artists who understand each other: Rosales and Luna."

Someone in the audience whispered to his companion. "Who is this Rosales?"

"The late Spanish realist painter Eduardo Rosales was like Juan Luna in that he also attended the Real Academia de *Bellas Artes* de San Fernando," the companion explained, "after he apprenticed in Rome and won the gold medal in the 1871 National Exposition in Madrid for his tragic rendition of the Death of Lucrecia."

A man in a nearby chair shushed the two friends and pointed to Graciano. "Let's listen."

"Rosales is the Voltaire who has created a new school with his revolutionary palette," Graciano said. *"Luna is the Mirabeau, who concludes, finishes, and perfects the work begun. Rosales is great for his school; Luna is great for his genius who understood the master. Rosales is dead. Long live Rosales in Luna!"*

The crowd erupted in applause! "Yes, long live Luna!"

Graciano motioned to the people to quiet down, and then he continued.

"Like the heroes who are the glory of their country, such as the invincible leaders, the veteran army of Lepanto that Luna depicted so well on his canvas, thereby attaining a heroic triumph in the art of painting, geniuses are the light, the blazon, the pride, the greatness of their nation. Luna as a genius exalts Spain, Luna exalts the Philippines, and the Philippines is exalted by Luna."

By now, the audience was on their feet. The people roared and applauded with approval and pride for their fellow countryman who spoke so eloquently about their favored son, Juan Luna. After paying ample tribute to Spain, Lopez Jaena took the opportunity to abase the weakness and shortcomings of the colonial authorities and friars in the Philippines.

"See there, gentlemen, how in glorifying genius, in speaking of Luna of his glories, of his triumphs, it is necessary, it is essential to speak of the Philippines, that beautiful corner of the Orient, his native country, a palpitating piece of the heart of Spain. Though she has cradled a genius to whom we are now paying a tribute of admiration, that most beautiful region of Oceanía still lies prostrate in the most abject condition, without rights, without freedom, rendering tributes to the friars, remaining helots of a government which is absolute, dictatorial, tsarist."

A murmuring around the room was smothered by a loud applause. And again, Graciano calmed the excited and appreciative crowd by holding his hands high in the air, palms out. And then he took the opportunity to hurl back at white Europeans who belittled the Filipinos for being of the Malay race and not intelligent enough to be at par with them.

"It is now time, gentlemen, to defend the Filipinos from the diatribes the sarcasms hurled against them by certain writers, our compatriots of the Peninsula, who say that we are good for nothing, pygmies of little acumen, unfit for progress, for sciences. Individuals who are pygmies, gentlemen, do not grow; on the other hand, pygmy nations with time become giants."

Lopez Jaena glanced at Luna, pointed his finger at him, and asked his audience to witness what a young and simple Filipino looked like. Although small in stature, Luna was a giant in distinction and genius. He went on and said:

"The providential fact that after the great Pradilla, it should be Luna, a Filipino, who was given the commission to do the painting that now forms a pendant to La Rendición de Granada, either means nothing or is a symbol of something like a mute protest, a reminder to

the fathers of the country that there beyond the seas, beyond the Suez Canal, far beyond the China Sea, exists a Spanish nation, as Spanish as the most. Although they have proven their loyalty in innumerable battles and have remained ever faithful and obedient to the Metropolis, until now they have no representative in the Cortes; and deprived of their rights, they are at the mercy of an oppressive theocracy and an exploitative bureaucracy."

By now everyone in the room agreed with Lopez Jaena's strong words, and suddenly there was an eruption of boos along with the bravos. But the orator continued with great force and conviction.

"La Batalla de Lepanto, gentlemen, placed in the temple of the laws, is the expression of the sublime lamentation of a people demanding from all the constituted authorities their representation in the Cortes, their rights, and their freedom. The Philippines, surfeited of friars, wants another dish.

Lopez Jaena expounded on the many freedoms that the Filipinos should be wanting for their homeland. Among those were freedom of speech, press and religion—if given the opportunity of these, Filipinos will prosper and experience progress.

I am going to conclude, Gentlemen," Lopez Jaena said, "where I began. *Luna's gigantic work, La Batalla de Lepanto, like La Spoliarium, is at the present historical moment the subject of great controversies, of contrary opinions, mostly unfavorable. And it is because the ideal of the artist has not been understood. An entirely new genus, new school, it sees horizons opening to all talents in its tempestuous sphere. Unthinking critics censure this new school, but those who think with their soul, judge with their spirit, and feel with their heart defend it."*

At this point in the oration, however, Lopez Jaena asked Luna's artistic detractors to be kind in their criticism of his work. He went on to distinguish the difference between Luna and the well loved and respected Spanish painter, Pradilla.

"Luna's palette, gentlemen, like that of Rosales, is in art what in the novel, in poetry, is the pen of Walter Scott, the pen of Alexander Dumas, the lyre of Lord Byron: innovators revolutionaries. Classical

works delight the eyes. The works of Luna are not only the delight of the eyes, they appeal to the sentiments, they dominate, caress, and subdue the imagination. They are like German music; they are like the magnificent works of Michelangelo: all philosophy, depth, grandeur, sublimity, not comprehensible to all, except in the course of time. Do not draw a comparison between Pradilla and Luna; between the two there is no parity. Each one is a colossus in his class. They are two stars that shine equally in the firmament of painting."

Several of the guests in attendance shouted, "Well done! Bravo!" After the audience quieted down, Lopez Jaena advised his listeners to not only look at the beauty of the artist's work, but also, to view and appreciate the harsh and brutal realities of life that Luna represented in his masterpieces—brush strokes that demonstrate the sublime and cruelty along side each other.

Lopez Jaena then took a glass of wine and raised it above his head, and proposed a toast to the honoree's wife, Maria Paz and their son, Andres, who journeyed all the way from Paris to grace and celebrate with them the talent and genius of her husband. He went on to recognize Luna's friend and renowned painter of *La Patria*, Antonio Benlliure, and although not present, his mentor, Alejo Vera.

Finally focusing his attention to the members of the press who were present, he raised his glass of wine once more and said: *"I salute and toast the press here worthily represented, so that with its powerful influence, it may secure from the constituted authorities equal representation, equal rights, equal freedoms, equal love, sincere affection among the Spaniards here and overseas, Cuba, Puerto Rico, and the Philippines, for we are all children of the same mother whose name is Spain."*

When Lopez Jaena stepped away from the podium, Luna went up to greet him. When the two men embraced, the audience erupted in frenetic applause that seemed to go on for a long while after, followed by enthusiastic admirers who smothered him with embraces.

CHAPTER 21

Rizal returned to Europe from his first and only trip to the United States. He wanted to learn more about the American society. His arrival was marred by the racial prejudice he saw against the native Indians, Chinese, and the African Americans.

"Would you believe I was quarantined at San Francisco's pier as a result of the Chine Exclusion Act?" Rizal said.

"Well, you cannot blame them for you are part Chinese," Antonio Luna snickered.

"Yes, but there is no civil liberty for people of color, having witnessed the inequality experienced by them, whether you are black, red, yellow or brown, is deplorable," Rizal responded.

"From what I have heard and read about American politics, I am saddened to agree with you," Antonio Luna replied.

"On the other hand, I saw much progress in the material affluence, the drive and the energy of the American people, the natural beauty of the land, the high standard of living and the opportunities offered to the poor," Rizal said.

"What cities did you visit?" Lopez-Jaena asked.

"I took the train from San Francisco to New York and got to see so many, but my favorites were Chicago and New York. I loved New York with their big buildings all lit up," Rizal said.

"There is no doubt that America is a great country, but it still has many defects," Rizal continued. "Hopefully not, but if the Philippines came under American rule, racism would be a problem."

"Impossible! What interests would the United States have if they occupied the Philippines," Marcelo asked.

"Based on reports from a leading newspaper in New York, it was insinuated that Spain has to go and that Cuba should be for the Cubans," Rizal answered.

"Hey, it could be the reason why the Cubans are better treated than us by Spain, and why they have representation to the Spanish Cortes."

"And the same reason why we should all work harder to be on the same status as the Cubans because as a last result, for us to revolt against Spain and succeed, we must align ourselves with a foreign power to provide arms, food, ammunition and diplomacy," Rizal said.

The Filipino reformist proceeded with the business of the Propaganda movement. Antonio Luna believed that Rizal was the most brilliant of them and that his writings had a wide impact in the Philippines. So he advised Rizal to spend more time in Madrid for he was the best person with the ability to lead and unify the Filipinos in Spain.

In 1889, Lopez-Jaena established a bi-weekly newspaper in Barcelona. *La Solidaridad* (Solidarity) became the principal organ of the Propaganda Movement, having audiences both in Spain and in the islands. In addition to Lopez Jaena, the major contributors included Jose Rizal, Marcelo del Pilar, and Antonio Luna.

The reformists were to make use of *La Solaridad* and to further promote Rizal's novel. They were to disseminate information to arouse and awaken the conscience of the Filipinos, to make the Spanish realize their mistake in the Philippines in order to initiate changes in their system, and continue presenting testimonials and evidences of abuse against native Filipinos.

Not long after Marcelo Del Pilar took over as Editor of *La Solaridad* from Graciano Lopez Jaena. The decision was made to move the newspaper from Barcelona to Madrid, where they had the opportunity to recruit more supporters and reach a wider audience of not only Filipinos, but also Spaniards.

Under the pen name Taga-ilog (from the river), Antonio Luna continued to contribute articles in La Solidaridad, where he recorded in significant detail the way Filipinos were perceived by Spaniards.

He wrote all of his own experiences from the day he arrived in Spain, and those of others regarding racial comments, insults, and the general ignorance of local customs and traditions. Luna ultimately compiled his articles into a book entitled, *Impresiones Madrileñas de un Filipino*.

Whenever Antonio Luna's essays appeared on the pages of *La Solaridad*, for some Spanish critics, it was a show of insolence, or worst, a shameless exhibition of ingratitude and disloyalty by a colonial subject of Spain. The editor of the newspaper *El Pueblo Soberano*, Celso Mir Deas, was outraged at what he saw as a depiction of Spaniards as backwards and barbarous.

Erroneously attributing the article of Taga-ilog to Antonio Luna's brother, Juan Luna, Mir Deas responded to the article with personal insults and accusations. Although Juan Luna wrote to the newspaper disclaiming being the writer, Mir Deas continued attacking the Filipino people in general.

In Madrid, the Filipino community, although used to the brothers Luna's fiery tempers, knew that Antonio Luna was prone to react violently to the insinuations Mir Deas was writing. His friends tried to calm him down and suggested that he forgive and forget since he did not even know the man personally.

Antonio responded, "With a name that sounds like *mierda*, — Spanish for shit— I would assault everyone in Barcelona who looked like shit."

Antonio Luna traveled to Barcelona and practically challenged a number of people to a fight before he found the right person. He went straight to the point and demanded a public retraction from Señor Mir Deas, or he would refer to him as "*mierdas*" in his column. Antonio Luna even challenged him to a duel, but Mir Deas declined.

CHAPTER 22

When Andres Luna turned a year old, his father invited the members of the *Kidlat*, a social club of young Filipinos residing in Paris organized by José Rizal, to a luncheon prepared by his mother-in-law Doña Juliana of all their favorite Filipino foods.

Later that evening when the rest of the party guests went home, Rizal, Felix, Antonio, and Juan Luna sat by the terrace to discuss the latest developments of Philippine propaganda movement.

"I feel so bad that I've not been as active as the both of you," Juan Luna said and pointed to Antonio and Rizal.

"What do you mean?" Rizal countered.

"You know, I am not directly involved with the journalistic and political activities of the reform movement." Juan responded.

"*Amigo*, you are very much part of our propaganda movement," Rizal said. "Your reputation as a renowned artist, your illustrated drawings in both my book and *La Solaridad*, your successes in your field of endeavor attract a lot of attention, and your connection to royalty brings respect to our cause and we truly value your support." Rizal went over to Juan and gave him a brotherly hug.

Antonio said, "You should not feel sorry for yourself, *hermano*. Not only are you the first Filipino artist to gain fame and be known all over Spain by winning a gold medal, but you are the first Filipino in any field to win recognition all over Europe."

Felix interrupted. "But, not so true. Looks like you have never heard of the two Tagal Filipino soldiers honored by the French for bravery and gallantry in action in Cochinchina."

Antonio cut Felix short. "What are you talking about? Did any of those ... whatever you call soldiers, ever get so close to a king and queen like my brother, Juan?"

"Tell us more about those soldiers," Rizal said to Felix.

"I only heard this from my father when I was a kid. I believe this occurred about forty years ago when France wanted a slice of the pie in Asia similar to the British, Dutch, Spanish, and Portuguese do at present. So they decided to invade a tiny Asian Annamite kingdom in Cochinchina ruled by an Emperor who wanted to expel all European missionaries in their land. Since this emperor beheaded a Spanish priest, the French asked for the assistance of Spain, who naturally sent an army contingent from Manila that was mostly made up of Indios. The rest is history," Felix said. "By the way, Tagal is what the French called the Filipino soldiers. Now don't ask me why, maybe because they spoke in Tagalog all the time."

"*Gracias* Felix, it's very interesting. Your story makes me proud to be an Indio," Rizal said.

"Amen," Antonio added.

An addition to the Luna household came in the form of a baby girl the following year. She was named Maria Del Paz and nicknamed Bibi. Their friend José Rizal accepted to be Bibi's baptismal godfather. A few months later, the youngest child of Juan and Paz Luna was baptized and all their closest friends and family were invited for the feast afterward. Later in the evening, José Rizal, Valentin Ventura, Gregorio Aguilera, Lauro Dimayuga, Felix Pardo, Antonio, and Juan Luna—all members of the Kidlat Club, as always the case—discussed Philippine politics over a bottle of French champagne. Also present was TH Pardo, who was in Paris to set up the Philippine Exhibits at the 1889 Paris Universal Exposition because of his wide knowledge of Philippine culture and the French language. He brought along his wife, Concha, and their only son, Carlos.

At one point, Rizal spoke out to his friends in honesty and suggested renaming the Kidlat Club to *Indios Bravos*, which meant brave Indians, since he discovered during his visit in America that the American Indians were proud of their heritage and to be called an Indian. He elaborated on his thoughts as to the type of organization he had in mind.

"We need an organization that envisions Filipinos being recognized by Spain for being excellent in various fields of knowledge," Rizal said. "But in doing so, we cannot expect that all shall have courage and know how, so I have defined three categories of people in Philippine European society today that we could initiate into our movement."

"What are they?" Felix asked.

"The actors are those among us whose interest range from the common good towards his fellow men to possessing the quality of self esteem, one who has the civic courage to publicly declare all evil and unjust acts, who would sacrifice their own interest for their country and the knowledge to choose and support great leaders."

"And the second," Antonio asked.

Rizal continued. "Spectators, I mean Filipinos with no clue as to what is going on in their country, apathetic to common ideals, and whose only desire is to make money and promote their own self-interest, and with no qualms of the abuses and injustices going on in his surroundings."

"And the last bunch of people I refer to are the claques or followers, leaner's, parasites, leeches or suckers, the common sheep without convictions and idea of the their own, who only know how to say yes and no when told to do so, and clap, cheer and be silent when told to be."

"I move that we only recruit actors and good looking Indios like me, "Antonio reiterated teasingly.

"I second the motion and proposed a toast to the *Indios Bravos*," responded swordsman Valentin Ventura, who at the same time raised his glass of champagne.

While the men gathered outside the house, the women gathered inside in the living room in front of a cozy fireplace. They were Doña Juliana, Paz, and Agustina Maginot, the Argentinean born fiancée of Felix Pardon. They talked about the upcoming October wedding of Agustina to Felix.

But right in the middle of the women's conversation, the men came inside to escape the cold.

Maria Paz called out to Rizal. "Listen Rizal, what is this I hear that you are going back to London in two weeks' time?"

"I may have to. Remember, I still have to finish my confrontation of the proofs with the original Morga in the British Museum."

"No, No, No, you have to stay for the wedding of Felix and Agustina," Maria Paz said.

"Yes, Rizal, it's not every day that I get married," Felix said. "You can be my third best man, after TH and Juan."

"I already delayed my return to London for the chance to join you at the World Expo sometime that week."

TH interrupted. "Yes, but we have a problem. Although the Paris Exposition opened last May 6, the Eiffel Tower is still undergoing some finishing touches, and spectators are only allowed to go halfway up."

"I think it would be best for all of us to go sometime in October, the week before Felix's wedding, and the day when the winners of the art exhibitions are announced. In this way, we can all fully enjoy the Expo," he suggested.

"Listen Rizal," Felix said. "You will also have the chance to witness the second Filipino to win a gold medal. I have joined the international competition for sculpture at the Expo."

They all got excited and gave Felix a congratulatory hug and wished him the best of luck, and at the same time continued to gang up on Rizal to stay for the wedding.

Rizal hugged Felix and said, “You are the actor I referred to earlier, and for that I am staying for the wedding.”

CHAPTER 23

When the Eiffel Tower was still under construction, the Luna brothers with Rizal and several other members of the *Indios Bravos* often walked routinely along the Seine River until they'd come to the benches along the river where they sat in full sight of the almost completed Eiffel Tower. The splendor and beauty of the massive steel structure never failed to amaze and mesmerize them.

Designed and built by Gustave Eiffel, an engineer known for building bridges of steel, he proved without a doubt that the battle between iron and stone building construction was over.

"I heard it's going to be 300 meters high when completed," Juan Luna remarked. "By the time it is completed, it will be the highest structure ever built in all of France."

"All these expenditures and activities just to commemorate the hundred-year anniversary of the French revolution," Antonio Luna stated in a confrontational tone.

"Felix, as a sculptor, maybe you can design a model of a giant structure in copper for future generations of Filipinos to build a hundred years from now in Manila," Antonio Luna joked.

"I don't know if one can ever gather enough copper in the world to build such a huge edifice," Felix replied. "Maybe, out of stone, like the Tower of Babel."

"They tried using stone in Pisa and it's now leaning on one side." Juan Luna snickered. "At the rate it's sinking, it won't be standing a hundred years from now."

"I wonder what the Philippines will be like a century from now." Rizal wondered.

"Actually there was this prominent architect from Paris who proposed building a thousand foot masonry tower, but the committee was not impressed with the foundation plan," Juan Luna continued. "But the strangest proposal of all was from a man who suggested building a giant guillotine to honor the victims of the reign of terror."

"Oh my God, that would have been a horrifying sight to see. Thank God for sanity," Felix said.

Rizal answered his own curiosity when from Paris he published a serialized article, "The Philippines a Century Hence" to supplement his novel, *Noli Me Tanghere*, and its sequel, *El Filibusterismo*, which ran from September 1889 to January 1890 on the propaganda movements newspaper, *La Solaridad*, based in Madrid.

Pandemonium broke loose all over Paris when the countdown to the opening of the international fair was but just a few days away. The fervor and anticipation of over a million visitors expected for such an event, the largest crowd ever in attendance, made it close to impossible to seek hotel and inn accommodations. Even private homes began renting out rooms at exorbitant rates.

Built on the Champ de Mars, the 1889 World's Fair was held in Paris to commemorate the centennial of the storming of the Bastille, the historical event that started the French Revolution, and as a result the collapse of the French monarchy. The total area covered almost one square kilometer, including the Trocadero, the quai d'Orsay, the Invalides esplanade, and a part of the Seine, where visitors could follow the winding course of the river along the Rue des Nations and visit the pavilions build by different countries displaying their own cultural motif, character, and tradition. Officially known as the 1889 *Exposition Universelle de Paris*, it finally opened for the public on May 6. However, the two powerful monarchial nations of Europe, England and Germany, boycotted the fair because of the theme to honor and remember the one-hundredth anniversary of the French Revolution.

The brothers Luna accompanied by Maria Paz Luna, José Rizal, Felix Pardo, and his fiancé, Agustina Maginot, were all so excited to finally go to their first World's Fair. They decided to meet at the Luna's home in Rue Pergolose for the purpose of sharing a carriage. TH and Concha left earlier to assist in manning the small Philippine Exhibits hall where paintings of Hidalgo and sculptures of Felix Pardo were being displayed.

However, the Spanish authorities did not allow Juan Luna's *La Batalla de Lepanto* to be removed from Spain for display in Paris.

"Ladies, let me be the first to compliment the both of you. You look gorgeous," Rizal told Maria Paz and Agustina.

"Thank you, but we give thanks to the Grands Magasins Au Printemps," Agustina replied.

"We practically spent the whole day at Boulevard Haussmann," Maria Paz interrupted. "We love shopping at such a first-class establishment like Au Printemps because it has everything and the best that Paris can offer to fashionable women like us." She giggled and then she spun around as she opened her new white and purple parasol, which perfectly matched her long cotton purple calico jacket. The jacket was trimmed in white ruffle lace with a hint of bustle in the back, a long row of front buttons with sleeves falling just below the elbow with a ravishing lace-trimmed calico flounce. The lace-trimmed matching purple skirt was shirred up and bustled revealing a charming coordinated attached white underskirt, like those worn by the ladies of the French Revolution.

"No more of that huge rear bustle from the eighties that made us look tremendously big from the back. So what do you think?" Maria Paz directed the question to her husband.

"You look ravishing, my dear," Juan Luna said warmly.

"Wait till tonight when you see my new seductive corset and crinoline underneath," Maria Paz said in a cooing voice.

"Looks like tonight is going to be the night, Juan" Antonio kidded his brother.

"Not for you, Felix, you will have to wait until after our wedding next week to see more than my corset," Agustina teased as she, too, turned around to show her fiancé her simple French white cotton blouse with scalloped embroidered lace, trimming the front and back yoke creating an overlay over the long sleeves gathered to a buttoned cuff.

"You look simply beautiful my love," Felix said and blushed as he hugged Agustina. "I'm so glad this latest Paris fashion of skirts is returning to a relatively slender shape."

"Here comes our ride," Rizal said, and they all stepped up into a large four wheeled horse-drawn carriage pulled by two horses to transport them to and from the fair.

Along the way to the fair, Maria Paz and Agustina noticed a majority of the ladies in the streets of Paris, and later on at the fair, still wearing the old fashioned dresses with bustles. They felt so gratified to be a few of the first to wear the latest style of dress and complimented each other for looking fashionably simple, but also elegant in their attire and matching parasols.

The main entrance to the fair was by walking underneath its symbol—the majestic Eiffel Tower. Constructed of tempered iron steel, one of the four elevators was built by Otis Elevators from the United States and carried visitors to the top viewing deck. Another example of American ingenuity was a telephone pavilion positioned at the foot of the tower to serve as the telephone communication center of the World's Fair, courtesy of Thomas Edison, who was in attendance.

The four main halls of the fair were ideally located next to the tower on the Champ-de-Mars. They were the Palais des Beaux-arts and Palais des Arts Liberaux, both designed by architect Joséph Bouvard; and the Palais de Expositions Diverses designed by Jean-Camille Formige; and the largest building of them all and considered the most beautiful pavilion, the Galerie de Machines by Ferdinand Dutert.

Like children going to a circus for the first time, they were all mesmerized by the magnitude and attraction of the World's Fair. "I hope you don't mind if we enter the des Arts Liberaux first," Rizal said, "since it contains exhibits on medicine and surgery, precision instruments, and of the other sciences."

"Sure," Maria Paz said as she examined her copy of the map that depicted the location of all the exhibits. "But what is pedagogy?"

"Pedagogy!" Agustina answered excitedly. "It is the study, process, or style of teaching. And since my ambition is to be teacher someday, I too am interested. Let's go to that one definitely."

"Interesting, I see that it also contains exhibits on different types of musical instruments, photography, archaeological, astronomical, and geographical dioramas," Felix said.

"I only have one suggestion," Juan Luna said. "Let's do the Palais des Beaux-arts last, since that is where the results of the art competition is going to be held tonight."

It did not take Maria Paz Luna long to get bored inside the Palais des Arts Liberaux. Except for Rizal and Antonio Luna, who by now were captivated by the latest chemical instruments and theater of military arts, Maria Paz managed to persuade Juan, Agustina, and Felix to move to the next pavilion, which displayed the exhibits that interested her the most—the Palais de Expositiones Diverses showed the latest furniture designs, crystals, art decor, mosaics, clothes, and jewelry.

"Rizal, you can take your time here, because you can be sure with Maria Paz around, we are going to spend some time at the Pavilion Diverses," Felix said.

At one point inside the pavilion, Maria Paz Luna, amazed by the size of the rectangular cut, with fifty-eight facets of diamonds, on display at the French section of the pavilion sarcastically remarked, "My dear husband, I wonder how many paintings must you have to sell to be able to buy me the 145 karat Imperial Diamond."

Juan Luna ignored her remarks and headed toward the exit of the pavilion to wait on a park bench for the rest of the gang. They were all together again and intent on going to the next pavilion when Agustina Maginot called the attention of Felix. She pointed to a sign that read: Negro Villages. "My love, what is a Negro Villages?"

"I believe that is the most controversial exhibit in the whole fair," Felix responded, "The displays inside are of real primitive human beings from Africa that show the cultural and ethnic differences between the white and the black people. This exhibit is also referred to as a human zoo."

"Can we go in? I have never been inside a human zoo before,"

"Hey guys!" Felix called to the rest of the group. "This Negro Villages seems to be interesting."

Maria Paz followed Felix and Agustina inside with José Rizal and the Luna brothers. Upon entering, they were surprised to see a makeshift open air village, except that each village representing African native tribes was referred to as savage and displayed in dioramas along walkways that led to each one, the most famous and fearless being of the Zulu tribes. Each village was secured by a fence and iron grilles separating spectators from humans like trapped animals inside a zoo cage.

"Look inside this cage." Felix called the attention of his friends to a poster that indicated the savages evolved from apes.

"Oh my god, there are people throwing bananas, oranges, and apples to the savages, and they are picking them up to eat" Maria Paz howled.

"Maria Paz, would you please not refer to them as savages," Juan Luna said complainingly. "They are people like us, with two legs, two hands, two eyes, a nose, and a mouth. The only difference is the color of their skin and certain body features different from Europeans. I, too, am slightly different and dark, so will you now refer to yourself as being married to an ape?"

"I am sorry, but you are being so sensitive. You know very well

I did not mean it that way," Maria Paz apologetically corrected herself.

"This is too much, I cannot take this any longer," said Rizal. "Let's get out of here"

"I agree," Juan Luna responded, "how can the organizers of this event allow such a deplorable, degrading, and racist panorama?"

"Now if we can only find the nearest exit," remarked Antonio Luna, "and the irony of this all, this year France is celebrating one hundred years of liberty and freedom from the monarchy, but what about the liberty and freedom of people in their colonies, and for that matter, all nations under the thumbs of European colonial power?"

As they were walking out of the village and passed the Egyptian pavilion, where a large crowd of people was falling in line to take their chance to ride in a large balloon holding passengers in a basket, the discussion on what they had just witnessed inside the human zoo continued. Being Filipinos, they knew firsthand what it was like to be subjected to a foreign power in their own native land, as Malays and especially the Aeta and Negrito tribes in the Philippines.

"There is no such thing as savages, primitive or uncivilized groups of people," Rizal said. "Everyone should have the right to live, act, and behave the way they want to. They should have the right to decide on what happens to their own identity, culture, and traditions in their own ancestral lands."

"I'm glad that the United States now has laws to protect their native Indians, granting them their own land," Felix said.

"Talking about the American Indians, let's head for the Buffalo Bill Wild West show. If we rush we can get there right at the start of the show," Rizal suggested.

"Great idea!" Juan Luna agreed.

The *Indios Bravos* were amazed at watching the other most popular attraction at the Exposition, the Buffalo Bill Wild Wild West Circus at Neuilly. They were astonished at how proud the American Indians seemed when they performed their act. Rizal told his friends, "The Spaniards have left their trademark on calling us Indios, a mindset that will never be erased and will always be there. Why not be like the

Indians? They are proud and unashamed of their name. Let us be like them."

"As for me, I found Annie Oakley truly fantastic," Antonio Luna commented. "If we can produce a military regiment full of women like Annie Oakley, the Philippines would be an independent nation by now. Oh my God, that lady can shoot!"

"Hey, why don't we see who is the best marksman among us. We should go target shooting tomorrow," Juan Luna suggested.

"Not a bad idea. I haven't fired a pistol for some time now," Rizal replied.

"Me too," Felix answered.

"Let's meet at Juan's studio no later than eight in the morning. We'll ask TH and Hidalgo if they may want to join us," Antonio responded.

"Come on guys, it's getting late. We need to rush back to the Palais d Beaux-arts. I want to know if my metal sculpture won any award," said the very anxious Felix.

Immediately after the Buffalo Bill extravaganza ended, they all practically ran toward the art pavilion with time to spare and a chance to view the large number of Naturist and pre-Raphaelite paintings on display before announcing the winners of the Expo's art competition.

The competition inside the exhibit hall was open for all artists and divided into five group classifications: paintings, sculpture and medal engraving, architecture, and lithography. Blacklisted from the competition were works done by painters of the Impressionist artist who were told point blank by the organizing committee that their style of arts was not real and had no creative value.

Imagine their excitement upon learning that Felix Pardo had just won a bronze medal for sculpture! They stood together, arms linked, jumping, crying with joy so proud to support and honor one of their own in victory.

"Congratulations on your win!" A fully bearded, pale Bohemian man with thick dark hair and deep-set eyes with a ring of perspiration coloring the collar of his wrinkled, white shirt greeted Felix.

He then focused his attention on Juan Luna. Unsure, he hesitated, but then in a slow voice asked, "Are you Juan Luna of the *Spoliarium* fame?"

Juan Luna's eyes drifted for a second as he tried to place him. Knowing a fellow artist when he saw one, he replied, "Yes, may I be of any assistance?"

"My name is Gauguin, Paul Gauguin. We were once neighbors at the Cite Fluerie in Boulevard D' Arago."

"Paul Gauguin, oh my God, of course, I remember you. I did not recognize you at first because of your facial hair. You only had a mustache then," Juan Luna responded.

"I would appreciate very much if you could join us for a cup of coffee." He pointed to his two companions waiting by the exit door of the pavilion. "My friend manages an art gallery here in Paris and would like to meet you."

Juan Luna introduced Paul Gauguin to his wife and friends. "Why don't you go ahead to the *Galerie de Machines*, and I'll catch up with you all later."

Next to the Eiffel Tower, the other most significant building structure of the World's Fair was the Galerie de Machines. The visitors to the pavilion were at awe of the enormous size of the hall's interior, a span of 111 meters long, 380 feet wide and a height of 148 feet, which made this iron and glass structure the world's largest interior space ever constructed, made possible by using a system of parallel made of steel or iron.

CHAPTER 24

Juan Luna remembered Paul Gauguin as a frustrated and destitute artisan when they were neighbors at Boulevard d'Arago. Juan's studio was but a few meters away from Gauguin's. He would see Monsieur Gauguin making ceramic vessels to sell in order to augment the slow movement of his paintings.

"What have you been up to lately?" Luna asked.

"Actively painting, but they don't like our art work inside there." Gauguin pointed to the Exposition. "So, we have our work displayed outside the exposition along the Champ-de-Mars."

"Do you have any of your paintings on display?"

"Oh, yes, in fact one of them is *Arearea*, one of my favorites, since it reminds me so much of Tahiti. I hope you find the time to take a look at them inside the Café Volponi." Gauguin said hopefully. "And bring your friends along."

"I will do just that," Juan Luna responded.

Gauguin introduced Juan to Theo van Gogh, who managed an

art gallery in Paris, and his older brother, Vincent van Gogh, who was visiting Paris from Arles in the south of France, and like Gauguin, was an Impressionist painter.

"Thank you for accepting our invitation for coffee," Theo said. "We've heard so much of your success and hope you find some time to share your thoughts on Impressionism with us."

"Should it be the other way around since you men are the masters of this new style of French art?"

"Let me be honest with you Monsieur Luna," Theo said, "there is a struggle going on at present here in Paris between the traditionally educated artists supported by the State and large salons, like yourself, who I believe is a product of the *Bellas Artes* in Madrid; as against a growing number of artists like Monsieur Gauguin and my brother, Vincent who prefers to work with specks of primary colors in their own independent style of art."

"Whether realistically innovative, or just splashes of paint sketches and short brush strokes on canvas," Vincent added.

"Now tell me, Vincent, who would splash paint on canvas?" Juan countered. "It is something that my son or any other kid playfully can do."

"You may think that I am only kidding, but someday, someone, or somewhere it may even be accepted as the latest form of art," Vincent predicted. "Our work will be so much in demand that those narrow minded officials in the Exposition will be begging for a piece of the action."

"Precisely," Gauguin said. "As you are aware, not a single impressionistic piece of art is on display inside the Exposition. Those anachronistic and doctrine minded salon officials believe that our paintings are not good enough, but the public is starting to move toward our direction."

"I have completed hundreds of paintings and not given the chance to display them in any official Paris Salons, as a result of no one knowing who I am. I've sold but one painting, *The Red Vineyard* and that's thanks to my brother who sold the painting for me." Vincent laughed.

"And you gave two away," Gauguin said.

"What did I give away?" Vincent asked.

"Those two silly sunflowers you had me hang on my bedroom when I stayed with you in Arles," Gauguin said. "Just kidding, I loved it, love sunflowers."

"You'd better because those darn flowers would wilt so fast that I had to complete the painting in a whole day."

"Perhaps your work deals a lot with the splashing of paint on canvas," Luna said laughing.

"And also mercilessly applying rough thick paint onto raw canvas," Gauguin said.

Juan Luna noticed that the man with the lower part of his left ear almost gone frowned.

"I am sorry. Please accept my apology. One should not make fun of anyone's work of art."

Surprising to Theo and Gauguin the volatile Vincent simply uttered, "Apology accepted. "I, too, have started lately transforming my heavy palette into short brush strokes."

"Monsieur Luna, drop by my gallery at 19 Boulevard Montmartre to see a work done by Vincent," Theo suggested.

"I would love to and maybe you can also display some of my paintings," Juan said.

"It will be an honor to do so," Theo said warmly.

Theo, the branch manager of Goupil's gallery, had Vincent's latest work of art for sale. It was an oil painting measuring 28x36 that depicted on a clear and starry night the reflections of the lights of a town over the Rhone River. He had completed the work months earlier, but still no one would buy the piece even at a low bargain price.

"Great, now tell us your thoughts on Impressionism," Theo asked once again.

"One of the reasons I moved to Paris was to study and learn firsthand this new and exciting school of Impressionist arts. I was attracted to the idea that it emerged from a much more liberated society in which, I think am heading, in my own painting," Luna said. "We do have one thing in common, the love of art in whatever forms the artist may desire."

Juan Luna had the attention of all three around the bistro table as they sipped on their second cup of fresh French brewed coffee and continued. "I once wrote to a friend my misgivings on historical paintings, starting with the very concept of its composition, the bright colors and numerous detailed adornments imposed on the canvas and finally to the antiquity of its subjects. "Yes, sometimes I find historical paintings false."

"False, what do you mean?" Theo asked.

'They are nothing but intangible realities. They may look realistic from the offset, but in reality the characters and actions are all staged and not really one hundred percent a product of one's imagination."

"I'm gratified to hear your favorable evaluation of Impressionism in comparison to what we now know of realism and its neo-classical world of limitations," Theo responded.

"Yes, there is a difference, like in my interpretation of *The Battle of Lepanto*. When I placed myself in the middle of a naval conflict at sea and managed to captivate and merge the sounds and movements of battle and the sea, it enabled my senses to visualize the whole scenario in vivid color as compared to the historical art of Pradilla hanging a few feet away."

"Oh, I how I wish I had the money to travel and see your award-winning paintings," Theo said.

"Come to think of it, you would have liked Lepanto, since I did interject a bit of my own style of Impressionism, and now I know why it was deplored by some old fashioned Spanish critics."

"I personally believe that the realistic classical art has been placed on a pedestal above the society by patrons for whom the work was intended. However, Impressionism will speak for itself when society comes to realize the significance of its artistic and commercial value." Gauguin interjected.

"Yes, but when will it stop? When will the people on top of the pedestal stop looking down upon us?" Vincent asked.

"By us not giving up where Manet started, and by us being more assertive and demonstrative to our cause," Theo replied.

"Yes, and where did most of his paintings end up—in the Salon de Refusee?" Gauguin countered.

"As I said in the past, we should stop questioning and accepting things just the way they are, and how we've always seen them," Theo replied, "Especially nowadays with this new generation of liberalism in our Parisian society, the so called *La Bella Epoque*."

"How true, it's time to deal with the matter from another point of view. It's time that we make or move and bring more of our kind to climb on top of the pedestal. Monsieur Luna, would you join us in our quest for recognition?" Gauguin asked as an invitation to Luna.

"I have done some work in the past, since my relocation to Paris. And in fact, my last three works of art bordered on Impressionism." Luna said. "However, I still have to maintain my commitment with the academic traditions of the various Salons of Europe."

"I don't see any reason why, for the meantime, you cannot do both," Theo said. "Why not continue competing for prizes at the so-called prestigious art salons of Europe with your classic Greco-Roman style and still paint like an Impressionist to display at Champ-de-Marche?"

"We are not advocating you abandon your traditional art of painting, but we invite you to support our movement. We need well-known artists of your stature in our drive for recognition," Gauguin said.

Although not much impressed with the individual styles of Gauguin, Van Gogh, and some of the Impressionists, who tended to diminish the importance of the subject into a non-traditional matter in the background—their preference for "rainbow" colors even on shades and shadows and brush strokes creating a pure pictorial form—Luna still took their advice and started shying away from the ancient classic style of Michelangelo, Da Vinci, and Rembrandt and into his own modified style world of Impressionism.

In support of their movement, Luna immediately began work

on *Le Chifonier*, The Rag Picker. The painting was an impressionistic depiction, in his own style, of an old man in tattered clothes carrying a basket of rags, which was displayed at the Champs-de-Mars the following month. Other paintings he created during this period were the *French Woman, Heroes Anonymous*, and numerous landscapes and seascapes of Normandy. *La Parisians*, a portrait of a liberated French woman seated inside a French bistro waiting for her companion to return while being admired by three men turned out to be the painter himself with Rizal and a friend, Ariston Avelino. Juan Luna considered this painting as one of his favorite in the impressionistic style for the woman reminded him so much of his beloved Maria Paz.

But Luna still had to complete a painting commissioned by the Spanish Senate in the academic tradition, *Peuple et Rois*. The work depicted a disgruntled crowd of passionate citizens of Paris looting and desecrating the Royal necropolis of France in the Cathedral of St. Denis during the French Revolution. Human remains of previous French Kings were removed from their tombs and thrown together into one single pile, which later became impossible to sort out and be reburied in a common ossuary. It would be Luna's last work on European historical classic arts as he progressed towards the more fashionable art of French society.

CHAPTER 25

Impressed with the shooting expertise of Buffalo Bill and Annie Oakley at the *Exposition Universelle de Paris* the brothers Luna, Rizal, Felix Pardo and Hidalgo got together the following morning to go target shooting in an open field that was just a few kilometers away from Paris. After a couple of rounds of firing their pistols at empty wine bottles, the men started to really wonder who was the best shot among them.

"There is only one way for me to prove to you that I shoot the best," Antonio said.

"And how do you intend to do that?" Rizal was skeptical.

"With my self confidence that I can blow your top hat off your head with one shot from about, hmmm… twenty paces," Antonio said.

"You're crazy! Why don't I blow your top hat off?" Rizal said and offered Antonio his hat.

"Wait a minute, let me settle the score," Juan Luna suggested.

"Why don't the three of us shoot each other's top hats off?" Juan said, and looking at Felix, he added, "Felix, give your hat to Antonio, unless you want to join us, too."

"No way, but are you guys serious? I know that you three are great marksmen, but to shoot at each other is crazy. The whole idea makes you look more like madmen than marksmen," Felix said while walking towards Antonio to hand him his hat.

"Let us form a triangle, standing at twenty paces from each other. I fire the first shot at Antonio"

Antonio interrupted Rizal. "No, no, I fire the first shot at you and not at my brother."

"Hey, what happened to all that self-confidence? Besides I am more confident to have Juan aim at me than you," Rizal said.

"I agree with Rizal. Let's take our back-to-back stance before one of you chicken out. Felix, make sure that Antonio takes twenty steps." Juan instructed him in a stern voice.

The brothers Luna and Rizal were completely so relaxed and at ease in forming a triangle at twenty paces apart, and exuded much confidence in their ability to handle a pistol with Rizal blowing the top hat off Antonio's head first, followed by Antonio on his brother's hat, and lastly Juan on Rizal's hat. All of them showed no sign of being afraid. In fact they were smiling at each other.

During the *despedida de soltero* of Felix, after downing a couple of bottles of red wine from the Rioja region of Spain, the *Indios Bravos* reminiscence and talked about their experience at the World Fair, which was about to conclude in a few days. They decided to further work on the goal of their new organization, the goal of which was the propagation of all useful knowledge about the Philippines and the redemption and dignity of the Malay race.

Rizal would later be persuaded to extend again his stay in Paris by the brothers Luna and the Pardos so they could all spend the Christmas holidays together. José Rizal postponed his return to London until January 1990.

By this time, a new generation of Luna and Pardos were added to the family that necessitated Doña Juliana to hire a live-in French maid, Brigitte Blanc into their household. In addition to Luna's children, Andres and Bibi, there was Carlos, the only son of TH and Concha.

A few days before Christmas there was still a little bit of confusion in the Luna household on how to celebrate Christmas Eve. Juan Luna preferred a combination of Filipino and Spanish food, a tradition begun by his mother back in Binondo, Manila. Doña Juliana and Maria Paz vehemently opposed the Manila tradition in favor of a French style.

"Now, why don't we wait and see how TH and Concha want to celebrate Christmas Eve. After all, they just got back from Manila early this year." Doña Juliana made the suggestion.

"Look, they don't live here. They come tonight as our guests so they have no say. This is my house and we are going to celebrate Christmas my way," Juan Luna said in a demanding and forceful voice.

"Listen to me, Juan. I believe my contribution of five hundred francs a month to this household gives me a lot to say," Doña Juliana said, "especially since I am the one spending and preparing the dinner, and not you." Doña Juliana crossed her arms over her chest and stared at Juan.

"Damn you, why do you always have to rub your money in my face during our conversations. I'm out of here!" Juan slammed the front door and stormed out of the house.

Maria Paz immediately ran after her husband to console him. "Juan, wait for me. Sometimes you and Mamita behave like children. Stop please and let just you and me talk this over."

Juan did as his wife asked, but he was not happy. "What's there to talk about? She always gets her way with you and your brothers."

"It's only food, my God! Since we are having a number of guests, why don't we serve a buffet of Spanish, Filipino, and French? Except for the food? The traditions of all three countries are not much different."

"I have no problem with that, but I don't feel like returning to the house at this very moment." He started to walk away again. "I'll be at the studio, my love. See you later tonight." But then he turned back one more time to his wife. "Wait, my love, let me turn that frown upside down by giving you a big hug."

On the evening of December 24, family members and guests gathered in Villa Dupont to partake of a sumptuous buffet of Filipino, Spanish, and French foods. Popularly known as *Noche Buena*, the whole family traditionally attended the midnight mass. But lately, the meal was served any time before midnight.

Antonio Luna, who had to do some last minute shopping, arrived just after the Pardo family. TH, Concha, and their son showed up together with Felix and Agustina.

"Don't you look like a little prince, Andres? Come and give your godfather a big Christmas hug. Merry Christmas," Antonio Luna said and handed little Andres his present to put under the Christmas tree and for him to open not until midnight.

"Andres, don't forget to say thank you and greet everyone Merry Christmas," his mother told him.

Last to arrive was José Rizal, who walked in with his roommate, José Albert.

"Brrr, it's freezing outside. I thought I was going to turn into a snowman it's so cold out there," Rizal said.

"Here, let me give you a warm hug," Maria Paz said to the shivering Rizal.

"Maria Paz, here is a little something for my goddaughter, Bibi." Rizal handed her a nicely wrapped present.

"Thank you so much for making it here tonight, José," Juan said.

"My God, you have a beautiful Christmas tree," Rizal said.

"Yes, our very first Christmas tree. Maria Paz saw one on display at a variety store and she just had to have one." Juan Luna smiled at his wife as he spoke.

"In fact, last Christmas in Germany I saw my first decorated Christmas tree and I thought it would be a nice Christmas tradition for Filipinos, too," Rizal said.

"I guess we could make trees out of wood because I don't recall seeing pine trees in the Philippines," Juan Luna said.

"The only way to find out is to plant a couple of trees in our northern highlands," Rizal said.

"Yes, and we can drink to that," Juan Luna said in agreement.

Juan Luna opened a bottle each of French red wine and sparkling French champagne. "There is a saying, open your best wine in the company of friends and the worst when surrounded by your enemies. Let me pour into your glasses the very finest from my collection, Cabernet d'Anjou and Pommery."

When all of the wine and champagne glasses around the dining table were filled halfway to the rim, Maria Paz stood up and said, "I would like to make a toast … for all of us to celebrate, being young and forever beautiful."

"Amen, to that," Agustina responded.

Antonio Luna lifted his wine glass and said, "To our first and maybe only Christmas together."

"De brevitate vitae, gaudeamus igitur," Rizal said in Latin.

"Wait a minute, that does not count, we don't know what it means," Concha said.

"It's not our fault that you did not attend school in Ateneo or you would have understood Latin," Antonio giggled.

"It simply means, life is short, so let us rejoice." Rizal translated. "All of us drinking and celebrating life around this table reminds me of a poem sung by university students in romantic Heidelberg."

"Can you sing it for us?" Agustina asked.

"No, I am not a good singer, but I can recite the first stanza of the song. Let me see … let us rejoice, therefore, while we are young, after a pleasant youth, after a troubling old age, the earth will have us."

"That reminds me, I heard you once wrote a poem about the beautiful blooming flowers of the Neckar River in Heidelberg," TH said.

"Yes, during spring time in Heidelberg."

"How morbid of you guys, come on. Where is your Christmas spirit?" Maria Paz lifted her glass of French champagne. "We hope your holidays are filled with fun and cheer. So, have a Merry Christmas everyone!"

"Enough with the speech. Let's eat. I am hungry!" Antonio cried out.

"Wait a second; we need to say a prayer first." Doña Juliana said.

"Ohhh, nooo, here, let me do the honor to say a short prayer." Antonio said. "We all hold our hands together." He made the sign of the cross. "Good food, good meat, dear Lord, let's eat!"

Antonio was the first to serve, and the others filled their plates without delay amidst complaints coming from Doña Juliana, who thought the short prayer recited by Antonio was not proper enough. But no one listened to her as they devoured chicken and pork adobo, paella marinara, pâté de foie gras, a fat turkey, and chestnuts served in burgundy. And finally, there was the traditional French cake shaped like a log, *Buche de Noel*, and in addition a bowl of Spanish *crema de Catalan*.

"Guess what? I brought a bottle of homemade 28 percent alcohol liqueur, nature chilled Patxaran." TH Pardo proudly announced and then asked his wife to hand him the red package that was behind her. "Concha, give it over here."

"Did you make it yourself?" Maria Paz asked.

"No way, it was given to me as a gift by my neighbor who hails from Navarre," TH said.

"What is it made from?" Agustina asked.

"Sloe berries, collected from the blackthorn shrub and mixed with some kind of coffee beans and anisette," TH said.

"Doña Juliana, please bring out the liquor glasses and thanks," Juan Luna asked.

"Why don't we move to the next room where we can be served Patxaran by the fireplace?" Maria Paz said.

"Mamita, can Carlos and I open our presents now?" Andres tugged at his mother's skirt.

"No, not until past midnight," she said.

"But Bibi and Carlos are about to go to sleep," Concha said in protest.

"Listen, why don't you all take a short nap and we will wake you up when it's time to open your presents," Maria Paz said.

"Can we sleep out here so you don't forget to wake us up?" Andres pleaded.

"Of course, sweetheart," Maria Paz replied as she called on Brigitte, who was in her black and white maid's attire, to make Bibi and the two boys go to sleep in the same room next to her. Brigitte covered the kids with a woolen blanket and began singing a most beautiful Christian tune that called the attention of all those present, especially the ladies who were brought to tears.

"What a beautiful French Christmas carol," Agustina said.

"You have a beautiful voice," Concha said.

"I've heard you sing that before, but what is the title?" Maria Paz asked.

"It's a fairly new French song called, Cantique de Noël (Oh Holy Night)" Brigitte said.

"Beautiful, and thank you Brigitte," Maria Paz said. She then turned to her son. "Andres, look at Bibi and Carlos. They are already fast asleep. Now it's your turn. Now go and close your eyes."

"Mamita, can Brigitte tell me a story first?" Andres begged.

"All right, just one story," his mother said.

"Little Andres, would you like to know why we cover Christmas trees with bright candle lights?"

"Yes," Andres replied, rubbing his eyes and laying his head down.

"Once upon a time, there was this little homeless girl with a box of matches sitting all alone in the snow on the sidewalk. By nightfall, when everything around her became very dark, she struck one matchstick at a time in order to imagine what would be like inside a warm and lit house." Brigitte paused awhile when Andres gave a big yawn, seeing that he was still awake. She asked, "Little Andres, do you believe in miracles?"

"What is a miracle?"

"When you wish for something impossible, but it is granted to you by baby Jesus," Brigitte said.

"Ahh ... ok, I guess I do," Andres replied.

"Since Christmas is the season for miracles, when the homeless girl ran out of matches, shining golden angels from Heaven came down and took her to Paradise, a place of everlasting light."

Brigitte had hardly finished her story when she noticed that Andres was asleep. "Madam, looks like they are all sleeping now," she said to Maria Paz.

"Good, we will all be leaving soon to attend the midnight mass," Maria Paz said.

To attend midnight mass during the eve of Christmas was a tradition among Catholics all over the world. Churches, no matter the size, were magnificently lit and decorated with a creche or manger as their focal point and would usually accommodate their faithful with joyful tunes of carols sung by well-rehearsed choirs, in tune with the sounds of bells and carillons at the same time.

As with many families, the spirit of Christmas did not end after the midnight mass for the Luna's and their guests as they looked forward to what the French referred to as *le reveillon*, a late supper after the opening of presents. The Lunas were so gratified to have spent the Christmas Eve of 1889 with family and close friends they mutually loved and trusted.

CHAPTER 26

Antonio Luna returned to Madrid while José Rizal traveled to London for the last time after living there for over a year. He liked London for so many reasons: the chance to speak, read, and write in English, study and annotate Antonio de Morga's work on the colonial history of the Philippines up to the end of the sixteenth century, *Sucesos de las Islas Filipinas* (Events in the Philippine Isles), for the purpose of publishing a present day edition of Morga's work for Filipino readers to enjoy.

He also felt free and safe to work on the Philippine reform movement as well as an opportunity to be with Gertrude Beckett, one of the many women he loved—although this time Rizal would only spend less than a month in London. He moved to a boarding house in Brussels where he worked on his second novel, *El Filibusterismo*. He also continued to contribute propaganda articles and essays for *La Solaridad*. But his ideal life did not last for long as news from the Philippines regarding his family's financial setbacks made him think it might be time for him to go home.

Rizal returned to Madrid and attempted to seek justice, to no avail, for the return of agrarian land confiscated by the Dominican friars from his family. Like most people sidetracked with personal problems, Rizal at times was irritable of events and with friends surrounding him.

At one point, he even accepted the challenge to a duel made by his good friend, a very drunk Antonio Luna, when he heard him say offensive remarks about his girlfriend, Nellie Boustead, a French-Filipina, who picked him over Antonio Luna. But later on, they realized that a duel between compatriots would damage their cause in Spain. Both agreed to settle their personal problems amicably by signing a carefully worded resolution, thus saving their honor and pride.

Later on, Antonio Luna told his housemate and second for the duel, Galicano Apacible, that he was very sorry for the way he behaved toward his friend, Rizal and that he would rather have himself be killed than hurt Rizal, whom he respected and held in high esteem.

The straw that broke the camel's back was the rivalry between José Rizal and the editor of *La Solaridad*, Marcelo del Pilar, for the leadership of the association of Spanish and Filipinos in Madrid. Losing the election to del Pilar, Rizal felt betrayed, rejected, and he temporarily moved back to Belgium to complete his second novel in the wool town of Ghent, where he shared a lodging space with another Filipino, José Alejandrino, who assisted him in the publication of the book.

It was during this time when Rizal strongly contemplated going back to the Philippines. At about the same time, Antonio Luna felt that he too could no longer work well with del Pilar and returned to Paris.

Having completed his latest novel, *El Filibusterismo*, Rizal, after an honest self-evaluation of his objectives in life and for his fellow countrymen left Ghent for Paris at the beginning of October 1891 to bid farewell to the Lunas, Pardos, and other compatriots.

On his last night in Paris after having spent two memorable weeks reminiscing with friends, Rizal, Antonio Luna, and Felix Pardo were walking on the Boulevard de Capucines on their way to meet up with Juan Luna, TH Pardo, and three other Filipino friends for dinner.

When the trio reached the intersection of Place de l'Opera, close to the Opera de Paris, they could not help but notice the words, "*Liberté, Egalité, Fraternité*," emblazoned in bold letters on top of the building.

"Liberty, Equality, Fraternity … the three most beautiful words brought about by the French revolution," Rizal said and added, "Yes, free from servitude to a foreign power, equal opportunities for all Filipinos living in an ideal society. Don't you wish we could apply the same motto for our country someday?"

"All we can do from Europe is for that to happen. The only way we can take those three words back to our country is by getting our feet wet and you are taking that giant step tomorrow, my dear friend," Antonio said.

"Do we have a few minutes to spare? I want to take a closer look. I have no intention of coming back to Europe and this may be the last time I see Paris, the capitol of freedom and the arts," Rizal said.

As they walked toward the Opera de Paris, Felix pointed at the beautiful building structure and said, "Are you guys aware that the Opera is sitting on top of a small lake?"

"No." Antonio and Rizal answered almost in unison.

"Apparently during construction while they were digging the foundation, an underground lake erupted from some kind of springs."

"Amazing, and you know what? I've not been to the Opera," Rizal said sadly.

"Me too. Too bad you are leaving tomorrow or we could have gone to see a performance. Have you been inside the Opera, Felix?" Antonio asked.

"Yes, only once. The auditorium is breathtaking and the largest crystal chandelier I've ever seen hangs from the ceiling."

"Really?" Rizal responded.

"Hey, let's get going to the café. Since you are the guest of honor, we shouldn't keep them waiting," Antonio said.

"I don't know if it's a good idea for you to go back to the Philippines," Felix said. "I'm worried.

"I have done all I can in Europe…my place now is in Manila.

My passage has already been paid for by José Basa, and we have eight hundred copies of *El Filibusterismo* to sell."

"But what is to become of the propaganda movement in Madrid with Antonio back in Paris and you in Manila," Felix asked.

"Although Marcelo is capable of running the movement, there are a number of people in his inner circle who don't like me, and do nothing but gossip that I do more harm than good to the Filipino people." Rizal shook his head. "I want nothing but the best for my people."

"Once they read your book, don't blame anyone but yourself if your head ends up at the guillotine," Felix said.

"Don't you worry. If that ever happens, I will make sure they mail my head to you," Rizal said.

"Ha, ha, ha, that was funny. But if one is to die for a cause, why not get killed in battle?" Antonio countered.

"I've had the same discussions with you guys some time ago, and we were all in agreement that without funds we cannot start a war and win," Rizal answered.

"Yes, he who owns the gold makes the rules," Antonio replied. "However, it's only through a bloody revolution that one gets to own the gold."

"In a way, what you are saying is true, but I am dead set on a peaceful revolution," Rizal said, his face seemed set in determination. "All kidding aside, what is worse than being dead is being miserable alive. I have no choice. I must return to the Philippines to lead the crusade for reform even if it means that I die."

"Are you stopping in Hong Kong?" Antonio asked.

"Yes, for several months perhaps before continuing on to Manila," Rizal said.

"Well, my friend, you are the one about to face the music back in our motherland. So leave knowing that you are highly valued by all of us, and you can count on our support and best wishes." Antonio clapped Rizal on the back.

"Amen," Felix agreed.

They dined at the Café des Nouvelles in Place Pigalle, a very popular café personally picked by Juan Luna not only because it was frequented by Impressionist painters, but also because the ambiance was his inspiration for his painting, *The Parisian Life*.

CHAPTER 27

Meanwhile in Paris, Juan Luna's life was about to change dramatically. Progressive social ideas displayed during the recently held *Exposition Universelle* upon the bourgeoisie and in particular, regarding the social status of women began to take root throughout Europe, but especially in Paris. So transformative was this era that it became known in history as *La Belle Époque* or the Beautiful Era. For Juan Luna, however, the change felt more like ominous storm clouds over his perfect life with his beautiful wife, Maria Paz and their children, Andres and Bibi.

Juan was already distraught over the death of his father. He received the news from the Philippines in late spring of 1892 and had not seen the elder Luna since they bade farewell in the Port of Manila.

And now Maria Paz, incited by the feminist movement, which encouraged women to be their own bosses, began staying away from home more than ever, socializing and shopping. But she was no different than many French women that were suddenly seen frequenting social clubs and places, such as cabarets, like the *Chat Noir* and the *Moulin Rouge* in the Montmartre district.

In the world of art, *La Belle Époque* also made it possible for the art nouveau and the Impressionist styles of paintings to be recognized by critics and patronized by the bourgeois over the realists, such as Juan Luna.

The biggest emotional crush to Juan Luna was when three-year-old Bibi got sick. He came home one evening to find a very worried Brigitte waiting for him.

"Monsieur Luna, I'm so glad you are back early," Brigitte said.

"Why is there something wrong?"

"Yes, Bibi is very sick. Her cough is getting worse, and she has difficulty breathing.

Juan Luna rushed to his daughter's side with the nanny right behind him. "My sweet daughter, how do you feel?"

The little child was so weak and cold she could only manage a whisper. "Not good, Papi"

"Don't you worry, Papi is here, and I will take care of you." He placed his right hand on Bibi's neck. She was hot, and he knew her fever must be high.

"Where is my wife?" Juan asked Brigitte.

"She went out shopping, but said she would be back soon"

"Papi, I'm so cold," Bibi said.

"Here," he said and pulled her blanket under her chin. He turned to Brigitte and asked her to bring more blankets.

"Papi, am I going to die?" Bibi asked with tears in her eyes.

"No, my child, don't even think like that," he said.

But as soon as the words were out of his mouth, Bibi's body began shaking so hard he was afraid she was going into a convulsion. She was hardly breathing and the color of her skin was taking on a bluish tint. Luna immediately ordered Brigitte to bring him all the ice that was in the cooler and then, to go for the medic.

When Brigitte returned with the ice, Juan placed a piece on Bibi's head and neck. He put some in a towel and wiped down her hot skin. But then suddenly, her body began to seize. The horrible shaking continued for several minutes. Juan tried to hold his daughter tight against him but her shaking was out of control.

Finally, the convulsion began to subside, and she fell into a feverish sleep.

The doctor arrived about an hour later. When he saw that Bibi was sleeping soundly, he assured Juan not to worry. He explained that febrile seizures were normal for a child her age. So he left again with the caution that Juan should watch over his daughter closely for the next twenty-four hours.

"What's really wrong with her doctor?"

"She may be suffering from an acute case of Pertussis or whooping cough. However, her neck is a little swollen so she could also be suffering from diphtheria. In that case, she is contagious so keep your son away from her."

'What else can we do?"

"Just keep an eye on her and if she gets worse, call me. I'll be back in a day or two with the results of the test and to check on her again."

"What test?"

"A throat culture that I took from her," the doctor said.

As a precaution, the doctor left a couple of hospital face masks to wear around the house and then, he was gone again.

About an hour later, Maria Paz and her mother returned from their shopping spree and were immediately confronted by Luna.

"Where the hell have you been? How could you have been out for hours knowing that little Bibi is very sick?" Juan Luna screamed at his wife.

"Why, we were just out for a few hours," Maria Paz responded, thinking that her husband had just come home, too.

"You've been out since noon, and Bibi got so sick that I had to call for a doctor."

"How is she now? Is she awake?" Maria Paz headed toward Bibi's bedroom followed by Doña Juliana.

"Wait, you have to wear the face mask," Luna said.

"Why?" Maria Paz asked.

"The doctor explained that her disease might be very contagious." Juan held out the masks to her and Doña Juliana.

Maria Paz snatched them from him and thrust one at her mother. They went into Bibi's room and after ten minutes came out again.

"She seems to be sleeping fine," Doña Juliana said. "Children recover so quickly. She will be good as new by the morning."

However, the next morning when Brigitte went into Bibi's room and felt the child's cold skin, she began to scream so loud that she roused the whole family.

Juan was the first to enter the child's room. "*Dios mío! Dios mío!*" Juan wailed as he knelt next to her bed and cradled Bibi in his arms.

Maria Paz dropped to her knees next to Juan and burst into tears as she stroked the top of her daughter's head. "Let me hold her," she said to Juan.

"No. I cannot let her go just yet," he said and held Bibi as tight as he could.

"Call the doctor and tell him what happened," Doña Juliana instructed Brigitte.

But Brigitte kept staring at Bibi and did not move.

"Go!" Doña Juliana yelled command causing the maid to jump and run from the room.

Before long, the child was pronounced dead and taken away. All through the night, overwhelmed with sadness over his daughter's death, Juan mourned both silently and aloud. Every so often cries of despair came from his bedroom.

Maria Paz sobbed and fretted. She tried to get comfort from Juan, but he pushed her away.

"How horrible to lose Bibi," Doña Juliana cried. She embraced Maria Paz. "I could not imagine losing you, my only daughter."

TH was notified, and he came over immediately. "I am so sorry," he said to Juan and then consoled Maria Paz. "She is in heaven now at peace."

"But I cannot see her anymore… or kiss her sweet face," Maria Paz wailed.

TH made the burial arrangements under the guidance of Doña Juliana. A sad event, all of the Luna's friend and family paid their respects. Juan and his wife stood next to each other as they accepted condolences from the line of people who came to say a final goodbye to Bibi. But they did not speak to each other. Nor did they hold each other's hand for comfort. Juan could not say anything to Maria Paz without anger seeping into his words.

The day after the burial, Juan finally spoke to his wife but with anger and sarcasm. "Bibi is dead because of you. You wanted to shop more than to spend time with your sick daughter."

"That's not fair," Maria Paz said. "Bibi was not that ill when mother and I left. I never would have left her otherwise."

"I will never forgive you for this," Juan said.

"It was only by chance that you were home before me. You spend all of your time working in your studio," Maria Paz said.

"It is my work. What do you expect?" Juan replied.

"And having drinks with your friends. Is that work?" Maria Paz said in a huff with her hands on her hips.

"It is work because I talk to them about my art. I am in the process of my largest masterpiece, *People and the King*, while all you do is spending money shopping instead of taking care of your children."

"I refuse to listen to you tell me I am a bad mother," Maria Paz said and stormed out of the room.

Juan collapsed onto a chair and wept. Coping with the devastating loss of his beloved Bibi was the hardest thing he ever had to endure. His whole world seemed to be crumbling. The fact that his little girl was no longer around for him to hug, talk, and enjoy made a lot of difference, as he tried to understand what really happened and who was at fault.

Matters worsened in July when Maria Paz, ill with asthma, left with Andres, also sickly, and her mother for Mont Dore in Auvergne in Central France to better recuperate, leaving the still grieving Juan

Luna alone in Paris.

Depressed by the loss of his daughter and missing an absent wife and only son who he adored, he spent much of his time in the cemetery talking to his daughter's grave or behind the desk in his bedroom writing notes to his wife, persistently reminding her to take good care of their son.

CHAPTER 28

Maria Paz stayed in Auvergne for a month. When she returned to Villa Dupont, she was like a new person—happy and laughing again due to a new friendship with a man, Rene Dussag. At first, Juan wasn't interested in hearing about her friend. He still mourned Bibi, and to see his wife in such good spirits made him angry. He wanted her to be as grief-stricken as he was. In addition, he was hard at work on *People and the King (Peuple et Reis)*, which he planned to complete in time for the 1892 Chicago World Exposition. The canvas was to be almost as large as *La Spoliarium*, measuring 4.2 meters high by 6.3 meters long, and it depicted the madness and horror of the French Revolution.

Not long after her return from Mont Dore, Maria Paz received a telegram from Monsieur Rene Dussag.

"Love, do you remember the Englishman of French descent I told you about, Monsieur Dussag, who befriended and kept us company in Mont Dore, the one who has heard of you and of your arts and who wanted to meet you?" Maria Paz asked Juan. "He will be in Paris next month and plans to drop by for a visit. I hope you don't mind. He was really very kind and nice to us."

"How did you meet this man again?" Juan asked.

"He was a good friend of a neighbor where we stayed," his wife said.

"What do you mean by being nice to you? Did you go out with him?" Juan's tone was tinged with jealousy.

"Oh my God, the man is almost fifty years old! He is old enough to be my father. Go out with him—that is funny."

"What do you expect when out of nowhere a complete stranger is suddenly nice to you because he has heard of my art?" Juan Luna said sarcastically. "So I will ask you once again, did you go out with him because you must like him for you to invite him here?"

"All right, forget I ever mentioned him. I am going to write and tell him not to visit because my husband thinks he is screwing me," Maria Paz said.

Her response temporarily silenced Juan. In the end, however, he agreed to Dussag's visit, but then as soon as he laid eyes on the man, he felt unease at the pit of his stomach.

Rene Dussag was tall and slender with beautiful Caucasian skin—the complete opposite of Juan's Malay features. Thoughts of his wife in the arms of this handsome stranger were too much for Juan to bear. Immediately, he said, "Please excuse me but I need to leave. I have to unexpectedly be at an art gallery in Paris today. I won't be able to join you for lunch."

"That is a shame," Dussag said. "I was looking forward to discussing your art."

"Perhaps another time," Juan said, but could not make eye contact with the man. He turned to his wife. "Maria Paz, I need to speak with you in private."

"You reassured me that everything was fine," Juan whispered. "You said that nothing is going on between the two of you, but I feel that there is something wrong. I saw the glow in your eyes as soon as he walked into our house. I am sorry, but I cannot handle this."

"You are crazy! Go if you must, but you are completely wrong and out of your mind," Maria Paz hissed.

Juan started for the door and then turned back to his wife. "And by the way, have Dussag out of my home before I return."

Juan left and headed to his studio to work when he was interrupted by the sudden appearance of his old friend, Felix Hidalgo.

Juan welcomed him warmly. "Welcome, and so good to see you."

Felix shook his head. "I am here to break bad news to you, my friend," Felix said.

"What happened? Tell me quick," Juan said and gestured for Felix to sit down.

"José Rizal has been arrested in Manila for the alleged possession of anti-friars pamphlets," Felix said.

"What do you mean, alleged? He either had them or not," Juan said.

"It is true, but he is telling the authorities otherwise. His newly formed group, *La Liga Filipina* (The Philippine League) made them up for the purpose of seeking reform."

"Oh my god, what will happen to him now?"

"He is under house arrest there until the authorities can prove his wrongdoing," Felix said. "As soon as I hear more about him, I will let you know. Until then, let our prayers be with him."

"Yes," Juan said.

That night in bed, Juan tried telling Maria Paz about Rizal's troubles. She looked blankly at him and then turned her back on him in silence. Her complete rejection of Juan began a pattern of existence in the same house but hardly communicating. She went about her own business as if she lived alone.

That is, until one evening when Juan confronted her. "Where did you go tonight? Why are you home so late? You were with the Frenchman."

"Questions, questions and suspicions… why do you treat me like you care when we don't even speak or make love anymore? If you cannot trust me then leave and you won't have to worry anymore who I am out with."

"I remember well when you were mine and only mine. I was your first experience… when you lost your lost innocence with me and used to tremble at my touch. When only I gave you the love you desired." Juan Luna lamented softly to Maria Paz.

"Yes, when I thought you were a man of honor and dignity, someone I could change in time into a man with class and elegance—someone I could be proud of."

"Like your Monsieur Dussag," Juan responded angrily

"Yes, like my Monsieur Dussag," Maria Paz shouted back.

Juan Luna lashed out at his wife. "I knew it! I was right all along. So answer me now…is he your lover?"

Juan began to shake his wife, and when she tried to get away from him, he shook her more violently.

"I am not! I am not," Maria Paz screamed. "Let me go. You are hurting me!"

Juan shoved her aside. "You better not or I will kill you and him."

"I am not having an affair with anyone, and one thing for sure is that I no longer love you. You can kill me, beat me up…do anything to me because I don't care about you. I only put up with you for the sake of our son." Maria Paz stormed out of her room, crying and headed to her son's bedroom where she spent the night.

The following morning, Antonio Luna was concerned with the commotion that took place the night before and went to his brother's studio to check on him. "I heard you arguing last night. Have you settled your problems?"

"It's complicated. Nothing I do seems right to her anymore and I feel so bad that every time something goes wrong, it's always my fault." Juan blurted out. "But more than anything, she continues to deny any infidelity, and yet, swears she is not in love with me anymore. My life feels like a tangled mess."

"Don't get mad at me, my dear brother, but could you be wrong about her infidelity and it is only a product of your imagination? You don't have any proof."

"Antonio, then why do I have these strong feelings that my wife is attached like a magnet to this Frenchman?"

"Again, you have nothing to support your accusations." Antonio tried to reason with Juan.

"Prove me right or wrong then, Antonio, The next time she leaves the house alone follow her."

Antonio did exactly what his brother asked of him and followed Maria Paz, to the Louvre area of Paris along the rue de Rivoli and into an apartment hotel building at the rue du Mont Thabor. Antonio felt devastated for his brother, and trembled when he discovered Maria Paz rendezvous with Monsieur Dussag. He felt sorry for his brother and knew he would never look at her the same way again.

Antonio decided not to tell his brother anything in case this was only a chance meeting. But after he witnessed a second meeting between the two lovers the following day, Antonio knew he had to inform Juan.

Antonio went to Juan's studio. "Brace yourself, but you were right. I witnessed your wife meet with Dussag—two times."

Juan sunk into a chair and shook his head. "I am relieved so at least now I know that I am not crazy. But I am also so very sad." But within minutes, as the information settled in Juan's head, he gradually got angry.

"Hold your temper until you see for yourself," Antonio said. "The next time Maria Paz goes out, you will be the one to shadow her.

CHAPTER 29

Later that day, Juan Luna decided to follow the advice of his brother to control himself and not confront Maria Paz on her adulterous affair until he caught her at the domicile of Monsieur Dussag.

However, as the evening progressed, every time he gazed at his wife, he felt the intense rejection by her. Jealousy consumed him, leading to resentment and anger for this woman who betrayed him, shattered his trust, and stomped on his love for her. He was hard put to keep his overwhelming emotions in check.

Maria Paz could sense that there was something wrong from the moment she walked in the door of their home. "What's wrong? You don't seem to be feeling well," Maria Paz said as she walked to their bedroom.

Juan followed her and once inside he asked, "Where were you the whole day?"

"Oh no, don't even go there again." She tried to make her voice strong, but she felt fearful and walked toward the door.

Juan Luna blocked her from leaving the room. "I am only going to ask you one more time. Where were you?"

"I spent the day shopping from one end of Rivoli to the other. Satisfied?"

"I do not believe you were shopping. Where are your purchases?"

Maria Paz huffed. "I could not find anything to my liking."

"You're a liar. You found a lot to your liking—your lover!" Juan shouted.

Juan suddenly grabbed her and lifting her off her feet against him, he sniffed her whole body like a dog from her hair, neck, shoulders… the front of her dress.

She tried to struggle out of his grasp, kicking and screeching at him.

Finally, he dropped her, but not without punching her in the belly with his closed fist and screamed with rage. "God damn bitch! You've been fucking the whole day! I smell sex all over your body. Slut! *Hija de puta*!"

She grimaced in pain and began screaming for help," Help! Mama, Antonio, please help me! Juan is trying to kill me!"

Juan shoved his wife on top of the bed, "If you have not been fucking him the whole day, then you have enough energy to fuck me right now?"

"You are crazy… a madman. Get away from me." She cried out again for help.

"Bitch!" Juan raised his fist and was about to punch her again when he heard his brother yelling at him. His head snapped in the direction of the voice.

"Juan stop right now. Don't hit her!" Antonio said in a commanding voice as he pulled his brother off her.

Juan stood shaking in rage and then in a flash, he sprinted to their bedroom and began grabbing dresses out of Maria Paz's closet. "From now on you will wear simple dresses made out of sacks so men will no longer lust for you."

"Don't you dare take those? I bought them with my own money

since you are a pauper without my mother's wealth."

"I am your husband and will do whatever I please," Juan said in a threatening voice.

Antonio stepped in between them. "Maria Paz, please for your own safety stop yelling at him." You can always buy more dresses. Stay here and don't leave. I'll take care of him."

Antonio walked in just as Juan threw the dresses into the fireplace. He watched them burn.

"Juan, come on. Sleep in my room tonight, and tomorrow when you feel better you and Maria Paz can discuss your troubles."

"Antonio, you are not married, so you have no idea how painful it is to have an unfaithful wife, especially someone like me, who has remained loyal to our wedding vows."

"But, if you truly love her, then you will find a way to forgive her and forget this nightmare ever happened," Antonio said. "You have to get that poison out of your mind. I have heard that a discovery of an affair is a painful blessing, and may rekindle a blissful union."

"I wish it was that easy, Antonio, but how does one erase the thoughts of my wife in bed with another man? It is so demeaning." Juan knelt on the floor by Antonio's bed seized with self-pity and cried out loudly. "Oh God! I hurt so much I feel like I am being crucified. Help me, my Savior, please!

Antonio lifted his brother gently onto the bed and tucked him in.

"I'm so cold," Juan said.

Antonio wrapped him in the bedspread.

A wave of loneliness and depression fell hard upon Juan; he began to slide sideways on his bed, exhausted and almost numbed, curled up like an infant waiting to be born.

CHAPTER 30

The following day, Doña Juliana took her daughter to the house of Felix and Agustina, since TH was there in order to try and ascertain a solution for the abusive and unhappy couple, Juan and Maria Paz.

Meanwhile, the next time Maria Paz left home alone, her husband trailed her along the same route leading to the Mont Thabor apartment hotel where Antonio had spotted her and the Frenchman. He walked at a distance, and as a result, he lost her when she turned right into rue Mont Thabor, but quite unexpectedly, he bumped right into Monsieur Dussaq.

"Oh!" Dussag said startled. It took a moment for him to compose himself. "How do you do, Monsieur Luna?"

"I am doing fine," Juan replied cautiously. "Is this where you live?"

"No, I'm just here waiting for a friend, but it seems I've been stood up," Dussag said.

"I really have nothing to do today and you mentioned when you visited my home that you would love to chat about my art. I can keep you company now while you wait"

"Thank you, but no. I've been waiting already for almost an hour, and it will be dark soon. I have to run along now." Monsieur Dussag excused himself and scurried away.

"Hmmm," Juan murmured to himself as he stared in the wake of Dussag.

He walked across the street past a bunch of sweaty little boys kicking around a soccer ball and entered the apartment hotel. He approached the woman behind the desk. Her name was Charlotte.

"*Bonjour madam*, would you happen to know if a Monsieur Rene Dussag resides in the hotel?"

"Yes, he shares an apartment with a friend," Charlotte replied.

"Would that friend happen to be a redheaded female and about this tall?" Luna raised his hands slightly above his head to indicate the height of his wife.

"No, not with a lady, he shares with a Monsieur Fermy."

Juan smiled warmly at her. "Could you please direct me to their room?"

"I'm sorry, Monsieur, we are not at liberty to give out a tenant's apartment number," Charlotte said.

"*Merci beaucoup*, but oh, one last thing, the redheaded lady I just described to you, did she ever come here to see Monsieur Dussag?"

Charlotte giggled. "Dussag and Fermy are so good looking; they have so many different women walk in and out of their apartment, although one of them sort of fits your description."

"*Merci*," Juan Luna said, and walked out of the building once again depressed and broken hearted.

When he got home, he was surprised to learn that his two brother-in-laws were waiting for him, concerned about his rage and how he had beaten Maria Paz.

Juan related his side of the incident and assured the Pardo about his unending love for their sister and was willing to forgive and forget all her infidelity on one condition—the chance to regain his honor through retribution.

"Why go on living as a man when a Frenchman dishonors and puts him to shame?" Juan said sadly. "And so I want nothing from that Frenchman but his blood on the tip of my sword."

The Pardo brothers realized that blood-vengeance was the only way their sister's marriage would be saved so they agree with Juan Luna and arranged for a duel with Monsieur Dussag. However, Dussag refused the challenge based on his vehement denial of ever having an affair with Maria Paz Luna.

As a counter suggestion, TH said to the Frenchman. "Monsieur Dussaq, if we prepare a sworn declaration of your innocence, would you be willing to sign such document?"

"Yes, I would do anything to get out of a situation that is driving me crazy," Monsieur Dussag said agreeably. "I am so sorry for the inconvenience my friendship with your sister has caused your family."

The following day Monsieur Dussaq signed the declaration in which he added that he had only met Maria Paz Luna briefly in Mont Dore the previous July and considered her merely as a friend.

TH presented the declaration of innocence to Juan who read the letter and snickered. "Do you think that son of a bitch can hide behind this crappy piece of paper? Nor do his words absolve your sister's infidelity. She will always be an adulterer, a Madame Bovary, and I would prefer she no longer be part of my life."

"Does this mean you are amenable to a legal separation?" TH offered congenially.

"It is very sad when love is unfair. And to love someone who does not love me in return, or love forever is not for me. I believe one of the most important things in a relationship is trust. I don't think I can ever trust her again. So yes, maybe, it's only best to end this marriage. That is how life is sometimes, full of pain but one still has to survive the agony." Juan Luna responded with such bitterness in his voice.

TH immediately accounted the latest development of his sister's marriage to his brother and mother, who decided it would be best to summon their family lawyer, Antonio Regidor to Paris to settle the separation of the couple.

"Thank God!" Maria Paz responded when told about the imminent divorce. "I don't want you to worry because someone will cross my path one day and give me the love and care a woman like me desires." She felt relieved that she could now live the way she wanted without her husband telling her otherwise.

But the more that Juan considered living without his wife and son, shattered and alone, made him so miserable that the following day he explained his change of heart to his brothers-in-law. "I cannot lose Maria Paz! I will leave Paris this Sunday and move away from the likes of Monsieur Dussag to Vigo, Spain where we can live as a family once more. I will force myself to forget about Dussag and all the ugliness that has transpired here."

"What does Maria Paz have to say about your plans?" Felix asked.

"She agreed to come," Juan hesitantly replied.

"Is she in her bedroom?" Felix asked.

"Yes," Juan said. "Go see for yourself."

But when Felix excused himself and confronted his sister, she said, "Felix, please I beg you to hold him off. I am leaving first thing tomorrow morning without saying goodbye. I hate farewells. Tell him that I was in love once, and that it does not matter anymore whose fault it was, but I do not love him anymore. Please, talk to him, and try to make him understand it's impossible to love him again."

"You cannot just walk away and disappear with your son."

"But, there is no sense to go on living with him for the rest of my life. Please Felix…please, understand my situation."

"You will make matters worse. Wait here while TH and I talk things over with Juan."

Felix rejoined TH and Juan. "Juan, be reasonable. You have everything here in Paris . . . your friends, your art studio, and family. How can you start all over again in a small town like Vigo? There is nothing to look forward to in that God forsaken place. You don't even have money saved to leave so soon." TH protested.

“I have eighty francs, enough to take my family there and get by for a few days,” Juan answered.

“You are so hardheaded! You cannot move your family out of Paris with so little money,” Felix said.

“Then I’ll prove you wrong, because you have no idea of what I’m capable of doing.”

“Hold on for a moment. Since I cannot convince you to stay then please let me give you some money so I am assured of my sister’s well-being.”

Luna refused. "I don’t want anything to do with your family. I can manage to live from the sale of my paintings. Nothing. . . I want nothing from your family. My mind is made up!"

The Pardo brothers were worried for their sister who they believed would be alone in faraway Spain with a madman.

TH whispered to his brother. “All will be well when Antonio Regidor shows up. The entire Filipino community respects him so even Juan Luna must listen to reason. He is due to arrive next Wednesday, September 21.”

CHAPTER 31

Early on the morning of September 22, Juan Luna woke up very early to finish packing for the move to Vigo. He went to bed late the night before to complete gathering all the things he needed to bring with him, but he perplexed that Maria Paz wasn't objecting about leaving Paris. But also, neither was she making an effort to pack her personal items or those belonging to Andres.

Not long after, the Pardo brothers showed up without notice accompanied by their family lawyer, Antonio Regidor.

Juan had only one thing to say in a cold, determined tone. "If you think you come here to change my mind, you are mistaken."

"No, we are here to say farewell to Maria Paz and Andres." TH lied. He could not bear tell his brother-in-law the real intentions of their visit.

Juan nodded toward the stairs leading to his bedroom where Maria Paz was supposed to be packing for Spain. The brothers went up and found their mother and sister already waiting and packed lightly as suggested by the brothers, ready to move out from Villa DuPont but not to Vigo. Instead, the plan was for her to go away with them. Meanwhile, Antonio Regidor stayed downstairs and waited for them.

"Why are you here?" Juan asked Regidor.

"TH telegraphed me to come and help settle your separation with Maria Paz."

"Separation! There is no separation anymore. We are on our way to Vigo today," Juan Luna snapped angrily.

"No, I am here to represent Maria Paz…"

"Get out of here! Get out of my house! Out!" Juan Luna shouted, not allowing Regidor a chance to explain himself.

From the bedroom, the Pardo family heard the commotion downstairs with Juan and Regidor. The brothers advised Maria Paz and their mother to bolt the bedroom door and then lock themselves inside the adjacent bathroom while they attempted to bring Juan Luna to his senses.

"How dare you go behind my back in concocting this conspiracy to separate me from my wife, and yes, kidnap my son in the process?" Juan Luna screamed at the sight of his brother-in-laws.

"Look, we are not trying to break up your family. All we suggest is a temporary separation for both of you to think things out, and to reminisce on the past events of your marriage. Perhaps, you will learn from your mistakes and can once again re-build your relationship with your wife," TH calmly replied.

"Enough! *Basta*! Leave my house immediately before I do something crazy." Juan screamed as he advanced toward Regidor and his brothers-in-law. His eyes bulged in rage, and both hands were clenched into fists at his side.

The men felt that they had no other recourse but to scramble out of the house.

Before closing the door behind him, Felix turned around and said, "I am sorry, Juan. I hope you understand."

Juan watched them cross the street and enter a small bistro across from his house as if they had no care in the world. "That does it!" Juan Luna said aloud to himself in anger. "Who do they think they are treating me this way, just because they have all the money in the world to hire a lawyer?"

A strange, raw, and almost indifferent emotion suddenly took hold of him, but only for a moment. Because then images of Monsieur Dussag came back to haunt him, and rage turned into uncontrollable hatred now clearly reflected on his face. He ran to the second floor where he reached for his revolver that was secretly hidden above the linen armoire.

"If you all think she can leave me for a Frenchman, you are crazy. I will kill all of you first. Before you ever leave this house, I will kill you!" Juan Luna screamed so loud and kicked the walls and doors that his family and neighbors all heard him.

Brigitte rushed out of the house and dashed into the bistro and warned the men of Monsieur Luna's threats to kill everyone in the family.

"Brigitte, listen to me, I want you to sneak back into the house, and go tell my sister and mother to hide in the toilette and make sure all doors are locked." TH ordered her.

"But I am afraid he might kill me too," she cried.

"He has no reason to harm you. Just go and do what I told you and we will be right behind you," TH said.

At the same time, Felix asked a passerby to go to the police.

Not long after Juan Luna heard footsteps coming from the first floor. His first thought was that it must be the conspirators coming back to destroy his family. He saw them entering the villa from the top of the stairway and blindly fired a shot.

Felix Pardo was hit on the chest. He slumped backwards against his brother who caught him, and then TH and Regidor dragged him to safety by the entry foyer outside the house. TH began screaming for help.

A crowd of on-lookers started to build up along the Rue Pergolese. TH offered 100 francs to anyone in the crowd willing to assist in pacifying his brother-in-law. No one accepted the challenge.

Maria Paz and her mother hid inside the bathroom and from a small window Doña Juliana screamed hysterically. "Help us! Help us! Please, for the love of God, don't let us be harmed."

Juan Luna continued to bang and kick on doors, swearing to kill anyone who dared contradict him. He felt a strong need for vindication and the urge to punish, to inflict pain.

Frantic for someone to help them, and with their eyes large in fear at what Juan was going to do to them, mother and daughter pressed their bodies against the bathroom door to prevent him from breaking it down.

"I hate you! I hate you! I wish you were dead and in hell with the devil!" Maria Paz cried out in sudden passion.

Frustrated that he could not break the door down, and with the deafening voices of his wife and mother-in-law on the other side, Juan's nerves continued to rage. He felt as if his brain was splitting and running in all directions, causing more anxiety and irritability.

"Crucify them! Yes, crucify them all for being nothing more than a bunch of Judases!" Juan screamed with these thoughts foremost in his mind.

And so without a clear thought in his head, he pointed the revolver point blank at the bathroom door and pulled the trigger three consecutive times killing Dona Juliana and wounding Maria Paz.

What may have been a partial loss of memory for Juan, he nonetheless had no idea how he got inside the bathroom. But seeing the bloodied bodies of his wife and mother-in-law made him drop to his knees in shock. He stared at the revolver that was still in his hand and cried out, "Oh, my God, what have I done!"

But then without reason, he felt a sudden release of emotions—a numbed feeling that it was all over, the end of the line, and a closure on being alive. He stepped out of the bathroom into the adjacent bedroom, and saw his son trembling in the protective arms of the housemaid. Juan looked at them, and then very slowly raised the revolver to his right temple, his index finger on the trigger, when Brigitte stopped him.

"Monsieur Luna! For the sake of little Andres, please don't hurt yourself," Brigitte cried out.

With a stunned, blank stare, he began walking toward Brigitte. She was so afraid that she pleaded, "No! Please, not us, too!"

But Juan calmly handed her the revolver and said, "Take this from me but be careful. It's still loaded."

Brigitte gingerly took the revolver that dangled from Juan Luna's hand.

Juan, still in a trance-like state, retreated to the bathroom and one at a time, moved the lifeless bodies to the bedroom, on top of the bed.

Brigitte slowly moved out of the bedroom with Andres and yelled for assistance. "Someone call for a medic. Both Madame Maria Paz and Madam Juliana are badly hurt. They have been shot."

Upon hearing the housemaid, TH and Regidor rushed to the bedroom to check on the conditions of the victims.

Upon seeing the men enter, Juan Luna asked for their forgiveness and inquired on the condition of his friend, Felix.

TH advanced on Juan. "You, crazy son of a bitch, what have you done? If you have killed them, then I am going to kill you."

Monsieur Regidor reacted swiftly and grabbed TH from rushing at Juan and beating him to death.

TH glared at Juan. "I will get my revenge on you and your family someday. Mark my words"

Just then the police tramped up the stairs and rushed into the bedroom where they apprehended Juan and took him away. He was arrested, booked, and detained at the Mazas Prison in Paris not far from the Gare de Lyon. Built in 1841, the structure was designed by Emile-Jacques Gilbert to be a geometrical model of Utopian architecture for 1200 detainees. There was a centrally located tower with a glass dome at the very top where guards kept a watchful eye on all prisoners inside their cells. The cells were equally distributed throughout all six three-story buildings surrounding the tower.

On the following day, TH exhausted his frustrations by destroying all the paintings he and his late mother had bought from Juan Luna.

CHAPTER 32

When Juan Luna completed narrating his life's story to Adriano Gomez, the newspaper journalist stood up and walked a few steps towards the cell bars, speechless. He had accepted Antonio's invitation to write about Juan because of the Filipino's reputation as a great artist, but to hear this blood-curdling tale of betrayal and murder momentarily overwhelmed him.

Juan sat quiet. He felt anguished and embarrassed and he could not bear to look at Adriano.

The mood inside his 2.60 m high, 1.85 m wide and 3.85 m long prison cell was somber and the hot air aeration system did not help at all in warming up the cold atmosphere.

Adriano Gomez turned around to face Juan and spoke finally. "I want you to understand that the story you just related to me I felt was coming from deep within you, as an ordinary man trying to find a metaphor for life."

"Yes," Juan replied.

"Then try to remember that we are all human, and making mistakes is a part of what we do," Adriano replied, without taking his eyes from Juan's face.

Antonio Luna reached out and grabbed his brother's shoulder from his seat on the wooden footstool. "Señor Gomez is right, Juan. We all do make mistakes, sometimes horrific, but what is important is that you have admitted your act and are now very remorseful."

By then, a guard showed up accompanying a young man of average height with rosy cheeks and smiling eyes—a comparison from the vulture-like eyes of the guard beside him. The guard tapped on the steels bars of Luna's cell with his baton and informed Antonio and Adriano that their time was up and they had to leave. And anyway, the court-appointed defense lawyer wanted to talk to his client in private.

"Sir, I would appreciate very much if my brother could stay longer," Juan requested.

"No, that's not permitted," the guard said.

"If we can this one time, I would prefer that his brother hears what I have to say so we can better help Monsieur Luna," the lawyer said.

The guard unlocked the cell to let Señor Gomez out as the young lawyer walked in and joined the Luna brothers. Antonio jumped when the heavy steel door clanked shut behind him.

Before he left, Adriano Gomez looked back inside the cell and assured Juan Luna of the full backing and support from his newspaper.

The lawyer spoke up next. "My name is Albert Danet and I will be representing you in court during your trial so from now on you are not to give any interviews without me present. And for now, let's hope that newspaper man keeps his word."

"He will," Antonio said.

"Normally I don't meet with my clients until they have been officially charged, but I had to make an exception in your case." Monsieur Danet looked sadly at Juan and then reached over and pressed his hand on Juan's arm." I have tragic news for you"

"What is it?" Juan asked.

"Your wife died last night," Monsieur Danet said.

"Oh no, all of my hopes to see her again, and apologize for what I did…are gone. All hope taken away from me." Distraught, Juan looked at his lawyer with tears in his eyes and said, "Go home, I don't want a lawyer. I am guilty and want to die."

"Juan, please don't talk this way. I worry for you. Please don't give up hope," Antonio said in a pleading voice.

"I am a murderer and deserve to die. I deserve the guillotine." Juan broke down in tears.

"Then go on living for your son," Antonio said.

"Monsieur Luna, if you want to continue taking care of your son then you have to start thinking positive. Your wife was not the only victim in this case. You had no control over your emotions and senses when you discovered her infidelity. You went insane. Isn't that true?"

"*Crime passionnel!* Committed due to a sudden rage or heartbreak is an acceptable defensive plea in France. I am very confident to win this case but only if you have the complete desire to win—for the sake of your son. For in winning the case, you win him back as well."

Juan Luna remained silent and still, except for when he looked at Danet and gave him a slight nod in understanding.

"I have to go now," Danet said. "But I will get back as soon as you are officially charged with the crime. Also, if needed, would you agree to have little Andres testify on your behalf?"

"I don't know if that will be a good idea," Juan Luna said. "He may have been influenced already by his Uncle TH to hate me for the loss of his mother. But also, I don't like the idea of him being grilled in court."

"Juan, you've got to start living again. You've got to see your son. If you go to prison, the Pardos will bring him back to Manila." Antonio Luna warned his brother. "Even worse, if they send you to Devil's Island, you will never see him again."

"But I don't know what to say to him. He must hate me so much and not want to see me," Juan said.

"Let me be the judge of that," Antonio responded.

"You have the right to see Andres. I will arrange to have him brought here for a visit." Monsieur Danet assured Juan.

"I love and miss him so much. Yes, I want to see him and give him a huge hug and tell him how much I love him and am sorry for taking his mother away from him," Juan said with tears in his eyes.

Monsieur Danet signaled for the prison guard to open the cell.

"Monsieur, you have to leave now as well," the prison guard said to Antonio.

Antonio wrapped his arm around his brother's neck and kissed him on right cheek. He whispered, "You will be all right, my dear brother. Take good care."

On the 16th of December 1892 Juan Luna was officially charged for murder by the Procurator and the Prefect of Police, arraigned at the Paris Court of Appeals under Case Number 1750, Assize Court de la Seine. The full indictment arrest: Juan Luna San Pedro, and included the following count, as recorded on the Paris police archives:

I. Of having, on 22 September 1892 in Paris, tried to commit voluntary homicide on the person of Felix Pardo, an attempt [which was not carried out due to] circumstances independent of the intention of the accused, with these circumstances the said attempt was committed:

1. with premeditation;

2. that it was followed by the crime of murder, committed on the woman Juliana Gorricho, widow Pardo, as specified below.

II. Committed voluntary homicide on the person of Juliana Gorricho, widow Pardo, with these circumstances:

1. that the said voluntary homicide was committed with premeditation;

2. that it preceded, accompanied and followed the crime of murder, committed on the person of Maria Paz Pardo, wife of Juan Luna as identified above;

3. that it followed the attempt to commit the crime murder on the person of Felix Pardo.

III. Of having committed voluntary homicide on the person of Maria Paz Pardo, wife of Juan Luna, with these circumstances;

1. with premeditation;

2. That it followed the crime of attempted murder as aforementioned, committed on the person of Felix Pardo;

3. That it followed the crime of murder as aforementioned, committed on the person of Juliana Gorricho, widow Pardo.

CHAPTER 33

A few days later, with the assistance of Monsieur Danet, Antonio brought Andres to see his father in prison for the opportunity to hear Juan's side of the tragedy. There was a brief startling silence between them until Juan Luna offered a chance to reverse their misfortunes.

"We need to talk, my son. You don't need to say anything, but you must hear me out. I know from what Uncle Trinidad tells you that you see me as a monster and a madman. And I still wonder myself what went wrong. How could I have not realized she was so unhappy?" Juan Luna said, and then saw that Andres was sobbing. "You look so big, and I miss you every single day. It's okay to cry; I do, too. All I have done is weep since your mother left us to go to heaven."

"Uncle Trinidad tells me Mamita and Grandmama are happy in heaven, but when are they coming back? Will they be here for my birthday?"

"My son, it's important for you to understand the difference between being in heaven and going away to a place like Spain or the

Philippines. I love your Mamita so very much, there is not a day that I don't think of her all the time, but she is in heaven and is not coming back to us."

Andres became frantic. "It's my fault! I made you and Mama fight, and because of me, you killed her! It's my entire fault."

"No, Andres, what happened between your mother and me had nothing to do with you. You must believe that and erase that notion from your mind."

"Then why did you kill her?"

Now in tears and his pulse beating faster than normal, Juan responded, "There is nothing I can do to bring your mother back. I did not wake up that morning with a revolver in my hand prepared to take your mother away from us." As his emotions built up, he cried unabashedly. "The devil took possession of me and I lost control. I committed the unthinkable and snuffed a living beauty like my beloved Maria Paz, your mother and your grandmother."

Juan Luna paused and nervously gritted his teeth, then continued. "I could have taken my own life, but the thought of you, all alone, stopped me. Instead, I am cursed to live out my life burdened with the guilt of my actions. Even worse is the threat of being found guilty in the courtroom and then you will lose me as well."

Andres was taken aback by what his father said and then in a small, choking voice he said, "Please don't let them take you away from me like what happened to Bibi, my grandmama, and mamita. I don't want to be left all alone, papa. I am so afraid."

Juan Luna hugged his son tightly. "With the help of God, I am not going anywhere, my son. I love you so very much and will do my best never to leave you. But I may need your help."

"Yes, Papa, I will do anything for you to stay with me."

"All right, then listen to your Uncle Antonio and do whatever he tells you. I love you, my son."

"I love you too, papa," Andres said in between his tears. "But I dream of Mamita and Grandmama. I miss them so much too."

"What happened to your mother has happened. It makes no

difference to us now, but you are sweet to remember her in your dreams and prayers. Your mother loved you and would not want you crying. She would want you to go on with your life and be a happy, healthy, strong and good son."

Father and son remained locked in each other's arms Juan Luna tells Andres, "Son, forgive me, please. We cannot change the past, but we can change on how we react to the past. We've got to let go and let everything be as it is now."

A jail guard escorted Antonio back into the cell to take Andres. "It's time for us to go, Andres," Antonio said. "Say goodbye to your father."

"Good-bye papa," the boy said as he walked away hesitantly, still sobbing quietly and holding on to his uncle's right hand. He turned around to face Juan once more and said, "I forgive you papa."

"Thank you my son, I am now in peace," Juan Luna, said. And then, he turned to his brother. "Antonio, come as often as you can with Andres. I feel my son is my only motivation to go on living."

CHAPTER 34

On February 7, 1893, Juan Luna was arraigned and subsequently charged by the Clerk of the Court of Assise at the Palais de Justice de la Seine, on the Ile de la Cite, 36 quay des Orvefres, in Paris, a stone throw away from the richly hued stained-glass windows of the majestic *Sainte-Chapelle* that was erected in 1246 by King Louis IX to house the Crown of Thorns and a fragment of the true cross, precious relics of the Passion of Christ.

The counsel for the defense, Albert Danet, arrived at the courthouse the day of the trial early in the morning for a last minute briefing with Juan Luna. Upon entering the newly renovated building, he headed down to the lower floor at the end of the corridor, beyond the office of the secretaries, into the middle rooms allotted to the police department for a holding jail.

Juan Luna was waiting for his turn to face the judge and the jury of men who had the power to set him free, or place his head under the blade of a guillotine or even worse, send him to the French Guiana, in the

French penal colony, *Ile du Diable*, better known as the Devil's Island.

Antonio Luna, hoping to sit close to his brother, also arrived early. He waited alone in line by the entry door beneath a beautiful wood curving that hang above the door. When allowed by the sentry guard on duty to enter the chambers, Antonio could not help notice the room was brightly lit by a large window facing the courtyard of the Sainte-Chapelle.

Antonio Luna sat on the right side of the center aisle of the courtroom allotted for family, friends, and members of the defense counsel. He rightly assumed that his brother would be seated at the center table facing the twelve jurymen who occupied the seats behind a u-shape table in front of him. The president judge directed the jury. He sat on an elevated podium with four magistrate judges on either side of him; all five of them were next to the registrar at the right endpoint of the table closest to the accused.

The courtroom started to fill with spectators, but still there was no sign of the Pardo family. Antonio spotted Adriano Gomez, and motioned for the journalist to sit next to him.

"Whoa, where do you come from?" Antonio asked Adriano as he was about to seat in an empty chair beside him, "Why do you smell so good, like you've just been with a woman?"

"When in Paris, you do what the Parisians do: go shopping," Señor Gomez replied. "This is the latest Eau de Toilette by Perfumeries Lubin at Rue Sainte-Anne, not far from here. You should go there."

"No, thanks, you are not going to have me wear cologne," Antonio said.

"So Antonio, how are you doing?" Adriano asked.

"I am doing well, but also a bit nervous. I feel like I am about to watch a duel-to-the-death match with my brother as one of the duelers."

"Don't worry too much, my friend. Your brother will be acquitted as a result of my daily columns as translated and posted in the French newspapers. Juan Luna has the sympathy of the French public on his side. The Pardo family can deny all day long that Maria Paz was faithful to your brother, but the French people know better. French men think they are the best lovers in the world and believe in making love all day long. They also believe that Maria Paz was having an affair, and so will the ten married jurymen that your brother will face today."

"Rene Dussag is an Englishman," Antonio said in explanation.

"But he is of French descent and name. That makes him a Frenchman in the minds of the public."

Adriano Gomez explained the French Assize criminal trial court system as best he could to Antonio. "The twelve jurymen are French citizens selected at random, but before the trial, both prosecution and defense can refuse a juror for no reason. The judge, referred to as president of the court, is there to more than supervise the proceedings and guide the jurors. He also has the power to interrogate anyone in the quest to discover the truth," Señor Gomez said.

"What about the witnesses?" Antonio asked.

"The defendants and witnesses give their testimony without taking an oath, so as not to force them to self-incriminate. At the end of the trial, the decisions by the judge and jurors carry equal weight in deciding to acquit or indict the defendant, as well as on sentencing," Señor Gomez said.

Just then, the Pardos arrived with little Andres in hand. Sounds of murmurs echoed inside the courtroom when the double doors swung wide open as Monsieur Danet and Juan Luna walked inside the room, flanked by four guardsmen. A tall and husky man built more like a bouncer in one of so many bars in the Montmartre district of Paris stood up and asked everyone to stand as he announced that the court was now in session.

The jury walked in and took their places. The magistrate judges, the president and two clerk assessors followed them. The president judge presided over the hearing. He called for the jury to be seated and instructed them of their duties.

The Court of Assizes President Judge, donning a black robe over his shoulders and a wide white scarf worn like a necktie covering his chest, addressed Juan Luna. "You are charged with the first-degree murder of Maria Paz Luna, Juliana Pardo, and the attempted murder of Felix Pardo. Do you understand the charges against you, Monsieur Luna?

"Yes, your honor," Juan said.

"How does the defendant plead?" the judge asked Monsieur Danet.

"Your honor, the defendant pleads not guilty on the grounds of temporary insanity."

"Very well, you may proceed," the judge said.

In his opening statement, the prosecutor Magistrate Felix Decori expressed to the court that the prosecuting counsel would be able to prove without a reasonable doubt that Monsieur Juan Luna willfully and with premeditation murdered in cold blood his loving wife, Maria Paz Luna, his very generous mother-in-law, Juliana Pardo, and attempted to murder his brother-in-law Felix Pardo. He also informed the court that he would be presenting detailed evidence regarding what had transpired before and after the murder, and from the moment the police arrived in the scene of the crime. The prosecuting lawyer went on to describe other means of proving Juan Luna's guilt and ended his statement by saying, "We have a signed confession that proves beyond a reasonable doubt Monsieur Juan Luna is guilty."

During his opening statement, Monsieur Decori also managed to read a letter written by Juliana to her oldest son, TH, which documented the constant beating and abuse upon Maria Paz from the accused and the psychological attempt to manipulate Maria Paz into admitting, in writing, to having had an affair with Monsieur Dussag.

The prosecuting lawyer concluded by characterizing the crime with the chilling words. "But to murder rather than be separated, how can you understand the accused? You will never … because he is a mad monster. Your honor, in all honesty, this is among the most hideous crime of murder I have ever faced in my career."

Albert Danet began his opening statement by clarifying to the court that the defendant had the right to withdraw any pre-trial confessions when arrested and questioned by the police last September 22, 1892. He explained to the jury that the court was expected to disregard the signed confession and instead examine the evidence against the defendant.

After going through the motion of shedding light on other pertinent items favorable for the defense, Monsieur Danet continued. "Monsieur Luna considers his brother Antonio and the Pardo to be his only family in Paris. What would drive a man with such impressive Catholic background and illustrious career to commit such an undignified act on family members he not only loved but also, adored."

Monsieur Danet continued. "What appeared to be a marriage made in heaven to his family and friends turned out to be a nightmare for a man who felt he was not being treated well by both his wife and mother-in-law? The constant insults on his character made this quiet man swallow his pride and keep to himself. That is, until he burst like a crack in a water dam when he discovered his wife was having an affair with a married man. Yes, a handsome, elegant, and wealthy married man with three children."

Danet pointed to Juan Luna as he spoke to the jury. "The defense is not contesting that Monsieur Luna fired his revolver. But to prove beyond a reasonable doubt that Monsieur Luna did so when he was not in a proper state of mind. I repeat, not in a proper state of mind on the day the Pardo brothers and family lawyer stormed into his house to kidnap his son, Andres, and his wife, Maria Paz. Monsieur Luna panicked and fired a shot with his revolver, accidentally hitting his brother in law. From that moment on, he completely lost all control of his mind until he was brought back to his senses by screaming and crying from the maid and Andres. It was then, and only at that moment, that Juan saw the lifeless bodies of his wife and mother-in-law. Only then he realized he may have done something horrific, and he surrendered the revolver to the maid and remorsefully broke down and cried."

The president judge of the court brought forth the first question of the trial. "Can you narrate to the court any evidence or proof of your late wife's alleged paramour relations with Monsieur Dussag?"

"I can your honor. I suspected my wife was having an affair with Monsieur Dussag from the moment he walked into our home. My wife was beautiful, but on that particular day she never looked more exquisite, and what hurt me was that it was not for me, but for the other man." Juan paused, cleared his throat and continued. "I had my brother, Antonio follow her twice to an apartment hotel in 25 Rue du Mont Thabor on the mornings of the 10th and the 11th of September and on both occasions she was seen in the company of Monsieur Dussag."

"But did *you* ever see your late wife with Monsieur Dussag?" the president judge inquired.

"No, your honor, but I did follow her once when she told me that she was out of eyebrow pencils and some cosmetics and had to go out and buy them near the Louvre, which happened to be very close to Mont Thabor. I was so sure then that she was going to meet up with her lover but suddenly lost her when we got to Mont Thabor."

"What happened next?" the defense counsel asked.

"I proceeded to the apartment hotel where my brother saw her rendezvous with Monsieur Dussag a few days before, and to my surprise I bumped into Dussag." Juan Luna pointed to where a very handsome man dressed in a dark business suit sat inside the courtroom.

"Gentlemen of the jury, let the record show that Monsieur Luna had just identified a man seated in the back row of this court as the man who was having an affair with his late wife."

"Objection, your honor!" shouted Monsieur Decori.

"Sustained, Monsieur Danet, you are out of order, so please refrain yourself from any theatrical outburst," the president judge instructed.

"I am sorry, your honor." And then facing the accused Danet asked, "What did you do next?"

"I told him that I found it to be a very strange coincidence to see him standing in the same area where my wife had just disappeared, and he told me that he had just left a friend who had an apartment inside the hotel."

"What made you believe that Monsieur Dussag even resided in the said apartment hotel except for the mere fact that you only saw him standing outside the building?"

Luna took a deep breath and said, "He lied because I found out from the concierge that he shared the apartment with a Monsieur Fremy and that a lady befitting my wife's description had been a constant visitor to the apartment. The incident can be substantiated and confirmed by Mademoiselle Caron, the hotel concierge, when she testifies on my behalf."

"Monsieur Luna, please explain to the court how you don't remember shooting at the locked door of the bathroom that killed your wife and mother-in-law, if in the transcript of the police report, you acknowledged and remembered talking to your mother-in-law, who was already dead at the time?"

Juan Luna replied, "I don't remember firing the revolver at all. It was like being in the middle of a dead calm, and my senses were only awakened by the cries of Andres and Brigitte. I felt so much pain and sorrow, seeing both Maria Paz and Doña Juliana lifeless. I did not want to leave them on the cold tile floor, and moved them to the bedroom. As I dragged the body of Doña Juliana, I expressed how sorry I was for hurting her since she was a very kind and generous grandmother, most especially to my son. I did the same for my beloved wife."

"Objection, your honor!" Felix Decori interrupted and pointed to the defendant. "What is a dead calm? One thing for sure, this man *calmly* shot dead his mother-in-law and his wife in their house in Paris, with a revolver that he bought barely a week before the shooting. Thus, he planned the whole incident and was awake the whole time when he brutally—and in front of his only child—committed the murder."

"Conjecture on the part of the prosecuting lawyer," Albert Danet countered for the defense.

"Sustained," the judge ordered.

"Can you explain to us what you mean by a dead calm?" the president judge asked.

"As a mariner in my youth, I experienced violent hurricanes while at sea, when suddenly out of nowhere, a dead calm came upon us with the sun shining brightly and the wind tamed. Nothing but peace, tranquility, and quietness enveloped your whole being, and then. . . I'm sorry! I'm sorry! I just wanted the infidelity to stop. I should have taken control of my emotions, but I could not help it. Please understand, I loved them both dearly, but like a storm brewing on the horizon, my blood boiled to the top of my head and I temporarily lost the ability to think rationally. I am so sorry," Juan Luna responded, and hung his head in shame.

But when Juan sat down, he was overcome by emotion and sank to his seat sobbing aloud and clasping his hands to his head.

Monsieur Danet, worried that Juan Luna might completely breakdown and incriminate himself, and the favorable impact of his testimony to the jurors, took advantage of the situation and wisely said, "Your honor, the defendant has already been subjected to a battery of questions, and due to his current state of mind, may we request a short recess?"

"Objection, your honor," the prosecutor bellowed. "I do understand the request of the defense, but the trial just started and the prosecution requests that the case moves on."

"Your honor, all we asked for is a short recess," Monsieur Danet pleaded to the president judge.

The judge looked at Monsieur Danet then turned his focus on Monsieur Decori and said, "Monsieur Prosecutor, if you very well understand the plea of the defense, then I see no reason for not approving their request."

He gazed back at Monsieur Danet, hit his gavel once, and said, "The request for a short recess is granted."

The president judge turned his attention to the jury, "Gentlemen of the jury, it's now almost noon. The court will resume at 1:00. Until then, I warn you not to discuss this case with anyone."

When the trial resumed, the prosecuting panel failed to break down Juan Luna who came back calm and rested. Danet also took the opportunity to coach his client on anticipated questions during cross-examinations. Juan was so composed and credible that the hearing ended that day with Monsieur Danet confident the jury would decide ultimately in favor of Juan Luna.

CHAPTER 35

There were a total of five people asked to testify for the victims by its prosecuting lawyer. They included Inspector Michel Legrand who summarized the police report he had filed, followed by the oldest son of Doña Juliana, TH Pardo, the younger brother of the defendant, Antonio Luna, a Monsieur Bonn, and the last one called was Brigitte Blanc, the nanny.

TH Pardo testified that on the day of the murders he saw Juan Luna suddenly become very upset at everyone, especially his wife for wanting to leave him. TH said, "Like a true Malay, he transformed into a body of anger—a madman, accusing his sister of having an affair with Monsieur Dussag. At one point grabbing one of his sister's already well-packed suitcases, he attempted to unload all of the contents into the fireplace in the living room, where Juan had a roaring fire going."

TH paused and then continued. "All the while, Juan repeated how moving to Spain was the only way to rekindle their relationship as well as keep Maria Paz from spending so much time shopping for fancy and expensive Parisian designer wear."

TH then testified that his sister did not admit to him of any adulterous affair. After this, TH related the events leading up to the shootings just as he remembered them, emphasizing how badly Juan mistreated his wife.

"If Maria Paz Luna was being beaten and abused, why did not she or any other family member report the incidents to the police?" Albert Danet questioned.

"We thought that we could handle the problem by ourselves, but of course, we now regret that we did not call the police," TH replied.

When Antonio Luna took the witness stand for the prosecution, he was reminded by the prosecutor that he should answer all questions truthfully.

"Where do you reside, Monsieur Antonio Luna?" asked the prosecuting counsel.

"I have been, what you may consider a long staying guest at my late sister-in-laws and my brother's house in Rue Pergolese since I moved there two years ago."

"All the time that you stayed at Rue Pergolese or anywhere else outside the Luna's home, did you ever witness or have seen Monsieur Juan Luna ever hit, beat, punch, or accost his wife, Maria Paz?"

"From the day my brother, Juan, and his wife, Maria Paz, got married and until she passed away, they would fight once in a while over the issue of debt, like for having spent too much shopping, but only once did I have to stop my brother from hitting his wife, and that was over her love affair with Monsieur Dussag."

"But did you see your brother, Juan hit, beat, punch, or accost his wife?" The prosecuting magistrate demanded.

"He hit her left shoulder with his open palm, more like a hard shove," Antonio Luna replied.

"He hit her on the left shoulder, as witnessed by Monsieur Luna's own brother," Monsieur Decori repeated.

"Your honor, that's all the questions I have for this witness," Decori said.

The president judge asked the defense counsel if he had any questions for the witness.

"Yes, your honor." Monsieur Danet walked slowly toward Antonio Luna.

"Monsieur Luna, how close is your relationship with the defendant, your older brother, Juan?"

"Very close, and as I said earlier, I've been staying at their house for the past two years."

"Do you love your brother?"

"Yes, not only do love him as a brother, but I respect and admire him as a friend, and as a gentlemen," Antonio said.

"Gentlemen of the jury, here before our presence, you find a most honorable man," Danet said and pointed to Antonio. "Although he loves his brother, he did not hesitate to testify against his brother for the sake of the truth."

The prosecutor raised his hand and objected, "Your honor, speculation by the defense counsel."

"Sustained," the president judge said.

"Now Monsieur Luna," Danet said. "Your older brother has been portrayed by the prosecuting lawyers and witnesses as a violent man and uncontrollable killer who deserves to be put away forever. Do you find their statements to be true or false?"

"Objection, your honor. The defense counsel is badgering the witness." The prosecuting magistrate bellowed.

But before the president judge could respond, Antonio quickly replied. "False, my brother has a big heart. He is a very caring and good man."

The president judge found the question not to be admissible in court, reprimanded the defense lawyer, and told the jury to disregard both the question and the answer to the question.

"Monsieur Luna, do you believe the late Maria Paz Luna was unfaithful to her husband by having an affair with Monsieur Rene Dussag?"

"Objection, your honor! Leading the witness," the prosecuting magistrate protested. "The opinion of the witness should not be used in court if not substantiated."

"Your honor," Monsieur Danet responded. "The question is relevant, which I intend to show."

"It better be, Monsieur Danet, or I'll find you in contempt of court," the president judge said."

"Monsieur Luna, would you please describe to the court why you concluded that the late Madame Luna was committing an adulterous affair with Monsieur Dussag."

"When my brother started to suspect that his wife was seeing another man he asked if I would follow her the next time she left the house alone. Of course, I wanted to help Juan and so I followed her number of times when she went shopping along Rue de Rivoli or browsed around the d'Ellysee. But on two of those occasions, I trailed her onto a side street off the Rivoli and into Rue du Mont Thabor where she entered a hotel. The first time, I waited outside for about an hour. But since she was taking a long time, I waited out the next hour inside a café with a full view of the hotel lobby entrance. Maria Paz finally left the hotel with Monsieur Dussag."

"You said on two occasions. Can you narrate to us the second time you saw your sister in law rendezvous with Monsieur Dussag?"

"Not much different from the first time, except on the second occasion they took much longer inside the hotel—as a good Frenchman would."

His comment was followed by snickering and applause from the public seated inside the courthouse. The judge pounded his gavel on the table to silence the crowd.

Satisfied with his round of questioning, and with a smile on his face, Danet said, "Your honor, at this time I have no more questions for the witness."

CHAPTER 36

Monsieur Bonn testified next for the prosecution by defining the syndrome referred to as Malay Madness, a condition to describe Malays who kill because of a sudden rage. He explained the feeling is similar to being high on opium where a person will kill for no reason. The prosecutor concluded it was the same cause that drove the defendant to commit murder. He argued that the crime of passion did not apply to the defendant in this case.

The prosecutor magistrate's final witness for the day was Brigitte Blanc, who was the star witness for she witnessed the crime.

"Mademoiselle Blanc, how long have you been working with the Luna family?"

"Since 1889, so for about three years."

"Did you live with the Luna family at the time of your employment?"

"Yes," she said."

"During the time you worked and lived with the Luna's, would you say the couple was happy together?"

"Well, like every other couple, they had their misunderstandings, but it was civil until the death of their only daughter last March of 1892," Brigitte said.

"What changes occurred in the Luna family after the death of their daughter?"

"The couple began blaming each other."

"In what ways did they cast blame?"

"Well, Monsieur Luna spent a lot of time in his studio and his wife got into the habit of shopping and socializing outside their home, so neither of them realized how sick their daughter Bibi was."

"Can you narrate to the court what you witnessed and heard between the couple from the time you came back from Mont Dore to the day before the crime was committed on September 22, 1892?"

"The first few days after we got back from Mont Dore the couple was happy to see each other again, especially Monsieur Luna when he was reunited with his son, Andres. But the casual relationship between the couple did not last long, for as soon as Monsieur Dussag showed up in the house everything turned into hell. Monsieur Luna and Maria Paz began bickering and fighting; interference by Maria Paz's mother did not help. Monsieur's temper would flare to a boiling point and we all began to fear him," Brigitte said.

"Did you ever witness the defendant hit his wife during this time?" the prosecutor asked.

"Yes, Monsieur, it was about the time Monsieur Luna announced his plans of returning to Spain with his wife and son. As soon as Madam Luna came home from shopping one day, the couple had a big fight. He accused her of discarding her black mourning dresses honoring Bibi for colorful dresses in order to attract the attention of Monsieur Dussag. After screaming at each other, Monsieur Luna became very upset and beat madam once in the side of her buttocks with his cane right in front of her mother, Doña Juliana."

"Can you now narrate to the court what you witnessed at 28 Rue Pergolese on September 22, 1892 the day the crime was committed?"

"Yes, the problem started early in the morning when the brothers of Madam Luna showed up in the house. Monsieur Luna got very angry and kicked them out, while Madam Luna locked us all in her son's bedroom and also locked the bathroom door, which led to the same bedroom from the outside hall. We could hear Monsieur Luna rant and rave when Madam Luna refused to open the bedroom door. And when he started banging on the bathroom door, Madam Luna asked me to sneak out and get help from her brothers, which I did. No sooner did I get back inside the bedroom when we heard a single shot fired. We all panicked. Madam Luna and her mother began screaming for help."

Shaken, Brigitte began to cry and brushed away her tears with her hands. The prosecuting magistrate walked up to the witness and handed her his own clean handkerchief embroidered with his initials "FD" and said, "Are you alright? Would you like a minute to compose yourself?"

Brigitte Blanc still sobbing said, "I'll be alright." She took a deep breath and continued. "There was such a confusion of noise. Monsieur banging on the bathroom door—the screaming from Maria Paz and her mother was so deafening and frightful that I covered both of Andres' ears with my hands when suddenly, I heard three consecutive shots from a gun. . ."

Brigitte looked up at Decori, her eyes filled with tears. "I saw both Madam Luna and her mother drop to the floor. There was blood all over. I ran out to get medical help and that's when I saw Monsieur Luna in shock at the reality of what he had done."

"You honor, I have no more questions for this witness," the prosecutor said and returned to his seat at the table.

The defense counsel waited a few minutes for the witness to control her emotions and then approached her. "Are you alright now?" Monsieur Danet asked.

"Yes, I'm fine," Brigitte Blanc replied.

"I only have a few questions to ask you so please bear with me.

Brigitte nodded.

"Mademoiselle Blanc, did you travel to Mont Dore with Madam

Luna, her son and Doña Juliana?"

"Yes, Monsieur"

"How long were you at Mont Dore with them?" Danet asked.

"About two months."

"Do you have any idea as to when Madam Luna met Monsieur Dussag for the first time?"

"Yes, about two to three weeks from the day we arrived," Brigitte said.

"Two to three weeks would be about 17 to 18 days," Danet said.

"Yes, Monsieur"

"Do you know if Madam Luna went out alone with Monsieur Dussag from the day they met in Mont Dore?"

"Yes, she did."

"How many times would you estimate—once, twice, five times, more than ten times. . . how often?"

"Objection, your honor, the defense counsel is leading the witness."

"Objection sustained," the judge said.

"Mademoiselle Blanc, did Madam Luna go out alone with Monsieur Dussag more than ten times in Mont Dore?"

"More or less," Brigitte said nervously. She fidgeted in her seat.

"More than fifteen times?"

"I'm not sure. I only remember about ten times, alone, because oftentimes she would leave the house with her mother."

"Mademoiselle Blanc, do you know or have any idea why Monsieur Luna beat Madam Luna once with his cane?"

"No, Monsieur."

"*Porque me case con un chongo*," Monsieur Danet said in Spanish. "Did you understand what I just said?"

Brigitte shook her head.

"Those were the same words uttered by Madam Luna to her husband when he hit her for the first time on the buttocks. In essence, she called Monsieur Luna a monkey, a term that Filipino men find derogatory and insulting," said Monsieur Danet.

"Objection, your honor. The defense counsel is stating his own opinion. We cannot know for sure the exact words said by the late Madam Luna."

"Your honor," Danet said. "According to Monsieur Luna, those were the exact words uttered."

"I would like to instruct the defense counsel to refrain from personal remarks," the president judge ordered, and then turned to the court reported. "Remove defense counsel's comments from the transcript."

"Mademoiselle Blanc, do you speak, read, or understand Spanish?"

"No, Monsieur."

"Objection, your honor, her language skills have no bearing on the case," the prosecutor said.

"Overruled," the president judge said. "If the witness does not communicate in, or understand Spanish, then much of her testimony is under question since my notes on the case clearly show that Spanish was the language of the household."

"What my eyes see and my heart feels and understand does not need translation," the witness replied sarcastically.

Danet spoke up immediately. "Your honor, I ask that you instruct the jury to disregard the last comment of the witness since her lack of Spanish language skills has already been proven."

The president judge nodded and noted his instruction to the jury and to the court clerk.

"Your honor, I have no more questions for this witness," Danet said and returned to his seat smiling.

CHAPTER 37

After a thirty-minute break, the court hearing resumed for the afternoon with Felix Pardo, Antonio Regidor, and Rene Dussag testifying for the prosecutor while Charlotte Caron and Dr. Georges Felizet were present for the defense.

Felix Pardo and Antonio Regidor reiterated a similar testimony given by his brother the day before, that his sister was true to her husband, and that she was being physically and mentally abused by the defendant prior to the crime committed.

Rene Dussag admitted having met and spent some time as friends with the victims while vacationing in Mont Dore. He testified that his friendship with Maria Paz continued in Paris when she would stop by for a quick visit at his place in Mont Thabor for coffee and pastries and of course to chat, and nothing else. He denied the accusation made by the defense counsel that he had sexual contact with the victim, Maria Paz Luna.

Dr. Georges Felizet gave his opinion of Malay Madness for the defense when he expressed that a crime of passion is due to temporary insanity and should be used as a legal defense if the situation applies.

When asked by the defense counsel to clarify himself, Dr. Felizet said, "The defendant is an Indio and therefore should be judged according to his native genetic and cultural traits, that of a Filipino. In the Philippines, a crime of passion caused by adultery is commonly grounds for acquittal, which in some cases are no different from our own French customs and traditions."

As Danet expected, the prosecutor objected to the witness testimony for stating his personal opinion, in which the defense counsel quickly rebutted that the witness was merely stating his expertise on the subject matter and went on to present as an exhibit, a copy of the Spanish Penal Code of the Philippines supporting the witness's testimony. The president judge overruled the prosecutor.

When it came for Charlotte Caron to testify for the defense, all eyes were on the petite, browned-hair woman walking down the aisle and into the witness box. For not only was she beautiful, but she and Antonio were the only people who could verify seeing the victim and Monsieur Dussag together on more than one occasion.

Adriano Gomez poked Antonio Luna on his arm when the witness stood in the courtroom and said, "She must have taken the advice of the defense counsel because she not only is she appropriately dressed, but she put her veil over her face as if was either going to church or to a funeral."

"Mademoiselle Caron, for the record, please state for the court your name and place of employment," Danet asked.

"My name is Charlotte Caron, and for the past three years I've worked as a front desk concierge at the Mont Thabor Apartelle here in Paris."

"Do you work on the day shift or the night shift at the apartment hotel?"

"Nights for my first year of employment, but on the day shift for the past two years," she said.

"During the course of your work as a concierge at the hotel, were you familiar with the names and faces of all the guest or tenants of the apartment hotel?"

"All the long-staying guests and some of the new guests, especially if they were young and good looking."

A burst of laughter was heard in the courtroom making the president judge reprimand the witness. "Keep your answers relevant to the question."

"But I am, Your Honor," Charlotte Caron said with all honestly. "Who remembers the ugly ducklings they meet?"

The president judge cleared his throat. "Proceed," he said to Danet.

"Your Honor, I ask that Monsieur Rene Dussag be instructed to stand and face the court," the defense counsel said.

"Mr. Dussag, please rise for the court," the judge said.

After Dussag rose, Danet asked, "Mademoiselle Caron, have you ever seen Monsieur Dussag before today in the courtroom?"

"Yes, Monsieur"

"Where?"

"He is a long-term guest at the Mont Thabor Apartelle so I have seen him many times in the lobby," she said.

The defense counsel plucked a photograph from the defense table and then approached the witness box and showed the picture to Mademoiselle Caron. "Mademoiselle, I want you to examine the photograph very closely and please tell the court if you have ever seen her at the Mont Thabor Apartelle."

After examining the photo of the woman, Charlotte Caron responded, "Yes. Monsieur"

"Do you remember how many times you have seen her inside the lobby of the apartment hotel?"

"I don't know exactly, but I would say very often," Charlotte Caron said.

"How often during the month of September 1892?"

"Over a dozen times for sure," she replied.

The defense counsel displayed the photograph in full view of the jury and said, "Let the record show that the woman identified by Mademoiselle Caron in the photo is the victim, Maria Paz Luna."

There was a chattering among the members of the jury.

Danet continued. "Mademoiselle Caron, please state for the court if you ever seen Monsieur Dussag and Maria Paz, the woman in the photograph, together?"

"Objection your honor! The defense is again leading the witness," the prosecutor said.

"Objection overruled," the judge declared. And to Mademoiselle Caron he said, "You may proceed with your answer."

"The woman in the photo and Monsieur Dussag oftentimes walked in and out of the apartment hotel with their arms locked together. Other times, she came alone and went upstairs by herself and then came back down with Monsieur."

"Your Honor, I have no more questions for the witness," Danet said and pushing his shoulders back, strutted back to his seat. When he sat down, he touched Juan Luna's arm.

The prosecuting magistrate realized there was no chance to break down this witness and instead faced the possibility that any questions on his part might only further convince the jury of Madam Luna's infidelity. "Your honor, I pass on any cross-examination."

CHAPTER 38

Felix Decori stood in front of the jury and motioned toward the Pardo family and then he pointed at Juan Luna. "Guilty!" he said in a loud voice.

The jury members looked at Juan and then to each other, nodding their heads.

At that moment, the prosecutor started by highlighting what he believed were the critical moments of the trial—those facts that were going to prove Juan Luna guilty. He concurred with the defense and said, "Passion is a compelling feeling of either love or hate. In the case of the defendant, he first abused his wife as testified earlier by witnesses, and then he forgave her. Next, he trapped her into submission, and then he finally killed her by shooting her in the head."

The prosecuting lawyer took a short pause as he glanced around the courtroom to detect any reaction. He then continued. "As a young lawyer, I have defended people who have committed a crime of passion due to jealousy. But none of them compare to the heinous and abominable crime committed by Juan Luna, not only to his lovely wife, Maria Paz, but to his generous mother-in-law, Doña Juliana. In this case, neither infidelity nor adultery should be accepted as a valid defense for first-degree murder."

"Gentlemen of the jury, this trial is not to judge if Maria Paz was not a good mother, or unfaithful. Neither is it a trial to determine whether or not Doña Juliana was nice to her son-in-law, even though, it has already been shown that Juan Luna was known to be very temperamental and like true Malay, possessed the tendency and extreme nature to become violent, and thus prone to commit murder."

Decori concluded by asking the jury to punish Juan Luna because if he truly was passionately in love with his beautiful wife, Maria Paz—the mother of his son, Andres—then he would have walked away and hoped to win her back someday. Instead he chose the path to a cold and premeditated murder. Like London's notorious murderer Jack the Ripper, instead of a knife he purchased a revolver. "This man," he argued loudly, and pointing to Juan Luna, "possesses a level of rage that is like a hurricane, which when it passes over leaves nothing but destruction, pain, and death in its wake. This man is a lunatic and a danger to society—a time bomb ready to explode—and he deserves to be strapped in irons inside a cargo ship of criminals, put away forever in Devil's Island." He paused, and then said, "thank you," before sitting down again.

The counsel for the defense, Albert Danet, took his turn to speak. He showed how good and loyal Juan Luna was as evidenced by numerous letters of commendation from high Spanish politicians and other well-known persons in the fields of art who supported Luna. He then addressed the jury directly. "Yes, gentlemen of the jury, marriage is a partnership, a commitment of love between a husband and his wife. Thus, a wife's adultery is to be treated with the utmost gravity and seriousness. It is an act that profanes not only the sanctity of marriage, but also destroys the respectability of the entire family. And as proven in past cases, women who were found guilty were banished from their family."

He walked closer to the jury panel and continued. "The Spanish Penal Code prescribes harsh punishments for adulterous women from heavy fines to imprisonment. And if the husband discovered his wife and her lover in the midst of sexual activity, he had the right to kill them both on the spot."

Albert Danet paused, and then reminded the court of the letters from Juan Luna to his wife, which he had presented earlier, that demonstrated how much in love the accused was with his wife. "Gentlemen of the jury, Juan Luna was more than a good husband. He was a good father, a man deeply in love with both with his late wife and his only son, Andres—seated over there." Danet indicated Andres sitting next to his Uncle TH. Danet turned slowly toward the little boy, trying to make sure that the eyes of the jury gazed upon him, and then turned back to address them. "Andres told his Uncle Antonio how much he loves his father. So how can you, the jury, now find his father guilty and allow poor Andres to be orphaned?"

"I plead with you to understand Juan Luna, father and husband, passionately in love with his beautiful wife, to be suddenly heartbroken, disappointed, and consumed by anger and jealousy upon learning of his wife's affair with another man."

Monsieur Danet continued his argument for the defense. "Gentlemen of the jury, it is common for any man in a similar situation to be an emotional wreck, and in a rage not to think rationally. And even to the point of committing the worse crime of all—murder. But I must remind you that the Spanish penal code clearly states that if a person catches his spouse in *flagrante delicto* with another person and as a consequence, or out of passion and temporary insanity, kills one or both of them, he shall be acquitted of the crime and only suffer the penalty of being exiled for the purpose of protecting him from revenge from any relative of the victims."

Danet picked up a book from the table and read to the jury a report on the character traits of a Malay written by Frank Swettenham, a British journalist. "The Malay is a brown man, rather short of nature, thickset and strong, capable of great endurance. His features are open and pleasant, and he smiles on the man that greets him as an equal. His hair is black and abundant and straight. The native upbringing and culture of Juan Luna is a key element to deciding his guilt or freedom. So take into serious consideration what Juan Luna and the generations of Filipinos before him who had to endure despotism and domination from the Spanish, which resulted in the denigration of their native character. Consequently, gentlemen of the jury, in order to arrive at a morally fair decision you must put the testimony given by Dr. Felizet foremost in your minds when the doctor stated that Juan should be judged as an Indio, and a native of the Philippines."

The counsel for the defense took a few short steps toward the jury and said, "Gentlemen of the jury, the key question to ponder: what was the state of mind of the repentant Monsieur Luna when the crime was committed? And I believe that we have proven beyond a reasonable doubt that Monsieur Luna was provoked and from a perspective of temporary insanity, fired from behind a locked wooden door, and accidentally committed an act in the heat of passion that resulted in the death of Maria Paz Luna and Doña Juliana Gorricho. I plead with you for your understanding, compassion, and forgiveness when you deliberate the outcome of this trial."

At this point of the trial, the president judge instructed the defendant to rise and asked if he had anything more to say.

Juan Luna stood up and apologized to the Pardo family. He told them of how truly sorry and remorseful he was for the tragedy and he asked for their forgiveness. He looked back at the president judge and begged for clemency, uttered that he used to be a happy and honorable man who really loved his wife. "Now," he said, "I cannot even imagine how miserable my life is going to be trying to endure each day with the remorse." Looking at the jury, he said, "I beg you not to convict me so that I can continue taking care of my son, Andres." And then he put his head down and started to cry.

Ultimately, the court found Luna not guilty on two counts of premeditated murder and one count of premeditate attempted murder, and again, not guilty on two counts of first-degree murder. In spite of the fact that the court accepted a guilty charge of voluntary manslaughter, Juan Luna was acquitted of criminal charges filed against him on February 8, 1893 on the grounds of temporary insanity. The unwritten law at the time forgave men for killing unfaithful wives and immediately set him free in consideration for the time he had already spend in jail. However, he was ordered to pay the Pardos, a sum of one thousand six hundred fifty one francs and eighty-three cents for civil and moral damages and an additional twenty-five francs for postage and court fees, in addition to the interest of damages.

"I am so glad that the court arrived at a positive conclusion," Adriano said to Antonio.

It was believed that the Queen Regent of Spain, Maria Christina of Austria, the second Queen consort of King Alfonso XII of Spain and Queen Regent during the minority age of her son, Alfonso XIII, intervened through her emissaries on Luna's behalf. She was said to have been impressed with Luna and pleaded that he was "an artistic genius we cannot afford to lose."

Four days later, without waiting for the decision in the appeal against his immediate release filed by the Pardo family, Juan Luna moved back for Spain with Antonio and Andrés.

CHAPTER 39

The brothers Luna eventually crossed the Pyrenees and settled down in Portugalete, a town to the west of the city of Bilbao in the province of Biscay in the Basque regions of northern Spain. Juan Luna began to paint again to complete *Peuple et Reis*, which he had set aside due to his own personal tragedy in Paris. All in all, it took Juan Luna more than a year to complete *Peuple et Reis*, a painting that showed the reign of terror and tragedy during the early nineteenth century.

Juan was inspired by two famous works during this time: French painter, Eugene Delacroix's *Liberty Leading the People*, which depicted the French revolution of 1830, and was displayed at the Palais de Louvre in Paris; and *The June Rebellion of 1832* by Victor Hugo in his book Les Miserables.

In the second one, Juan Luna managed to transform to perfection the images of an uncontrollable mob led by a bare-breasted woman with her hands raised high and clenched into fists as they all ran around berserk and screaming inside the Saint Denis Cathedral in Paris. The mob desecrated the Royal tombs and relics in the church, displaying the evil transpired in a revolution. It was to be his last important work of art intended for the 1892 World's Columbian Exposition in Chicago, which he set aside to unveil for another time.

Meanwhile, the Spanish Governor-General, Eulogio Despujol, who had exiled Rizal to Dapitan was replaced by Ramon Blanco in 1893. An officer and a native of San Sebastian of nobility, he dealt with the ongoing rebellion led by Andres Bonifacio of the Katipunan. He wanted so badly to improve the good image of Spain not only among the Filipinos, but also to the rest of the world. The installations of electric street lights in the city of Manila had started; and so was the attempt for Governor Blanco to compromise with the very conservative Spanish authorities in the islands and the Dominican friars, whom he secretly referred to as *frailocracias* because they exercised more power than the civilian government.

Back in Europe, the brothers Luna spent most of the year inside the Salas de Armas in Bilbao. They mastered the art of fencing and sharpened their skills at target shooting a pistol with accuracy.

Juan remarked to Antonio. “I guess your sword playing as a kid has carried on to adulthood. I don’t think I’ll ever beat you at this sport. You are so really good, dear brother.”

“For the same reason, I cannot beat you in pistol shooting,” Antonio responded. “We each have our special talents, and you have a great eye to hit a target in the same way you have an eye for the arts.”

Antonio looked at his brother straight on and said, “I have been thinking. Ever since we heard that Rizal was exiled to the island of Dapitan, I have felt such guilt that we are here enjoying the sport we love best while he is out there fighting for what he loves best—equal rights and representation for the Filipino people. I think it is time for me to go back home.

“I think it’s time for all of us to go back home so that Andres can experience what being half a Filipino really means,” Juan shot back.

And so it was that in April 1894, Juan, Andres, and Antonio left Barcelona to board the steamship that took them back to the Philippines. When they landed a month later, the whole Luna family was on hand at the Port of Manila to welcome the brothers Luna and the new member of the clan, the young Andres.

"*Ang tataba ninyo at ang guapo ng apo ko*," their mother greeted them by saying they had gained so much weight and for having a handsome grandson.

Although the brothers felt good being back in Manila, it did not take long for them to discover that life in the city they knew as children had not changed much. Besides now having electricity, there were a few other things the brothers noticed right away since their departure when they were in their twenties.

First, the pace of life was still so slow compared to the cities of Europe they had either visited or lived in. And second, the power to self-govern still seemed a distant dream. They were amazed to also still find the same old mansions with pillared columns owned by wealthy Spaniards and Filipinos of Spanish descent among the beautiful rustic surroundings of the barrios with its wet and muddy road trails when it rains.

And so it was that Juan and Antonio accepted the invitation of an old friend Galicano Apacible to spend a weekend at their house in Balayan, Batangas with a side trip by boat to the Taal Volcano. Rizal's former roommate in Brussels, José Alejandrino, joined them. The twenty-five year old clean-shaven young man, born in Arayat, Pampanga from wealthy parents had also just arrived from Europe after having been away to obtain a degree in engineering.

Even in this remote town there was a sense of anxiety in the air as the Dominican friars became suspicious of the gathering of distinguished Filipinos and former members of the Propaganda Movement in Europe. The friars feared the gathering was setting up for a rebellion when all the Filipinos wanted to do was to relax, eat, have fun, and reminisce about their experiences in Europe. Even with their intentions to party, however, thoughts of José Rizal politically exiled and all alone in the far away land of Dapitan in Zamboanga del Norte Province in Mindanao were ever present in their minds; they never had the chance to visit him.

In February 1895, a revolution similar to the Philippines had broken out in Cuba and concurrently, there was an epidemic of yellow fever. The Spanish government appealed to all doctors under the age of forty-five to volunteer for service in the military. By December of the same year, Rizal received a letter from an old friend from Europe, Ferdinand Blumentritt, who suggested that Rizal volunteer as an Army surgeon in order to end his exile. Rizal took his friend's advice and immediately wrote a letter to Governor Blanco offering his services as a doctor in Cuba. Meanwhile, with financial assistance from the Spanish Government, Antonio Luna proceeded in the study of tropical and communicable diseases, which led to a post as the Head Chemist of the Municipal Laboratory of Manila, As head chemist, Antonio was the first to conduct environmental science studies. The studies included researching the contents of several sources of water, which he found to be unfit to drink. He also was the first person to conduct a study on Philippine forensic science, studying human blood and how it could be used as evidence when investigating crimes.

Since his return to the Philippines, Juan Luna vacated his studio in Calle Alix in Sampaloc and moved to Calle Jolo in Binondo, where he completed portraits of family members and friends. But he also finished one of his favorite paintings, Tampuhan, which depicts a sentimental misunderstanding between a young and loving Filipino couple.

For his venture, Antonio took over the lease in Sampaloc and opened a *sala de armas*, a fencing school, which became a very popular hangout for family and friends; a number of Spanish military officers were also members of his academy. Not long after Antonio opened the doors to his school, a very serious looking man with a stocky physique and short, cropped hair wearing a white shirt, pants, and a bow tie showed up just before dark at the Calle Alix school. The man walked straight up to Antonio, who was alone and about ready to close shop, and he introduced himself as Dr. Pio Valenzuela.

"*Buenas noches*, how may I be of assistance?" Antonio Luna asked.

"I just got back from Dapitan, and José Rizal sends his best wishes to you and your brother," the man said

"From Dapitan? Oh my God, you just made my day." He pulled a chair out for the doctor. "Here, have a seat."

"Tell me all about my Rizal … how is he doing? Is he healthy and in good spirits? Are they treating him well?"

"Rizal has been keeping himself very active and healthy in his barrio Talisay in Dapitan," the man said. "He's been practicing medicine. But in addition, he built a classroom to teach young boys about farming and horticulture. Why, he even provided the barrio with a water system and formulated a system to light the streets with coconut oil lamps that hang on wooden posts."

"I'm so glad to hear my dear friend is doing so well. But, wait a minute … how did you manage to get through the civil guard to see him?"

"As a doctor, and with a help of an assistant, I brought along a blind man to be healed by Rizal."

"How ingenious!" Antonio said.

"But it was not the real reason."

"What do you mean?"

"I was in Dapitan as a personal emissary of our leader in the Katipunan, Andres Bonifacio, for the purpose of updating and consulting with Rizal on our revolutionary plans," the man said, and to determine if he was still with us. And if so, we were going to help him escape."

"What was his response?" Antonio asked.

"That it was not a good idea, and that the Filipino people in general did not wish for war, but reforms. He did not think that we are ready for armed rebellion due to the lack of arms and money."

"Exactly what I expected Rizal to answer," Antonio said, and then asked with excitement in his voice. "But what about escaping?"

"I told him the Katipunan had a plan, but he declined. He

explained that he gave his word to the Commandant that he would not escape."

"Oh," Antonio said disappointed.

"But here is good news," the doctor said. "Rizal also mentioned that he is expected to be released soon."

"When?"

For a brief moment, Dr. Valenzuela sat as if he was suddenly uneasy. He scanned the room, cracking his knuckles at the same time as if he was trying to avoid the question.

"Why are you not answering me," Antonio asked.

The doctor hesitated, and then spoke. "Rizal suggested we see you because he thinks you are the best man capable of attracting the rich and educated Filipinos into our fold. He wants you to become our liaison officer."

"No way," Antonio said, "I do not want to get involved with your premature and poorly planned revolution that is bound for failure," Antonio said sarcastically. The doctor was so taken back by Antonio's abruptness that Antonio softened his attitude. "I'm sorry, Dr. Valenzuela, but without military strategy, organization, funds, ships, weapons, and equipment, you are not going anywhere with your little war."

They both remained silent for what seemed to be about a minute, and then Antonio said, "I'm so grateful to you for sharing the news about Rizal, but I have to leave now."

The man stayed put, said nothing, hardly daring to breathe. And then finally, with a stern voice he said, "Supremo Bonifacio will be very disappointed. Is there any chance we can still make you change your mind?"

"No chance at all," Antonio said. "I'm sorry but I really have to go."

Although José Rizal wrote his last novel *El Filibusterismo* to motivate and prepare Filipinos for potential hostilities against Spain, he still believed that the best approach was through dialogue and peaceful means—that the pen was mightier than the sword. His writing angered the friars who referred to the book's author as a sympathizer of heresy, impious to Christianity, and detrimental and disrespectful to both the colonial government and the church.

But in the mind of Andres Bonfacio, the book awakened his emotional patriotic beliefs that the only way to free themselves from the Spanish colonizers was through a bloody revolution. Andres Bonifacio, not giving up on the suggestion of Rizal, this time asked José Alejandrino to convince Antonio Luna to join the Katipunan as its liaison officer and was turned down again for the same reasons he gave Pio Valenzuela.

A month later Governor Blanco, who personally met with Rizal two years earlier in Dapitan during one of his sojourns to visit the rest of the Philippines, took his time to decide, but eventually approved Rizal's petition to heal the sick in Cuba. José Rizal immediately boarded the first ship for Manila, the *España*, hoping to be able to transfer to another ship for Spain without stopping. But faith was not on his side for he arrived a day late and was faced with the consequence of a month's delay.

Alarmed that once the knowledge of the popular Filipino patriot was known to be in Manila, the Spanish authorities detained Rizal, not in Fort Santiago and not as a prisoner, but as a guest of the Spanish navy aboard the cruiser Castilla, anchored at Sangley in Cavite Province, where only the members of the patriot's family were allowed to visit.

It did not take long for the Katipunan to find out that Rizal had just been released and was stranded in the tiny peninsula named by Spaniards after the Chinese merchants, *sangleys* who used to frequent the area to smuggle their goods. Rizal's photo image was displayed at most of the revolutionaries meetings in Cavite and excited its members, which by now had grown to a point it no longer became secretive.

Consequently, it did not take long for a Spanish friar to gather information from a disgruntled member of the Katipunan that there was talk about starting a revolution and in the process possibly free Rizal before he was transported to Spain.

While Rizal waited aboard the Castilla, the Spanish Guardia Civil were deployed along key points of the city and along all roads leading to Cavite. They searched and detained any person for questioning they had suspicions of being a rebel. Bonifacio was left with no other alternative but to set the end of August as the date for their first salvo, the capture of a Spanish garrison in San Juan del Monte. Two days later, the Isla de Panay was set to sail for Spain with Rizal on board carrying a letter of endorsement from Governor Blanco for the Minister of War in Madrid.

CHAPTER 40

After a brief visit to Japan, Juan Luna returned to his homeland in time for the August 1896 failed uprising by Bonifacio under the banner of the Katipunan, against the Spanish colonial leaders and friars. As the result of the rebellion, Governor Blanco offered amnesty to any revolutionary who would surrender their arms and themselves. At the same time, he placed eight provinces under Martial Law. They were Manila, Bulacan, Cavite, Pampanga, Tarlac, Laguna, Batangas, and Nueva Ecija.

Andres Bonifacio blamed the defeat on the wealthy and educated class of Filipinos because out of fear they failed to support the revolutionary movement either morally or financially. On the other hand, the Katipunan leadership distributed letters implicating various prominent Filipinos as leaders, members, and supporters of the revolutionary movement. Dr. Pio Valenzuela was the first one to be detained and questioned at Fort Santiago when he availed of the amnesty.

Fort Santiago, known for centuries as the *Real Fuerza de Santiago*, was named after the patron saint of Spain, Saint James the Great. The hard volcanic stone fortress was erected like a castle, surrounded by water but without the towers. That was in 1593 by the Spanish Governor-General Gomez Perez Damarinas inside the established walled city of Manila, as the last line of defense for its soldiers and residents. The constant threat of invasion from Japanese leader Hideyoshi, who feared the rise of Spanish power in the region and possible influx of Christian missionaries to Japan from Manila, swayed the decision to build the stone walls and citadel around Manila.

Antonio and Juan Luna were arrested on September 16 and jailed separately inside the historical but unpleasant Fort Santiago. The charges against them were for subversion and conspiring with the Katipunan reform movement. Their makeshift cell room on the ground floor of the Fort was completely bare of furnishing, except for a single cot. There was a small window and a door with bars; a guard stood outside in the hallway.

As a result of the August revolution, Fort Santiago became overcrowded with prisoners; a number of them had no idea the reason for their arrest. The most controversial of all the men was taken into custody thousands of miles away off the Port of Said in the Mediterranean when José Rizal was arrested and transshipped back to Manila from Barcelona.

When the Spanish friars found out Rizal was allowed by Governor Blanco to sail back freely to Spain at the start of the Filipino rebellion, they went berserk! They did everything in their power to reverse the decision, especially after the results of the initial investigation completed on prisoners inside Fort Santiago were disclosed. Apparently, the name of José Rizal was predominant among any of the others. Thus, in the eyes of the clerics, he clearly was the leader of the revolution, leaving the Governor-General no other alternative.

On October 3, 1896 the steamship Isla de Panay arrived in Barcelona with Rizal on board as a prisoner. Rizal was kept under heavy guard in his cabin for three days. They finally woke him up at three in the morning and, escorted by foot soldiers, he was forced to carry his personal belongings to the prison at Monjuich. Later that evening, he was transferred to the military transport ship Colon, which was filled with soldiers and officers returning to the Philippines. One month later, José Rizal landed in Manila, but was taken directly to Fort Santiago.

Meanwhile, the Spanish colonial authorities had no evidence against the brothers Luna, except for information gathered from arrested members of the Katipunan, and by way of association with their relationship to José Rizal and the Propaganda Movement in Europe.

The authorities, backed up by the Dominican friars and led by their Archbishop of Manila Bernardino Nozaleda, were very much aware of Juan Luna's popularity in Spain and to the royal family. They thought it was best to leave him alone, and instead, concentrated on his younger brother in order to garner information regarding the Katipunan and its alleged leader, José Rizal.

Antonio Luna's interrogators showed him a long list of friends and allies who had testified that he was a member of the secret society to overthrow the Spanish authority in the Philippines. But he insisted that he had nothing to share. Moreover, Antonio asserted his denouncement of the Katipunan and Liga Filipina to his supervisor at the Municipal Laboratory

However, the prison interrogators did not accept Luna's declarations and remained adamant to obtain a full confession one way or another. He was not only kept imprisoned, but his captors tried to starve him into submission. But Antonio remained strong until one early November morning when he was taken outside and into an alley where his captors pointed at to a 10 x 10 inch solid wood post about four feet in height. About halfway up, a wooden plank acted as a seat, and a steel vice with a leather neck strap was attached at the top of the post.

"You better cooperate with us," the interrogator said, "or you will suffer the same fate as your compatriots did when we strapped the garrote on their necks and squeezed slowly until their faces turned blue, as they grasped for their life, but to no avail because in the end, their eyes popped out of their heads."

The interrogators laughed. One of them clasped his hands around his own neck and mimicked a man choking.

Another one said, "Or if you are lucky, the firing squad may be your salvation."

Antonio was then taken into a long cell chamber that was equipped with different types of torture. The former Filipino propagandist who had just turned thirty years old less than a month before was subjected to horrendous torture one could imagine inside the chamber of horror. For hours, he was heard screaming in pain that he was not a rebel, nor a conspirator, and not even a revolutionist, but a pacifier and a reformist like Rizal.

It did not take long for Antonio Luna's mind and body to disintegrate; after all, a man can only take so much punishment. However, as weak as he became and so close to seeing the end of his life either with the continued torture, or the firing squad, the more he gradually became determined to live—to die fighting on the battlefield rather like a victimized animal in this cell.

And so Antonio began feeding his captors information of no value, and made sure that none of his friends were implicated by his actions. Now he wanted nothing more than to stay alive and strong and to live for another day in order to get even with them.

At the same time, having experienced prison four years ago in Paris, Juan Luna hated to be inside a cell. There were times when he was so restless that he laid down on the floor and counted the lines of ants that climbed along the walls of his cell. He tried to figure out how ants thrived to survive and remembered an old fable with a grasshopper. The ant worked hard during the long hot summer, building his house, to store supplies for the cold winter, while the grasshopper thought the ant was crazy to work so hard on a nice and sunny day and instead, used his time sunning himself and eating all the abundant food. But come winter when the ant was warm and well fed, the grasshopper had no food, nor shelter, and died out in the cold.

Juan Luna became very still on the mossy stone floor of his jail, thinking he was turning into a grasshopper, languishing in and out of jail for the rest of his life, not thinking straight nor looking ahead. He could not help but think that he was incarcerated again as a form of punishment from God for the deaths of his wife and mother-in-law. And then he realized that he had not painted for some time, and to maintain his sanity he stood up, and inspired by the lesson learned by the fable, he pulled out his sketchpad and pencil and started to draw again.

He drew anything from the ants he saw on the floor to sketches of his cell and faces of the prison guards. He kept himself busy even sketching on the walls of his cell. He even completed a drawing depicting a portrait of Jesus Christ, which he gave to a visiting Jesuit. But he missed using his easels and real canvas, oil paints, and brushes and started writing letter to anyone he knew, demanding art supplies and materials. He made clear to his warden that the governor-general or the queen would not want to learn that a man of his stature in the arts was decaying in prison doing nothing.

CHAPTER 41

About a month later, Juan Luna was awakened unexpectedly at early dawn by the prison guards and carted away along the cobblestones streets of Manila across the Pasig River and into Malacañang Palace, the official residence of the Spanish Governor General Ramon Blanco, who wanted the Filipino master to paint his portrait in complete secrecy.

Malacañang Palace was a Spanish colonial style home along the Pasig River built in 1750 by Don Luis Rocha, a Spanish aristocrat. In 1825, the house was purchased by the Spanish civil authorities in the Philippines and converted into the official residence of the governor-general.

Once inside the palace, Juan Luna was mesmerized by the large quantity of curved woodworks made from a type of local hardwood called the narra, cushioned furniture, crystal chandeliers, and historical paintings. He was directed into a sunlit room in which on one side stood a large professional wooden studio easel with a canvas measuring 195 cm x 258 cm. There were also two wooden palettes, all types of brushes, palette knifes, a variety of large oil paint tube colors, and all other tools and equipment consistent to the needs of a great artist.

"*Buenos dias*, Señor Luna, my name is Arsenio, an aide and good friend of the governor-general. He instructed me to have you taken here in order to paint his portrait."

The aide walked toward the large easel, "Please check what we have for you and if you need anything else, I'll be glad to get it for you."

"What happens if I refuse?" Juan Luna responded.

"You won't because you are a great artist with the unending desire to paint, and besides you've been making so much noise in prison asking for the tools of your trade, and that's the main reason you are here now. And by the way, they are yours to keep."

Juan Luna nodded. He knew very well this was a great opportunity for him to personally get to know and speak with the governor-general in the course of painting his portrait.

"Make yourself comfortable, the governor-general will be joining us soon," the aide said and walked toward the armed guard instructing him to wait outside.

A minute later, Governor Blanco entered the room and walked straight to Juan Luna. "It's an honor to meet a great painter like you, Señor Luna, and a much bigger honor for you to grant me my wish."

"It will be my pleasure, Governor Blanco," Juan said.

"Shall we start then? Where do you want me to pose?" the governor asked.

Luna looked around the room, pointed to a wall and said, "How about under your family crest?"

"Perfect!" Governor Blanco exclaimed.

"But before we begin, I need to ask for your full cooperation," Juan said.

"In what sense?"

"As an artist, I need to connect with my subject in order to capture the likeness that is then reflected on the canvas"

"Like how?" the governor asked.

"Show me your best stance as to who you think you are," Juan said.

"You mean like this?" The governor shifted his body a little bit toward his right to face the window. His hand rested on a wooden cane, his head tilted a bit to the left as he faced Juan with a serious smile indicating he was a man of power, but Luna could see right through him—this man had a big heart.

"Maybe you can place your left arm a bit forward right beside your sword," Luna said as he traced the governor's footing on the wooden hardwood floor.

The governor adjusted his position.

"Perfect! Now if you can please hold your pose for about fifteen minutes. And then you can take a short break. But your facial expression has to remain the same for me to mirror your true character."

After a two-hour session, the governor-general said he was tired and still pressed with so much business to take care of. He thanked Juan Luna and said that the guard would take him back to the palace the same time tomorrow morning. He then excused himself.

The next day, Governor Blanco got into his pose and asked Juan, "What did you mean yesterday when you talked about mirroring my true character? That has puzzled me all night."

"The most important factor of portraiture is how your subject feels deep inside himself at the time he is being painted, and I can see you are a fair and honest man, but I also wonder if you wrangle over your love and loyalty for the queen and Mother Spain against the injustices and upheavals going on in her colony driven by a group of powerful friars and their cohorts? We are no different from you. We, too, love Spain and the queen has been good to us. But we need her and your honor to intercede on our behalf before it's too late."

The governor-general remained calm and still and did not utter a word. Instead, he looked at Luna, captivated on how this man—his prisoner—spoke so openly to him as if he was one of his advisers. The governor wondered if Luna spoke the truth or because it was contrary to what was reported to him by the prison interrogators.

Juan Luna continued. "We, Rizal, my brother, and myself, and so many others are innocent of the charge of sedition and rebellion, and our only hope is for you to champion our freedom."

Governor Blanco walked toward the painter and raising his voice answered back. "Then explain to me why your brother was named by some in prison to be a be an active member and liaison officer of the Katipunan,"

Juan Luna was about to reply but the Governor went on talking. "As for your friend, José Rizal, I personally met with him once during my sojourn in the south. I was impressed with all the great things he did for the people in Dapitan, so I approved his request to serve as a medico in Cuba. I felt so bad sending him back to Manila, but reading the report that practically all prisoners questioned by the authorities identified him as their titular and iconic leader and the pressure coming from the *frailocracias* left me with no alternative but to put him on trial … Don't worry, your brother cooperated with the authorities and won't be tried."

"We were set up by the Katipunan to be used as a tool for recruitment in their secret society," Juan said.

"You may have a point, and for that the reason I will work for your release, but I cannot promise anything for Rizal and your brother. They may have to languish in prison … On second thought, I will see what I can do about your brother."

"If the court found Rizal guilty and recommends he be executed, will you be able to revoke the decision?" Juan asked.

"Definitely! Executing him will only make a him a martyr and turn his followers into ferocious dogs that bite you in return," Governor Blanco replied.

CHAPTER 42

When the brothers Luna discovered that José Rizal was also imprisoned in Fort Santiago, they tried their best to get in touch with him but never had the chance. Rizal was being held incommunicado. Unbeknownst to the brothers, the Spanish authorities had issued an order also placing them as officially incommunicado from visitors and any news about the trial of José Rizal.

Meanwhile, a conspiracy led by the Dominican friars in collusion with a number of conservative Spaniards in the colony secretly exerted their efforts and influenced the queen regent to replace the governor with his newly appointed assistant, Camilo Garcia de Polavieja, who was a puppet of the powerful Archbishop of Manila.

Two days after Governor Blanco was deposed, Rizal wrote a manifesto of his own accord to the Filipino people to stop the bloodshed and to achieve their liberties by means of education and industry.

All alone in their individual prison cells, the brothers Luna and Rizal found themselves depressed on Christmas Eve. Juan Luna could not help but reminiscence about their good times in Paris, especially the Christmas Eve of 1889 in Villa Dupont.

On December 27, 1896 José Rizal was brought in front of a military court inside Fort Santiago. His trial was proof of Spanish injustice and misrule. The court accepted all charges and testimonies against him and ignored all arguments and evidence in his favor. He was considered guilty before the trial even began.

When asked by the court if he had anything more to say in his defense, Rizal solemnly replied, "After four years of exile in Dapitan, all I wanted was to serve our colonial mother country as a volunteer doctor in Cuba. I have written a manifesto attesting my position against the revolution, the leaders of which used my name without my permission. All I desired for my country is liberty. But the only way to realize freedom is through education and not rebellion."

After a short deliberation, Rizal was found guilty, supposedly for sedition, rebellion, and conspiracy in connection with the outbreak of the 1896 rebellion led by Andres Bonifacio and his secret revolutionary society, the KKK.

The military court unanimously voted for the death sentence. As soon as the verdict of death was announced a Spanish Dominican friar representing the Archbishop of Manila, who was a spectator during the trial of José Rizal, ran from the courtroom as fast as his feet could take him to his single horse drawn carriage waiting for him outside. He rode fast and hard along the cobblestone streets of Intramuros, headed toward the Manila Cathedral to report the outcome of the trial to Bishop Bernardino Nozaleda, who was in control of the Diocese of Manila for the ailing Archbishop and fellow Dominican Pedro Payo.

Upon entering the room, the friar dropped onto his knees and kissed the hands of the Bishop. Breathless, he blurted, "Your Grace, I am happy to report the outcome of the trial. The court found Rizal guilty and sentenced him to death."

"It's about time we have colonizers who know what they are doing," the bishop replied. "I was starting to believe they were turning into Indios. We cannot be blamed for doing what is right. If anyone is to blame it is Rizal. His ideology caused the death of so many Indios, who speak of freedom, of wanting freedom … give them freedom and they will not know what to do with it. Except for a handful, they are all ignorant people."

"Your Grace, we may have cut off the source, but what about Rizal's writings? We need to do something about his books. Otherwise, they will continue to persist and poison the minds of future generations against us," One of his assistants warned.

"Anyway, we can work on having Rizal admit he made a mistake against his Christian beliefs and retract all his ideology," a second assistant said.

"I like your idea, but how do we put it into action?" the bishop asked.

The friar who attended the trial suggested. "We can write our own books, declarations, and manifestos that express our views of the whole matter, and then relate how Rizal recanted Free Masonry, repented for his sins, and died a good Catholic."

"Let us dilute the memory of Rizal, and what he wrote and championed until it weakens the resolve of his people enough to make them skeptical of his beliefs," the first assistant said.

"Excellent, let's go for it!" the bishop said excitedly. But we may need the assistance of the Jesuits."

In what way?" the first assistant asked.

"Without knowing our hidden agenda, we can suggest that they visit Rizal in prison with the hope that he may want to go to confession one last time, or rekindle his faith before having to face his Creator," the friar said.

Bishop Nozaleda ordered the first assistant to invite the Jesuit priest known to have been his mentor at the Ateneo to visit Rizal in prison. He also sent another friar to remind the governor-general not to hesitate and immediately approve the execution of Rizal or have to suffer the same fate as his predecessor.

On December 28, Governor-General Polavieja approved the decision of the court-martial and ordered Rizal to be shot at 7:00 in the morning of December 30 at Bagumbayan Field. As soon as TH Pardo heard of Rizal's death sentence, he managed to pull some strings and was allowed to pay his old friend a visit. He brought along an alcohol burner to lighten up Rizal's cell room.

Rizal hugged TH. "I am so sorry for the loss of your mother and sister. I love Juan like a brother, but I love you as well and can only guess the pain you all went through with everything."

"Thank you," TH said. "I try not to hate Juan, but wishing him well even now in his hour of need is very difficult."

"What do you mean?" Rizal asked. "Tell me."

"Both Juan and Antonio have been detained at Fort Santiago since the Katipunan August revolt," TH said.

"Why?"

"Like you they were both implicated as leaders of the uprising. Even worse, there are rumors that Antonio snitched on you."

"Antonio wouldn't throw me to the wolves," Rizal said. "But whatever, what is their fate?"

TH shrugged.

"Hand me my note paper and pen," Rizal said. "I am going to write Juan and Antonio each a short letter expressing my support of them."

TH sat and waited while Rizal penned the letters.

When Rizal handed TH the folded notes, he said, "Please deliver these to each of them."

TH nodded and put the letters in his pocket, but knowing full well that Rizal was going to be executed in a few days and was never going to know that TH had no intention of passing the letters along to Juan and Antonio.

Shortly after, TH and Rizal embraced and then TH left the cell, never looking back.

The night before Rizal's execution, family members visited him, led by his beloved Joséphine, several Jesuit priests, a Spanish newspaper correspondent, and some of his friends.

He also finished his last poem, *Mi Ultimo Adios* (My Last

Farewell), and hid it in the alcohol burner given to him by TH. To his old friend and confidant Ferdinand Blumentritt, he wrote a farewell letter affirming that even though he was going to be executed, he was innocent of the crime of rebellion, and that he was prepared to die with a tranquil conscience.

By very early morning of the next day, Rizal was up and ready to face his executioners. The thought of retracting from being a Mason to marry Joséphine Bracken in the Catholic rites of matrimony kept him up the whole night. He called for Fr. Victor Balaquer and informed him of his retraction from Freemasonry and impending marriage to Miss Bracken, who was already waiting for him at the Fort's Rajah Sulayman chapel.

Soon after the ceremonies, Rizal gave his new bride a religious book entitled, *Imitation of Christ*, and then bade her farewell. To his military lawyer, Luis Taviel de Andrade, he formally asked that his personal possessions in jail including the alcohol burner be handed over to his family.

At 6:30 in the morning, a trumpet sounded at Fort Santiago. A squad of Filipino soldiers of the Spanish Army and a backup force of regular Spanish Army troops, who were ready to shoot the executioners should they fail to obey orders, aligned formation and moved to their designated positions.

Rizal wore a black suit, shoes, and tie. His shirt was stark white. He began his walk to his place of execution flanked by two Jesuits: Father José Vilaclara, one of his professors, and Father Estanislao March, whom he had known in his student days.

Juan Luna was still asleep in the early morning of December 30 when awakened suddenly by the sound of a single trumpet followed by the rolling of drums and drills, which he first ignored since it was a common sound inside Fort Santiago.

Only when he realized it was the day of the execution, he jumped out of bed and ran to look outside the steel-barred window. He saw Rizal with his arms hogtied and escorted by soldiers marching to the sound of the drums toward gates that led out of the fort.

Juan yelled, “Rizal, Rizal!” But his friend did not seem to hear him, so he yelled much louder, “Rizal, Rizal, Rizal!”

Rizal marched briskly, but in calm dignity. He was just about to leave the gates when he slowed down, almost stopping as he slightly turned his face to the left with a strange feeling that he heard a familiar voice calling his name. He never looked back, however, due to the distance of the gate from Luna’s cell window and the sound of drums and marching footsteps drowned the sound of Juan’s voice.

Inside his cell, Juan remained with his hands clasped onto the rusty steel bars, preventing him from physically running after his friend. He lowered himself to the floor, still hanging to the window bars, and feet still not touching the floor, he burst into tears and cried out loud.

Rizal continued to walk at a normal pace and when he passed the Ateneo, he turned his face toward it several times. Upon reaching Bagumbayan, he looked back again, and seeing the towers of San Ignacio Church, he asked the Jesuits: "Is that the Ateneo?"

"Yes," they replied

"Well, I spent seven years there," Rizal said.

Then addressing his lawyer, Don Luis Taviel de Andrade, who walked on the side of Father March, Rizal said: "Everything that the Jesuits taught me was good and holy."

The Army Surgeon General requested to take his pulse: it was normal. One of the priests blessed him and offered him a crucifix to kiss. Rizal reverently bowed his head and kissed it. Then he requested the firing squad commander that he be shot facing the firing squad, but his request was denied since he was being executed for treason and rebellion.

In front of a thousand spectators, mostly of Spanish descent, the death ruffles of the drum filled the air as the squad commander ordered the firing squad to get ready, to load, to aim, and above the drum-beats, the sharp command, “Fire!”

At the precise moment of the order to fire, Rizal spun around and stared down his executioners.

Rizal fell to the ground with his face up to the morning sun.

He was thirty-five years old. His last words were those of Christ—*consummatum est!*—it is finished. It was exactly 7:03.

The execution of Dr. José Rizal on 30 December 1896 marked the beginning of the end of Spain in the Philippines.

Antonio Luna's single cell located in the ground level on the north side of the fort's dungeons was small and sludgy due to moisture and lack of sunlight, and though near the river it did not flood, for those right by the river would fill with water and at times drown the prisoners.

When Antonio Luna heard the sound of the one single bugle so early in the morning, he got up from his bed. With tears in his eyes he looked out from his single jail window at the Pasig River flowing westward to its final destination, the mouth of the river as it blended to the sea.

He was fatigued from being up the whole night thinking that, although in different cells, this was the last time that all three of them: Rizal, Juan, and himself, were going to be together.

Antonio wondered how Rizal—a man who treasured and believed in a peaceful revolution—was handling all of this unfair, horrific, and unimaginable experience. In honor of his good friend, Antonio recited: "As you walk to your final destination, stand tall for you are an honorable man, a patriot dying for your beliefs and for your country."

After a few minutes, he heard the sounding cracks of rifle shots; he continued staring outside the window and uttered a short prayer.

As for Juan, he became very depressed. He hardly ate, and his only consolation was the knowledge that his younger brother was well and alive and not having to face a firing squad. He had befriended a young man, Kiko, of Filipino and Chinese descent that kept Juan informed, including news about Rizal.

"Good morning, Señor Luna," Kiko, said. The jail guards let him into Luna's cell with a breakfast tray.

"I have great news for you," Kiko said to Juan. "But before I tell you, promise me first that you finish this whole tray of food instead of one small bite."

Luna grabbed the breakfast tray, which held a piece of bread, an enchilada, and a cup of coffee with milk. He came to understand that proper nourishment was tantamount for him to survive.

"All right give me the good news," Juan Luna said.

"I heard that you and your brother may no longer be incommunicado. I can start passing short notes again to him from my friend who services his jail room." Kiko told Juan as he started sweeping the floor inside the jail.

"Thank you Kiko. I will have one ready when you bring my lunch tray later," Juan Luna said.

"And for the bad news, I can tell you how Rizal died. My cousin was at Bagumbayan Field and witnessed the execution."

Kiko related the incident. "My cousin tells me that he never saw brave men like your friend Rizal. He died valiantly."

"Thank you, Kiko," Luna responded. "Did he die facing his executioners?"

"My cousin said that at first Rizal's back was to them, but when the order was shouted to fire, Rizal twisted around. I cannot say for sure, but it is very possible that he was facing them."

Kiko finished cleaning the room, picked up the empty breakfast tray and cleaning supplies and said, "Have your note for Antonio ready by noon."

"You did it, Rizal!" Juan said to himself with tears in his eyes, as he recalled the many times since their visit to the Prado museum when Rizal had played out the scene of facing a firing squad. "You got what you wished for my friend. I am so proud of you."

CHAPTER 43

Through the intercession of the Spanish Queen Regent and support from the former Governor-General Ramon Blanco, who was back in Madrid serving as their intermediary, the brothers Luna were pardoned by the Spanish courts on May 27, 1897.

However, their freedom was not total. Antonio was exiled to the newly inaugurated Cárcel Modelo, a prison known as Carcel Celular. It was the main prison for men in Madrid during the last quarter of the nineteenth century. Juan Luna traveled to Spain with the hope that he could just one more time influence the queen regent to release his brother from jail.

During the August months of 1897, Europe experienced one of its worst heat waves on record with when the temperature peaking as high as 39 degrees Celsius. The heat did not bother Juan Luna at all, because after having just been notified by the Military Supreme Court that the case against his brother had been dismissed, he was on his way to take Antonio away with him.

Juan Luna was grateful to the Benlliuere brothers for their assistance in convincing the queen regent to release his brother from prison. During those times, the Propaganda Movement in Spain was no longer in existence. Panganiban, del Pilar, Lopez Jaena, and others had passed away or gone back to the Philippines while the brothers Luna were once more united together.

A month later, the Spanish Prime Minister Antonio Canovas Del Castillo was assassinated at Santa Agueda, Alicante in Spain by a known militant anarchist. The new Prime Minister Praxides Mateo Sagasta appointed General Ramon Blanco on October 31 as the new governor-general of Cuba to replace the highly unpopular General Valeriano Weyler, also known in Cuba as the butcher, who placed almost 300,000 Cubans in concentration camps all over the island.

When the sinking of the USS Maine in the Cuban harbor off Havana on February 1898 occupied the headlines in all newspapers of Madrid, the main concern of the Spanish people was how the United Sates would react to the incident. They were the newest and most powerful nation in the Western hemisphere and Spain worried the United States would call war on them. This was in the mind of every single Spaniard and Filipino in Spain and in the Philippines.

Knowing well the good character of Governor Ramon Blanco, Juan Luna was convinced that Spain was not at all responsible for the sinking of the American battleship. In addition, there was nothing for Spain to gain but create an obstacle in their ongoing crisis with Cuban revolutionaries, and torment from the American people and its press.

A group of Filipinos immediately gathered inside a Madrid restaurant in Calle de Manuel Fernandez y Gonzales, a narrow street not far from the plaza of Puerta del Sol. The main bar located at the front of the eatery was loud and crowded with young university students. The Filipinos occupied the back room and sat around a large rectangular wooden table enveloped in a tin plate of metal tabletop and surrounded by a number of heavy, decorative spiral steel chairs. The room was spacious and its interior walls were plastered with antique blue ceramic tiles, artworks, and ornate crown moldings that enhanced the classic ambiance of the tapas bar and restaurant.

Juan Luna conjectured two possible scenarios. The first and most plausible was that the sinking might have been an accident due to combustion in the coal bunkers around the forward magazine, as reported in the Paris Tribune. Or revolutionaries planted a bomb in order to embarrass and blame Spain for the incident. The third and probable reason, which the brothers Luna found preposterous, was that the Americans sabotaged the Maine in order to declare war on Spain to force them once and for all out of the Americas.

"How much do you want to bet that the Cuban propagandist and investors in America with the assistance of the newspapers will take advantage of this crisis and seek American support against Spain?" Juan Luna said.

"A forgone conclusion that the United States will not only grab Cuba the way they did Hawaii, but will also take Puerto Rico, Guam, and the Philippines before the end of this century," someone at the table said.

Little did Juan and his friends know that in the absence of John Davis Long, the U.S. Secretary of the Navy, his Undersecretary, the energetic, and aggressive Theodore Roosevelt telegrammed Commodore George Dewey in the Pacific and informed him that in the event the United States declared war against Spain, his naval fleet would sail immediately for the Philippines and destroy the Spanish Armada.

Two months later, the brothers Luna and friends in Madrid were back on the same rectangular table in the same restaurant to discuss the American occupation of the Philippines.

"But I heard the United States has no plans to annex Cuba the way they did with Hawaii. In fact, they plan to grant and recognize Cuba's independence," Juan said. "You can be sure they would do the same thing in the Philippines."

"Have any of the Europeans with colonies in Southeast Asia ever left their colonies alone to governed for themselves? The answer is never!" Felix Roxas replied. He was visiting Juan from Paris.

"Well, the British captured and occupied Manila for about two years, but then returned the city back to Spain after their war with France ended," Valentin Ventura replied.

"Juan, remember the story of Felix Pardo when France invaded Cochinchina to gain a foothold in Asia?" Antonio reminded his brother. "Just like the French, America needs a foothold in the Pacific, especially now that Germany has seized and established a naval base in Tsingtao, China. As of now, America is the only naval force in the Far East without a military base. America is in the Philippines and Guam to stay. Spain has just lost its last frontier.

"This will happen, my dear brother," Antonio continued. "I wish I were wrong, but I will not be surprised if America already has a couple of naval ships loaded with invading infantrymen and heavy artillery in the Pacific and on the way to the Philippines, as we speak."

CHAPTER 44

From then on, foremost in Antonio Luna's mind was to study all he could on the subject of military warfare. His motivation was to be a soldier and fight for the independence of his native land. He'd come to realize that José Rizal's ideals of peaceful revolution did not work and got his friend nowhere but in front of a firing squad. Antonio was totally convinced that it was time to put away his pen and brandish his sword for the glory of his country.

He read books, studied maps, and collected all the manuscripts he could pertaining to military warfare, national defense, and organization from the General Library Archives and the Spanish National Library in Madrid.

He traveled to Germany and Belgium to study field military and fortifications, guerrilla warfare, and other aspects of military science. In Belgium, he studied military tactics and strategy at the Ecote Militaire under the brilliant military strategist Gerard Leman, who was responsible for the military education of King Albert the First of Belgium.

Upon his return to Madrid, Antonio Luna informed his brother that it was time for him to go back to the Philippines.

The thought that this might be the last time to see his younger brother dismayed Juan. And so on his last day in Madrid, and with the political uncertainty and unrest brewing back home, Juan invited Antonio for an early morning breakfast of *churros con chocolate* at the Chocolateria San Gines, a café at Pazadizo de San Gines by the passageway close to San Gines Church, walking distance from Puerta del Sol.

"This café must have just opened. The last time I walked by this area, vendors were selling *churros con chocolate* along the sidewalks outside the theaters," Antonio said.

"I believe they opened for business about two or three years ago. But isn't this place marvelous? Juan said. "Look at the walls covered with mirrors that make this room much bigger than what it is, and see how it blends well with the green wooden panels in between, and these wooden chairs and tables with green velvet seat cushions and marble tabletops. Looks great."

"Yes, I am amazed," Antonio said. "And I hope the churros con chocolate inside this beautiful place are as good as or even much better than the ones sold by vendors outside."

"Oh yes, definitely much better. The Spanish chocolate here is much thicker and darker, and fresh. And by the way, you can also order coffee and cakes here, too," Juan replied. "So what do you prefer?"

They placed their order and while they waited for their breakfast tray, Juan thought this was a great opportunity to discuss the purpose of Antonio's return to Manila. Juan warned Antonio about General Emilio Aguinaldo and his role in the assassination of the Bonifacio brothers. He advised his younger brother to try his best to be at the good graces of General Aguinaldo, and not to ever cross or even talk bad about the man since he had become the dictator general of the revolutionary forces in the Philippines.

"Listen Juan," Antonio replied. "Since I was released from prison, I did not waste my time studying and learning military warfare in Europe just to be a politician. I am going back as a soldier with no other intention but to defend and fight for the sovereignty of our new Philippine Republic, no matter who is our leader or enemy."

The brothers Luna kept quiet while the waiter served them. They both dipped at the same time. "Hmmm, you are right. Their churros con chocolate are the best," Antonio commented.

"I told you," Juan replied.

"There are awful things happening in this world of ours. Just today I heard that the great American Indian Chief Sitting Bull, the same man we saw in Paris during the Buffalo Bill show, was killed by his own tribesmen a few years back. He was shot in the head for nothing, just like Andres Bonifacio, betrayed by his own people," Juan said.

Antonio held his older brother's hands on top of the cold marble table and said, "I care for you so much, my dear brother. I know how much you would prefer that I stay with you here in Madrid. But I need you to understand how very important it is for me to go home now. The Philippine revolutionary forces are all over the place without real leadership. And the organization is without well-trained officers and soldiers. The first thing I will do is meet with our General Aguinaldo and convince him to create a military academy to train qualified officers and to establish a military camp for these officers to train soldiers just like they have in Belgium."

Antonio smiled at his brother and said, "I am going back not to command but to obey. I will struggle like the common soldiers for the liberty of our motherland."

Juan hoped and prayed that his brother meant every word he uttered, but he knew him better and was left to worry even though he needed to believe that Antonio's destiny was safe in God's hands.

"I had a feeling you were going to say that since I am your older brother and know and understand you well. And so I cannot help but worry about your welfare just like I've been doing since you were a child," Juan said. "You have my full support and cooperation, and that is the reason I already designed a uniform for the officers and soldiers of the new Philippine Republic army." He handed Antonio a Manila envelope with various colored sketches of military uniforms. Antonio, teary eyed, gave his older brother a big hug as they said farewell to each other.

Antonio was about to board the steamship to take him back to the Philippines when he noticed it was the *España*, the same vessel that brought him to Europe for the first time almost thirteen years before. Antonio's superstitious mind fretted about it being the same ship combined with the unlucky number 13. He tried to reason to himself that getting on the *España* was nothing but a coincidence. And as for the number 13…so what if the King of France decided to massacre leaders and members of the Knights Templar on a Friday the 13th or if Jesus chose twelve apostles, which meant that thirteen people sat at the table of the Last Supper, or if the makers of tarot cards had designated the number 13 as the card of death. "Come on, *basta*!" Antonio mumbled to himself, but still he worried.

On June 1898, the *España* set sail bound for Manila, stopping at the same ports as its trip to Europe, except this time, it sailed through Saigon, Hong Kong, and Manila en route to Singapore and back to Europe.

At the sight of Naples, Antonio could not help but think about the lovely Chiara Pagani. He wondered and calculated her age in his mind and thought about how she must have been twenty-eight by then and probably married with children. If only he had not lost her address, he might have been married to her and residing in her richly decorated villa overlooking the Isles of Capri, drinking a glass of … no, make that a bottle of Chianti and that bread with tomato sauce they call pizza. "I've got to have that as soon as we dock."

Leaving Naples, he promised himself, as he did on his last trip to the Philippines, that on the way back he was going to stay in Naples longer to look for his long lost friend.

PART TWO

CHAPTER 45

During the Seven Year War between France and England, Spain aligned with the French in 1762 to invade Portugal and capture Jamaica. Not only did the Spanish attack fail, but its defeat also resulted in the British capture of Havana and Manila.

The war ended with the signing of the 1763 Treaty of Paris. Havana and Manila were returned to Spain in exchange for the cessions of Florida to England, with the French giving up a portion of Louisiana to Spain for losing Florida.

Except for the brief occupation of Manila by the British, for over three hundred years the Philippines had been a possession of Spain in Asia. The island had grown and developed from a small colony of tribal warlords and natives to a Christianized and partially autonomous colony of Spain with enough infrastructures to support schools, hospitals, and universities.

In 1823, the United States, now an independent nation and in full control of Florida and Louisiana, proclaimed the Monroe Doctrine to protect the American interest in the Caribbean against any attempt made by European governments to colonize or interfere with states in the Americas.

Exempt from the doctrine were Cuba and Puerto Rico. The Spanish authorities and friars felt elated because it gave them a sense of security and freedom to continue subjugating the native people of both Caribbean islands in the same way Filipino natives were abused by the local authorities and friars, in most cases without the knowledge of the government in Madrid.

During that time, the United States had no plans to get involved in Asia in the same manner as the Europeans had. However, that changed in May 1895, when an armed rebellion led by José Marti, Maximo Gomez, and Antonio Maceo of the Cuban Liberation Army came to life. Wealthy Cubans residing in the United States supplied the rebels with the necessary armaments to keep the revolution going, which slowly weakened the Spanish military forces.

The execution of Dr. José Rizal in December 30, 1896 did not help to alleviate the troubles Spain faced with the Cuban Liberation Army and instead added fire to the mountain of problems by now having to quell the Philippine revolution movement led by an ardent admirer of Rizal, the fiery Andres Bonifacio, supreme leader of the KKK movement, the Kataastaasang Kagalanggalangang Katipunan nang manga Anak nang Bayan (The Highest and the most Respected Society of the Sons of the Country).

When José Rizal returned to Manila from Europe, he invited a number of Filipino patriots to join him in the formation of a new peaceful revolution movement known as the Liga Filipina. Andres Bonifacio, a self-educated warehouse worker, joined the movement. But after the execution of Rizal, he believed the Liga Filipina was ineffective and very slow in bringing about reform.

So instead, he formed the Katipunan, a secret society and nationalistic fraternal brotherhood for the purpose of attaining Philippine independence through armed rebellion. Bonifacio was convinced that only through brute force could they obtain their dream for independence.

Spain unexpectedly got a break and found a solution to their problems when another Filipino rebel leader General Emilio Aguinaldo, a native and former mayor of Cavite el Viejo, seized control of the Philippine revolutionary movement from the KKK Supremo Bonifacio during the Tejeros Convention in Cavite Province, when he was elected President by the Katipunan members. Bonifacio was not happy with the way the elections were held and in anger, bolted from the convention to conduct his own revolutionary movement. Andres Bonifacio and his brother, Procopio, were tracked down and accused of sedition and treason, tried, and executed by Aguinaldo's men on May 1897.

Camilo Garcia de Polavieja, the Governor-General in the Philippines who became a stooge of the Dominican friars and who signed the death sentence of Filipino patriot José Rizal was replaced by General Fernando Primo de Rivera y Sobremonte, who later issued a country-wide decree recruiting able-bodied men between the ages of eighteen to fifty years old.

The volunteers were to be trained and armed, paid and equipped at the expense of the government, and sent to battle at any time, and anywhere, as when Spain assisted the French in Cochinchina.

The Spanish forces under the new Governor General Primo de Rivera drove the demoralized and diminished members of the Katipunan into the mountains and highlands amidst a series of defeats suffered when they found out the true nature of the dead Bonifacio. As not to be embattled on two fronts, the Governor de Rivera offered President Emilio Aguinaldo a truce, which came to be known as the Pact of Biak-na-Bato.

The peace treaty called for the rebellion against Spain in the Philippines to cease immediately, and its civic and military leaders, including President Aguinaldo, to be exiled to Hong Kong with a compensation of $800,000. On the part of Spain, the government instituted reforms, which included the expulsion of abusive friars. The recruitment of Filipino troopers and the Pact of Biak-na-Bato was a relief for Spain, now they could fully concentrate with the rebellion in Cuba.

However, in February 1898, the USS Maine, a United States navy battleship exploded and sunk in the harbor of Havana killing close to three hundred navy personnel. The Maine was sent to Cuba to protect American interest in the region during an ongoing revolution in Cuba between its people and mother country, Spain.

The Spanish military governor of Cuba, Ramon Blanco, who previously served as Governor-General in the Philippines, vehemently denied any involvement in the sinking of the Maine. He formally paid his respects and extended an apology to the Americans, and he proposed a joint investigation of the incident with them.

When the investigation did not materialize, Blanco conducted his own search probing the spontaneous combustion of the coal bunker located near the ammunition storage as the cause of the internal explosion. The American government, through their board of inquiry, could not determine with clarity the true cause of the sinking. Despite the findings, the powerful American press led by William Randolph Hearst and Joséph Pulitzer insisted a mine planted by Spain blew up the battleship. The press and media in the United States made a spectacle of the alleged sabotage with slogans such as, "Remember the Maine, to Hell with Spain!" in order to incite and justify to the American people declaring war on Spain.

CHAPTER 46

The incident at Havana Harbor eventually led to the declaration of war against Spain by the United States on April 25, 1898. On the same day, the United States Navy Asiatic Squadron under Commodore George Dewey, aboard the cruiser USS Olympia, immediately sailed for Manila from Mir Bay of the coast of China with a fleet of seven ships, the cruisers Raleigh, Boston, Baltimore, and the gunboats Petrel and Concord, and dispatched boat McCulloch.

A few minutes after midnight, Commodore Dewey knowing that the Olympia was now entering the mouth of the Manila Bay, could not sleep, and instead, took command from atop the flying bridge. He ordered the squadron quietly into the Boca Grande, the calm, warm, and pitched dark sea water channel between Corregidor and Cavite Province.

"What's the latest condition of Captain Gridley?" Commodore Perry asked the first mate regarding an illness that had struck his close friend.

"The captain is very weak and still resting in bed, Sir," Lieutenant

Corwin Rees replied. “Do you want me to wake him now?”

“No, I would need him strong and able by dawn. Meanwhile, slow your speed to four knots,” ordered the Commodore.

“Yes, sir.”

“This will give our men a few more hours of sleep in their battle stations,” Perry said.

At dawn, when the rays of the sun begun to break and shone lightly behind the mountains, east of the city of Manila, the squadron sailed south toward Sangley Point in Cavite.

“Do me the honor of waking up Captain Gridley, and tell him that the ship is cleared for action,” the Commodore said to Lieutenant Rees.

It did not take long for the terminally sick Captain Gridley to join Dewey on the bridge. Alarmed by the frail and ailing condition of his old friend, Perry said, “You are a brave man Gridley, but you may be excused from duty for a much needed rest in bed.”

“Thank you, Commodore, but this is my ship and I will fight with her,” the captain replied proudly as he grabbed a cup of black coffee.

The commodore handed his binoculars to the captain and pointed for Gridley to look ahead toward the twelve ships of the Spanish armada under the command of Rear Admiral Patricio Montojo, which were anchored between Sangley and Las Pinas.

Captain Gridley enjoined his crew to swerve the Olympia and headed west, the rest of the squadron followed suit for all to face the Spanish Armada.

There was no need for Captain Gridley to ask Commodore Dewey when to commence firing its powerful alternating and port guns. He only had to look at the Commodore for him to transmit the signal that started the Battle of Manila Bay.

“You may fire when you are ready, Gridley,” Commodore Dewey ordered.

The antiquated and inferior Spanish ships for battle were no match against the newer American iron clad navy vessels. In just about six hours, when the heavy black smoke of constant bombardment cleared, the entire Spanish squadron, including cruisers Maria Cristina, and Castilla, gunboats Don Antonio de Uloa, Velasco, Argos, and Don Juan de Austria, transports Isla de Luzon, and Isla de Cuba were all sunk.

Commodore Dewey's jubilation in victory was short lived, for the condition of his good friend Captain Gridley had turned for the worse. He died a month later aboard the passenger ship Coptic on his way home to America. But then, with his navy ships out of range from the large Spanish cannons atop the walls of Intramuros, Commodore Dewey decided to blockade Manila Bay from any local or foreign ships entering the city of Manila, without boarding and inspecting its cargo as he waited for troop reinforcements to arrive for a secure harbor landing.

Upon hearing of the demolition of the Spanish armada, the insurgent movement in the Philippines still led by General Emilio Aguinaldo from Hong Kong renewed their revolutionary activities in justification that the newly appointed Spanish Governor-General in the Philippines *Basi*lio Davila was not abiding to the terms of its predecessor Fernando Primo de Rivera.

Two weeks after the sinking of the Spanish armada in the Battle of Manila Bay, Commodore Dewey dispatched the McCulloch to Hong Kong with orders to transport General Emilio Aguinaldo back to Manila. Aguinaldo departed Hong Kong aboard the McCulloch on May 17, arriving off the shores of Cavite in Manila Bay two days later. The Filipino rebel leader who was exiled to Hong Kong was able to rally enough Filipino revolutionaries, as well as Filipino soldiers employed by the Spanish army, to cross over to his command and join in the liberation of cities and provinces surrounding the city of Manila.

With the Filipino revolutionary forces now in control of most of the provinces, except for the Walled City of Intramuros, from an open window in his house in Cavite el Viejo in Cavite Province, General Emilio Aguinaldo proclaimed the independence of the Philippines on June 12, 1898. He established a dictatorial form of government, since the rebellion against Spain was not over and the American naval forces were still anchored at Manila Bay.

Meanwhile, at the outbreak of the Spanish-American War, the Spanish Ministry of Marine began to analyze different military options: deploying their naval squadrons and reinforcing their infantry in Cuba would be suicidal since the United States was just a stone's throw away from Cuba and its naval forces had formed a blockade of the island. Instead, Governor Ramon Blanco offered complete autonomy and reform to the Cuban Liberation Army on one condition: that they fight on their side against the American, since their language, customs, and traditions were similar. The Cuban rebels under Generalissimo Gomez refused and instead sided with the United States, who promised them liberation from Spain and recognition of their own independence.

Gomez's decision forced the Spanish Ministry to concentrate their forces at Cadiz, where their most powerful naval armada the Second Squadron was formed under the command of Admiral Manuel de la Camara, with the purpose of seeking and destroying any attempt made by the United States Navy to sail along the coast of Spain.

However, when news of the sinking of the whole Spanish fleet at Manila Bay by the Americans reached Spain, infuriated and with their pride on the line, the Spanish Ministry ordered the Second Squadron to relieve the Spanish garrison in the Philippine Islands.

With two of Spain's most powerful warships now available to join the squadron, the battleship Pelayo was undergoing reconstruction and the newly build armored cruiser Emperador Carlos V was not yet completed when the war started.

By the middle of June 1898, the Second Squadron sailed for the Philippines, escorting a convoy of ships carrying four thousand troops for reinforcement of the Philippines, with the mission to destroy Dewey's squadron in Manila. To ensure the safe arrival of the troops, the plan called for troops landing in the southern provinces of the Philippines, and then for the armada to continue sailing into Manila Bay and engage the United States Navy in battle.

However, the United States through their consulate in Egypt managed to pressure the Egyptian and British authorities from allowing the Spanish naval squadron to access coal owned by Spain in Port Said, the Suez Canal, and from other independent sources in the canal. Then the news came that the Spanish naval squadron had been destroyed and sunk in the Battle of Santiago de Cuba and that the Filipinos had proclaimed their own independence, and its troops now surrounded the city of Manila. The Spanish Ministry now had no alternative left but to deploy the Second Squadron back into securing the Spanish coast, a single decision that spelled the end of the last frontier of Spain.

The United States Navy began to transport artillery and infantrymen for the permanent occupation of the Philippines, as they secretly pursued a treaty with Spain to obtain their desire for a foothold in Asia.

CHAPTER 47

Arriving in Hong Kong, Antonio Luna met with some members of the Hong Kong Revolutionary Junta, a group of Filipino revolutionaries, and discussed the American occupation of the Philippines. After their conversation, Antonio received letters of military endorsement to serve with the self-proclaimed military dictator General Aguinaldo.

On a clear, crisp morning in July 1898, about a week since Antonio Luna had arrived in Hong Kong, he landed on the shores of Manila. After being received by his family, the next day he was on his way to Cavite to meet and present his credentials, recommendations, and military plans for the revolutionary army to the self-appointed military dictator Emilio Aguinaldo. A month earlier, Aguinaldo had declared the independence of the Philippines from an open window balcony of his house in Cavite el Viejo in Cavite Province.

Antonio felt freedom in the air among the town folks he met as he traveled through the province. Upon arriving in Cavite el Viejo, he was met by his old friend José Alejandrino who immediately joined the revolutionary forces as a Colonel upon the return of Aguinaldo.

"We've been expecting you since noon. What happened?"

"My mother thought I was too tired from my voyage," Antonio said, "and was hesitant to wake me up early."

"Well the general is waiting for you in his office." He directed Luna in the direction of Aguinaldo's office. "But before you see him, be advised that you are already a victim of intrigue from disgruntled Katipuneros who believed you mistreated them and would only be problematic to them who fought the Spaniards."

"I was a reformist then, but I am a rebel now, and if I have to atone to them, let it be, for my desire to serve the country is foremost in my mind," Antonio said with dignity.

They walked toward Aguinaldo's office passed some soldiers who were barefooted, and some who still wore their old Katipunan uniforms, while others were homemade in different colors styled after the Spanish uniform. Antonio thought of his brother.

Having heard so much negativity toward his character, Aguinaldo glanced with uncertainty at the man with a thick moustache standing in front of him.

"Good afternoon, sir. Antonio Luna reporting for duty." He handed his credentials to the general.

"Good afternoon, and at ease, Mister Luna. In fact, please take a seat," the general said from behind a desk and stretched out his right hand to grab Luna's documents..

"Your reputation and that of your famous brother precedes you, Mr. Luna."

"In what sense, sir?" Antonio asked.

"Your work as a propagandist in the reform movement and your contrary position to support the Katipunan rebellion two years ago. Tell me what made you change your mind?" General Aguinaldo asked as he continued glancing at Luna's credentials.

"I stopped being a reformist and became a rebel the day José Rizal was executed." Sensing that Aguinaldo was agreeable to his response, Antonio continued. "I was mistaken to think that freedom could be attained through reform. It can only be achieved through armed rebellion, and I am ready to do my part even if it means dying for the same flag you hailed and swayed from your window when you proclaimed our independence."

"I feel your sincerity in serving our country and our fight to maintain our independence from any foreign invaders, Mr. Luna," the general said.

"Thank you, Sir"

The general briefed Antonio on his meetings and arrangements with the Americans and told him, "The Americans thinks it is best to leave the remaining Spanish forces holed up inside the walls of Intramuros, as if they have been captured and detained by us without the loss of more soldiers. They cannot harm us nor get anywhere from inside the walls."

"It makes sense, and I believe you are right," Antonio Luna responded, remembering his brother's advice not to cross the dictator and president of the new republic. "I noticed that when I arrived at the Port of Manila that the American naval forces dropped anchor outside the range of the Spanish cannons mounted along the walls of Intramuros."

"I like and accept your credentials and recommendations, Mr. Luna." General Aguinaldo stood up from behind his desk and approached Antonio. "I have been looking for someone with the proper qualifications to one day lead the whole revolutionary forces, to prepare and defend us on the field of battle from any future foreign invaders. Once we get rid of the Spaniards with the assistance of the Americans, we will hold them to the same arrangement they gave the Cuban Liberation Army."

Antonio Luna refrained once more in contradicting Aguinaldo's opinion of the Americans and remained silent. He knew well that the Filipino forces were already in full control of the suburbs of Mandaluyong, Makati, Paranaque, San Juan, Navotas, Caloocan, Tondo, Binondo, Ermita, and Malate thus surrounding the Walled City of Intramuros, and all they had to do was walk in and Spain would have capitulated.

General Aguinaldo continued. "Let me be the first to congratulate you, General Antonio Luna. We have no time to spare but only to mobilize as fast as we can in building the most desirable armed forces."

"By the way, I also like your idea of a military academy to train future officers and soldiers for our armed forces," the general added, referring to Antonio Luna's suggestions included in his packet of credentials.

"Thank you, Sir, for your support and full confidence in my ability to lead." Gratified to be appointed a general on the spot, Luna said, "and with your approval I would like to implement the military academy as soon as possible, somewhere in the vicinity of Bulacan province."

"I may have the right man with proper military credentials to assist you, but we may have to wait until it can be funded. I will keep you apprised," Aguinaldo responded.

Meanwhile the Spaniards, although still a force to reckon with but trapped within the walls of Intramuros, were running out of food supplies and faced in an imminent land war attack by a revengeful Filipino revolutionaries. To save face from being defeated by Asians, they had no other alternative but to surrender the Walled City of Intramuros to the newly reinforced American forces under General Wesley Merritt, a West Point graduate and veteran of the Civil War, waiting outside the walls, afloat in Manila Bay and part of Admiral Dewey's fleet.

On the morning of August 13, 1898, the Spaniards to save their honor made a deal of orchestrating a fake battle of Manila with General Merritt. It paved a way for the unopposed American brigade led by General Arthur MacArthur to occupy and capture the Walled City of Intramuros and its surrounding land area. The maneuver caught the unaware Aguinaldo and the Filipino revolutionaries by surprise.

The next day, the Spanish authorities in Manila surrendered to

General Merritt who declared a military government and placed the city under Martial Law with himself as the military-governor. His main objectives, as ordered by President McKinley, were to complete the elimination of Spanish forces in the Philippines, to occupy the islands, to provide security and order to the inhabitants, and not to recognize the declaration of the Philippine Republic by General Emilio Aguinaldo. He named General Arthur MacArthur as provost marshal and the military commandant of Manila and suburbs.

General Merritt, who referred to the Filipino leadership as children for crying out in a letter to President McKinley with complaints against them, found it impossible to recognize Aguinaldo and his supporters. He deliberately avoided any contact with them and strongly believed the Filipinos were not needed in their complete subjugation of Spain.

He finally decided to meet with General Aguinaldo and his staff in Ermita, located outside the Walled City now occupied by the Americans in order to discuss the surrender of the Spaniards, concerns enumerated by the rebel leader in the letter, and misgivings the Filipinos had with regards to the outcome of the battle.

The following day, Generals Aguinaldo and Luna accompanied by Generals Pantaleon Garcia and Artemio Ricarte arrived at the temporary Headquarters of General Wesley Merritt. It was a two-story wooden structure that reminded General Luna so much of the house he grew up in as a kid in Binondo.

They were met by General Merritt and his staff, composed of Generals MacArthur, Anderson, Greene, and Bell—all of whom where magnificently dressed in white uniforms as they stood outside their headquarters and in front of a Roman water fountain.

"Who among them was the recipient of a typical Castilian old-fashioned bribery?" Merritt quietly asked General Anderson.

"Second to the right with a crew cut hair and medallion on his chest," General Anderson replied.

"You mean the amulet that he swears keeps bullets from hitting him?" Merritt smirked. His remark made his staff snicker as they walked to greet the Filipinos.

After Aguinaldo and Merritt introduced each of their respective staff, they proceeded to enter the wooden building structure to begin the meeting with an American soldier of Cuban descent interpreting for them.

"Gentlemen, yesterday after a brief exchange of military firepower with the Spanish forces, I am pleased to announce that our demand for them to surrender the city of Manila and of all their forces has been accepted."

General Merritt went on to inform the Filipinos the main condition given by Spanish Governor-General Fermin Jaudenes for them to raise the white flag of surrender in Fort Santiago besides finding themselves surrounded by American and insurrection forces.

"I gave them and the government of the United States my personal assurance for their safety and that of the non-combatants, the wounded, sick women and children who were lodged within the walls of Intramuros."

"We understand and have no problem with the conditions of surrender you have just reiterated. But we are very disappointed not to have been included in the attack, as if we did not exist at all," Aguinaldo said in an angry voice.

"Not only that, but you made it hard for us to advance toward the Fort by blocking off strategic gateways to the Fort with your soldiers," General Ricarte protested. He was in charge of the revolutionary forces in the city.

General Merritt glanced at his staff for a second to get a feeling for how to respond properly. He took a deep breath and said, "My apology for not giving you any notice of our attack on the Fort on August 13. We thought it was best for all that we approach any military interaction with extreme caution. From time to time, we have been in communication with General Jaudenes demanding a surrender for humanitarian reasons and their hopeless chances for victory, as they were completely surrounded by American and Filipino forces."

In reality, General Merritt all along did not plan on the military assistance of General Aguinaldo. He was concerned of rumors heard from American officers that the revolutionaries were all set to cut the throats of all Spaniards captured in battle. In fact, news of murder, kidnapping, pillaging, theft, and torture of prisoners and helpless Spanish civilians in some parts of the city controlled by the revolutionaries have been brought to his attention.

"The Spaniards are defeated, but when do we capture the spoils of victory?" Aguinaldo asked.

"Excuse me, but there is no war booty to be gained here," Merritt said countering.

"Oh yes, there is! And we've waited over three hundred years for it—the right to be free from Spain!" General Luna responded passionately.

"We expect a joint occupation, the same concessions your government proffered to Cuba," Aguinaldo demanded.

"As you well know, I'm in no position to offer you that and cannot promise you," Merritt said. "My orders are to occupy the city and take full control of Manila bay and its harbors, preserve peace and order, and protect persons and property. We expect your full cooperation on this matter and in return, I can assure that the government and the people of the United States will treat you fairly."

"How long must we wait for you to complete your task at hand?" General Aguinaldo asked.

"We had unexpected casualties during the attack. The Spaniards were about to surrender when a battalion of your men got past our blockade and fired on them. The Spaniards fired back killing 19 men and wounded 107 American soldiers. It's crucial that we increase the buffer zone between your forces and ours. In addition, we demand your assurance to keep your men strictly away from the demarcation line."

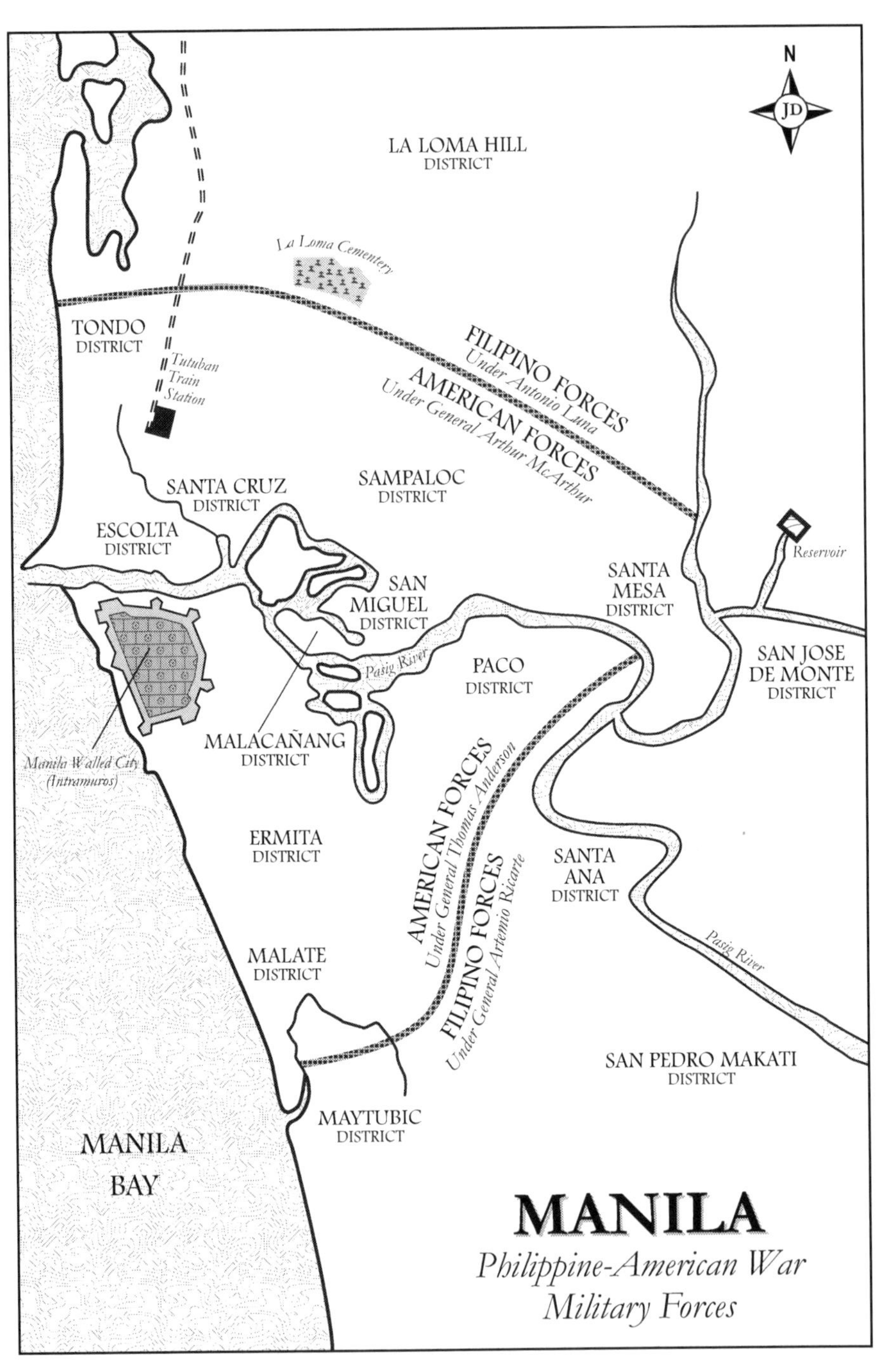
N
JD
LA LOMA HILL
DISTRICT
La Loma Cementery
TONDO
DISTRICT
Tutuban
Train
Station
FILIPINO FORCES
Under Antonio Luna
AMERICAN FORCES
Under General Arthur McArthur
SANTA CRUZ
DISTRICT
SAMPALOC
DISTRICT
ESCOLTA
DISTRICT
Reservoir
SANTA
MESA
DISTRICT
SAN
MIGUEL
DISTRICT
Pasig River
PACO
DISTRICT
SAN JOSE
DE MONTE
DISTRICT
MALACAÑANG
DISTRICT
Manila Walled City
(Intramuros)
AMERICAN FORCES
Under General Thomas Anderson
ERMITA
DISTRICT
FILIPINO FORCES
Under General Artemio Ricarte
SANTA
ANA
DISTRICT
Pasig River
MALATE
DISTRICT
SAN PEDRO MAKATI
DISTRICT
MAYTUBIC
DISTRICT
MANILA
BAY
MANILA
Philippine-American War
Military Forces

CHAPTER 48

General Antonio Luna was convinced that General Aguinaldo had been conned by the Americans into believing the Filipinos would get the same deal or arrangement given to the Cuban rebels. He did not know whether to feel sorry for the general's simple mindedness in allowing a foreign invader to control his ability to decide what was best for the Filipinos. But he also allowed them a foothold into the shores and like a cancer, spread throughout the island archipelago.

Luna knew that the Americans could not be trusted and sought the need to get much more involved with the revolutionary movement. He also wanted to prepare for the inevitable war and aligned himself with other generals who were like him, such as Pio del Pilar, Artemio Ricarte and others, like his old friend Colonel José Alejandrino.

Knowing that the revolution and the infant republic was a race to bring the majority of the people into their fold, Antonio Luna turned to journalism to strengthen Filipino minds with the ideas of nationhood and the need to fight a new imperialist enemy. He edited and published a broadsheet, *La Independencia*, in Malabon. The four-page daily was filled with articles and news pertaining to the American occupation, short stories, patriotic songs, and poems. The paper came out in September 1898 and was an instant success with as many as 4,000 copies printed. Much more than all the other newspapers combined, the paper attracted the city's leading manufacturers of beer, Cerveza de San Miguel and Cerveza Negra, to be advertisers..

The publication of *La Independencia* made Antonio Luna a household name among the young officers and soldiers of the revolutionary forces. But on the other hand, he became very unpopular with some of the senior officers and pro-American members of the Filipino society, who made known their feelings to General Aguinaldo to a point that he had General Luna summoned to Cavite for a meeting.

"Good afternoon, General Luna. Come and take a seat over there beside my new advisor and lawyer, Apolinario Mabini. "

Luna looked at the man seated at what seemed like a wheel chair, paralyzed from waist down and rumored to have been caused by a venereal disease.

"Mabini, you two have never met, but General Luna is the brother of the renowned Juan Luna. He came highly recommended with military credentials."

"A pleasure to meet you, General Luna and congratulations for *La Independencia*. It is a job well done," Mabini said as way of greeting.

"Amen, to that, but how did you managed to create a newspaper and at the same time run our military operations in the north of the city?" General Aguinaldo asked.

"Keeping our hands off the Americans gives us a lot of time on our hands, and with so many students out of school, I was able to pool together the best writers among them," General Luna replied. He was referring to his newspaper staff, which was composed of José Abreu, Fernando Ma. Guerrero, Cecilio Apostol, Epifanio de los Santos, José, and Rafael Palma.

"Very well, I would want you to continue running the newspaper but as a mouthpiece of the Philippine Republic and with Mabini as one of the contributing editors," the general said.

"Precisely the purpose the newspaper was established. Being a military officer is my priority and I leave the newspaper in good hands." He turned to Mabini. "And yes, it is an honor to have you join us in the press, Mr. Mabini."

"Where do I submit my news articles, General Luna?" Mabini asked.

"The printing press is located in Malabon inside a building called Asilo de Heurfanos," Luna said.

"Very well, you have traveled a long way, General Luna. Do you have anything else in mind to discuss?" General Aguinaldo asked.

"Yes, sir, and it's of utmost importance. Colonel Alejandrino and I believe that if war were to breakout against the Americans our best line of defense would be from Novaliches to Caloocan. We seek permission to dig strong trenches along the line."

General Aguinaldo quizzically looked at Mabini for an opinion, who in turn, nodded his agreement. "Although I see no reason for war with the Americans, I approve. Anything else?"

"Yes, permission to study the terrain along the Manila to Dagupan railway for possible more trenches to build," Luna said.

"And for what military purpose?" General Aguinaldo questioned.

"By controlling the railways, we control the dynamics of the war," Luna replied.

"And the ability to destroy the railways if overrun by the enemy," Mabini said, and once more nodded his agreement.

"Approved," General Aguinaldo responded.

"And one last thing if I may, I seek permission to proceed with the establishment of a military academy in Bulacan Province based on our previous discussion," General Luna said.

"Carry on with the plans, General Luna, and thank you," the general said.

La Independencia became one of the most significant tools of the revolutionary forces, for they continued to disseminate information and rally the citizenry to their cause. The newspaper had to move to different locations from time to time so as not to be neutralized by the advancing American forces, and the editors followed the advancing and retreating of the Philippine forces while writing their articles. At times, the press types were set by hand aboard a small banca ready to be printed in a railroad car. It was during this time when the very inspired editor José Palma wrote and published for the first time in *La Independencia* the poem of what would eventually be the lyrics of the Philippine National Anthem.

However, most of the generals in charge of the Filipino troops where the proposed trench fortifications were to be built objected to the plan, thinking it was a complete waste of time, manpower, and priority.

"The Filipino soldiers are not afraid to fight hiding behind walls. They prefer to fight unprotected in the open fields of battle," was the comment being made around their circle.

General Antonio Luna knew better; he and Colonel Alejandrino disregarded the arrogant opinions made by these generals and instead preceded of their own accord and limited resources into completing the trenches that would one day protect soldiers during battle.

Not long after these same trenches were dug, the distance from Commodore Dewey's heavy artillery and the proposed military academy became some of the leading factors for General Aguinaldo to move his seat of government from Cavite to Malolos in Bulacan Province, especially when Filipinos began questioning Americans credibility as an ally for demanding more land area within the city as a buffer zone between the two forces.

A few days later, Antonio Luna served as a representative in the Ilocos Norte Province and arrived in Malolos for the inaugural session of the Revolutionary Congress to be held at Barasoain Church for the purpose of drafting the constitution of the new Philippine Republic.

His older brothers, José and Joaquin, were also there to represent Ilocos Norte and Benquet Province, respectively. The Malolos Congress not only developed a Constitution for the Filipinos, but they also confirmed General Emilio Aguinaldo as the President of the Philippine Republic. General Antonio Luna was named the Director of War reporting to the first cousin of the President, the new Secretary of War, Baldomero Aguinaldo.

CHAPTER 49

It was during one of those sojourns to the north of Manila, when Antonio Luna walking along Calle de las Mestizas, where the elite of the town resided, spotted the most beautiful woman his eyes had ever gazed upon. She was a very attractive and slightly fleshy but not plump young lady whose high cheeked bone and exotic looking almond eyes gave her a Chinese mestiza looked.

She wore a wrap-around decorative skirt known as a *tapis*, and a light white blouse that hung loose on her neck baring one shoulder. A brown shawl wrapped her waist like an apron as she watered a row of rose plants properly arranged outside the front of a huge two-story house not far from the train depot, a walking distance from the Barasoain Church.

He smiled at her when he got close, and she pretended not to have noticed and went about doing her work. She placed a bunch of freshly cut red roses into a crystal clear vase. After smelling the flowers, she looked up, shyly smiled back at Antonio, and walked past him.

"Excuse me," she said and walked towards the two huge wooden entry doors to the house. Attracted to the young woman, Antonio walked right behind her. She glanced back at him once and then a second time, until she was on the threshold of stepping inside her house.

"Excuse me, my name is Antonio… Antonio Luna, and I was told you have a room for rent."

"Yes, we do," she responded without looking back.

"I work for the Philippine government here in town and I am very much attracted to the house and the people who live here" Antonio said.

"I have three brothers and was hoping to rent the bedroom to a woman," she said.

"What is your name, please?" Antonio asked.

"Sidra Gantuanco," she replied.

"Sidra, would you happen to be the landlord?"

"My father José owns the house, but I'm the oldest child and make the decisions," she said.

"Then it will be a great pleasure to be your tenant," Antonio said. "I can entertain you and your brothers, for I can play the mandolin and am an expert on the guitar. I also sing and dance, write, and recite poetry. I'll make you laugh and will forever be a great and loyal friend to you, almost like your fourth brother," he said with a smile in his eyes.

"You're so funny," she responded looking at him with hint of a smile and a new sense of appreciation.

"When can you move in?" she asked.

"Right this very minute. I travel light," he said.

"Oh! No, not without your guitar," she said.

Antonio laughed. "Just kidding, sometime tonight with all my stuff and my guitar."

"Follow me so I can show you your room," Sidra said.

For the next few weeks, Antonio's inner thoughts wondered off from his work in the Malolos Congress to his interest in courting Sidra

Gantuanco. The last time he felt the same for another woman was with Chiara Pagani. He could not help but compare the two: Chiara was very young then and married by now, while Sidra was already past the age of marriage and considered a spinster.

Antonio got in the habit of waking every morning with the hope of seeing Sidra before leaving for Congress. He complimented her on how pretty she looked so early in the morning. He also impressed her with his newly washed and pressed clothes, and his gentlemanly posture and actions. Whenever possible, in the afternoons after Congress was shut down for the day, he rushed back to the Gantuanco's for an early evening chat and chance to play his guitar for Sidra.

He would rearrange the chairs in order to position his to be closest to Sidra as a pretense to bump against her so they could touch. He tried to gauge her reaction. To his pleasure, she sometimes patted his shoulder or took a turn at bumping into him with her knees, which made them both laugh.

One night, pressed with so much work at the Barasoain, Antonio returned to the Gantuanco's much later in the evening and was glad to discover Sidra was still awake. She sat alone in a pensive mood on a chair by the grand piano, elegantly positioned on a thick piece of solid Narra hardwood floor. She appeared dwarfed by the high ceiling in the main hall. Antonio walked towards her.

"Have you eaten dinner?" she asked coyly.

"Yes, I was out with Alejandrino and my brothers," he said.

"Oh, because I kept a piece of fried fish and a bowl of steamed rice for you," she said.

"Thank you," he said and paused. "Is something bothering you tonight? Can I help?"

She did not respond and instead turned away from him so as not to face him. Sidra forever dwelled upon how she looked."

"Sidra, please tell me, so I can help you," he said in a pleading tone.

"Can you make me young and beautiful again?"

She could not accept that she no longer was young and beautiful.

Why, she was almost as old as Antonio, she thought, not realizing that Antonio saw her differently. He saw her as this girlish-looking half-Chinese who looked no more than twenty. He saw her as a girl so full of joy and intelligence, someone who could converse with him for hours.

Antonio knelt on the floor in front of her, holding both of her hands said, "Pretty lady, you glow with so much beauty that not everyone sees it. But my eyes and my heart are capable of seeing the beautiful, real you."

"I wonder if you really like me or am I going to be one of your conquests, a fling?"

Antonio knew it was time for him to make known his true intentions towards Sidra. "Don't move so I can lift away a tiny lint just above your eyes. Actually, it would be best if you close both of your eyes." And Antonio stood up and kissed her lips. "I am falling in love with you. And no one else on this earth has to know how beautiful you are but me."

Seeing no reaction but a blank stare on her face, Antonio said, "Sidra, we may have met by chance and mutually bonded like the best of friends, but I could not help but fall in love with you."

Sidra was numb, and did not know whether to be mad or happy, whether she should laugh or cry, and found it hard to believe that at her age, she had finally been kissed on her lips. She got up from her chair and walked toward an open window. She looked out and took a deep breath. Yes, she thought, I am in love, and called Antonio, her lover, to join her by the window.

"Do you see all those fireflies glowing in the dark by my garden?"

"Yes," Antonio said.

"You are the firefly of my life, for you have just lit up my lonely and dark existence."

"And what am I to you during the day, a bed bug that will bite you all over?" he teased, and began pinching Sidra all over her back until they both laughed so hard.

CHAPTER 50

Antonio Luna walked passed General Aguinaldo's office window located at the convent of the Malolos Cathedral also known as the Minor Basilica of our Lady of the Immaculate Conception. What he saw through the open window was disheartening. It was the general with his hands clasped on his back walking from one end of the room to the other end, staring at nothing, like he was clueless and lost with no direction to move forward.

Outside the General's office, Luna saw Mabini under the shade of a large acacia tree resting on the same hammock he had been carried on by his attendants a few months earlier when he offered his services to be the General's adviser.

Antonio approached Mabini, who was a reformist and like himself and became an activist for war when Rizal was executed. "Why do I have this gut feelings something is bothering Aguinaldo?"

"He is no longer sure of himself on whether he should continue trusting the Americans," Mabini said.

"Is there anything we can do to assist him since you and I seem to be on the same side when it comes to dealing with the Americans?" Antonio asked.

Although Antonio Luna promised his brother not to rock the boat and instead be an ordinary officer under General Aguinaldo, he no longer could control his desire for leadership in the revolutionary movement. Luna knew that General Aguinaldo was in a quagmire as to whether to continue supporting the military orders coming from the Americans.

After all, there were signs that the dilemma was coming from the direction being taken by the man who brokered the Pact of Biak-na-Bato with the Spanish colonizers, Pedro Paterno and all his former pro-Spanish—but now American-leaning cohorts—who got elected and were in control of the newly established Malolos Congress. The other alternative was to obey the advice of Mabini and his generals, who were in defiance of the American occupation of their motherland.

Luna knew he had to make his move now before General Aguinaldo destroyed his credibility with the Revolutionary Army, or the doves amongst them—the same people interested in advancing their own careers and aspirations—would hand over Philippine sovereignty to the Americans.

"Yes, but first we have to find out from Aguinaldo what the real score is between him and the American consulate in Hong Kong?" Antonio said.

"I was hoping he would have opened up to me, but he shows no signs of doing so," Mabini said.

"Then we have to ask him directly. And make it very clear that the Filipino people are beginning to think we are weak and easily pushed around by the Americans," General Luna said strongly.

"Ummmm, I agree with you Luna, and perhaps this time you take the lead and I will follow you." Mabini offered to assist Luna in getting answers from the president.

Without waiting for a response, Mabini signaled for his attendants to take him to General Aguinaldo and then gestured for

Luna to go ahead.

"Good afternoon, General." Both men acknowledged their presence upon entering the room.

"Come in, and what can I do for you, gentlemen?" Aguinaldo greeted them warmly.

"We would like to have a word with you regarding the American occupation of the areas surrounding Fort Santiago," Luna said.

"What about?" the general asked as he looked at Mabini being carried from the hammock to his wheel chair. Mabini then ordered his attendants to leave the room.

"General Aguinaldo, history dictates that there is no substitute for freedom," Antonio said. "The Spaniards, who ruled us for centuries and were dispelled not by us but by another more powerful invader, are here to stay. And the longer we wait, the harder it will be for us to drive them back into the ocean. We need to make our move now, so it's very important for us to know what really transpired between you and the American leadership."

"Honestly, I am beginning to wonder myself what really occurred during my secret meetings with the Americans last April. I was approached by the American Consul Spencer Pratt and a certain Englishman by the name of Bray, who with his little knowledge of Tagalog acted as my interpreter." General Aguinaldo stood up and walked away from his desk and continued, "Consul Pratt offered the same terms given to the Cuba rebels by the United States for aligning with them against Spain, which I accepted."

The general paused as if considering what to say next, and then continued. "While in Singapore, I met again with Spencer Pratt, who brought along Consul Rouceville Wildman, who convinced me to renew our fight to free ourselves from the Spaniards. General Thomas Anderson, who was also present that day, advised me that Dewey was fully aware of the plan and would assist us in defeating Spain and in recognizing our independence."

"Did you get anything in writing, a formal agreement from the Americans?" Mabini asked.

The general scratched the back of his head and responded, "No, they gave me what was supposed to be their solemn word because of their claim to be a powerful and honest country."

The general took a few moments again, glancing at both Luna and Mabini. "Upon my return to Cavite, I met with Dewey who assured me that they came as liberators and not as conquerors, and were prepared to recognize our independent nation."

"General Aguinaldo, they don't seem to come as friends or allies but as an invading force of occupation, and they are beginning to act like our enemies," Antonio Luna warned.

"We believe you, General Aguinaldo, but we have this feeling that your hope to return to the Philippines once more may have distracted your ability to question them thoroughly, or at the very least, have them clarify their interpretations," Mabini said in a respectful tone so as not to anger the general.

"What do you suggest we do?" Aguinaldo asked.

"We are a few months late for a frontal attack because they have plenty of infantry and artillery since their arrival on our shores. We have the infantry, but no armaments," Antonio said.

"But, either way, we have to set our feet in the sand. No more pulling back from any form of demarcation request made by the Americans," Mabini advised.

"We need to reinforce our existing defensive lines and secure funds pronto in order to purchase all the armaments we can get our hands on," Luna said.

"Move ahead with the development of a military plan of action in case war breaks out with the Americans," General Aguinaldo ordered.

CHAPTER 51

Antonio Luna saw the immediate need for establishing a military school similar to those in Europe. This time, with the newspaper to back him up, he had Aguinaldo issue a decree, which established the *Academia Militar*, a military academy at Malolos, Bulacan Province. Based on the recommendation from General Aguinaldo, he appointed a mestizo and former lieutenant of the Spanish Guardia Civil, Captain Manuel Sityar, as superintendent. Sityar was a mestizo and graduate of the *Academia Militar de Toledo* in Spain and had volunteered to serve with Aguinaldo in Cavite after Spain surrendered to the Americans.

Not long after, Sidra Gantuanco knocked at the bedroom door of General Luna. "There is a man by the name of Manuel Sityar waiting for you outside."

"Oh yes, good, please let him in, *mi amor*. I'll be down in a minute," Antonio said.

General Luna rushed out to meet the man who came highly recommended by General Aguinaldo. He seemed surprised to find a lanky looking fellow, well-groomed. He sported a mustache much like Antonio's, but appeared older and more European than an Indio.

"*Buenos dias*, General Luna. I would like to repeat to you what I told General Aguinaldo when I first met him. That since I have served the country of my father with blood, it's time for me to now serve the country of my mother with blood," Sityar stated with genuine sincerity.

"Very good, Sityar and the general recommends you very highly. So I want to show you the location I have in mind for the academia. Come, let's go," Antonio said.

Sityar and Luna recruited numerous *mestizos* and Spaniards who had fought in the Spanish army against the Filipino revolutionaries and of late, with the Americans. They believed that their services were of most value to the *Academia Militar* for their knowledge and skill of military warfare and ability to lead troops in battle.

One of them was José Bugallon, a handsome young man of twenty-five. He was polite, intelligent, and a recipient of Spain's highest military honor for great valor, the Red Cross for Military Honor. His experience, combined with his knowledge of the military were very instrumental in reorganizing the Philippine Army, particularly as a faculty member.

He captivated almost everyone who came in contact with him and as a result, recruited additional former officers of the Spanish Army to join forces with the Filipino Revolutionary Army.

The *Academia Militar* in Malolos opened on November 1, 1898. And having in mind that war with the Americans could explode at any time, General Luna had no other recourse but to figure out the best way possible to achieve maximum productivity with minimal wasted time, effort, and cost in converting young officers into the revolutionary army.

For all the work General Luna had done in such a short time for the revolutionary forces, he was not getting the support and cooperation from older officers, which was a shame because his prime objective was to develop an efficient, precise, systematic, disciplined, and orderly fighting machine.

The old officers of the revolutions were those who had fought in the first revolution against Spain, and whose loyalty would forever be with the generals of that revolution, especially Emilio Aguinaldo, but clearly not from a mere pharmacist such as he was.

Eventually, and to prove a point, he made it known to his friends and allies that he was ready to give up his life in order to earn the respect of those who doubted his personal courage. "When the time comes, we will see if those conceited asses who claim to be brave can remain at my side in the hour of death."

By late September 1898, the general's feelings towards those officers eventually ended up at the office of General Aguinaldo, who appointed him Chief of War Operations in order to calm him down. And as a show of his support for Antonio's achievements, the general promoted him to Brigadier General, which alienated him further from the older officers of the core.

He was now the third-ranking official in the military hierarchy, next to the Secretary of War, Baldomero Aguinaldo and the President.

The president, with his dictatorial powers, influenced the Philippine government to appoint Juan Luna as a member of the Paris delegation, which was working for the recognition and diplomatic relations of the newly established Philippine Republic to other countries.

A few days later, every one in the *Academia Militar* was in jubilation with the news coming from General Aguinaldo that a shipment of rifles and bullets from Japan had landed in Naic, Cavite province and was being transported to Malolos.

"As soon as the shipment arrives, I want all of our young officers and officer candidates at the firing range," General Luna said to Colonel Sityar and the rest of his military instructors.

"Yes, we finally have bullets and brand new rifles for target practice," said the excited Major Bugallon the day the rifles arrived.

"I only know of three Filipinos who get really handle a gun. One is dead, the other is in Europe, and the third is right in front of us," said Colonel Alejandrino referring to General Luna.

"I see two people in front of you—General Luna and Colonel Sityar," Major Bugallon said as a challenge.

"You can be sure, it's not me," Colonel Siyar responded and walked towards Alejandrino.

"And now my general and friend, would you do us the honor?" Colonel Alejandrino said as he handed Luna a loaded pistol.

"All right, only because I want to demonstrate to you guys that anyone can be good at handling a pistol as long as they have the confidence and the patience of constant practice for accuracy," Luna said.

"Do you know that General Luna can put out the flame of a lighted candle with one shot from a distance of about 10 meters and at 20 meters?" Alejandrino said. "The general, his brother, Juan, and our good friend Rizal shot each other's top hats off."

"I would love to see that," Colonel Sityar said.

"Follow me," General Luna said as they walked to his office and stopped about twenty meters away. He aimed the pistol at the wooden door of his office, took a deep breath, exhaled slowly, aimed, and began firing in rapid succession. When he stopped and lowered his pistol, every person in the room was shocked to see the rays of the sun in his office window pass through the bullet holes in the door that spelled his initials, A. L.

After the applause Colonel Sityar said, "I guess I'll have to order a new door for you."

"No, don't replace the door, my office is too hot so a little ventilation is just what I needed," Antonio joked.

Luna's shooting demonstration paid off well, because soon after, Major Bugallon assisted in the formulation of the most disciplined and elite unit of the *Academia Militar*, the cavalry and the sharpshooter's squadron, and eventually became General Luna's chief aide-de-camp.

"Gentlemen, please follow us to our office. We have presents for you guys. They arrived early this morning." Colonel Sityar said.

Inside a large number of boxes were brand new uniforms, caps, and black booths for rank and file of the revolutionary forces.

"We should be ready to issue them out in a few days, but meanwhile, take a look at a sample of an officer's uniform," Colonel

Sityar said and pulled out a complete set of black booths, a white cap with black shades, a bluish grey pin striped on white pair of pants, coat shirt, and a red sash to hold the sword.

"Oh, my God, these uniforms looks much better than our Guardia Civil uniforms," Colonel Francisco Roman exclaimed.

"The uniforms were designed by my brother, the artist Juan," General Luna stated with great pride.

"All these must have cost a fortune. We could have bought more guns and bullets for the money spent," Colonel Alejandrino said in criticism.

"You do have a point, Colonel, but it takes more than bullets and guns to run our military forces. A uniform distinguishes an officer from a infantryman, and brings honor, and a feeling of solidarity among comrades. Our uniform will signify to the world, and especially to the Americans, that we are an independent nation with an organized and uniformed military force ready to defend its freedom, rights, and constitution," General Luna said.

"I get the point," Colonel Alejandrino said.

Meanwhile, General Luna understood the importance of the railways that connected Manila to Dagupan, for they were important for communication and transportation, as when they were controlled by the Guardia Civil. He and Alejandrino begun laying out plans to defend and control the railways by building trenches along any chain of hills or long narrow elevations of land running from north to south that bordered the railways. With assistance from the revolutionary army, about twenty miles of defensive line trenches were completed stretching from La Loma to Caloocan.

Thus, General Antonio Luna had not only secured the sixty-year-old Ferrocaril de Manila, a Dagupan railroad line owned by the defunct colonial Spanish authority, but also, he was in the position to utilize train travel for transporting volunteer soldiers, goods, and relaying military information from the northern regions to Manila in less than eight hours when in the past, it took more than a day of travel.

During this period, relations between the First Philippine

Republic and the United States began to sour, especially with the continual American occupation of the Walled City of Intramuros and the lines of blockhouses outside Intramuros formerly occupied by the Spaniards, while the Filipinos maintained their positions after the mock war.

When General Wesley Merritt turned over the command of the American forces in Manila to General Elwell Otis to attend the Paris peace talks for the purpose of culminating the purchase of the Philippines from Spain, he gave strict orders to demand that the Filipinos withdraw their forces beyond the suburbs of Binondo, Tondo, Santa Cruz, Quiapo, San Miguel, Ermita, Malate, and Paco. And since the Americans largest contingence of reinforcement were on their way to the islands, the United States was strong militarily to annex the Philippines in the same way they did previously to Hawaii. Merritt also informed Otis that an alliance of supposedly Filipino patriots and businessmen where convinced that the Philippines would be better as a territory of the United States. Otis took full advantage of this group of Filipinos. Some of them who transferred information to him were even friends of Aguinaldo.

These latest demand for the Filipino's to deploy back beyond the proposed demarcation line made by the Americans was not well received by Aguinaldo and his generals. But ultimately, during the meeting to discuss the American request, Aguinaldo succumbed to the ultimate irony of faith for the Americans, and the wishes of his political advisors led by the Director of Foreign Affairs, TH Pardo. But the meeting had to be adjourned only after the heated verbal exchange between Antonio Luna and TH. Afterward, TH exuberantly relayed the message to General Otis.

CHAPTER 52

General Antonio Luna was upset and disappointed that the High Command would not listen to his military strategy, so he did not waste any time in rushing to his room in Malolos to get himself ready to fall in the arms of the woman closet to his heart and who listened to him—Sidra.

Antonio told a servant to prepare his bath and to have a horse mounted to his carriage with a canvas canopy on for the impending rain. With her parents out for the weekend in the neighboring province of Tarlac, the couple had earlier planned for a late afternoon picnic. Unknown to Sidra, he planned to take her to an isolated field outside Malolos by sunset and promised himself to be much more affectionate and loving to her this time since they had been seeing each other for almost six months.

He was going to profess his real intentions, and then seduce her, his only true love. He grabbed a bottle of red wine on his way out of his room and called for Sidra, who heard him arrive earlier. She'd waited anxiously with a picnic basket on hand outside the house.

Sidra was wearing a very light summer dress made of abaca fiber with a see-through blouse over her dress that pressed against her breasts and chiseled body when she quickly boarded his carriage. Although dark rain clouds surrounded them, he rode his carriage rapidly toward an imaginary field of love. On the horizon, the sun was the color of amber very appropriate for an evening like this, a perfect setting. He smiled.

A few kilometers away from Malolos along the large Calumpit River, and under the shade of rows of Ipil-Ipil trees, Antonio brought his carriage to a halt. He looked around as far as his eyes could see. They were all alone. *Perfect*, he said to himself.

After spreading their table cloth under a shaded area for Sidra's picnic basket, Antonio opened his bottle of Rioja red wine and poured it into two crystal drinking cups. After his toast, they began to partake in manchego cheese, cooked Spanish chorizos, slices of jamon Serrano, and a piece of large round bread.

"I hope you enjoyed the Spanish meal, since you've been away from Spain for a while now," Sidra said.

"I enjoyed every bite, and you were so thoughtful for thinking of me," Antonio said.

"I have a confession to make. The day we met was not the first time I saw you. A few days before, I saw you from a distance when you were coming out from the Barasoin Church, and since then I've always wished and hoped you would someday get to know you," Sidra shyly confessed and then took a sip of wine.

"Why did you not introduce yourself and then I would have met you earlier," Antonio said.

"I could not find the courage," Sidra responded, "but I am glad you are a soldier. It gives me a feeling of security like having my personal bodyguard."

However, she also had concerns about Antonio's character after hearing gossip from her brothers. So she gulped more wine to give her courage. "Antonio, you fill me with such joy, and you may be the love of my life, but …" she struggled with the question.

Antonio could not help but stare at her because she looked at him as if he were a different person.

Sidra took a deep breath and said, "I've been told that you have a bad temper like your brother who murdered his wife, and I don't know if I should be concerned.

Antonio tried to reply but was interrupted when Sidra placed her fingers on his mouth, "Let me explain … I am comfortable and feel good when I am with you, because I have fallen in love with you, Antonio. Can you promise me that you will always love me, and that you will not change but remain the same nice and wonderful man who sings to me and makes me laugh? Promise me Antonio."

"Since childhood I've struggled with the definition of a tough guy and don't deny that I am a bull toward my adversaries. But my mother taught me at an early age to be as meek as a lamb to people who are kind and caring, especially to those I love and trust. You ask about my brother. Rest assured that I don't want to suffer the same fate and remorse that can stretch into a lifetime of suffering and misery. I promise, Sidra, to take good care of you, my love."

Antonio sidled close to her and kissed her at the corner of her mouth. She held his face with her palms and softly told him that she felt she was living in a world of romantic fantasy. "Let us be as happy as we can. All my life I have fantasized about love, its longing tenderness, pleasures, joys, and ecstasy as well as its sadness and pain. And now I want to enjoy every moment of it."

Sidra was extremely attracted to Antonio who so far had only kissed her lightly. The thought of being passionately kissed by him sent shivers down her spine, better yet of her kissing him.

Alone in the world, Antonio revered Sidra as the beautiful and refined woman she was. He found her to be both an individual and a representative of her society, an emblem of a lost tradition. However, he noticed a subtle rise in her expression and in her exquisite, intelligent almond-shaped eyes when he caressed her lips with the tip of his index finger.

Sidra shrugged to his touch as if it did not matter. On the contrary, it did matter as she excitedly anticipated his next move.

"Darn, it's so hot and humid even under the shade. Look at my shirt sticking to my body with sweat. Do you mind if I take it off"

"We appear to be alone, so go ahead," she said.

"You can take yours off, too. Just kidding," he said laughing.

"No, you're right. It's so humid and if only I were alone I would take a dip in the river."

"Not a bad idea. Go ahead, I won't look," Antonio teased.

"Oh, yeah," she said and laughed.

"Well, you better close your eyes because now I think I will jump in," he said.

"Are you serious?"

'Watch me!" And then he sprinted to the river bank, took off his pants, and butt naked he jumped into the luke warm water of the river. All the time, Sidra pretended not to look, but she had one eye slightly open.

"You're crazy, Antonio!" Sidra cried with laughter as she walked toward the river.

"Whew, you don't know what you're missing, Sidra. The water is so nice and refreshingly cool and really nice."

"No, I'm not. It's embarrassing."

"Come on, you don't have the guts. I dare you to jump in the river and I promise you, I won't look."

"Then turn around and close your eyes until I am ready," she said.

"Very well," he said and turned around.

Sidra nervously removed all her clothes in a blink of an eye. She lowered herself into the water and swam to about two meters of Antonio.

"You're absolutely right. The water is so refreshing," she called out to Antonio.

"Good, but can I turn around and face you now?"

"Yes, but don't get close to me," she said.

Antonio turned and moved a bit towards her and said, "I love you, Sidra, so please tell me that you love me too."

"I do love you, Antonio, but don't get any closer," she said and dunked herself under water for a split second.

Antonio spotted a large long branch of a tree floating towards them and yelled out to Sidra. "Sidra, quick swim away. A python is right behind you!"

"Where?" She cried out and instinctively bolted toward Antonio and soon their bodies clashed in a tight embrace, so close that the hiss in her voice reverberated between them.

"Don't worry, it was just a piece of wooden debris," Antonio said calmly.

But they both felt each other's presence, and without saying a word they gazed into each other's eyes until he placed both hands on her face and kissed her tenderly, but not for long. For soon enough they laid in a deep embrace along the banks of the Calumpit River, passionately kissing, and then made love for the first time.

When it was over, she laid on the sand, flat on her belly, and with tears of joy in her eyes told him, "I've never done this before. Please believe me, I've not been with another man until tonight."

"Yes, I do and I am so glad and happy that you did for we have just proven our deep love and commitment to each other," he replied tenderly.

Sidra shifted her body to embrace Antonio. "I love you so very much, Antonio."

Antonio pointed to the dark clouds in the west above the Manila Bay and said, "Looks like it's going to rain. We'd better seek shelter in the carriage where there is a canopy and blankets to cover ourselves up when we take a nap."

"We take a nap. How romantic!" she said.

"Since we cannot sleep together in your house, the carriage will do," he said. "I just want to be close to you for awhile longer."

Once snuggled and comfortable in the carriage, it did not take long for the setting sun to be enveloped by the thick grey clouds in the horizon. The dark pressed down the mantle of silence, and soon after, the torrential rains began.

"I love the rain. It reminds me of when I was a child, and my brothers and I would play and take a shower in the rain. Did you not go out and play in the rain when you were little?"

"We used to all the time," Antonio said.

Sidra confessed. "I dreamt of you last night."

"About what?"

"Of you making love to me," she said.

"Was it as good as the real thing?"

"Of course not," she said softly. "Tonight was indescribable!"

"Great, so next time we don't have to go so far. You can sneak into my room."

"You are crazy. What about my reputation if word leaks out that we've been intimate? My father would disown me."

"Disowned you like a piece of furniture?" Antonio said.

"Yes, you have no idea about the Chinese culture and tradition," she said.

"Only the little I've learned since I met you," he said.

Sidra replied in words that helped define Chinese women. "Did you know that then, as well as now, a Chinese woman is always second to her brothers, her husband, and even to her sons? Marriages are arranged by the parents and once married, the woman is at the mercy of her mother-in-law. The wealthy women of society have more time to enjoy life, but suffer the consequence of having to share a husband with other women known as concubines. And a first wife can even be discarded for failure to produce a son."

"*Hombre*, I did not realize the men in China have it so good. How soon can we get married?" Antonio jokingly told Sidra.

"Get out of here. You are never serious, but thank God my mother is a Filipina and she controls my father," Sidra teased in reply.

"Kidding aside, your mother must have been quite a woman. She raised a priceless princess for me," Antonio said wanting to compliment her mother.

"Thank you, but let me change the subject. Did you know that the happiest people on earth are the poor? They don't have everything a rich man possesses and so they just do whatever makes them happy."

"Like what?"

"Like dancing in the rain," she said.

"Sounds great as long as you go first, and I dare you to do so," Antonio said.

"Are you serious this time?"

"Yes," Antonio said.

"Then let us live this night forever!" Sidra screamed as she jumped out of the carriage and began dancing in the rain singing loud. "Let us live this night forever!"

Antonio remained seated in the carriage, bewildered at the sight of Sidra dancing in the rain with nothing on but her soaking wet camisole that barely covered her private parts, exposing her exquisite pair of legs. He was elated to know that she had this liberated and joyful side of her, which made him love and admire her even more if that was possible.

"Come on, you don't have the guts to play and dance in the rain?" Sidra challenged him.

He stepped out in a gentlemanly manner humming Johann Strauss, Blue Danube and walked into her arms. They began dancing the waltz and then passionately made love once more on the ground and right under the rain. Afterwards, bundled in each other's arms inside the carriage to keep warm, they both fell asleep. A slight breeze of cold wind woke them up about an hour before midnight.

"It's getting very late." she said in a choked voice. "Can we go now?"

"Yes, before we catch a cold," Antonio said.

Their love affair intensified even more, and with war pending on the horizon, Antonio Luna took every opportunity to be free from his daily duties and obligations as a soldier, to be in the arms of his true and eternal love as often as possible.

CHAPTER 53

General Elwell Otis, uncertain of his military power and capability to subdue the Filipino revolutionary forces, utilized the down time and ponder military tactics. And at the same time, he used their power of persuasion to alienate the population, the rich landlords and Filipino businessmen—those who were brainwashed into believing that there was a lot to gain from the United States by supporting their occupation of the Philippines. This happened especially in the areas of education for the young and the commerce industry such as the production of hemp for making rope.

The deception was so great that at one point to appease General Luna, the American forces gave up one of the blockhouses in Caloocan. This simple gesture of appeasement by the Americans reinforced the belief of General Aguinaldo that the Americans had no intentions of permanently occupying the Philippines. As a result, the revolutionary troops surrounding Manila were ordered by the Filipino leadership to return to their respective provinces.

This infuriated Antonio Luna, and he wrote an exposé about the real intentions of the American in his newspaper, *La Independencia*. The unaltered proclamation of benevolent assimilation— in other words, the truth about the American occupation of the Philippines from Spain— made by President McKinley after the signing of the Paris Peace Treaty.

On New Year's Day 1899, General Emilio Aguinaldo was officially declared president of the new Philippine Republic by the Philippine Revolutionary Congress, which had just approved the Malolos Constitution a month earlier. The United States authorities refused to recognize the new government.

When Spain's secession of the Philippines to the United States was made public, the Philippine military high command met in Malolos, Bulacan province on January 23, 1899. At that time, Antonio Luna was appointed as head of the Philippine Army by General Aguinaldo. Luna began to reorganize the Filipino revolutionary forces and ordered all Filipino officers to recruit officers and soldiers of the former Spanish colonial army. He devised courses of instruction, planned the reorganization of the army, created a battalion of sharpshooters and a cavalry squadron, and set up an inventory of guns, ammunition, and arsenals using convents and town halls, quartermasters, lookouts, and communication systems.

As for the core of officers, most of them belonged to the upper class of society. Their appointments were decided on the strength of their connections to the generals who were remnants of the first rebellion against Spain. He insisted on strict discipline and qualifications over and above clan and clique loyalties. Luna proved to be a strict disciplinarian and thereby alienated many in the ranks of the army.

During the meeting with General Aguinaldo and his staff, Luna reiterated that only a quick and decisive military action could save the new republic. Their strongest unit at present in the military forces was the infantry. Their artillery and cavalry were neither strong enough nor ready for battle. Thus, Luna's strategy was to bottle up the Americans in Manila before more of their troops could land. He planned to execute surprise attacks at night while building up strength in the north. Luna also suggested building a military base in the northern highlands of Luzon should the enemy pierce his lines, wage a series of delaying battles while waiting for the shipment of guns, ammunitions, and other war supplies that he recommended buying from abroad.

Luna talked about the rudiments of guerrilla warfare that smaller nations employed a thousand years ago. He described how they would band together in smaller units of fighting men that would lure the larger invading forces into areas of the region that were alien and unfavorable for traditional warfare. By the time ambushes spread through the landscape, the smaller nations were able to gradually and methodically destroy the invaders.

"The main purpose here is to avoid direct confrontation and to continue with our plan of well-timed ambushes, letting the war drag on our enemy loses begins to pile up, and soldiers morale drops." General Luna concluded his deliberation. "When public opinion against this war spreads and intensifies in the United States, the government will have no other alternative but to withdraw their forces allowing us to uphold our sovereignty."

Even before General Luna arrived, Aguinaldo had already been pondering a different type of strategy. "I shall consider your position very thoughtfully, General Luna," he said. "Rest assured that I will do so. But at this point in time, we may still outnumber them, and we must show the Americans that we are serious about defending our liberty and our new republic. And toward that end, there is no better demonstration than a massive frontal attack, driving their forces back into the ocean."

"How can I make you all understand that we have one rifle for every three infantryman. The other two are armed with just a *bolo*, a long knife like a machete, ready to take over when the other has fallen." General Luna continued. "On the other hand, every American soldier carries pistol and a belt full of cartridges. Even before our soldiers can get to them, they will have to dodge bombs raining from their cannons and bullets from their Colt rapid firing machine guns. History is made with guns. No guns means no power, and no power spells sure defeat."

"Why are you afraid to fight the Americans, face to face, *mano a mano,* hand to hand?" General Gregorio Del Pilar asked. "If you don't have the necessary pride and courage, then I suggest you resign from your commission."

"There is no room for pride in military warfare. Pride is a sign of weakness. Common sense has to rule us in battle. To kill and be killed in a frontal assault may be honorable, if the rules of engagement are of equal par, but if they are one-sided in favor of the enemy, then I would prefer to hide and kill as many of the enemy before being killed in return," General Luna said in a rant. "So don't talk to me about pride. I will defend my country until I exhaust the last recourse for the cause, thus complying with my oath to the flag."

President Aguinaldo immediately interfered with the arguments by calling for order in the meeting and reiterated that to further discuss the situation is moot because he had already made up his mind. Except for the purchase of military armaments, the plan for guerrilla warfare was turned down by the High Command.

The newly appointed Foreign Affairs Minister Apolinario Mabini recommended purchasing war armaments from Japan since Mariano Ponce, their Filipino contact abroad, informed him that the Japanese officials, although hesitant of American retaliation, were willing to sell all the military armaments needed for the cause, they too were worried of the growth of American imperialism in the Asian region.

As requisitioned by General Luna, the President of the Philippine Republic approved an order of five thousand rifles, two thousand revolvers, three thousand swords, fifty thousand rounds of ammunition, thirty artillery guns, four tons of gunpowder, and one hundred bombs.

Unwilling to let things lie where national pride was concerned, the revolutionary forces made preparations for a frontal war with the intruding American forces. Pulling every string at his disposal, General Luna tried to thwart it, but failed. Having lost credibility with the High Command, he knew very well that Filipinos had the heart and courage to gallantly fight in battle, but given all the obstacles one had to overcome across the killing fields, left them nothing but prayers to survive, to overcome their fear and willingness to die in the struggle for their beliefs. His only consolation was his own fighting spirit and pride as a Filipino, which made him accept and follow orders from President Aguinaldo to lead the charge as a fighting general of the Philippine freedom fighters.

CHAPTER 54

It was the first day of the New Year in 1899, and foremost in the mind of General Elwell Otis was to discover ways and means to delay any military activity until his massive recruitment of soldiers arrived. He sensed the eagerness of Filipino military leaders to propel them out of the country, so he approved a plan for a dialogue between them, some kind of a commission as suggested to him by his pro-American Filipino friends. He named Brigadier General Robert Hughes to preside over the commission.

Nothing positive came out from their meetings because the Americans seemed to only pretend to listen to the Filipinos' demand for the recognition of their independence in return for a peaceful coexistence between the two governments in the Philippines.

At the same time, heated arguments between Aguinaldo's political and military advisors with regards to dealing with the Americans did not subside either. The president was still hopeful that the Americans would uphold their promises, and consequently continued to side with his political advisors who were in constant contact with the Americans.

The other wrench in the division between the Filipinos and Americans came about from the conception of the Schurmann Commission, which was an advisory group created by President McKinley in order to study the situation in the Philippines. The commission would then make recommendations on how the United States should proceed. Coincidentally, the commission became known to the Filipinos a month after the signing of the Treaty of Paris.

Using his newspaper as his public forum, General Antonio Luna began to attack the latest American ploy as another form of delaying tactics and with no sincere intentions of recognizing Filipino independence, but instead to permanently seize the Philippine Republic.

And a few days later, General Henry Ware Lawton, a veteran of the Civil War, Apache Wars, and Spanish-American War in Cuba and credited to have captured Apache leader Geronimo, arrived with the largest troop reinforcements at the end of January 1899. All negotiations and contacts with Aguinaldo's political advisors temporarily ceased. And all U. S. army volunteers were required to extend their duty of military service.

Now convinced of the United States' subterfuge regarding their alleged promise to pull out of the Philippines, General Luna tried once more to encourage the preparation for immediate armed hostilities with the Americans on February 1, 1899, but to no avail.

In fact, the Americans believed they had garnered a sufficient number of military reinforcements and armaments, and thus, on February 4, 1899 believed they were in a perfect position to commence hostilities with the Filipinos, while the Filipino leadership had no inkling or notion of the treacherous American strategy that was about to occur.

It was a weekend, a quiet and warm Saturday, and being a new moon, it was pitch dark in an open field close to San Juan del Monte, a suburb of Manila. Two Nebraska volunteers from Company B, who had taunted a pair of Filipino soldiers earlier along the declared neutral zone, were now on sentry patrol in the corner of Sociego and Silencio Streets in the Santa Mesa District.

"Oh man, I hate being on this boring patrol duty. By the way, what time is it now?" Private William Grayson asked in a whining voice.

"It must be around a quarter past eight by now. We still have a long night ahead of us," Private Orville Miller replied.

"Yup, a bloody boring night, as if we are going to see any action tonight," Private Grayson responded.

"You bet, Grayson, the best we can do is hurl insults at those short niggers on the other side of the fence."

"Why do we even have to bother strapping this bloody heavy rifle on our shoulders? It's not like we're going to even get a bloody chance to shoot any of those midget niggers, especially the ones who taunted us." Grayson laughed and continued. "On my next patrol, I plan to leave this bloody rifle behind."

"Well, we do have outstanding orders to shoot any Filipino soldier who might try to enter the neutral area," Miller said.

Both soldiers continued to pace along the American borderline fence when they heard a whistle that they thought sounded more like a signal.

"Grayson, did you hear that whistle coming from left field?"

"Yup, and wait a minute, now a whistle sound like a counter signal on right field"

"Do you see anything?"

"Nope, but wait, by the number seven blockhouse, I just saw a flash of red light. It may have been a bloody lantern. But maybe not. I never saw it before," Grayson said.

"Now I hear footsteps heading toward us from about twenty-five yards," Miller warned.

"Halt!" a nervous Grayson shouted.

"Halt!" he shouted a second time.

"*Alto*," responded one of the four Filipino soldiers, who continued walking slowly towards the Americans and stopped about fifteen feet away.

"Halt!" shouted Grayson for the third time, this time aiming his cocked rifle at the Filipino soldier leading the pack.

"*Alto, Alto!*" the Filipino soldier who seemed to be in charge snapped as one of his companions was interpreting in Tagalog the reason it was important for them to cross to the other side of the fence.

"You hard-headed bloody nigger. Here is what you get for not listening." Grayson fired and hit the leading soldier, who dropped dead. Private Miller fired off as well and hit another soldier. Grayson shot and killed a third soldier. The fourth Filipino got away unharmed. The Filipinos never had the chance to defend themselves since they did not expect to be fired upon.

By coincidence, the American military command that evening knew that most of the Filipino generals were on furlough, and that the Filipino peace commissioner had just updated the result of their peace conference with several members of the Malolos Congress.

The Filipino soldiers who were killed merely wanted to visit family members on the other side of the fence, had no given orders to attack and kill Americans, and were fired upon and innocently killed by an English immigrant who migrated eight years earlier to the United States, and who worked in a hotel in Nebraska before enlisting in the army.

Afterwards, the Americans claimed that the Filipinos opened fire first, giving the Americans no choice but to defend themselves. The reaction of the Filipinos was that the Americans had staged the whole incident.

The whole Filipino defensive line from Pasay to Caloocan returned fire the following day and the first battle of the Filipino-American War broke out. It had become a war of conquest, occupation, and annexation, which General Luna and Apolinario Mabini, among others, had predicted and repeatedly warned Aguinaldo and his military High Command against.

With the support and endorsement by U. S. President William McKinley, the incident was later on used by the United States Congress to vote for annexation.

Both parties in the conflict expected war to break out at any time. Thus, they were not really caught by surprise and proceeded immediately with their prearranged military plans and strategies. President Aguinaldo felt incredibly betrayed by the Americans as well as embarrassed before his own military advisors that he had been proven wrong in trusting the American government.

General Hughes rushed to Malacanang at the break of dawn and informed General Otis that the war with the Filipinos was on. He described in detail what happened in San Juan del Monte and concluded, "The Filipinos under General Luna in the north seemed to be the most organized and will be ready to attack us at any time."

"Is General MacArthur apprised of the whole situation?"

"Yes, sir."

"Then, let's go ahead as planned," General Otis said.

On the same day, General MacArthur's forces not only secured the bridge in San Juan, but also advanced at flank speed north to control all of Santa Mesa, Sampaloc, and the Binondo area, with an eye on devastating General Luna's troops in Caloocan, while in the south of Manila their military forces under General Anderson had occupied all of Paranaque.

Meanwhile, General Lawton spread out his forces on the embankments east of the Pasig River and with the support of their naval gunboats plying the Pasig River managed to control the territory.

President Aguinaldo was in complete disarray when his emissary informed him that his proposal to General Otis for an immediate cease fire and negotiations for a new buffer zone between the two forces was not approved. For one reason, the dye had already been cast and was no longer retrievable. He immediately had General Luna summoned to Malolos for a briefing on how to implement their military plan and strategy against the Americans.

"General Luna," Aguinaldo said. "I am so glad you made it back here so soon. You must know by now that the war with the Americans started early this morning, and as president I have more things to do than to just run a war. Therefore, I am giving you the authority to operate all our war efforts with the American. I have full and complete confidence in your ability to succeed, while I stay in Malolos, and continue running our operations from here"

When their military briefing with the president ended, Colonel Alejandrino, who accompanied General Luna to the briefing, asked him, "I don't get it, the president gave you the full authority to lead the war, but does he plan to continue running the war from Malolos?"

"I don't know, and the reason I kept quiet and did not ask for elaboration was that in this way I can lead the army my way and with his full authority."

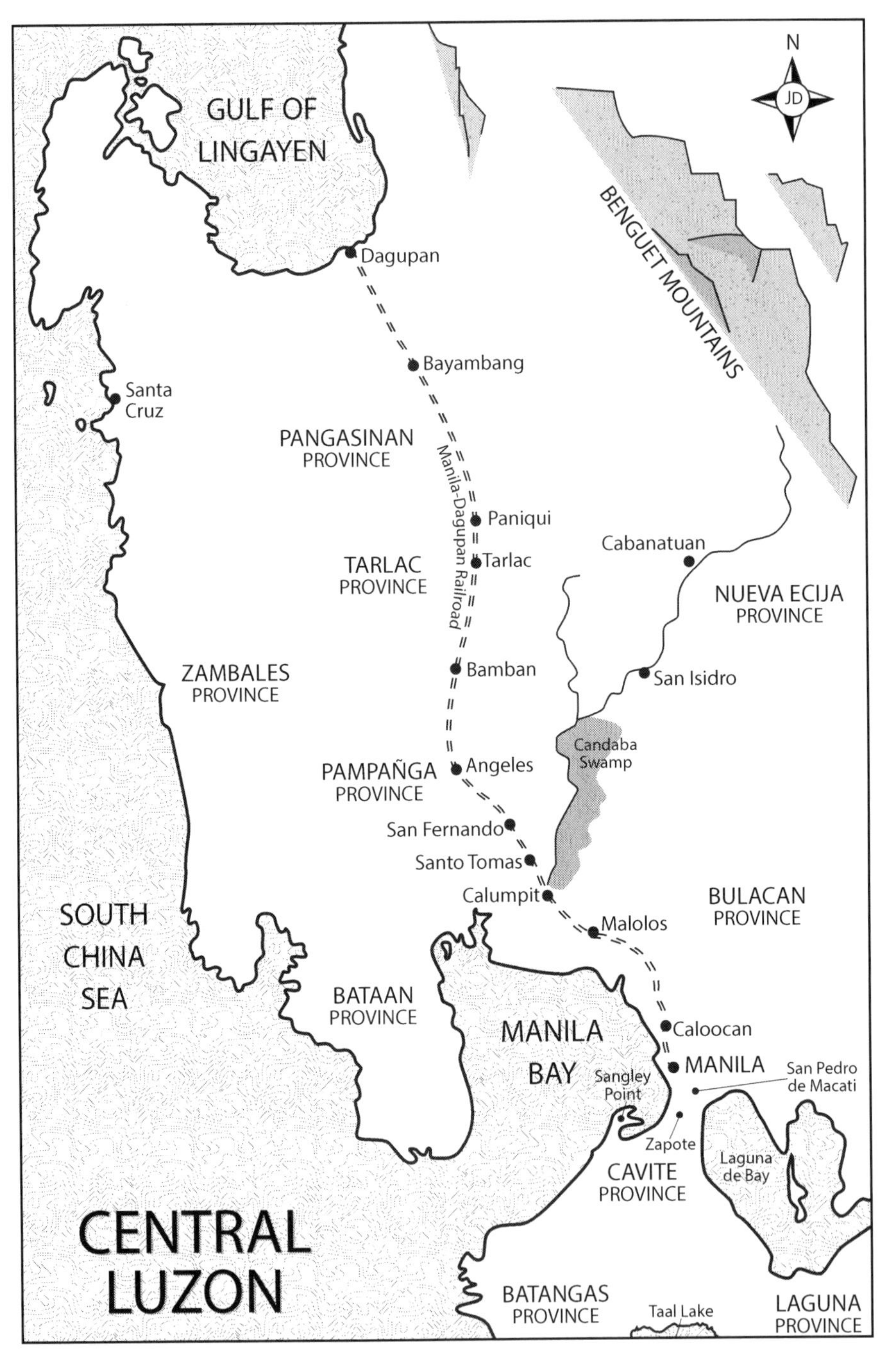
GULF OF LINGAYEN
N
JD
BENGUET MOUNTAINS
Dagupan
Bayambang
Santa Cruz
PANGASINAN PROVINCE
Manila-Dagupan Railroad
Paniqui
Tarlac
TARLAC PROVINCE
Cabanatuan
NUEVA ECIJA PROVINCE
Bamban
San Isidro
ZAMBALES PROVINCE
Candaba Swamp
PAMPAÑGA PROVINCE
Angeles
San Fernando
Santo Tomas
Calumpit
BULACAN PROVINCE
Malolos
SOUTH CHINA SEA
BATAAN PROVINCE
MANILA BAY
Caloocan
MANILA
San Pedro de Macati
Sangley Point
Zapote
Laguna de Bay
CAVITE PROVINCE
CENTRAL LUZON
BATANGAS PROVINCE
Taal Lake
LAGUNA PROVINCE

CHAPTER 55

Brigadier General Arthur MacArthur, Jr. commander of the First Brigade, 2nd Division, Eight Corps, was given the command of the north army division of the American forces. His principal strategy was to immediately mobilize his right flank coming from the east of Manila and the left flank from the west; and engage the enemy like a claw before they had time to organize as they march forward towards Coloocan. Their offensive line spread from the neighborhood of Santa Mesa in the east and westward to the outskirts of Tondo. They were set to engage any opposing forces along their path as they move fast to turn their flanks and envelope the enemy.

With all of their war machines deployed, and with over fifteen thousand soldiers, including a battalion of logistics and support, carabao drawn wagons to supply the army with food and other necessary supplies, MacArthur gave the orders to move his main force and left flanks in full toward the hills of La Loma on their way to Caloocan. This was on February 5, 1899, the first full day of the war between the

Americans and the Filipinos, who they still classified as mere insurgents.

MacArthur had also made arrangements with Commodore Dewey for the naval forces to support the army by sending an armed steamboat captured earlier from the Spaniards into the Pasig River.

The newly appointed fifty-four year-old Brigadier General Arthur MacArthur was born in Springfield, Illinois. He was a veteran of the Civil and Indian Wars, and his experience in the army included a Medal of Honor at the age of eighteen for his heroism in rallying and commanding his regiment at the Battle of Missionary Ridge during the Civil War. His appointment at such a young age to the temporary rank of Colonel in the Union Army was so rare that he became known as "The Boy Colonel." After years of distinguished service, he was shipped to Manila at the start of the Spanish-American War.

For the moment the Filipinos remained entrenched in their defensive line outside Caloocan waiting for the Americans to attack. General Luna hesitated to follow the invasion plan, but also was fretful to discuss the matter with the other generals for not wanting to be taken for a coward. Until he received orders from President Aguinaldo to attack the Americans at all cost. Against his wishes and better judgment, he met with his staff to inform them that instead of waiting defensively in Caloocan for a frontal attack against the Americans as ordered by President Aguinaldo, he proposed marching past the protective trenches he built in the hills of La Loma, and into its foothills in order to surprise the Americans.

Before setting out to La Loma, Luna quickly led and mobilized four companies of a thousand men. After he had deployed the rest of the troops to significant targets to engage General Arthur MacArthur's Montana Volunteers forces, Luna decided to take a preemptive action and attack at dawn.

And so before the morning light, the Filipino troops began slowly advancing down south past the Binondo and Chinese cemeteries and stopped to a halt when they spotted soldiers dressed in blue shirts and brown pants wearing large, light brown campaign hats. They sat and waited for the orders to begin firing.

On the American side, General MacArthur had no idea where the Filipinos planned their first assault until his scouts informed him of a column of dust rising from the direction of La Loma, and that the Filipinos were amassing enough troops for a major attack on the American positions close by. MacArthur immediately deployed a brigade of Pennsylvanian volunteer troopers towards La Loma to face General Luna's forces for the first time.

A few clouds on the early morning's blue sky blushed, as if anticipating the terrible clash about to take place in the foothills below as the Filipinos started to build makeshift defensive trenches among the bamboo thickets. Major José Torres Bugallon rejoined Luna in the fields of La Loma Cemetery located between Manila and Caloocan City.

Major Bugallon saluted and addressed General Luna. "Sir, I know you would prefer me by your side as you're aide-de-camp, but I beg of you, sir, make me lead a command in this battle."

"Thank you for volunteering yourself major, because you are the only one I trust like my own son to lead the battalion and mission I have in mind," General Luna answered.

"Major Bugallon, I need you to lead a battalion and at my signal charge toward the left flank of our target destination."

'Yes, sir I'm on the way right now," Major Bugallon said.

It did not take long for General Luna to communicate the order to commence firing, but not before every officer knew beforehand that they had to make every shot count during their first salvo. Their stock of ammunition was low.

As expected, the Americans countered fire with their heavy guns followed by an infantry charge supported by a number of Colt rapid firing guns and a signal core platoon, who would move ahead of the regular army to report the movements of the revolutionary soldiers.

Out of nowhere from the east side of the Chinese cemetery appeared a battalion of American soldiers crouching toward the domain of Major Bugallon's single company. Bugallon stood up when he heard Luna's command to commenced firing.

"*Amigo*s, take your time and make sure to every shot counts.

Get ready, aim, fire!"

The element of surprise worked well for Major Bugallon and his company as a number of the enemy soldiers dropped to the ground. Even an officer on horseback was felled.

After their second salvo of firing from their Mauser Fusils, Bugallon ordered his company to advance. But by then, the Americans were already firing back, forcing the Filipinos to take cover and fire back from behind tombstones in the Chinese cemetery with Bugallon leading ahead of the pack until he was hit by a bullet in his attempt to cross a road. Although injured, he managed to walk swiftly the few meters to a low-lying ditch where he dropped to seek shelter from the sizzling sound of bullets being fired at him.

The battle in La Loma continued with relentless American bombardment and in a matter of hours, casualties began to mount. When it became quiet in one of the battlefronts, Luna went out to investigate.

"What's up? Why so quiet down here?" General Luna asked.

"My general, we are out of bullets. I'm on my way uphill now to pick up more cartridges if there are any left."

"Where is Colonel Roman?" General Luna asked.

"He is covering our left flank and may also be out of ammunition soon."

"Here, take my pistol and go back to your sector. I'll have someone muster some cartridges for you," Luna said.

"Thank you, sir."

"Wait, what's your name officer?"

"Captain Hernando, sir," the young man replied.

"May God be with you, captain," Luna said.

Captain Eugenio Hernando nodded and then rejoined his unit leaving General Luna to ponder his next move. He was short of ammunition and acceding to the advantage of American artillery, he could not just pack up and call it a day. Such a decision would only invigorate the enemy into going for the kill, while a prolonged stand might spell more casualties, which would send a message to General MacArthur to slow down in his attack mode. The Filipinos were not going to be rolled over by his mighty military armed forces.

General Luna was about to get back to his outpost at the crest of the hill, when Lieutenant Colonel Queri informed him that Major Bugallon and his men were exposed to enemy fire by the side of a road and as a result, the Major was wounded and needed assistance.

Upon learning that Bugallón was wounded, Luna said: "We cannot let Bugallon die or fall into the hands of the enemy. He must be saved at all cost. His worth to us is equal to 500 soldiers, as he is one of my only hopes for future victory."

Dust-draped, Filipino revolutionaries bravely drove forward again and were met by musket fire. Luna joined the melee on foot. With his sword in the scabbard at his waist and a borrowed pistol in his hand, he gave the loud orders to his men to attack. "*Sugod mga kapatid!* (Attack my brothers!)"

General Luna and Colonel Queri managed to get behind a large boulder about five meters away from the badly wounded Major Bugallon, who did not look good at all laying prostrate in the ditch he had fallen into.

"Bugallon!" General Luna shouted.

The young major turned his head when he heard the general call his name, and moaning in pain, still managed to cry out. "My general, don't attempt to save me. Don't come any closer. It's too dangerous for you. Please save yourself."

"Colonel Queri," General Luna said. "Bugallon looks very pale and he is moaning in pain, so cover me while I make a run for it."

"Are you sure? Why don't you send me instead?" Queri said.

"No, I sent him on this mission, and I will bring him back. Besides, I'd better live up to my reputation as a madman."

"Please, don't risk your life for me," Bugallon begged in a whisper.

"Bugallon, Bugallon," Luna cried out. "It's too late for I'm here beside you. I want you to stay strong, and I will take you to a médico."

Major Bugallon was bleeding extensively. He had been shot in his right thigh and was hemorrhaging. Since the young Bugallon fought bravely in battle, Luna promoted him on the spot.

"Lieutenant Colonel Bugallon, did you hear what I just said? I just promoted you to a Lieutenant Colonel."

Bugallon smiled and whispered, "Thank you, my General."

Colonel Bugallon passed out and lost consciousness as General Luna dragged him out of the ditch while Colonel Queri fired his rifle to cover them in the midst of the extreme exchange of firepower. In an effort to take him away from harm's way, and hoping that he could be kept alive, Luna carried the young colonel on his shoulders until they got to the nearest safety zone.

However, it was too late; with his eyes swollen from dirt, pain, and tears, breathing slowly and labored, Colonel Bugallon died in Luna's arms. The thought of how his brother Juan would have felt if he was the one dying in his arms made General Luna painfully weep for the young colonel.

In the north of Sampaloc, more Filipino soldiers continued to be cut down by profuse gunfire from street intersections. Changing tactics, American fighters barged into houses, tore down doors, jumped over fences, advanced along rooftops. Artillery fire destroyed part of the perimeter wall, allowing the Americans to drive troops inside. Cannon fire continued pounding the city. While holding the line, American troops under General MacArthur charged and outflanked the Filipinos with the support of his Fourth U. S. Cavalry.

Luna began falling back across and up the hills of La Loma settling into the sanctuary of trenches that he had built, while sending the wounded back at the end of the line into Caloocan. When MacArthur's forces reached the foothills, the battle continued, but their advance was temporarily stalled due to the upland terrain advantage of the Filipino troops, until they brought in their howitzer cannons aimed towards the crest of the hills and commenced firing dropping six-pound bombs like rain on the trenches of the Filipino forces.

By late afternoon, the American firing salvo tapered off. Luna and his revolutionary army were outnumbered, outgunned, and most of his men were out of ammunitions, so they decided to regroup and save the day by pulling back their troops in an orderly fashion. Stage by stage, they retreated to the rear toward Caloocan.

When General Luna heard from his officers that a number of their soldiers did not make it back and were presumed either dead, wounded, or missing, he did not waste any time to organize a band of volunteer soldiers to go with him deep into enemy territory in search of their wounded and missing comrades.

"I would like to volunteer, sir."

"I know you. What's your name again?" Luna asked.

"Captain Hernando, sir," the young man replied.

"And he is a médico," Colonel Roman said.

"A médico is exactly what we need for this mission," Luna replied.

"Count me in, too, and some members of my company," Paco Roman said.

There was a long silence between them as the rescue party proceeded slowly walking, and at times, even crawled under the cover of darkness down the hills of La Loma. It was a new moon. They were careful not to be spotted by enemy scouts. They came out of no where, the humming sounds of mosquitoes all around. Finally, in the silence, they could hear from afar the sound of voices coming from all over the terrain below them. They heard the injured screaming in pain, crying for help, praying to God, and calling out names of their loved ones. The horrifying sounds became their beacon, as it led to their rescue and assistance.

Luna personally carried some of the men back to safety from the mission. One of those was a man shot in the leg that was just hanging freely loose and not complaining at all except for the wish to smoke a cigar. General Luna believed that it was upon the blood and ideals of men like this unknown hero that the foundations of the Republic was going to be built.

If there were any doubting Thomases in the military left to question the personal courage and fortitude displayed by General Luna in the battlefield, they still had not heard the news of what had just transpired in La Loma. Deep inside him, General Luna knew it was his shining moment since he was not only courageous, but also compassionate toward his brave soldiers, and he seized it with relentless purpose.

That same evening, Juan Luna was joined by his friend José Alejandrino, Colonel Queri, and Major Francisco Roman back at headquarters at Polo, Bulacan, not far from Caloocan. Also invited was Captain Hernando. Being a medical doctor, General Luna thought it best that he remain at headquarters to take care of the wounded.

Later on when he was alone, he prepared and sent to the Secretary of War his report of the activities of the day, informing him that they had engaged with the enemy from early morning until before the sun had set. It was only when they were out of ammunition and without any reinforcement and practically with nothing much to eat the whole day, that they had no other recourse but to retreat and fight another day. He also reported that his four companies of soldiers had a casualty count of 41 confirmed dead, and over a hundred wounded or missing in action.

The following morning, after a few hours of nothing but catnaps, General Luna received a report from his scouts that the enemy that had occupied La Loma was not advancing. Taking immediate advantage of the cease fire, Luna reorganized his forces and pressed on the best way he could with the soldiers on hand and others who had been coming from neighboring provinces. He then ordered the occupation of Caloocan by Filipino troops and pushed far south toward Binondo with the help of newly recruited volunteers that arrived from Malolos.

La Loma Church became General MacArthur's headquarters, and the top of the church dome was used by his signal corps to relay messages and spot Filipino insurgents on the field. With the vicinity all secured, MacArthur focused his attention on the preparation for the Battle of Caloocan and the burial of the dead.

Meanwhile, fighting went on at Marikina, Sta. Ana, and Paco. The Filipinos were subjected to a carefully planned attack from the American southern command forces under General Anderson, with naval artillery support from Dewey's gunboats plying the Pasig River.

Filipino civilian casualties and damage to personal property were horrific due to the indiscriminate shelling by the Americans.

CHAPTER 56

After capturing La Loma, General MacArthur was completely satisfied with the outcome of the battle and rested for the night in his La Loma Church headquarters to wait for additional reinforcements. He wanted to push forward toward Caloocan, an important railroad center eleven miles north of Manila. He did not want to spread his forces thin, so from La Loma he had his troops from the east and the west merge together in a pincer-like movement like a pair of pliers, planning to close in on the enemy and slowly squeeze them at Caloocan.

While General Luna issued detailed orders with five specific objectives to the field officers of the territorial militia, he reminded them to honor and not forget their fallen comrades in the battle of La Loma. He also encouraged them to continue their valiant stand against the American aggressors in their fight for freedom and independence, even if it meant their death.

Two days later in the early morning dawn, trainloads of high-spirited Filipino volunteers were seen landing in Caloocan. General Luna conveyed his battle plan to defend Caloocan to his military commanders and divided the territory in contention into various strategic sectors. General Panteleon Garcia, who was in command of his vanguard unit, was mobilized to the south of Caloocan; General Gregorio del Pilar was ordered into the cogon grass fields of Maypajo heights. Colonel Paco Roman was assigned to the urban area west of Caloocan, and Colonel Maximo Hizon stood guard in Polo available to depart for whatever post needed him the most.

It did not take long for General Otis to receive dispatches from paid informers on the movement of Luna's forces all around Manila, and reinforced more men traveling by rail from the north. Not to be outmanned, General Otis began spreading his Eight Army Corps composed of 831 officers and 20,032 men from the regular and volunteer combined forces strategically positioned to counter any advancing Filipino forces.

On February 10, the battle for Caloocan began with a massive, non-stop bombardment by MacArthur's forces from their position in La Loma making it impossible for Alejandrino and his men to dig last minute additional trenches to defend Caloocan.

From his command post in Manila, General Otis arranged with Admiral Dewey for his battleships to shell the field positions held by the revolutionaries northwest of the city continuously for forty-five minutes. At the same time, his artillery battalions were ordered to do the same from shore, and then wait, until the signal of ten-minute interval firing from MacArthur's big guns in La Loma was given, which marked the start of a synchronized infantry attack.

MacArthur's objective to occupy most of the city from San Juan to Caloocan was about to be realized in every step forward made by his men since their enemy had been shocked and awed by their mighty guns.

As for General Luna, he made sure earlier that all his field generals and their infantry of 4,000 courageous men were in their designated sectors and ready for battle. He then, together with his staff, decided to watch and monitor the battle from the house of the manager of Manila Railway Company, an Englishman named Horace Higgins.

By nightfall, a full moon had risen fully casting a bright light over the landscape of the battlefield. It did not take long for the range of American artillery to reach the Higgins home for soon enough, volleys of cannonballs rained on them too. From his vantage point, Luna could hardly see much for the air was dense with smoke, dust, and the thunderous sounds of exploding bombs and the rattling of machine gunfire.

"It's already bad enough that our men are poorly armed, but if only the president supported us earlier with more men to build trenches, then our men would have been better shielded from gunfire," Colonel Alejandrino said.

"Oh my God, please save my people from this holocaust," General Luna uttered.

"Jesus! Mary! Joseph! I cannot stand this horrible noise. I am afraid we are all going to die here!" Mr. Higgins cried out.

"Mr. Higgins, you don't have to stay here, if you are uneasy. I suggest you head north until the battle is over," Major Hernando suggested.

"You are probably right, so I'm out of here, but can you please make sure to lock up the house when you leave?" the very worried executive of the railways company said.

"I've never heard anything as loud as these before," Alejandrino commented.

"Well, if they believe they can obliterate us into submission through their constant and never-ending bombardment, then they will be disappointed for they cannot break the will of the Filipinos in their quest for freedom. We have waited long enough," Luna said in quiet control.

He walked to the nearest wooden rocking chair out in the garden and sat down. He rocked in his chair, and all alone, considered his options.

Not long after, a couple of bombs exploded near the house followed by ricocheting bullets from sporadic gunfire, hit the house, and shattered a window.

"General Luna, it's no longer safe to remain here. We better leave now," Colonel Alejandrino suggested.

"No, I can still see our men fighting ahead of us," Luna said.

Alejandrino approached General Luna to prod him a couple of times more until the general once and for all agreed and abandoned the Higgins house.

General Luna once more rode on his war horse to assess the battle situation in each of his sectors. When informed by his field generals of their poor chances of defeating the American forces in lieu of their much more effective firepower and the lack of ammunitions on the part of the Filipinos, he ordered his men to retreat north to their next line of defense in Polo, Bulacan Province.

General Luna and Colonels Natividad and Alejandrino decided to stay behind with rifles and strategically positioned themselves in the town church to continue the firefight with the American forces until he was positive that all his men had retreated north.

The Americans utilized the same military strategy of raining artillery fire followed by the infantry bursting forth sheets of flame from hundreds of rifles and captured Malabon, but only after suffering many losses. Not wanting to be outdone by MacArthur, General Luna immediately deployed all of his available forces at strategic areas along the Manila-Dagupan railways since the Americans now had in their possession the major railroad yard in Caloocan.

The fall of Caloocan convinced Luna of the necessity of imposing a vigorous injunction in the army of punishing with great severity whoever did not comply with this duty. This rule was to be applied above all when the one concerned was in an officer's position.

Luna believed that the resistance would have been more tenacious had there reigned solidarity among his various fighting units and this solidarity could only be obtained through mutual confidence among the troops. It was necessary that the soldiers were convinced that in dangerous situations they would not be abandoned by their chief officers and that they would be supported by the other corps of the military. After each battle, Luna received complaints from the different brigades, mutually accusing each other of having failed in their duties and blaming each other for the defeat.

In certain cases to solve this problem, Luna considered using disciplinary measures, starting with the incoming volunteers from Manila brought in by Colonel Queri after the loss of Caloocan.

Still smarting from defeat, Luna answered, "What! More recruits who had never been shot at before. Tell them to go to hell! I am fed up with hearing so many people who desire to fight but do not do so when the occasion presents itself!"

A moment later, he had second thoughts, as an idea flashed his mind. He asked the volunteers if they were prepared to submit to a test before being accepted. After they agreed, Luna smiled and turned to Alejandrino. "You will see the joke I will play on these men." He ordered Queri to pack ten rifles and cartridges on the train.

After breakfast, Luna separated the volunteers into groups of four and five. After arming each individual, he ordered them to board the train headed towards Malinta. Upon reaching the bridge before the destroyed house of Hacienda Malinta, Luna ordered the volunteers to disembark and march along the railroad lines heading south to search and destroy the enemy. He remained at the bridge, and commanded Colonel Roman to fire a couple of rounds in front of the marching recruits as he observed the volunteers in action with his telescope.

Later, Luna told Alejandrino. "You should have seen the admirable serenity with which these die-hard men marched along the railroad tracks even after being shot at."

No body among the volunteers was hurt and afterward, Luna exclaimed excitedly, "Now I have found some brave men who gave me the kind of satisfaction I have not felt from other units during the course of this campaign."

Luna formed a guerrilla unit from these men under the command of Rosendo Simon de Pajarillo, a mestizo. They were the same men who entered Manila at the end of February and exchanged fire with the Americans on Calle Bilibid until they exhausted their munitions. If instead of forty or fifty of these volunteers there had been two or three thousand as Luna wanted, perhaps the course of events would have changed. The heroic action of the guerrilla unit resounded heavily up north and aroused the morale of hundreds of soldiers, but unfortunately, the authorities in Malolos did not know how to profit from this fruitful lesson.

CHAPTER 57

After the battle of Caloocan, General MacArthur's forces marched all day along dusty cogon grass fields in ninety degrees heat and smoldering humidity. And with no clouds at all, the morning sky was featureless. Even though they moved slowly, they were able to advance all the way to where the Spaniards held their line of defense before their downfall. They were only about twenty miles north of Malolos, the capital of the Philippine Revolutionary government, but MacArthur was unfamiliar with the terrain.

In addition, he was ignorant of the strength of the enemy in the area and insisted that there was to be no engagement with the enemy until his army was concentrated and fully stretched between Caloocan to Binondo. His forces camped for the night in Caloocan with no idea what was in store for them.

General Luna gave a passionate address to his military staff. "The enemy believes we are just staying put like rats here in Polo and wait for them to attack us. We have been watching like a hawk every movement made by the American troops in Manila and suburbs. We cannot wait to give them time to deploy more soldiers and artillery against us. We have to take advantage of the element of surprise to achieve total victory."

Thus, with a clear mission in mind, General Luna planned a surprise attack against the American position, which gave him the opportunity to be more aggressive with his military tactics. He pulled out his vicinity map of the war zone and spread it on the ground.

The general plan, as visualized by General Luna and his staff and approved by the President, was for Filipino forces to attack from three different directions: advancing from the east were the forces from General Licerio Geronimo, from the south were Generals Miguel Malvar and Pio del Pilar, while the responsibility to surround and harass the Americans main garrison at Caloocan from the north was assigned to the brigade of General Mariano Llanera. Lastly, the *Sandatahans*, the armed guerrillas disguised as civilians and men working for the Manila waterworks, remained inside the city limits.

Since the Americans did not expect the Filipinos to attack so soon after the battle of Caloocan, Luna ordered the *Sandatahans* to camouflage attack by setting fire to a building, which would definitely attract the attention of the American forces to assist in putting the fire out.

The huge fire and its smoke was the signal to start the three-pronged attack by the revolutionary forces.

Meanwhile, General Pantaleon Garcia, with his two battalions from the Manila regiments and a battalion from Bulacan under Colonel Pacheco Soriano, marched toward the extreme right of his position in the west towards Maypajo and into downtown Manila.

Colonel Hizon's brigade composed of two companies from Pampanga under Major Canlas and four companies from the Kawit Battalion under Captain Pedro Janolino coming from the East—whose mission was to advance his forces toward the American forces—occupied Blockhouse 2 and the Binondo Cemetery. Once the area was secured, he advanced his troops towards San Lazaro. Colonel Aguino's men composed of six companies from Tarlac followed suit and, in turn, marched towards Manila via Sampaloc, where his troops merged with General Garcia's coming from San Juan passing through Calle Alix.

According to plan, on February 22 at around 10:00 in the evening, houses in the Santa Cruz district blazed with flames reading high up into the air. Thinking the fire was accidental in nature, it did not take long for the Americans to rush troops to save the neighborhood that commanded the highest price, and was the gathering place for locals to buy and sell merchandise, as well as being valued for the importance as a point of trading with huge warehouses that made it easy for goods to be transported through the *cascos* or boats moored along canals and Pasig River.

The Binondo market went up in flames very fast, so Colonel Lucio Lucas and his men advanced their prime objective, the *Meisic* police station manned by a detachment of American troopers. However, they were intercepted at Calle Azcarraga by a large company of American soldiers on their way to assist with the fire. In hand-to-hand combat, they broke through an American detachment and eventually managed to elude the enemy.

Colonel Lucio Lucas, a protégée of General Luna, was the first high-ranking revolutionary officer to be arrested a month later by the Bureau of Information. The bureau was a new secret service division created by General Elwell Otis responsible for finding meetings by insurgents and for searching and tracking down any subversives working against the military and government of the United States. It was manned by Lieutenant Charles Trowbridge, a combat veteran of the Eleventh Cavalry, and assisted by four Americans and a group of paid Filipino informers.

At the same time, Colonel Francisco Roman, commanding a company of revolutionary soldiers and assisted by Major Rosendo de Pajarillo and his forces, quietly marched in the dark through the swamp lands of Tondo ready to hit the left flank of MacArthur's forces stationed in Pritil not far from Calle Jolo. Upon reaching their destination, they dug themselves into makeshift trenches and waited for the signal of fire.

Not long after, rows of *nipa* huts along the tramway began to burn, and when a large group of American soldiers approached to investigate the cause of the fire, a barrage of gunfire forced them to retreat. The Filipinos shouted out with joy and pride as they watched the Americans run away. "Long live the Philippines! Down with the Americans!"

Major Pajarillo and his forces had infiltrated the rear of the American lines and pushed them toward Calle Ascarraga, while Colonel Roman's group rushed deep into Calle Jolo. In their attempt to cross the Puente de *España* and into the sanctuary of the Fort Santiago, the Americans were contained on the north side of the Pasig River. And it was only when reinforcements arrived that Colonel Roman's band of brothers were driven back. Their limited ammunition hampered what could have been a victory for them. But instead, they retreated through the marshes of Tondo.

Meanwhile, with very little supply of ammunition left, Paco Roman and his men while withdrawing encountered an American detachment of khaki-clad troopers. A vicious struggle raged at close hand, giving them the opportunity to empty out their revolvers. That struggle was followed by hand to hand combat, each man prepared to kill without blinking an eye. Colonel Roman eventually drew his saber and cut off the head of an enemy. It made him sick watching the blood gush out that was no different than slicing a chicken's neck.

It did not take long for the Americans to realize they were outnumbered, and they ran back to rejoin their battalion. The scrimmage also gave Colonel Roman the chance to continue the withdrawal of his troops back to camp, but not before they scrounged the area for cartridges from the three dead Filipinos and eight American troopers left behind.

Francisco Paco Roman was three years younger than General Luna and was born in Alcala, Cagayan Province. His father was a Spaniard who was an authorized distributor of the tobacco monopoly in his province, who married a Filipina and together with Paco became successful owners of a tobacco factory in Tondo, Manila. Paco Roman married a Spanish mestiza Juliana Piqueras and had two children, Juan and Carmen. In 1896, he joined the Spanish military in battle against the Katipunan, but after the Spanish-American War, he assisted in funding the Filipino revolutionary cause and eventually linking with General Luna in the *Academia Militar*. He eventually invited his first cousins Rafael and José Palma to assist Luna in running the revolutionary newspaper, *La Independencia*.

The surprise attack and battle skirmishes demonstrated by Colonel Roman and his company of men against the Americans the night before had given General Luna a new sense of confidence. More than ever, Luna was convinced that the best plan of attack was to wear down the enemy to a point of collapse by slowly delaying their march to the north of Luzon until the heavy typhoon season hit in July.

CHAPTER 58

Until then, in the vicinity of Caloocan, General Luna and his troops remained rested and confined in their makeshift barricades. Whether considered crazy or brave, General Luna continued to risk his life moving around the various military posts and inspecting battle formations. At the same time, he checked on the welfare of his troops and at times, joined them in battle. His presence gave them the inspiration and confidence to fight.

There was only one exception when General Luna spotted a group of soldiers sloppily dressed and bickering at each other. He dismounted his white horse and began horsewhipping them to get their attention and to manage control.

"You are all behaving and dressed like dogs fighting in street corners, while we have our brothers at this very minute fighting and even dying in the streets of Santa Cruz and Tondo," he said.

The horse-whipped soldiers did not utter a single word, but instead stood at attention, accepted their punishment, and apologized to their general. He then looked into their eyes with compassion, for some of them would never make it back home.

"You were all told how important discipline is to the military, and adhering to our uniform policy is one of them," General Luna said and then rode back to his command post in dismay at the conduct and discipline his forces needed in battle the following morning against the Americans.

Taking advantage of their higher terrain, the revolutionary army's signal to attack was made at early dawn by firing their only Single Krupp breech-loading cannon with a six-inch projectile weighing 80 pounds. Manned by Spanish volunteers, they fired upon MacArthur's forces at Caloocan specifically the Higgins House, which was now the temporary headquarters of General MacArthur.

General MacArthur and his staff were sitting under the shade of an abaca tree not far from the Higgins house on the foothills surrounded by stone fences in a state of disrepair. They had just finished a heavy breakfast of ham, sausage, eggs, and fried rice and were about to smoke Cuban cigars they brought from when they were in Havana. In a few minutes they were engulfed in a dense cloud of dust.

Although the weather was more than normally hot and humid, and realizing that it might only be another day of diversion attack coming from the Filipinos, General MacArthur ordered his own counterattack with fresh troops and additional artillery. He did not care how many sorties it would take and was convinced he would demolish the enemy. The singular artillery Krupp firing at them earlier was now neutralized by American counter-battery fire. The Americans captured their cannon. Even so, shaken by setbacks and continuous loss of territory, the battle was far from over for the Filipinos.

As American pressure increased, more bombs from seven American batteries lined up along their field of battle holding over twenty-five cannon guns, which rained upon the brave Filipinos, who began to reel and fall from their wounds. Some men were even cut in half as a result of shells bursting around them. General Luna ordered his men to hold their fire and remained slouched in their trenches in order to try and outlast the cannonade.

However, despite the fact that most of the bombing passed over their heads and missed their target, the waiting brought down the morale of the Filipinos. They were restless and chaffing in the hot sun, but also gratified to be alive. That is, until the Americans got within shooting distance and the order came from Luna for his men to attack toward their next offensive line of trenches.

An outburst of firepower was exchanged between them, rapid machine gun fires rattling like a hundred snakes, bullets hissing overhead or ricocheting on rocks—all of which created a deafening racket on the ears of the soldiers on both sides of the battle.

In one instant, as the result of the thunderous disturbance and commotion, a company of MacArthur's troops ran full force into a volley of shots from Spanish Mauser rifles at the hands of General Luna's vanguard troops hiding from behind a row of bamboo thickets, north of the main train depot in Caloocan. The synchronized attack seesawed back and forth in savage hand to hand fighting, and the toll on both sides was staggering. Many soldiers never made it home again.

Meanwhile, Filipino forces camouflaged by black smoke and rows of bamboo thickets returned safely back to camp for more ammunition, but then came out again as American shelling continued for the whole day.

By the following day, General Luna ordered his army to move northward toward the flat lands of Bulacan and to readjust their defenses. The ambitious counterattack planned by General Luna, although feasibly a good one, faltered for lack of support from the revolutionary government in Malolos, insubordination and unclear communication in the field of battle and overwhelming firepower by the enemy.

General Luna sent his report via telegram to President Aguinaldo. He cited the heroism and courage of all those involved in the counterattack that successfully pushed the Americans back to their original positions. He stated victory would have been complete except for the right wing of General Garcia's brigade who could not get past MacArthur troops by the Higgins House due the fact that the troops from Kawit Cavite failed to understand the importance of the battle plan and did not attack.

CHAPTER 59

The newly promoted Major Eugenio Hernando was a twenty-two year old medical doctor in the Spanish army before he volunteered to fight on the side of the Filipinos. When he arrived, Luna appointed him Chief of Staff of his General Headquarters.

When called upon, he narrated the incident to the general pertaining to the insubordination of Captain Janolino's command. "During the battle, the companies from Pampanga exhausted all their gun power and in as much as the time had come to attack, Captain Janolino was ordered to advance with four companies of the Kawit Battalion and jointly, with the companies from Pampanga, attack the enemy at the point of bayonet and drive them away."

Hernando paused, and General Luna nodded for him to continue.

"General, we were surprised, when upon receiving the order, Captain Janolino told us that he could not obey our orders, for he had been instructed to obey only General Aguinaldo. I immediately informed Colonel Hizon of the attitude and inflexible resistance that the soldiers from Kawit put forward, and our indignation knew no bounds. The battle was lost in our sector. In our other sectors, the movement was a little bit delayed and it was also not successful."

General Luna became increasingly angry as he listened and soon became so berserk that he ordered an immediate conference with his most trusted staff. "Major Hernando, I demand Major Pajarillo and his premier squad report to my office in 1000 hours."

"Yes, sir," Hernando rushed out of the General's office to summon Pajarillo.

"How do we reprimand Captain Janolino?" Luna asked Roman and Alejandrino when they showed up at the specified time.

"I would send him to jail awaiting a court martial," Colonel Roman said.

"Yes, you need to make an example of him," Alejandrino advised.

"As soon as Pajarillo and his men get here, let's all head to Balintanwak so I can personally make an example of the son of a bitch. I'll shoot him right between his eyes with one shot."

"You're not serious," Alejandrino said, stunned by Luna's extreme reaction.

"Yes, he is," Colonel Roman replied.

"Janolino is a coward," Luna said determinedly.

A short while later, they rode toward Balintawak to reprimand Captain Janolino. Upon their arrival, Luna's staff tried once more to talk him out of shooting Janolino.

"General, please hear me out. Captain Janolino's offense calls for a trial by military court martial and if you take the matters into your hands, then you become as guilty as the accused," Major Hernando said.

"General Luna, besides, there are only nineteen of us against four companies of soldiers from the president's hometown of Kawit. We don't know how they would react to what you are about to do," Colonel Roman said.

"Yes, my general, let the two Aguinaldos take care of their own people, and send them to the president," Major Hernando suggested.

Alejandrino clasped his hand on Luna's shoulder. "My friend, don't gamble your life on a coward. He is not worth it. You are too valuable to lose. We need you for the revolution."

Luna let out a long breath. "All right, all right, you win. I'm not going to shoot him, but I still intend to reprimand him personally."

They began to walk into the encampment of the Kawit regiment toward Captain Janolino's *nipa* hut, but he must have been warned of their arrival because Jamolino was standing outside his hut waiting for them.

General Luna walked and stopped about meter in front of the taller Janolino, who did not even bother to salute. "Stand at attention, Captain," Luna ordered.

Janolino walked towards the general with a smirk on his face.

Luna did not take kindly to his insolent attitude, and he slapped him with the back of his hand so hard that Jaonlino's head snapped backward.

Everyone watching was stunned.

Major Pajarillo and squad immediately surrounded Janolino and Luna with their rifles pointing toward the soldiers from Kawit who witnessed the incident making sure no one interfered with the general's actions.

"We come here to reprimand Captain Janolino only for insubordination, and we demand that none of you get involved." Colonel Alejandrino shouted to the crowd of soldiers.

Captain Janolino covered his left cheek where the general's hand had landed and listened to Luna's orders.

"Captain, as you are aware, it is customary in the military for a subordinate to respect and salute a senior officer. You have not only acted disrespectfully toward me, but also willingly disobeyed the orders of your commanding officer when you failed to attack the enemy yesterday morning in Caloocan. You are therefore being charged by the president and the High Command for insubordination and discreditable conduct unbecoming to an officer of the Philippine revolutionary forces."

General Luna then asked Major Hernando to read Captain

Janolino's directions to follow, which was that he and his men head back to Aguinaldo's Headquarters were he would be disarmed for improper conduct and insubordination and placed under house arrest.

General Luna mounted his horse and cried out to the officers and men of Kawit. "In the future, whoever disobeys the orders of any senior officer may immediately incur the death penalty by facing a firing squad."

Luna and his men then rode away to return to his headquarters, leaving Captain Janolino behind to await his fate. They returned to the headquarters at Polo, and the next day the companies from Kawit were relieved from Balintawak and placed more to the rear. Eventually, they were let go for misconduct and sent to a third zone to a different unit under different leadership in lieu of proper punishment.

CHAPTER 60

By this time, Luna was incredibly frustrated with his career on two fronts. First, he was disillusioned with Aguinaldo and the lack of support for Luna's military efforts. Luna always admired the president, but with each new decision Aguinaldo was faced with regarding military strategy, Luna began to lose faith in his leader.

Luna considered that perhaps Aguinaldo was jealous of him. Luna made a great impact on the men underneath him, as well as a reputation for a committed and fearless officer. At the same time, Luna was well aware of how little control he had over some officers close to Aguinaldo, causing him to exclaim more than once: "I hate them because they hate peace, order, and justice!"

The second major problem that Luna faced was the fact that the organization within the army did not grow as he had anticipated. He had great plans for mobilizing his men and their fighting strategy, but even though some officers were extremely loyal to Luna, he did not have the kind of respect and loyalty from enough of the officers to lead effectively.

Luna's frustration became so intense that he handed in his resignation, which was initially returned to him by Aguinaldo, who promised Luna that the miscreants would duly punished. When they were not, Luna insisted on his resignation. But after some months of watching from the sidelines, he burned to lead again. But he waited until he returned to service on his own terms and under the most opportune circumstances.

Since the outbreak of war, the U.S. forces had continued bombardment of the towns around Manila, burning and looting whole districts. And so it went during Luna's absence from the field of battle for almost a month. Battle after battle, incident after incident, and the Filipino forces suffered major defeats and setbacks.

Luna realized very soon that quitting and merely watching from the side lines was not the right decision for his county. Consequently, he took a chance and met with President Aguinaldo with the intention of asking for his old post back.

The president reinstated Luna with no questions asked. In fact, he gave Luna even more of a leadership role. He had power over the whole military, which soon came to know that the newly reinstated general was all for doing away with conventional warfare in favor of guerrilla warfare.

From that day forward, Luna woke up with so much hope and thoughts of how to inspire support for the revolution as demonstrated by the poor Filipino masses and the likes of the late Bugallon, Roman, Hernando, Pajarillo, and Alejandrino, all who abandoned their families, businesses, and professions for the cause.

Since Malolos was about to be lost to the Americans, Aguinaldo ordered Luna to fortify a line of defense at Bagbag and Calumpit. Thus on Good Friday, March 31, 1899, the president ordered his military to set everything on fire, beginning with the Malolos Cathedral and its huge silver altar.

For the time being, General MacArthur, somewhat puzzled, rode his black castrated stallion unopposed toward Malolos. The sun was up in the sky almost above his head. It was noon, blazing hot and humid. He felt a great sense of accomplishment until about three miles away from his destination when the dirt road turned uphill. He witnessed the Filipino rebel victims of the cannonade that had rained upon them at first light earlier in the day. There were more than a hundred bodies partially covered in a mantle of dirt and sand mixed with dried out blood with flies swarming all over them. The stench of mangled bodies, eyes shut and others widely opened, laid in a row on the ground following the contour of the trenches that were supposed to protect them. A burial party was organized to gather up the dead for internment by laying them on atop another to save time and shoveling.

By the time the Americans captured the capitol, the town was ablaze and Aguinaldo escaped to San Fernando to energize the reinforcements before the American forces arrived.

As the Americans entered Malolos, they noticed a number of Chinese flags raised and flying over rooftops of houses. This was to inform the Americans that they were Chinese residents and merchants and were non-combatant and neutral about the war, thus sparing Chinese lives and property. In addition, the Americans often hired the services of the young and strong Chinese men to carry heavy supplies, work in the kitchen, and do laundry as they advanced to the battlefront.

Meanwhile, upon the American occupation of Malolos, General Otis called for a meeting with his commanders to determine their next plan of action after having just been advised by the Schurmann Commission about their desire to have the Americans call for a cease fire in order to inject some credibility in their reports to the Filipino people.

"Our forces have been pursuing this crafty so-called Filipino general for months with no real success. I think we have underestimated the battlefield skills of General Luna, a one-time pharmacist, and a man who deserves our admiration. I will be honored to retrieve his sword when he surrenders," General Otis said.

"We outnumber the Revolutionaries and have the greatest artillery in the world at our disposal. You have nothing to worry about," MacArthur responded.

"Of course." General Otis nodded as he took a deep draw of smoke from his cigar and exhaled slowly through his mouth, letting it drift upwards, and with a slight hesitation added, "but I still believe it would be best to stop and refit your troops before proceeding further north."

"Yes, sir," MacArthur replied and wasted no time beginning his soldiers on training and drilling exercises. Since it was the start of the long hot summer season in Malolos, MacArthur made sure his forces were fed and rested well for their next march ahead.

As the top ranking officer, Luna had to reckon with a couple of things: one was of a popular leader who would do anything for his men. On the other hand, many of those same men were jealous of his popularity and power and saw him as a rival. A lesser consequence and none the less important to his reputation was the constant advances of the American military with its dispiriting effect on the men under Luna.

Meanwhile, General Luna, in command of the Philippine revolutionary forces again and with renewed backing from the president, doled out orders with full confidence.

"Major Hernando I want you to facilitate the deployment of some of our troops to Pandi, Hagonoy, and Baliwag with the plan of surrounding American forces when they attack."

"Colonel Alejandrino, I want your company to continue the demolition of all railways and bridges leading to Calumpit. I want MacArthur's forces to toast in our summer heat when they march toward us."

"Yes, sir, and should we dig trenches?" Alejandrino asked.

"Yes, along our defensive line north of the Bagbag River," Luna said.

"Sir, except for a few officers, I don't have enough men to complete the task as fast as you would like." Alejandrino informed the general.

"How many men do you need?" Luna asked.

"About two thousand men with pickaxes, hoes, and shovels," Alejandrino said.

"You will have your men and tools within four days," Luna said.

"Gentlemen, send out patrols scouts at night. We need every piece of intelligence we can get our hands on so we can plan to ambush all American outposts not heavily manned"

General Luna and his staff then proceeded to divide their remaining main forces into two sectors in the defense of Calumpit, one brigade under General Gregorio del Pilar and the other under the command General Mariano Llanera.

CHAPTER 61

General Luna used his influence as an Ilocano, and with the assistance of Pampangenos Colonel Hizon and Alejandrino, began an immediate and extensive recruitment campaign in the provinces of Pampanga and the Ilocos region. His efforts resulted in more than seven thousand new recruits to the revolutionary forces. Most of them were able-bodied Ilocano and Macabebes from Pampanga who served diligently and loyally in the Spanish army.

Colonel Alejandrino was amazed and praised Luna, not only because they were close friend since their European days. Rather, for his ability to reinvent himself after the battle of La Loma. Luna believed there were no world of difference in the battlefield between officers and men, the rich and the poor, the educated and the uneducated. Luna saw them all as equal. Thus the people from the Central plains of Luzon reciprocated in great numbers in the fight for freedom and independence. Alejandrino truly admired Luna for his geniality and capability to plan, lead, and organize—a military genius who would not shy away from his principles and from the common people.

Meanwhile, at the American Headquarters, Elwell Otis was distressed and uneasy because his army volunteers were beginning to complain and wanting to go home. In addition, he worried that his superiors in the United States would start to question his ability in suppressing what he reported to them as mere insurrections were threatening to blow up into war.

Otis blamed the turnabout in control on the cunning and genius of General Luna's military maneuver of attack and retreat and attack all over again, which had now delayed Otis' timetable to control all of northern Luzon before the rainy season. He too began to wonder if General MacArthur may not be up to the job of leading his army alone.

A dispatch was sent to General Henry Ware Lawton in Colombo, Ceylon, begging for his presence in Manila. Because of the critical nature of the situation, Lawton rushed to Manila with his troops. Otis decided to send two expeditions: one was to send 116 officers and 4,473 men under Lawton to march to Nueva Ecija and Bulacan. The second expedition of 4,000 men and officers was led by MacArthur and expected to move north toward Pampanga by rail. The forces would eventually meet at the San Miguel junction.

Lawton's forces left by the end of April and by May 2, they marched into Baliwag. On May 18, the Americans captured San Isidro but were disappointed to discover that Aguinaldo had already fled to his new headquarters in Cabanatuan, Nueva Ecija Province.

MacArthur's division left by the third week of April. By the time he was near to confronting Luna's army, the American general was faced with crossing the Bagdag River.

During the early hours of the battle and under the direct command of General Luna, the Filipino revolutionaries moved forward expanding their coverage of the battlefield with the support of a brigade each commanded by General Gregorio del Pilar and General Mariano Llanera.

The forces of General MacArthur ended up being almost surrounded and under attack on both sides of the river banks by sporadic musket firing and assistance from Luna's marksmen. Challenged by the cross firing from different directions by the Filipino troops in their attempt to encircle them, the Americans forces had no alternative but to deploy in readiness for combat at a right angle to each other.

General Luna could sense his first victory in battle and for the kill, he telegraphed for General Tomas Mascardo, the provincial military commander of Pampanga Province, for reinforcements to assist General del Pilar at the Bagbag River.

"Colonel Roman, send out Major Pajarillo with his men to the front for precise information on how many men and cannons the enemy have and their strategic positions in the field of battle," General Luna ordered.

"Great idea, I will have an answer to your inquiry no later than tonight in time for the grand entrance of General Mascardo's unit," Roman responded.

"Precisely, my friend," Luna replied confidently. "By the way, can someone update me on General Mascardo?"

When informed that General Mascardo had not responded at all, Luna screamed. "What? The future of our struggle falls on his forces. Don't stop contacting the son-of-a-bitch!"

However, it only fell on deaf ears for Luna kept repeatedly ordering General Mascardo via telegraph again and again to deploy his forces to Calumpit, and he just kept ignoring Luna's command and authority toward him, believing that his seniority in the military gave him the right to report directly to his province mate President Aguinaldo.

CHAPTER 62

Instead, General Mascardo moved his troops to Guagua, Pampanga and prepared himself for battle with General Luna in case he asserted his authority on him by force. The enraged and very furious General Luna had no option but to make an example of anyone not following his orders, especially from a high-ranking officer and a friend of the president.

Luna had to find a way to cease the mutinous activities rampant in the military command. He acknowledged that most of the troops had no respect for the chain of command, which included pledging their loyalty to officers from their home province. General Luna was stereotyped as a European-based *ilustrado* and not regarded well by the Caviteños.

General Luna walked into Major Eugenio Hernando's office. "Hernando," he said loudly, and directed the young major. "Go, right now, and immediately gather two companies of sharpshooters, and one section of cavalry and leave at once for Pampanga. Arrest Mascardo and bring him back to me."

Major Hernando thought it was not a wise decision and would only result in further chaos between two adversaries. He cleared his throat and swallowed. And although nervous about what he was going to propose, he spoke up anyway. "My general, you know very well I would do anything you ask of me, but any time now the Americans can charge us, and you would not want your best and most experienced unit missing in action. Instead, let me ride alone and convince General Mascardo that he was wrong and encourage him to expedite his forces to Calumpit."

"You don't expect me to go against my principles, my ideals of what constitutes an efficient military force. On the other hand, it takes a noble man to know when to compromise, and to the extent that MacArthur is practically knocking at my door, I will accept your suggestion."

"I'm out of here, my general." Major Hernando took off with a fresh and fast horse that got him through a number of mesas and canyons along the way to Guagua in no time at all.

About an hour past noon, Major Hernando arrived at the headquarters of General Mascardo. He was disappointed to learn that the general was taking a nap.

"Major de Leon, I come with a very urgent and life-saving message for all of us. Please wake up the general."

"I'm sorry, but the general gave us strict orders not to be disturbed unless the enemy was in sight."

"If you consider General Luna to be his enemy, you'd better wake him up," Major Hernando said.

It did not take but a few minutes for General Mascardo to come out of his room, anxious over General Luna's latest dispatch..

"My deepest apology for disrupting your period of rest, sir, but I come here as a peacemaker. I was able to restrain General Luna from personally coming here to arrest you ..."

"Huh! I believed you just saved his life for we were prepared to fight him all the way," General Mascardo interrupted sarcastically.

"My general, for the good of all, please bear with me. Give me a chance to explain myself."

"Go ahead," Mascardo said.

"What I have to say is something that the president himself would have said to you if he were here, sir. Since President Aguinaldo appointed General Luna as Commander-in-Chief for Operations, he was given the military jurisdiction of Central and Northern Luzon, which the province of Pampanga is part of. Thus, all of your officers and men including yourself fall under his command."

"Excuse me, he may out rank me as the General-in-Chief of Operations, but as the Military Commander of Pampanga…" Mascardo pointed to himself while sitting behind his desk. "I fall under the jurisdiction of the Secretary of War."

Major Hernando realized the futility of arguing with General Mascardo, who was skeptical about Luna's position in the chain of command, and decided not to waste any more valuable time in Guagua. He returned to Calumpit, but not before warning the general of the consequences.

"Sir, fighting one another is detrimental to our revolutionary cause and General Luna is aware of its effect, but no one can control his emotions when he gets mad. I suggest you really think twice before you go against his orders."

This angered Mascardo, and pounding both of his hands on his chest, he stood up and boasted, "Tell your General Luna, that if he has any *cojones* left to come here himself and not send his ordinary messenger to arrest me."

Major Hernando excused himself and by nightfall was back at Calumpit to report the outcome of his mission, deliberately excluding the challenge made by Mascardo to Luna.

"General, but I have not yet given up. I still believe in the power of dialogue for a peaceful solution to the problem," Major Hernando said as he concluded his report.

"And what would that be, Major Hernando? It better be good or you will have no choice but to carry out the orders I gave you this morning."

"Let me submit your written report of the incident to President Aguinaldo. I can leave for Baliwag tonight."

Not wanting to take the gamble of Americans suddenly attacking from the south, General Luna decided not to take the chance to travel north to arrest General Mascardo. While Luna was writing the incident report, Major Hernando had a quick bite of rice with mongo stew offered to him by the general. He was then back on a fresh horse and sped through the night for General Aguinaldo's headquarters in Baliwag.

After reading the incident report of General Luna, the president found himself in a predicament. He either had to disregard Mascardo's act of defiance or have to reprimand his very close friend. Aguinaldo sat behind his desk and wrote a letter of reprimand and punishment for insubordination to General Mascardo. With a heavy heart, he handed the note to Major Hernando and ordered him to update him of Mascardo's reaction.

Major Hernando was back on top of his mount and riding his horse to the fullest, with his primary focus being the reaction of General Mascardo when reading the president's memorandum. By the time Major Hernando arrived in Guagua, the first light of dawn had peaked over the eastern horizon of the central plains of Luzon, partially blocked by the mystical and volcanic Mount Arayat, a complete contrast to defensive military formation in the plaza by the troops loyal to General Mascardo. He was immediately escorted to see Mascardo, and to the delight of Major Hernando, had no other alternative but to submit to a higher authority.

After Major Hernando left for Guagua, the president ordered Felipe Buencamino to Calumpit to pacify and inform Luna of his instructions regarding the matter of General Mascardo. However, before Buencamino got to Calumpit, Colonel Roman got hold of the news that Mascardo not only disregarded Luna's orders, but also of the threat and readiness for armed rebellion. He advised his friend General Luna of the information, suggesting it would not only bring down the morale of his officers and soldiers, but also might affect his reputation and his ability to lead the revolutionary forces.

"Who does he think he is?" General Luna burst out. "I cannot take this any longer!" he turned to Colonel Roman. "You are coming with me, but not a word to anyone until we are on board the train. And Major Hernando, get ready as soon as possible with as many men, artillery, and horses you can spare."

Still dazed and confused from his lack of sleep, Major Hernando had a hunch of what was going on, and sensing Luna's resolve, gave up on his peaceful crusade. He went about and had a special train ready in an hour. He was able to deploy a couple of companies from within the post and decided not to pull anyone from the front line.

On board the train with Luna and the soldiers were Colonel Francisco Roman, Captains José and Manuel Bernal, Major Hernando, and three more officers. It was only then when Luna told them the purpose of their mission: to impose his superior authority over Mascardo.

Disembarking at San Fernando, Luna immediately had Major Hernando proceed to Bacolor with his cavalry so as to secure all exits by making sure no one entered or left. Luna was met at the train station by his brothers José and Joaquin, who pleaded for him to go back to Calumpit and to forgive and forget Mascardo for the greater good and glory of the revolution. The brothers even went to the extent of blocking and grabbing Antonio Luna, preventing him from moving forward. But Luna had them temporarily detained under guard at a nearby railroad car.

On their way to Bacolor, General Luna was once more interrupted, this time by a group of women belonging to The Red Cross Ladies of Bacolor, all begging and some even on their knees, crying, asking for clemency for Mascardo.

"I am sorry," Luna said, "but imposing discipline, for me, is a matter of life or death. So, I leave it all up to General Mascardo whether he submits to my authority or faces the extreme punishment from my forces."

The Red Cross Ladies managed to convince General Luna to give them a chance to talk to Mascardo, and leaving some of their members with Luna, the leaders of the group rushed toward Guagua to negotiate for peace between Filipinos.

Meanwhile, General Luna received an urgent telegram from Calumpit that the Americans had started bombing the revolutionary forces' defensive line along Bagbag and the forces of General Gregorio del Pilar, at Quingua, were now in need of assistance.

Soon after, the ladies were back at Bacolor excited about the news that General Mascardo had agreed to present himself at the Betis town plaza. General Mascardo arrived at the plaza in a carriage surrounded by officers. Luna rode on his horse beside the carriage. General Mascardo stepped out and stood at attention.

"General Mascardo, do you acknowledge me now as your commandant?

"Yes, sir."

"Will you carry out all the directions you receive coming from my command?"

"Yes, sir," General Mascardo added, "I will honor and follow your direction as my commandant. But I swear I did nothing wrong, for I was obeying the orders of President Aguinaldo when he appointed me provincial commander of Pampanga.

"I understand," Luna responded.

"Major Hernando, get into the carriage with General Mascardo to make sure he gets to Aguinaldo's General Headquarters. I will see you both at the San Fernando train depot.

CHAPTER 63

Upon arrival at Calumpit, Luna got another urgent telegram to send assistance to General Gregorio del Pilar. The Americans had deepened their attacks along del Pilar's line of defense. When the battle shifted in favor of the Americans, Luna immediately sent General Mascardo's men by train to assist General del Pilar with a battalion of sharpshooters and a canon.

As General Luna got ready to face the invading Americans with the same officers and troops he deployed with him to Pampanga earlier, his conscience begun to bother him, as he wondered if he had made a big mistake. But his core belief that for an army to be strong, there had to be no substitute to discipline convinced him that he made the right move and would easily defend his actions from any criticism thrown to him by his cowardly detractors in the Cabinet.

General Antonio Luna now rode briskly among his army at the front line of Bagbag, talking to the men, calling them by their names, mingling and making eye contact, and offering words of encouragement.

Reflecting the confidence he transmitted, men were no longer tired, but rather, eager to give a good fight.

The Filipinos had an advantage over the Americans because they knew the topography so well. The Americans had to aim horizontally very close to the ground because if they aimed a little higher they would shoot over the heads of the Filipinos.

Trained to create havoc with sudden, lethal actions, and recoils, Luna's mission was to confuse the enemy. For most of the day, both forces blazed away at each other and in some cases, almost at point blank range, but not for long. The overwhelming number of MacArthur's forces and confusion in the Filipino ranks forced the defenders back. For some in the south flank, the advancing American presence across the river and the extensive attack on the bridge was a bit too much to take. And when almost out of munitions, the Filipinos were forced to retreat and stirred into position into their backup trenches as cannon shells still fell steadily, polluting the air with drifting clouds of smoke and phosphorous.

Sensing that Calumpit was going to be lost, General Luna ordered General Gregorio del Pilar to destroy the railroad bridge over the Bagbag River to prevent the Americans from crossing and slowing down their movement of troops and armaments towards Malolos. General Luna also ordered all telegraph wires cut as they retreated to the north.

Within a short time, the Filipino defenses began to crumble when MacArthur's forces came upon them with all their mighty armaments. By nightfall, Calumpit fell in the hands of the Americans, but only after inflicting much damage to a less-equipped Filipino army.

General Luna was left with no other alternative and again reinforced his next line of defense with the construction of trenches in the town Santo Tomas in Pampanga Province. But to finally put a halt to MacArthur's driving land forces, he traveled to San Isidro, Nueva Ecija Province to garner the full military support of President Aguinaldo.

"Good afternoon Mr. President, Senor Mabini. It's great to confer with both you again." General Luna greeted them.

"How are you doing?" Mabini asked.

"Not well, that's why I am here," Luna said.

"What do you need?" Aguinaldo asked.

"General MacArthur is resting in Calumpit while waiting for his reinforcement of infantry and artillery. We need the same from you, since if we are going to stop MacArthur, it's got to be in Santo Tomas."

"Why there?" Mabini asked.

"By the simple fact that the locality is very defensible, the roadway as well as the railway are like land bridges from Calumpit. Both sides are flanked by swamps, turning the territory into a large funnel, which slows the passage of soldiers.

The president nodded for Luna to continue.

"You have over a thousand soldiers here with you, not counting your Presidential Guards from Kawit. Please deploy a thousand men to Santo Tomas," General Luna said.

President Aguinaldo looked at Mabini for his opinion.

"Can you guarantee us that if MacArthur learns we deployed our defensive forces here to you, he won't change his mind and attack us instead, especially since the road to Santo Tomas is not suitable for his large army," Mabini asked.

General Luna could not help but only nod his head in disbelief of what he just heard. "Mr. President, I can assure you that MacArthur is not going to change his plans. His mind is set on controlling the whole railroad line, all the way to Dagupan. I can most assuredly guarantee that he won't go after you here in San Isdro but will pursue me in Santo Tomas."

"Are you trying to say the Americans are more interested in defeating you than the president?" Mabini smirked.

"No!" Luna raised his voice and said to Mabini. "Don't you get it? MacArthur is not stupid. If he breaks his line and advances here, he opens the door for me to recapture Calumpit."

"All right, I've made my decision," Aguinaldo said. "We need to keep our reserved forces here. I'm sorry, General Luna, but you will have to do with what you have. And also, I'm giving you military control of Pampanga in place of Mascardo," President Aguinaldo concluded.

"At least more ammunitions," Luna pleaded and then realized something was wrong when Aguinaldo and Mabini looked at each other like they were hiding something from him.

"Very well, what's going on here? Don't tell me you refuse to also release arms," Luna said.

"We have bad news for all of us," Mabini said. "We were just notified that the ship transporting our arms and ammunitions from Japan sunk in a typhoon over China Sea."

"Darn it, no way, no way!" Luna exclaimed. "This happened at the worse time for our war!"

"My only consolation to you is that we placed another order and expect the shipment to arrive by the end of June or maybe even earlier," Mabini said.

"And for now we fight them with hatchets, spears, bows, and arrows?" General Luna said sarcastically.

"We fight them the best we can with what we have and then when need be, we retreat," Aguinaldo responded with a note of finality to his voice.

"Understood," Luna said. "We'll try and outsmart the Americans using guerrilla warfare, ambush and sabotage. It's the only way."

Luna sought the support of Apolinario Mabini, who agreed with him that it was now time to maneuver into guerrilla units. Apparently, Aguinaldo did not adhere because he did not act upon the suggestion. However, with the tide of battle turning against him, Luna asked for a ceasefire. Aguinaldo approved Luna's proposal to sue for an armistice with the Americans through the Schurmann Commission. General Luna thought the process would give him the necessary time to organize his forces, wait for the new shipment of arms coming from Japan, and to train his soldiers into the rudiments of guerrilla warfare in time for use against the Americans during the monsoon rains.

President Aguinaldo immediately created a commission headed by Colonel Manuel Arguelles to meet and discuss the armistice among other issues with the Schurmann Commission in Manila. Nevertheless, the Schurmann Commission and General Otis did not agree on the ceasefire and instead asked the Filipinos to completely surrender and only then would they be granted amnesty.

It was not long after the sun had just risen beyond the surrounding hills and valleys, when the mighty American forces led by General MacArthur, after a much needed rest in Calumpit, approached Pampanga. The ground trembled as the sun poured its soft textured light into the river but then began to ripple when MacArthur's division crossed the Rio Grande heading towards Santo Tomas.

CHAPTER 64

Meanwhile, a regiment of volunteers under Colonel Funston arrived at a wooden railroad bridge that spanned between two lagoons near the Santo Tomas train depot. They managed to cross the bridge, slowly one man at a time, when the Filipinos running out of munitions vacated the trenches defending the bridge. Virtually undefended, Funston traversed the bridge with two companies of soldiers as they march toward the railroad station.

The town of Santo Tomas in Pampanga Province was located along the rail route to Dagupan, and it had its own train station made of brick and wood. General Luna, when informed that the company responsible for securing the railroad bridge leading to the train station abandoned their post for lack of ammunition, decided to counterattack the advancing American forces. They remained secretive under cover behind the solid structure of the train station and its adjoining town structures and bamboo thickets.

As the mighty American forces approached, the sound of hooves grew even louder in the ears of the waiting and tense Filipino forces led by General Luna, who was on his white horse behind the railroad station with a detachment of soldiers.

They did not make a move until Funston's men were about 75 meters away. Luna fired a shot and an enemy dropped from his horse, and then the rest of the Filipinos started firing on the attacking American forces.

The exchange of deadly volleys continued until Colonel Funston, the sorely perplexed commander across the river, called for his forces to fall back and take cover behind rows of bamboo trees and started firing back at about 300 meters away.

The American forces would have been shredded if the Filipino forces did not run out of ammunition again. Luna had no alternative but to order a sound retreat making sure he was the last man out of danger.

After a brief exchange of fire, General Luna, still astride on his horse, was shot in the abdomen and fell. His horse spooked, and Luna was left on the ground alone. He crawled a foot and took cover behind a grove of bamboo trees, seriously wounded. He was scared, but also ready to fight and die for his country. He continued firing his revolver until left with only one bullet.

Cold shivers ran down his spine due to the loss of blood and in an attempt to stop the bleeding, Luna clenched his finger muscles hard against the single bullet hole. Shock gave way to confusion, and the thought of the Americans capturing the highest-ranking general of the revolutionary forces made Luna believe he would rather die than be capture.

He pointed the tip of his revolver on his temple and was about to fire the only bullet left in the chamber when he spotted Colonel Alejandro Avecilla heading toward him on a horse. Avecilla was grazed by a bullet in his thigh, but still managed to grab Luna's left hand and with all of his might lifted Luna up onto his horse behind him and galloped out of the line of fire. A red silk belt, which his mother had given him sewn with gold coins inside took the brunt of the bullet and saved Luna's life.

General Antonio Luna had cheated death, and every day after, he thought it was a gift from God. He was promoted to the rank of brigadier-general and received a medal for valor from President Aguinaldo.

Meanwhile, General Venancio Conception temporarily took over his command, headquartered at Angeles, Pampanga. However, General Luna ordered Alejandrino, who was promoted to a general, to lay out and prepare the grounds for his proposed headquarters in Bayambamg, Pangasinan.

CHAPTER 65

Although General Luna was still under medical care, he was continually updated on all military activity. In that way, he was able to still issue orders regarding guerrilla warfare activities done by the Filipinos, who continued harassing the enemy through smaller units in territories formerly lost to the Americans.

General Otis called for a meeting to discuss and evaluate the performance and status of their military operations in the Philippines since the start of the Philippine-American War. The meeting was held at his Malacanang headquarters in Manila.

"Good morning, Arthur. How are you doing?" Otis said to General MacArthur.

"Good morning, sir," MacArthur replied.

"Please sit down. Would you like some coffee?"

"No, thank you. I had coffee earlier," MacArthur said. "You are the first one here. How are Pinky and your sons, Art and Douglas, doing?"

After a few minutes of chatting about MacArthur's family, General Henry Lawton and General Robert Hughes walked in and greeted the rest of the generals already present. After going through a small list of details and items listed on his agenda, General Otis begun to discuss, one by one, the concerns voiced by each of his staff.

MacArthur began. "For four months, my men have been under arms night and day, exposed to a scorching sun almost as destructive and much harder to bear than the enemy's fire. The toll has been so severe and unwavering that many of them are broken in health."

"On the other hand, the enemy is used to the heat of the sun and can march the whole day long with nothing but a handful of rice in their knapsacks. Likewise, they fall asleep anywhere in the rain without getting sick. We lost close to a thousand men to malaria, dysentery, sunstroke, and dehydration."

Major Lawton spoke next. "The Filipinos are a very fine set of soldiers. They are far better than the Indians. The latter never fought unless they had the absolute advantage. The Filipinos are far more advanced. Taking into consideration the few facilities they have, and the many drawbacks, they are a very ingenious and artistic race. I must say that they are the bravest men I have ever seen. These men are indomitable. I am very impressed with the Filipinos."

"But we are winning battles," General Otis asked.

"Yes, but at a great cost because as we move forward, Filipino soldiers seem to appear out of nowhere, dressed as civilians, but fighting like guerrillas in territories we already do," General MacArthur said.

General Hughes added,. "Since the start of the war, our army had moved as far as only 40 miles to the north and less than 20 miles to the south and east of Manila. There is not much to gain. We need more than the 70,000 men we have at present to end this war; and to control all the islands, we may need as many as 120,000 men."

"When I first started in against these rebels, I believed that Aguinaldo's troops represented only a fraction. I did not like to believe that the whole population of Luzon was opposed to us, but having come thus far, and having been brought into contact with both insurgents and *amigos*, I have been reluctantly compelled to believe that the Filipino masses are loyal to Aguinaldo and the government he leads," General MacArthur said.

"Maybe it's about time to change our strategy of conquest from military to political or a combination of both. We can concentrate on all the peace-loving Filipinos and hope they come into our fold. Let them know that we mean well. Let them have an autonomous government under an American governor-general or prime minister," General Otis said.

"And we already have a number of influential Filipino politicians and prominent businessmen on our side. Let's take advantage of them by supporting them to wrest the leadership of their government from the likes of Aguinaldo, Luna, and Mabini." General Otis said, and his face creased into a grin.

"Are you suggesting a cease fire? Listen, give me two regiments, and I will end this war within sixty days. As you are my witnesses, I will even present to you the head of Aguinaldo and his cohorts on a golden platter," Lawton challenged.

General Otis thought for a moment about what he just heard from Lawton, and looking at him and then to the rest of his staff, he laughed.

The disgraced General Lawton never forgot nor forgave Otis for ridiculing him in front of his peers.

It was almost May, and the heavy rainy season would soon be upon the American forces, who were worried about their natural survival. They still had not subjugated the revolutionary forces of the new Philippine Republic led by General Luna, which they vowed never to recognize, especially when the so-called Filipino "Americanistas" were beginning to approach them with ideas on how to end the war amicably.

On May 5, 1899, the Schurman Commission proposed what they called "autonomy" for the Philippines, but the U.S. president would hold absolute power. On cue with the Americans, the pro-autonomy Filipinos led by Pedro Paterno and Felipe Buencamino and a number of prominent Filipino businessmen all clamored for peace and had no problem surrendering the country to American sovereignty. The remaining partisan members of the Philippine Congress held in Malolos met and accepted the offer made by the Commission, and at the same time dissolved the Mabini-led cabinet. They voted for a new cabinet under Pedro Paterno and Felipe Buencamino as the new Secretary of Foreign Affairs.

This sudden and latest development gave President Aguinaldo no alternative but to approve and recognize the formation of a new cabinet, forcing Mabini to dissolve his own cabinet.

Pedro Paterno replaced Mabini on May 7, 1899, which ushered in the start of a favored Philippine autonomy under the tutelage of the United States. The new Cabinet did not waste much time to propagate their cause and spread the news to the Filipino masses that peace with the Americans had been declared. Paterno also appointed a commission of nine members, chaired by his Secretary of Foreign Affairs, to negotiate with the Americans.

Even TH Pardo went to the extent of launching *La Democracia*, a daily newspaper, for the purpose of promulgating peace with the Americans, the separation of church and state, Philippine autonomy with representation in the U.S. Congress and eventual admission as a state in the American Union.

CHAPTER 66

Like Mabini, Antonio Luna was very vocal against entering into any deal with the Americans. He was a man with vision, integrity and courage who vehemently advocated a fight to the finish for independence. So it drove him crazy to sit around all day and night recuperating from his wound confined to his bedroom at his headquarters.

One evening, Luna was entertaining his confidant, Major Hernando who had dropped by for a visit. Not long after, a very excited General Alejandrino walked in to update Luna on what had just transpired with the Malolos Congress led by Pedro Paterno.

"Good evening," Major Hernando said and stood at attention and saluted General Alejandrino.

"General Luna, you won't believe what I have just heard from Manila," said Alejandrino.

"Major Hernando and I were partaking of *basi*. Would you want a glass of this Ilocos region wine? You will be surprised what it takes to brew a jar of this very exquisite wine."

"I am not fond of *basi*, but for being a messenger of bad news, I might have to consume the whole jar."

"Go ahead with the disturbing news from Manila," Luna said, while Major Hernando handed General Alejandrino a glass full of rice wine.

"Paterno and Buencamino managed to convene Congress with mostly partisan members, and they have mustered enough votes to overthrow Mabini's cabinet. They also appointed a new cabinet with Paterno as president and Buencamino as foreign secretary." Alejandrino chuckled to himself, turning his head from side to side to address both Luna and Hernando.

"Oh, no! We've got to get rid of those leaches, pronto," Luna responded.

"Listen to this," Alejandrino continued. "The cabinet led by Paterno intends to approve the autonomy proposal of the United States Secretary of State Hays on behalf of the Filipino people, and through the Schurmann Commission."

"Son of a bitches! What a bunch of crap. I hope Aguinaldo realized that he is now surrounded and advised not only by leaches, but also by traitors to the country!" Luna said. Barefooted, he stood up and walked toward the corner of the room and bent to pick up his pair of boots. "Ouch!" Luna grimaced in pain, but still managed to pull his boots on.

"Oh my God, Paterno did it again. He brokered the Biak-na-bato deal with the Spaniards against the Katipunan and now this Schurmann deal with the Americans against the freedom-loving people of the Philippines," Major Hernando protested.

"Yes, but this time we are going to make sure they don't succeed. We have to find all means to stop them, even to the point of having them arrested, tried, and executed for sedition and treason," General Luna said, striding from one end of the room to the other wiping his fingers on the back of his pants.

"Wait a second, what was Aguinaldo's reaction?" General Luna asked.

"He recognized the new cabinet and forcibly coerced Mabini to dissolve his own cabinet," Alejandrino said. "He had no other choice."

"Well, where does he stand on Secretary Hay's proposal?" Luna asked as he shook his dead in disbelief.

"He did not commit to the cabinet, but he agreed to pursue further negotiations with the commission."

"Aha! To pursue further negotiations when he should instead have all the coward autonomist, Americanistas, and recalcitrants faced against a wall and shot in the back as traitors," General Luna yelled, shaking his fists and bursting with uncontrollable emotions.

There was an intensity in General Luna's eyes that Alejandrino had not seen before, and it scared him. "Antonio," advised Alejandrino, "you need to do your best to control your emotions and temper. There are people who have started labeling you as another madman, like your brother."

"By people, do you mean like the autonomist American lapdog Pardo, who had been against my family ever since the incident with his sister and mother?" General Luna laughed sarcastically. "What he has to say does not mean anything to me."

"Yes, but he also talks against you with the president, the cabinet members, and some of the Old Turks of the revolution," Alejandrino said.

"I don't give a shit about them. I may be frail, but no one will ever break my will to fight on." Luna shook his head from left to right. "What's wrong with the president? When will he ever stand up to his word?

General Luna was convinced that Aguinaldo's mind no longer dictated his actions.

"Why does he always have to switch from one side to the other? Due to his character flow, his weakness, we have not been able to instill complete discipline in our military and unity among ourselves, politically and militarily," Luna said.

Luna paused. "However, who else but Aguinaldo has the prestige and is in the position to handle both branches? Aguinaldo is evil, but nevertheless, a necessary evil. We have to work with him."

"Meanwhile, Major Hernando, I have been on a sick bed and away from my men for three months and I am ready to fight again. Get my gear ready first thing tomorrow morning and send a telegram to all pertinent officers and to the president of my return to active duty."

"But, my general, you are in no condition to travel. First, you need to be cleared by the medics."

"You are my medic," Luna said and grinned. I just gave you an order. They have not heard the last of me. We are back in business."

CHAPTER 67

On May 27, 1899 at the Presidential Quarters at Cabanatuan, Nueva Ecija Province, General Antonio Luna walked into the meeting room to discuss the proper steps to be taken by the cabinet during the transition to autonomy, which he opposed. Looking around the room, he was clearly and incredibly uneasy with the people invited to attend the meeting. Besides General Gregorio del Pilar and the cabinet secretaries, also invited were TH Pardo, Cayetano Arellano, and Colonel Manuel Arguelles, who were now on the side of autonomist.

Things were initially cordial, but hostilities inside the room turned sour by the minute. Tempers flared and men began arguing loudly, their emotions to the boiling point, especially when Buencamino stood up to defend and justify the position and conduct taken by the cabinet members. And General Luna confronted the cabinet members on the issue of autonomy. "We should not be influenced by the enemy just because of the color of their skin or the size of their wallet. Think about it! To be ruled by Americans will be as intolerable as the Spaniards, or maybe even worse. I see no reason why we cannot rule ourselves."

"Or be ruled by you," Buencamino rebutted.

Luna shot up, walked toward Buencamino, and pointing his index finger at him yelled, "I hope you understand that to compromise with the enemy is treason and the beginning of a new era of slavery and suffering!"

"And you, General Luna," Buencamino responded with rage. "You were responsible for the defeat and deaths of so many of our countrymen. My own son perished when you abandoned your post at Bagbag for your own satisfaction and personal gain."

Being blamed for the death of his beloved soldiers who fought in Bagbag infuriated Luna. He slapped Buencamino and knocked him down on the floor and said, "You are an autonomist, a traitor, and a shame to the memory of your son, Joaquin, who volunteered to serve with me and died as a hero for the price of freedom and liberty."

President Aguinaldo and his aide, Colonel Sityar, immediately jumped between the two men, and as they were being separated, Buencamino threatened Luna. "This is the end of you. Your conduct here will cost you big some day."

Felipe Buencamino was a plump man no more than fifty-five years of age. He had once been an ardent defender of Spanish rule and of the friars and a commander of the militia set up by Spain to fight the Americans. Captured by Filipino revolutionary forces, he immediately became an advisor and speechwriter for President Aguinaldo and now was a leading proponent for American rule.

"Please, trust me just this once." Luna pleaded to the Paterno-led cabinet members in the meeting chaired by President Aguinaldo. "We are starting to see public opinion in Europe and the United States sway to our side."

General Luna pulled out a news clipping from his pocket and held it up so the gathering could see it. "This is an interview given by the famous American author, Mark Twain on where he stands on the issue of subjugation. Mr. Twain made the following comments: 'We have gone there to conquer, not to redeem. It should, it seems to me, be our pleasure and duty to make those people free and let them deal with their own domestic questions in their own way. And so I am an anti-imperialist. I am opposed to having the eagle put its talons on any other land.'

In addition," Luna continued, "I also have read the treaty of Paris very carefully, and I have concluded that the people of the Philippines are certain to be under subjugation forever if we don't change our course of action.

After much discussion, the majority of the cabinet members decided that since the issue was complicated and not clear enough, a committee chaired by the Secretary of Foreign Affairs needed to be set up to determine the strengths and weaknesses of the Schurman Commission's proposal, but all efforts by the Cabinet had been toward ending the war and regaining a peaceful coexistence in the country.

General Luna became more and more angry and could not take what he heard in the room. He stood up with slow deliberation and said, "I cannot bring myself to believe that there are individuals within our midst who would do anything to collaborate with the enemy for their own personal gain."

A loud protest was heard inside the room from most members of the cabinet, who were appalled by the accusations made by Luna. They addressed their concerns to President Aguinaldo that the general was out of line and should be censured.

"General Luna, we are here to discuss what would be best for our countrymen and if you don't have the patience or cannot control your emotions in our open discussions, then it would be best for you to excuse yourself," the president said.

"Forgive me, Mr. President, I will take your advice and leave. But I have one more thing to say since we are gathered together."

"Have your say," Aguinaldo said.

"I would like to have an investigation as to the sinking of the vessel that carried our arms from Japan," Luna said.

"Explain yourself," the president said.

Luna nodded. "Most of us have experienced taking the same

shipping route, one way or another, through thick and thin fog, rough and calm seas, stormy days and nights. But then without warning, the one steamer carrying arms for the Filipinos all of a sudden sinks during a typhoon in the South China Sea." General Luna shook his head from left to right in disbelief. "Come on, for God's sake, don't you think that merits an investigation from us?"

"No, not for a natural disaster at sea. What are you implying?" Pedro Paterno asked.

"Those rifles and ammunitions meant as much to those of us who cherish independence from foreign rule as the Americanistas and the defeatists, who in our mist loved the sinking of the vessel."

"Who do think you are?" Pardo stood up and shouted back at Luna. "You are a madman like your brother."

"If you don't conduct an investigation, then I will conduct my own because there must be a traitor, a Judas Iscariot within our ranks!" Luna shouted back.

A clamor of boisterous protests and indignations by leaders of the Paterno-led Congress continued from inside the meeting room when General Luna left. Unknown to them, a certain Lieutenant Colonel John Mallory from the Forty-first Infantry had been detailed as one of the officers to obtain military information abroad and serving as military attaché in the American Legation in Peking received a tip from someone in Hong Kong about an arms shipment ready to be delivered to the Philippines. He immediately relayed the message to the U.S. Secretary of War.

Knowing in which direction the majority of the cabinet was going to vote with the issue, Luna lost his head and called everybody a traitor, including the president. As soon as Luna left, President Aguinaldo called for the meeting to be adjourned and excused everyone out of the room except for some key cabinet members and advisors who he was certain were loyal. Behind closed doors, they proceeded to further deliberate the serious matter pertaining to General Antonio Luna. The president had been falsely informed that Luna was planning a coup d'etat. And Luna's rage made it easy for the president to believe that

Luna wanted to oust him.

"Who does he think he is, making demands as if he is the president instead of you?" Buencaminino said.

"We know the problem. I want a solution," President Aguinaldo said as he looked around the room for the first man to respond.

"Mr. President," Buencamino said. "More than once, General Luna has disobeyed you. When you asked him for a regiment, he did not comply until the enemy was on hand. He did not comply when you told him not to confront General Mascardo in San Fernando. I am warning you, he will not stop until he takes over your chair as president!"

"Are you trying to imply that we should condemn a man for his ambition?" the president said, staring at Buencamino.

"But even your presence did not stop him from slapping Mr. Buencamino, your loyal minister. And if you had not interceded, he wanted to arrest all the members of your cabinet," Pardo said.

"He will go on doing things his own way because he believes that only he has the power to dictate to the army. And now wants to have the power—your power—to dictate to the entire country!" Buencamino gestured toward the president. "General Luna is turning to be a very dangerous man." He paused and looked directly at each man sitting in the room, ending with the president. "He is guilty of sedition and has to be either exiled or condemned to death."

Although President Aguinaldo had doubted in the past the validity of all the intrigues presented to him against General Luna, the latest revelations affected him to the point of distancing himself from Luna and his allies. In the days that followed, the president had Luna's senior officer of the military quarters in Cabanatuan transferred to another unit because he was known to be a Luna sympathizer. Aguinaldo was secretly undermining and making decisions contrary to the recommendations and ideals of General Luna. He even had Luna's closest friends, especially the two generals from the Pampanga province, Maximino Hizon and José Alejandrino, closely watched by his secret agents.

At the same time, the propaganda promulgated by the proautonomist Filipinos against General Luna immediately started in full swing all over Manila. Rumors that Luna had now taken over the command of the military and of the government were being spread around. In fact, at one point, rumor was that Luna was the new dictator and that Aguinaldo was fighting back with the support of his old compatriots.

Another rumor was that of an anonymous letter received by Apolinario Mabini earlier that Antonio Luna was the one responsible for the Spanish execution of José Rizal, that he was now out of control, acting like a madman, ordering the summary arrests and executions of Filipinos, and that he had lost the confidence and respect of most officers and soldiers because of his arrogance and showmanship and madness.

CHAPTER 68

Fully aware that he had stepped on the toes of his fellow revolutionaries, Luna knew that he was walking on thin ice. But he had no regrets hitting the son-of-a-bitch. In fact, he felt good and given the chance, he would hit him again.

On his way back to Bayambang in Pangasinan after the meeting in Cabanatuan, Luna stopped by Paniqui in Tarlac to spend the night at Sidra's house. Frustrated with everything that happened at General Headquarters, he blurted out all of his problems, ending with the incident that when he hit Buencamino.

"Why did you do that for?" Sidra said annoyed.

"Because the man is a traitor! He is pro-American and should be pro-Filipino," Luna said. "They want me to be calm and not get emotional, but how can I not get angry when they betray our quest for sovereignty."

Sidra shrugged. "You still cannot lose your temper whenever you think you have been wronged. What happens if I disagree with you? Will you hit me too?"

Antonio kicked at the floor. "Enough of this. I am bone-tired," he said, and went into the bedroom.

A short while later, Sidra regretted the way she responded to Antonio. She realized how much the success of the Philippine revolution meant to him. She followed him to the bedroom, closed the door, and slowly climbed into bed next to him. "Are you awake?" she asked softly.

Antonio's back was turned to her but he moved slightly.

Sidra put her arm on his shoulder. "I'm sorry, Antonio, if I upset you."

"It's frustrating, like there is nothing left for me. But it's okay. Let's both get some sleep now," he said.

An hour had passed, and thinking Sidra was fast asleep, Antonio stood up from bed and went to the wooden desk at the corner of the room. He wrote his last will and testament that left everything he owned to his loving mother. In case he got killed in battle, he wanted his body wrapped in the Filipino flag and he wanted to remain in the same clothes as when killed. Lastly, he wanted everyone to know that he had died willingly for his country and for its independence.

Luna pocketed the document inside the side coat pouch of his uniform. It started to rain. He stood up and walked toward an open window and gazed outside at the dark sky through a couple of overgrown banana trees. He wondered about his destiny and that of his country, and thought about it for a long time. He looked sorely disappointed. He saw fireflies glowing in the dark. He smiled.

But all the while, Sidra was still awake. Tears dripped onto her pillow as she gazed at Antonio, and thinking that she was going to have his baby. But how could she break such news to him that he was going through so much. She was so happy about her pregnancy, and wanted to know that he would be joyous as well. But for now, she closed her eyes again, thinking that she would just have to wait for another day.

Within a matter of days after the slapping incident in Cabanatuan, Colonel Joaquín Luna, Antonio's brother, traveled to Bayambang to warn him about a rumor he had heard from close friends. They told Joaquin about a plot pertaining to a group of pro-American revolutionaries who were bent on accepting autonomy under American sovereignty in order to stop the suffering of the Filipino people and the existing terror and rampage destroying the peaceful coexistence of the country. Included in the conspiracy was a clique of army officers whom Luna had disarmed and arrested.

"And the strangest of them all, the Revolutionary Army may be splitting and leading into a civil war between two factions," Joaquin said. "The new elements of the revolution led by you and the old elements that fought the Spaniards are for Aguinaldo."

"I feel sorry for them. They don't know anything." Antonio shrugged off the threats. "Aguinaldo has no idea what's going on in the battlefield. He only depends on the advice from a battery of leeches to assist him in making military and political decisions."

"But according to them, the tenor of the telegrams of Aguinaldo to General Tinio asking for his support mentions a serious plot against you. And that I find very credible."

"There is really nothing to fear. I have heard many rumors against me in the past, but they have always amounted to nothing but a plain simple case of intrigue, which resulted in me being promoted. Hey, you might be looking at the next premier and secretary of war."

Joaquin shook his head. "This time your things are very different. You have a lot of people angry with you."

"What do you think happens after you die? Your life is not over; maybe it has not even started." He suddenly corrected himself. "You know how it goes, dear Joaquin, one should not fear death, because one way or another, we are all going to die," Antonio said. But don't worry. I won't go after death because the longer I stay alive, the closer I get to accomplishing my objectives for our country."

"Then be very careful and watch your back at all times. I will keep you updated if I hear of anything more."

"Joaquin, the big secret is not taking things too seriously. Again, don't worry, and let me handle any rumors in my own way," Antonio said. "President Aguinaldo appreciates all that I have done for him, his army, and the country, just as I appreciate him, too."

The brothers hugged for a long time without saying a word, as if this was the last time together. They bade farewell.

CHAPTER 69

The following day, General Luna and General Alejandrino continued designing plans for guerrilla tactics and defenses, the preparation of trenches, and the fortifications of Pangasinan where Luna suspected the Americans were planning a landing from Lingayen Gulf. After working the whole day, inspecting troops at the front line and the construction of trenches, General Luna had high hopes that he would soon be promoted. Luna invited his military staff composed of General Alejandrino, Colonel Roman, Major Hernando, Major Simeon Villa, Captain Eduardo Rusca, Major Manuel Bernal, and Captain José Bernal for dinner at his office.

Waiting to eat, they all sat in conversation on the porch outside Luna's office when one of them asked the general about his relationship with José Rizal. The question brought back so many great memories of his time in Europe.

"I found him to be a very extraordinary man. He was far beyond us in stature." General Luna gestured towards Alejandrino. "My friend here can attest to that since he also knew him well."

"Most of us have read his novels and writings and were so amazed by his passion for Spanish colonial reforms one for the betterment of the Filipino people and the country as a whole. His stand on progressive reforms knew no bounds. He might not have known, but he inspired us so we listened with respect and conviction to his ideals. We were ready to follow him in his crusade for a peaceful revolution."

"General, perhaps this is the time to dispel the rumor of your role in the execution of Rizal that's been going around. We don't believe them to be true and neither should anyone else," General Alejandrino said.

"As long as you don't believe them, then there is nothing for me to explain." The general paused for a second, and then he said, "On second thought, what I just said are the words for reporters and busy bodies, but you are like my family so this is what I have to say."

Luna walked to the center of the room and faced his nine loyal officers. "Like Rizal, my brother and I were against any form of armed rebellion toward Spanish authority. The leadership of the Katipunan used our names to inspire others to join them and was the main reason we were arrested and sent to Fort Santiago."

The general took a deep breath and continued, "Once in jail, I was first whipped with a rattan belt for my silence. Later, they tortured me by pricking pins in each of my fingers every time I would not answer to the demands of my interrogators. And then, my fingers were placed between two iron clamps and tightened until I passed out. Once revived, they covered my head with a hood and with my hands tied behind my back, they kept me suspended in the air by my wrists with pulleys. They kept asking me questions that I had no answers for because I did not know much about the Katipunan and their armed rebellion. But they did not believe me and kept lifting and dropping me, which sent me crushing to the stone floor."

"When I heard them laughing that they could drop me all the way from the ceiling, I stopped being a pacifist and vowed to take my revenge as a revolutionary. But first I had to survive and so I began feeding them with lies and useless information that did not incriminate a fellow Filipino, especially my dear friend Rizal."

All nine officers stood at attention, saluted the general, and started clapping their hands in appreciation and loyalty.

A few minutes later, a vendor walked by carrying two bamboo cages of chickens for sale with one chicken nestled on a piece of cloth on top of his head for prospective buyers to see how fat and healthy they were.

"What are we having for dinner?" Colonel Roman asked Antonio.

"I'm not sure," General Luna replied. "I left that up to the cook."

"Most probably fried fish again, but I suddenly have the urge for a hot chicken dish," Colonel Roman said. "And I am willing to pay for the chicken."

"You would need more than one chicken to feed all of us," the general said.

"I will buy all the chickens that man is selling." Colonel Roman pointed to the vendor. "On one condition."

"And what is that?" Antonio asked.

"Hey, you guys, listen to this. General Alejandrino can attest to what I am about to say about our General Luna. He is the best shot in the whole darn country. He can shoot the chickens from that vendor's head from about twenty meters away."

"No way, maybe from a fixed target like an empty bottle of wine on top of a wall. Besides, that is crazy and although the Americanistas think of my general as a madman," Alejandrino laughed and pointed to Luna, "he is crazy enough for this."

"Did you just say you are buying all the chickens from the man selling them?" General Luna reiterated.

Roman nodded.

"Call the man," Luna said.

News of the sharp shooting challenge immediately swept like wildfire inside the perimeter of the camp, and in no time there were more than a hundred onlookers mingled together in curiosity.

The man selling chickens approached the group of officers and started trembling when told of the conditions to purchase his chickens. He was about to walk away when General Luna called him back and said, "You have nothing to worry about. If my father was alive today and he was in your position, he would not worry at all knowing that his son can shoot accurately, even blindfolded."

"No, sir, not blindfolded, please"

"Okay, no blindfold, only with my eyes closed. I am just kidding," Luna said and laughed. "All you have to do is to relax, close your eyes, don't move at all, and think of all the money you will be stuffing in your pockets in just a few seconds from now. By the way, I will have the chicken standing on your head instead of sitting down." He tapped the man with both hands on both of his shoulders and reassured him again.

The general pulled out his pistol, walked twenty paces away from the vendor, slowly turned around, and ordered everyone to keep quiet and not to move. The general took a deep breath, aimed, and fired one single shot. The man walked away a little bit shaken, but pleased with the monetary outcome. Besides fried fish, a flask of La Campana gin and three bottles of red wine, they all had chicken adobo and stew for dinner that evening.

General Luna, however, realizing that a large crowd of compatriots had gathered to witness his accuracy of handling a pistol under pressure called on all of them to come and move closer to right in front of his veranda. Based on an interview he made and posted in the local newspaper a few months earlier, Luna delivered a motivational speech for unity against the oppressors and to reaffirm his ideological stand and passionate belief to attain freedom for all Filipinos.

"Compatriots, fellow revolutionaries…" Luna paused when a sudden gust of wind blew in their direction.

"Compatriots, can you hear that wind blowing? It's like a song, the song of freedom heading toward our shore. We must continue fighting until all Filipinos are able to spread their wings and fly on their own."

The general was interrupted with loud cries of "*Mabuhay*, long live my general!"

The Filipino nation seeks its independence, and I will sustain the cause of my country until my last breath in compliance with the oath I made to my flag."

"I confess to you that it is always better to die in battle than to be under foreign rule. I say to you, we must not hide from fear, for it is the path to courage and glory in our struggle for liberty.

I have spoken to most of the generals, and they are all of the same mind. Our revolutionary forces, together with the people, will not deliver their arms or accept autonomy. I am sure of my beliefs because I have asked the people what they want." Luna raised his voice loud and clear. "Long live independence! May autonomy die!"

"Long live independence! May autonomy die!" the soldiers shouted repeatedly with pride.

"I hate war as much as anyone else. But for our freedom, it is necessary. The Americans understand what it's like to have to fight for freedom and why we rebel. It is because our war with America is no different from her war against England."

"Luna! Luna! Luna! Luna! Luna!" shouted all those gathered in front of their general. They shouted, mesmerized with glee, and some of them shed tears of happiness for their leader. Only after General Luna motioned for them to stop yelling his name did they became quiet.

"The Americanistas who favor a puppet government under the strings of the President of the United States. The Americanistas who demand that we surrender and give up our weapons. This is impossible because we have no trust in them nor America or their leaders. Our arms and passion for freedom are our only defense. Once we give them up, we lose our right to bear arms and instead will be leashed like dogs."

"We will not surrender! We will not surrender! Will not surrender!" The revolutionaries replied in unison.

"We have not won a single major battle since the war with the Americans began three months ago, but be patient. The monsoon rains will be upon us soon, and they will bring to us the winds of change that will turn the tide in our favor. Remember that we have a legion of armed patriots who know guerrilla warfare, and will be able to lead our motherland to victory!"

The crowd in front of Luna had continued to grow as he spoke. They all began to chant in deafening voices. "Death to the enemy! Death to the enemy! Death to the enemy!"

"We will win by our desire to never give up and be victorious! The Americans spend a large fortune every day to keep up their military in our domain. In addition, they are not used to the climate and lose men daily. We can sustain ourselves and exist on next to nothing. And in time and with patience, we will forbear, and they will be forced to give up.

"My fellow Filipinos, what will the Philippines be liked without you? Look around you, and believe in this war. Believe in what we are fighting for. They cannot break our spirit or our will because our principles lead us to fight for sovereignty. There is but one cry for Filipinos. Long Live Liberty! Long Live Freedom! And Long Live Independence!"

CHAPTER 70

On the morning of June 2, while at his headquarters in Bayambang, Pangasinan implementing guerrilla bases along the northern provinces of Luzon, General Luna received two telegrams. One was from Angeles in Pampanga Province summoning him to a conference to seek assistance and help in a counterattack operation against the Americans in San Fernando. And the other, supposedly signed by Aguinaldo was ordering him to come to headquarters, a convent at Cabanatuan, Nueva Ecija Province, to head a new cabinet.

Luna set off for Cabanatuan accompanied by his aides, Colonel Francisco Roman, Major Simeon Villa, Captain Eduardo Rusca, the brothers Major Manuel Bernal and Captain José Bernal, and twenty-five cavalrymen.

A few hours after departing from Pangasinan, a typhoon with powerful winds and rain hit the central and northern Luzon region. They took shelter for the night in a couple of *nipa* huts near a railroad station.

They traveled first by train, and then in three carriages and eventually, they continued on horseback. On the way, they came upon a bridge swept away by a strong river current caused by the torrential rains the night before. The rain had stopped and the sun was shining bright through pockets of openings in the sky. Since he was only going for a conference in the friendly and familiar surroundings of Nueva Ecija, the impatient general left his escorts at the bridge. This time with only Colonel Roman and Captain Rusca as escorts, General Luna continued on their journey with the intention for him to return and spend the night in Paniqui, Tarlac with Sidra.

Upon reaching the outskirts of Paniqui, Sidra saw him from a long way off. She had been waiting hours for her true love, Antonio to show up. She had planned on waiting until he got closer, but she couldn't resist and ran out in the road. "Antonio! Antonio! I cannot believe my eyes that you are here."

Antonio ran toward Sidra and when their bodies met, they embraced with such intensity that Sidra had to pull away slightly. "Antonio, you are holding me so tight, I cannot breathe."

"I cannot help myself," Antonio said. "I am so much in love and so excited to see you."

"Let's go inside the house," Sidra said. "I have something very important to tell you."

"Are you okay? Are you ill? Tell me," Antonio said.

Sidra smiled. "Nothing bad so don't worry."

They headed inside the house and Sidra made something for Antonio to eat and drink. Afterward, they sat next to each other, holding hands.

"So what is it you want to tell me?" Antonio said. "I don't want to wait any longer. You know how impatient I am."

"I hope you are as happy as I am." She paused. "Antonio, I am…we are going to have a baby."

For a moment, Antonio could hardly believe her words. And in a soft whisper, he asked, "A baby?"

This time Sidra laughed. "Yes."

Antonio embraced Sidra and then gave her a long, loving kiss.

"I am over the moon with happiness. You made me the most joyful man in the world!"

"So now you must stay safe for your new child," Sidra said.

Antonio kissed her again. "Yes, my love. But what do you want, a son or a daughter?"

"My only wish is for a healthy baby. I don't mind having either a boy or a girl. What about you?"

"I agree, a healthy baby first, but I would like a boy to follow in his Papa's footsteps," Luna said with pride.

Later in bed, Luna was so dead tired after making love to Sidra that he dropped like a log asleep in her arms. She stared for what seemed like hours at the face of the soon-to-be father of her child. She dozed off only to be awoken by the splattering of heavy raindrops on the roof.

She rose from bed to close the window, but instead of returning to Antonio, she cracked open the window a few inches and watched the rainfall outside. She had always looked forward to the start of the monsoon season and knew that this downpour had no signs of letting up. And by the rains, she would never forget the night she had told him she was pregnant.

A short time later, Antonio woke for a bit. He was so excited that he jumped out of bed onto the floor. He promised her and God that he would be a good father and a husband and asked her to marry him. She had never been so happy and thanked God for making her wait so long for the right man to come along. Now, after he returned to bed, she smiled with tears of joy streaming from her eyes like the falling rain.

The next day was sunny, and the sky appeared much sharper and brighter than normal. A solitary arc the color of a rainbow reflected the sun. It was a beginning of a new day to start a new life with the man and baby of her life as she rested both hands on her belly, and with her relationship to the general no longer a secret, and with his marriage proposal, she took a deep breath of relief.

"Are you worried" Antonio asked as he held her in full embrace.

"No, I just think that there will never be a day like this again." Sidra sobbed and clung to him tightly, unwilling to let go.

She shook her head. Her black hair loosened at the back of her shoulders. "I lied. I am really worried." However, having become accustomed to sad farewells, Sidra was ready, hurtful as it was, to let duty have his way.

"You don't need to worry about me. I promised you last night that I will be back as the Philippines second-most powerful man, next only to Aguinaldo. And the first thing I'll do is talk with your father and mother and ask for their blessings to marry you," Antonio said.

He then removed the red sash full of gold coins his mother had given him, the same one that saved his life, and gave it to Sidra.

"Here take this and spend it wisely for our child's future."

On his way out, he kissed Sidra on her lips, hugged her for what seemed an eternity, kissed her exposed shoulders once, and said goodbye.

"Antonio," Sidra cried our loud enough for him to turn around on his horse. "People say you are crazy and a madman out of control, but they don't know you my love. You have a big heart, and to me, you are a living patriot and a most honorable man."

Although her voice trailed away, the scent of her body and the sweetness of her lips remained on Antonio as he rode away to meet his destiny. She tearfully waved goodbye to her everlasting love, kissed her own exposed shoulder, on the same spot her lover had just kissed earlier and in a whisper said, "Travel safely, my love, and may God be with you."

CHAPTER 71

On the road to Cabanatuan, two barefooted Franciscan friars in dark brown wool robes carrying a statue of the Virgin Mary, Our Lady of Lourdes, walked ahead of Luna and his men.

"Why are they walking without shoes?" Colonel Paco Roman asked.

"They belong to the Order of the Friars Minor, also known as the Discalced, Capuchin, and the Recollects," Captain Rusca replied.

He further explained. "The roses peering out from the bottom of the Virgin's white mantel signifies the souls she protects. It's a good omen, so you see, we are in good hands for having seen her."

"Thanks, now I feel better," Paco Roman replied.

"We can only hope for the best and see what lies ahead of us," General Luna said.

On that same day, June 5, they arrived at General Aguinaldo's Cabanatuan headquarters office located in the second floor of a convent. About a dozen presidential guards mulled about anxiously. General

Luna proceeded to the second floor alone. As he went up the stairs, he ran into the hated Felipe Buencamino.

Buencamino told Luna that General Aguinaldo had to leave for San Isidro in Tarlac Province. Enraged, General Luna asked why he had not been told the meeting was canceled. As he was about to depart, a single shot from a rifle on the plaza rang out.

Outraged, and furious that the Americans may have fired the shot at one of his aides waiting by the entrance to the plaza, Antonio Luna rushed down the stairs but was met by Captain Pedro Janolino, whom he had previously disarmed for cowardice. He was accompanied by some of the same Kawit troops that Luna had previously dismissed for insubordination.

Captain Janolino swung his bolo at Luna, wounding him at the temple above the left ear. At the same time, Janolino's cohorts fired at General Luna. Others stabbed him, even as he tried to bring his revolver to bear. He staggered out to the plaza uttering, "Cowards, Assassins, Traitors!" He dropped to the cobblestone floor of the plaza.

Colonel Román and Captain Rusca rushed to his aid, but they too were shot and ran for cover behind the side wall of the convent.

Captain Rusca said, "I've been hit on my right leg."

"You won't get anywhere with that wound. Run and save yourself while I can still cover for you." Colonel Roman ordered Captain Rusca. "And let everyone know what happened here."

Although shot in the leg, Captain Rusca managed to escape and elude the assassins, but not until being grazed in the forehead by another bullet. He managed to crawl toward the church portals and escaped for his life. Captain Roman finally out of bullets ran to the house of Colonel Sityar to seek help.

"Manuel, Manuel, where are you? I need help," Paco Roman called hysterically.

Colonel Sityar heard Paco Roman coming to seek refuge at his house, jumped out of the window and pressed himself against the wall out of sight. He muttered. "Oh! Paco, why did you have to be on the wrong side of the fence? I am so sorry… so sorry, but I can not help you. You're a good man and may God bless you."

Colonel Roman walked out of the house brandishing his sword and tried to escape but was killed by two assassins. They shot him in the back the moment he stepped out of the front door. He dropped his sword and fell on his knees, dead. One of the assassins walked toward his lifeless body and stepped at the back of his uniform to extinguished the flames caused by being shot at such a close range. He was only thirty years old.

As Antonio Luna laid dying with blood gushing from multiple wounds from his badly butchered body, deadly cold and scattered look in his eyes, numb and emotionless; he knew it was all over. He felt his heart sink, like his soul and fighting spirit had been emptied. He heard voices coming from his assassin's transition to that of his departed father and brother Manuel consoling him. He thought of his beloved Sidra and mother. Their image in mourning imprinted in his mind.

He silently whispered to himself, *"No llores por mi, Madre mia. No llores por mi Sidra porque te amo mucho."* (Don't cry for me my mother. Don't cry for me my Sidra because I love you so much."). From the corners of his teary eyes, he saw Captain Janolino with a pistol on hand about to fire a final shot at his head that would silence him forever.

The local townsfolk, for fear of reprisal, would not even dare to get close to his body as it lay on the plaza under the heat of the sun for about an hour. The assassins gave up on their search for the injured Captain Rusca and returned to the plaza as some of them began verbally insulting the general while stabbing his dead body all over again with a machete and at the same time looting his boots, pistol, and saber.

"Stop, stop, whatever you are doing and leave his body alone," Colonel Sityar yelled. "I have a telegram, a direct order from President Aguinaldo."

"What are his orders?" Buencamino asked, who by now had stepped out of the convent to join the crowd gathered at the plaza.

"That they deserved to be fully honored and buried with a military funeral merited to all officers and gentlemen," Colonel Sityar said.

"Very well." Buencamino ordered the presidential guards from Kawit, the same men who had just mutilated the general's body earlier. "Remove any letters or telegrams in their possession and give them to me. And then take their bodies inside church and lay them on the floor by the altar until the funeral services tomorrow morning."

After their bodies were wrapped in an old tattered floor mat to carry inside the church, the telegram Luna got telling him to report to Cabanatuan and the letter he had written for his mother a few nights before his assassination were removed from his uniform.

On the morning of the day after the murder of Luna and Roman, the two officers and friends of the revolution, their bodies wrapped with the flag of the Philippine Republic, were buried at the church yard in two shallow graves, side by side, and with full military honors as his assassins stood guard.

PART III

CHAPTER 72

Sidra waited for Antonio the whole day in anticipation of their trip to her parent's house to announce their wedding plans. By sunset, she had not yet given up hope for his return, but by nightfall, she was miserable when there was no sign of him. She was up the whole night thinking of what might have become of him. Was he ambushed and killed by the Americans or held captive by them? She was crazy with worry.

Scrunched up in bed that night, her thoughts percolated from Antonio's welfare to the first time he made love to her until slowly drifting away to sleep by midnight. Within two hours, she was awakened by the sound of thunder and flashes of lightning.

It started to rain and the wind was blowing harder than normal. She suddenly got up from bed because she thought she heard her lover calling her name. She rushed downstairs upon hearing a knock on the door. It was only a window left opened and being blown by the wind creating the sound, but maybe not she thought. She opened the front door and stepped out. There was nothing out there but rain, wind, and darkness. She remained glued to her sight, for she was positive Antonio had called her name until brought back to her senses by her housekeeper.

"My girl, you're all wet. Get back inside so I can close the door," the housekeeper said.

"Senorita Sidra, what made you go out in the rain? Wait here and I'll get you a towel."

"I thought I heard my Antonio calling my name," Sidra said.

The housekeeper came back with a fresh towel and nightgown. She dried her and assisted her back to bed and reassured her that Antonio would be back first thing in the morning.

The following day, she woke up to the sun coming in brightly through her windows. She was smiling and knew in her heart that she would soon see her beloved, Antonio. How could she not be happy when she had a brave and handsome man to love her passionately and raise a beautiful family with.

She was beaming, and her excitement grew when she went to the window because she heard hoof beats in the distance coming toward the house. She immediately grabbed her hair brush and in front of a mirror fixed her hair to make sure she was pretty enough to receive him. She even changed her mind about them seeing her parents. All she wanted was to stay in his arms and make love to him the whole day and night. And then she tore open the door and rushed out of the house to receive her beloved Antonio. That's when she saw the carriage with three people on board heading toward her house.

But she was disappointed when she recognized her brother Dencio and his wife, Becca accompanied by their housekeeper in the carriage.

"Good morning, and glad to see you." Sidra lied and peeked inside the carriage as if she was looking for someone. "I thought you were Antonio."

Her brother looked sadly at his sister. "Can we come in?"

"What's wrong, Dencio?" Sidra asked.

"Let's go inside where we can talk," Becca said.

"Why? What's going on? You know something about Antonio."

Becca took Sidra's arm, but Sidra pulled away. "Tell me now, please. You are making me so nervous that something is wrong."

"Come inside," Dencio begged.

"No, it cannot be. It's not true. He promised to return," she cried and dropped down onto the steps leading inside the house.

Becca sat down next to Sidra and held her when Dencio explained that Antonio Luna was killed by the Kawit Presidential Guards of the President in Cabanatuan. She became hysterical and fainted.

When Sidra awoke, she said in a hushed voice as if speaking to Antonio, "You promised to make me laugh, not to cry."

"Don't worry, Sidra," her sister-in-law said. "After some time, you will find another man you can love and cherish."

"No, I will never love another man. I only love my Antonio."

"Time will help to heal you. You will find love again. I promise," Becca said.

Sidra cried out. "You don't understand, I'm pregnant. I'm going to have Antonio's baby."

"Oh Sidra," Becca said. "How wonderful."

"No, not anymore. We were planning to be married. He was going to talk to our parents tonight," she said to Dencio. "Now the whole world just turned upside down for me. There is nothing more to live for," Sidra cried out.

"You're wrong. You are bearing his son," Becca said. "You are carrying Antonio Luna's future and his destiny."

"No, my Antonio is gone from me," Sidra said in tears.

"No," Becca said. "Because you have his baby inside of you, your love, Antonio will be with you forever."

Although her lover was gone eternally Sidra found it hard to believe that she will never hear Antonio speak again, nor smile and laugh at her again. All she thought about were their nostalgic moments together, how much he cared for her. She grasped onto her memories of him and was determined that he would never be just a figment of her imagination. She memorized the sound of his voice. She vowed to never stop loving him. She adored the man.

CHAPTER 73

On the same day and about the same time of the funeral services of General Luna and his aide, a wire telegraph was sent on President Aguinaldo's behalf to all five northern provincial military commanders. With no mentioned of Luna's assassination the orders within the telegram were effective immediately, stating that he would be directing all military operations. He also stated that he was temporarily moving his headquarters to Bamban, Tarlac. President Aguinaldo's credibility later was suspect when it came out that General Venancio Conception of Pampanga province received the same telegram, but a day early, about the same time of the assassination.

Meanwhile, on the same morning of the funeral, the American forces having just captured the town of Antipolo and satisfied with the direction of the war in the south of Manila met at the Malacanang Palace headquarters of General Otis to plan their military operations in the conquest of all towns and garrisons being held by the Filipinos, south of Manila from the Pacific coast in the west to all of Laguna de

Bay in the east. General MacArthur, who normally was the first one to arrive during these meetings, came late. He barged excitedly into the meeting room "Have you heard what happened to General Luna?"

"No, what?" General Otis asked bewildered.

"It is the main reason I am late. I had to double check the validity of the report. General Luna was assassinated. Yes, murdered by the presidential bodyguards of Aguinaldo yesterday afternoon in Cabanatuan."

"You have confirmed this news?" General Otis asked.

"Yes, I am positive. He was a victim of power politics." MacArthur proceeded to narrate exactly how the incident occurred as told to him by a pro-American autonomist.

"I don't know what to say. I have very mixed emotions toward the man. On one hand, we hit him with everything but the kitchen sink and he kept coming back. On the other hand, he is now gone forever and we are left with the knowledge that we failed to completely annihilate the man in battle."

"I foresee a complete demoralization among the ranks and file of their military forces in the north. Should we review our military strategy now that General Luna is out of the picture?" General MacArthur asked.

"No, in fact I would prefer we go for the kill," Otis said.

"But with the hawkish general gone and Aguinaldo's cabinet under the leadership of our autonomous sympathizers, why not offer them a peaceful way out?" MacArthur countered.

"Ah! Ah! *Divide et impera*, which is Latin for divide and conquer. We will follow the lead of Julius Caesar and take advantage of the loss of General Luna by seeking out his loyal sympathizers and assist them in avenging the death of their beloved general in the capture and torture of Aguinaldo."

"Now back to our original agenda, the capture of Filipino garrisons from the coast of Cavite to the banks of Laguna Bay," General Otis said.

He looked at Generals Henry Lawton and Lloyd Wheaton and inquired, "What's the latest update on your Southern command?"

"We have started deploying all our forces and set camp in the vast open fields of San Pedro de Macati," General Lawton reported.

"How many men do you expect to gather at Macati?" General Otis asked.

"About 4,500 troops in 20:00 hours," General Wheaton replied.

"We should begin to advance our forces no later than 07:00 hours on June 11 and enter Cavite through Las Pinas by 09:00 on June 13," General Lawton added.

"Do you expect any resistance from the Filipino forces?" MacArthur asked.

"Our intelligence reported possible skirmish from enemy soldiers guarding a tiny bridge in Zapote," General Hughes said.

"We will just roll over them," General Wheaton commented.

"Remember, this battle can crush the insurrection once and for all. Anything else pending or any other questions?"

"All I can say," General Robert Hughes said, "is that the Filipinos only had one general, and they have killed him."

The Americans developed an astonished admiration for General Luna—so much so that they stood for a minute in silence for the repose of his soul.

However, the reign of terror did not end in one day. Loyalty checks among military ranks and file were carried out by Aguinaldo's men, and anyone known to have been loyal to General Luna was purged. They were detained, tortured, or killed, as in the case of Major Manuel Bernal, who was liquidated. His younger brother, Captain José Bernal, was imprisoned and released, but then he was assassinated during a secret military mission.

The tragic demise of Antonio Luna at age thirty-three, the most brilliant and capable of the Filipino generals, was a decisive factor in the fight against the American forces. The retaliation, coming from officers and men who sympathized with General Luna, was simply to bolt the revolutionary army and organize their own unit, *Guardia de Honor* (Guard of Honor), to continue fighting the Americans and avenge the death of their beloved general.

But the heaviest blow to the revolutionary movement was the disgruntled soldiers from General Luna's home region of Ilocos and Pampanga, especially the Macabebes. Their ancestors were Yaqui Indians, also known as Yoeme from the valley of Rio Yaqui in Mexico. They were brought into the Philippines by the Spaniards and for their proven loyalty were given land in the region and in time the Yaquis intermarried with the local Kapampangan natives.

When Spain surrendered to the Unites States, the Macabebes switched their allegiance to General Antonio Luna and his Philippine revolutionary northern forces until his assassination. Disenchanted, they approached and were accepted by the Americans to serve under them in fighting the diminishing forces of President Emilio Aguinaldo.

Eight days after the death of General Antonio Luna, the bloodiest, largest, and crucial battle of the war occurred at Zapote Bridge. The struggle was in a deserted area of the Cavite province, commonly referred to as *El Desierto*, an area covered with high grasslands and rice fields.

The battle started when about one thousand Filipino soldiers stood ground in defending the tiny bridge from two advancing companies of American forces under Major Boyle. Both sides immediately called for reinforcements: five thousand Filipinos and four thousand Americans in total.

By noon, the Filipinos led by Generals Artemio Ricarte and Mariano Noriel, fighting with an arsenal of obsolete firepower, slowly started withdrawing to the rear when the big accurate field cannon artilleries and American gunboats pounded on strategic Filipino positions. They were followed by a number of properly positioned Colt rapid-firing machine guns, which started to take a toil on the Filipinos who had no such weapons of mass destruction.

By the end of the day, the invading United States forces under Major General Henry Ware Lawton started to drive the Filipino freedom fighters out of the their trenches until finally withdrawing further inland.

The battle at Zapote River was a decisive victory for the Americans that made President Emilio Aguinaldo finally realize that the only way to continue fighting the foreign invaders was the way the late General Luna suggested to him from the very beginning of the war. Luna had wanted to engage the Americans by establishing pockets of guerrilla units all throughout the country. But now it was too late to follow what General Luna advised.

CHAPTER 74

Juan Luna was in Paris when he heard about Antonio's murder. He exploded in rage, and was so horrified and grief-stricken, that he abandoned his duties as a member of the delegation to Washington, DC to press for the recognition of the Philippine government.

Juan wanted revenge in the worst way. He began patronizing the *salas de armas* clubs of Paris once more in order to sharpen his self-defense skills in order to get even with his brother's assassins.

At night, however, he would lock himself alone in his hotel room with a deep feeling of loss and sorrow. That was until the evening of Bastille Day when all of Paris celebrated their freedom from monarchial rule with military parades, communal meals and binge drinking all day long,

Felix Roxas stood holding a bottle of chilled French champagne outside Luna's hotel room not far from Rue de Rivoli.

Caucasian looking, but of Spanish descent, Roxas was seven years younger than Juan Luna, and had moved to Paris from Manila three years earlier. He was a civil engineer turned lawyer who was overshadowed by his father, Felix, the first Filipino architect. The Roxas family owned haciendas and large tracks of land in Batangas Province.

"Juan! Juan! It's me Felix, Felix Roxas and not the other Felix, the boring and unattractive painter," the fair-skinned, baby-faced Roxas screamed loud enough for Juan to hear him from his second floor hotel room window.

But Juan Luna sat staring blankly at the wall as if in a trance.

"Hey, let me in. It's the craziest time of the year in Paris to go out hunting for women," Roxas yelled up.

Roxas went up without being invited. Once inside the unkept and messy room that smelled like sweat, he saw Juan. There was an innocence about him that made Roxas wonder what was on the mind of this once great Filipino genius of an artist. Roxas popped the champagne cork and spent an hour convincing Juan to join him for an evening of fun and boisterous parties and dances that Bastille Day was always known for.

"I see no reason why you should stay all alone tonight," Roxas pleaded to Juan after extending his last glass of champagne, having emptied the bottle in no time at all.

In what seemed almost an apologetic, and sad expression, Juan Luna agreed to go out drinking with Roxas, much to his shock as if a miracle had occurred.

Felix Roxas and the other Felix, the painter Hidalgo, were the only two people Juan Luna liked and continued to communicate with in Paris since the death of Antonio over a month earlier.

The summer of 1899 in Paris was notably hot, even at night. Roxas and Luna walked past so many bars along the Rue du 4 Septembre to drink, and for the chance to meet some willing Mesdemoiselles. They got as far as Rue Vivienne when they came upon two young Parisians, who accepted their invitation to drink, dance and enjoy the remaining hours of Bastille Day.

Although not beautiful, they were both slender and young, and without a wrinkle of blemish on their skin. Roxas felt great seeing his friend, Juan leaning in very close to the shorter girl of the two, chatting and laughing his heart out as in years past. Or were the bottles of French champagne and red wine they consumed the cause for Juan's fun as they danced the night away, which culminated in sweet embraces for both couples.

In the autumn of the same year, Felipe Roxas asked Juan Luna to accompany him to a party given by a famous Italian contralto, Madame Bertrami. Juan Luna was so impressed and practically in tears listening to her sing Bach's, Erbame Dich. Her voice moved with ease from the low female singing voice to the upper regions.

After her performance Roxas and Luna invited her for drinks at the exclusive Restaurant Payet.

"Oh, I would love to but only if two of my friends could join us," Madame Bertrami said obligingly.

"Of course, it would be our honor to have you as our guest at the Restaurant Payet," Roxas said.

"Lovely, let me introduce you to my friends," Madame Bertrami said. "Ladies, come here. I want you both to meet these two good looking gentlemen."

The two women looked Roxas and Juan Luna up and down.

"Gentlemen, this is Camille, my favorite French pianist," Madame Bertraimi said.

Roxas recognized her earlier from when she was behind the piano and was enamored by her at first glance.

"And this is the lovely Lara, a soprano and my close friend from Russia," Madame Bertrami said.

Juan felt a knot in his stomach twist like a corkscrew the moment he focused his eyes on Lara—the Russian soprano was the spitting image—more like a reincarnation of Maria Paz. A scalding breath of desire for Lara hit him as the five of them headed for Payet. They drank all night long so that by two in the morning Juan Luna was dead drunk and out of control.

"Lara, you are as beautiful as my late wife. If you ever marry I hope you will faithful to your husband." Luna began recounting his personal tragedy at Rue Pergolese to the group, but especially directed to Lara. "You see Lara, I loved my wife so much. The thought of her being with another man hurt me so much."

"Juan, I believe Lara gets the point and understands how you feel," Roxas said, but at the same time attempted to change the subject of conversation.

Juan shook his head. "No, No, I don't want Lara to end up like Maria Paz. She needs to know—"

Roxas abruptly interrupted Luna. "Excuse me ladies, but we need to go to the toilette."

When Roxas forcibly pulled Luna away from the group and towards the toilette the three ladies grabbed their coats and purses and practically ran out of the restaurant scared and in complete shock.

"Where is Lara? I need to find her," Juan said when he staggered back to their table and discovered the ladies were gone.

"No, Juan, you need to find your bed. You've had too much to drink. I'll take you home."

"Maria Paz, why? I loved you so much, Maria Paz. Why… why..." Luna slurred his words while Roxas dragged him out of Payet and into a carriage.

For Luna, the chance to spend all the time he could to visit the graves of his beloved Maria Paz and lovely Bibi was the only reason he stayed in Paris. But he missed his son Andres, and the call to continue what Antonio had started were the emotional magnets that pulled him to return to the Philippines.

Roxas and Hidalgo dropped by to say good-bye and see him off at the train station. As a going away present, Hidalgo gave him his personal revolver. He was worried that Luna may also be a target of an assassination by Antonio's enemies when he returned to Manila.

From a distance, the façade of Gare du Nord looked like one of so many triumphal arches made of stone slabs found all over Paris. The U-shaped terminal building crowned with majestic statues along the cornice line and whose main beams and pillars were made out of cast iron for support brought back memories of Rizal and Antonio.

By coincidence, inside the terminal a group of Filipinos stood waiting for someone. One of them recognized Juan Luna and called out, "Don Juan, for the sake of our country, do not avenge the death of Antonio!"

"Fuck you, traitors! Juan Luna screamed back in anger.

Felix Roxas immediately managed to restrain Luna from confronting the group but not until he himself turned and shouted back, "Fuck you, brown Americans."

CHAPTER 75

Juan Luna traveled back to the Philippines in November 1899. As the steamship entered the Hong Kong harbor, Juan knew that he would be in the Philippines in a few days. He longed to see his son, Andres, who he had not seen in more than a year. But in all honesty, the only real thing on his mind was revenge.

The smell of smoke, fried fish, and fish balls being sold by sidewalk vendors along the harbor mingled with uncollected garbage on the streets greeted him as he hailed for the first rickshaw. The island of Hong Kong reminded Juan Luna very much of Manila. As a child growing up in the commercial district of Binondo, he and his brothers would run around the vicinity mingling with hundreds of sweaty Chinese coolies, some half naked, scattered along busy streets balancing heavy loads on a bamboo poles. He remembered hearing the loud clacking sound of wooden sandals of the people in the street. Chinese amahs, in trousers walking, as if on tiptoe, across the cobblestone streets, in tiny cloth shoes.

Once inside the hotel room, Luna looked outside the French windows of his bedroom, where he gazed upon the harbor, multi-colored sampans and square-sailed junks displaying colors of red, white and yellow sails. Looking down the alleyways and streets he could not help but stare at the mushroom of overflowing stalls of vendors selling silks, jade, and bamboo products.

One thing Luna desired from Hong Kong was their authentic Chinese Cantonese and Mandarin foods, which tasted much better than the Chinese food served in Paris and even more so than what he used to get in Madrid.

Rushing out from his hotel room to get to the nearest Chinese restaurant recommended by the hotel's desk clerk, Juan Luna, bumped into a couple of Filipinos. It did not take but only two hours for TH Pardo to learn that Juan Luna was in town and staying at the Imperial Hotel.

After dinner, Juan Luna returned to his hotel room and found a flask of red wine on top of his drawer table with a note attached, "Compliments of the Hotel." He drank almost half the bottle when he began to feel sharp pains in his chest just above his stomach. He laid down, and wondered if the wine was not reacting well with the Mu Shu pork, Pancit Canton stir fry noodles, and the hot and spicy soup he had consumed for dinner earlier.

"Oh, my God, how do I get rid of my stomach ache?" Luna mumbled to himself as he tossed from side to side on his bed thinking that there must be some logical explanation to what he felt.

"Maybe, I am just tired," he thought. "I just need to close my eyes, to rest, and go to sleep."

But his body became more and more disabled and in great pain. His heart pounded so hard in his chest and his legs began to shake uncontrollably. And when the heartburn and excruciating chest pains worsened he felt cold and started to shiver.

Juan began to panic. "What's going on? I feel like I am having a stroke. Could I be dying?"

"I hope not," he mumbled. "And if so, please God, get rid of all the demons polluting my mind." He took a deep breath and contemplated for a second. "And to those I have hurt and offended, my sincere apology, please forgive me."

Juan attempted to get up from bed and call for help. But a severe drowsiness took over him. The cold shivers and excruciating pain prevented him from moving. He was glued to his bed. Thoughts of death and visions of Antonio calling him made him feel like he was losing his mind. He had journeyed to his homeland to avenge his brother and now, he was going to join him in death.

Juan thought one last time of Maria Paz and Bibi and Andres, and soon, his thoughts took him further back to his childhood with his brothers and parents, when all their dreams and ambitions were still ahead of them. Juan gently closed his eyes and never opened them again.

The cleaning lady discovered his body in the morning. It was rumored that Juan Luna might have been poisoned since his brother-in-law, who had a motive for revenge, was also in Hong Kong. Being a doctor, TH Pardo assisted in the autopsy conducted by the Hong Kong medical examiners.

The official statement given by Dr. Pardo to the Hong Kong press was that Juan Luna, the famous Filipino painter died at the age of 42 of a heart failure on December 7, 1899 en route to his motherland, the Philippines.

EPILOGUE

Juan Luna became the greatest Filipino painter that ever lived. He achieved numerous international recognitions from the finest salons of Europe, but foremost, his name will be associated with the *Spoliarium*, his spectacular masterpiece on display at the National Museum in Manila.

General Antonio will forever be remembered for his fighting spirit and relentless patriotism. His efforts to free the Philippines from American rule gave him the reputation for being the greatest general of the Philippine military, an honor that is still recognized today. His legacy as a capable and efficient soldier, as well as a scientist, all left their mark in his country.

Dr. Jose Rizal became the national hero of the Philippines. His books, poetry, courage, determination, and educational and intellectual deeds awakened Filipino national consciousness and spirit to pursue freedom and liberty.

Sidra Gantuanco recovered the remains of her secret lover and after exhuming his body, buried him in Tarlac. She gave birth to a boy and named him Antonio but she gave the baby to her brother, Dencio to raise as one of his own sons. When Sidra died in 1960 at the age of 93, she was buried together with the bones of her one and only lover, Antonio Luna.

General Arthur MacArthur was appointed by President William McKinley to become the Military-Governor for the Philippines. He replaced the unpopular General Elwell Otis. He ordered Colonel Frederick Funston to hunt down President Aguinaldo.

General Emilio Aguinaldo suffered successive and disastrous losses in the field of battle over the next eighteen months. As a result, he was forced to retreat toward Palanan in Isabela Province. With the assistance of Luna loyalist Macabebe Scouts from Pampanga Province, he was captured on 23 March 1901. He was released from prison only after declaring allegiance to the United States. He was accused for collaboration with the Japanese at the end of the Second World War, and was sent to Bilibid Prison. Arthur's son, General Douglas MacArthur wanted him hanged. But Manuel Roxas, the President of the new Philippine Republic, had him pardoned.

General Henry Ware Lawton, who as a young Captain during the Indian Wars in the United States was credited in capturing the Apache chief Geronimo, would later be shot and killed by a lone Filipino sharpshooter, ironically under the command of General Licerio Geronimo at the Battle of Paye, southeast of Manila. General Lawton was the highest ranking-American commander to be killed in action in both the Philippine and Spanish wars with the United States.

Finally, in July 1902 the Philippine-American War officially ended with over 7,000 U.S. soldiers, 20,000 Filipino soldiers, and 100,000 Filipino civilians dead and wounded. The New York Times recorded the Filipino army to be the largest and best organized body of men the American troops ever fought.

My Last Farewell

~Dr. José P. Rizal

Translation by Charles Derbyshire, 1911

Farewell, dear Fatherland, clime of the sun caress's,
Pearl of the Orient seas, our Eden lost!
Gladly now I go to give thee this faded life's best,
And were it brighter, fresher, or more blest
Still would I give it thee, nor count the cost.

On the field of battle, 'mid the frenzy of fight,
Others have given their lives, without doubt or heed;
The place matters not—cypress or laurel or lily white
Scaffold or open plain, combat or martyrdom's plight,
'Tis ever the same, to serve our home and country's need.

I die just when I see the dawn break,
Through the gloom of night, to herald the day;
And if color is lacking my blood thou shalt take,
Pour'd out at need for thy dear sake,
To dye with its crimson the waking ray.

My dreams, when life first opened to me,
My dreams, when the hopes of youth beat high,
Were to see thy lov'd face, O gem of the Orient sea,
From gloom and grief, from care and sorrow free
No blush on thy brow, no tear in thine eye.

Dream of my life, my living and burning desire,
All hail! cries the soul that is now to take flight;
All hail! And sweet it is for thee to expire;
To die for thy sake, that thou mayst aspire;
And sleep in thy bosom eternity's long night.

If over my grave some day thou seest grow,
In the grassy sod, a humble flower,
Draw it to thy lips and kiss my soul so,
While I may feel on my brow in the cold tomb below
The touch of thy tenderness, thy breath's warm power.

Let the moon beam over me soft and serene,
Let the dawn shed over me its radiant flashes,
Let the wind with sad lament over me keen;
And if on my cross a bird should be seen,
Let it trill there its hymn of peace to my ashes.

Let the sun draw the vapors up to the sky,
And heavenward in purity bear my tardy protest;
Let some kind soul o'er my untimely fate sigh
And in the still evening a prayer be lifted on high
From thee, O my country, that in God, I may rest.

Pray for all those that hapless have died,
For all who have suffered the unmeasur'd pain;
For our mothers that bitterly their woes have cried,
For widows and orphans, for captives by torture tried,
And then for thyself that redemption thou mayst gain.

And when the dark night wraps the graveyard around
With only the dead in their vigil to see,
Break not my repose or the mystery profound,
And perchance thou mayst hear a sad hymn resound;
'Tis I, O my country, raising a song unto thee.

And even my grave is remembered no more,
Unmark'd by never a cross nor a stone,
Let the plow sweep through it, the spade turn it o'er
That my ashes may carpet the earthly floor,
Before into nothingness at last they are blown.

Then will oblivion bring to me no care,
As over thy vales and plains I sweep;
Throbbing and cleansed in thy space and air
With color and light, with song and lament I fare,
Ever repeating the faith that I keep.

My Fatherland ador'd, that sadness to my sorrow lends;
Beloved Filipinas, hear now my last good-by!
I give thee all: parents and kindred and friends,
For I go where no slave before the oppressor bends,
Where faith can never kill, and God reigns e'er on high!

Farewell to you all, from my soul torn away,
Friends of my childhood in the home dispossessed!
Give thanks that I rest from the wearisome day!
Farewell to thee, too, sweet friend that lightened my way;
Beloved creatures all, farewell! In death there is rest!

Acknowledgements

I would like to offer thanks to several people for various reasons known to me and to them: Elizabeth Crespo, Bob Garcia, Sabsy Palanca, Butch Belgica, Myles Garcia, Angel Ortiz, Adrian Gomez, Juan Del Gallego and Lorenzo Maria Guerrero III.

I thank Buddy Abello and Joey Valenzuela for going out of their way in taking me to museums and various historical sites in the Philippines.

To Raffy Esteva, I am grateful for his contribution to the life of his great grandfather Eugenio Hernando.

To Ricardo Ongpin, great grandson of Jose Luna, my appreciation for sharing his knowledge and photos of his great granduncles Juan and Antonio Luna.

My gratitude to Charles Derbyshire for his beautiful and poetic translation into English, during the early part of the 20th century, of some of Rizal's words used in their entirety in this novel.

During my research, I consulted valuable published sources. Among them were 100 Years of the Paris Trib, La Vanguardia 1892, 1898 and 1899 issues, Rizal by Austin Coates, From Indio to Filipino by Domingo Abella, Little Brown Brother by Leon Wolff and Juan Luna, the Filipino as Painter by Santiago Albano Pilar.

Special recognition to Vivencio T. Jose, author of the Rise and Fall of Antonio Luna by for his vivid and entirely compelling account of General Luna and the Philippine-American War; and to my cousin Mike Ripoll for introducing me to the book.

I am grateful to Esperanza Navarette of the Academia Royal de Bellas Artes San Fernando for making their "Bibliographia" available to me.

To Karen Coccioli, my thanks for her guidance, insights, thoughtful and superb editing of my manuscript.

To my daughter Penny Delgallego, my gratitude for the cover design, illustrations, E-book and hardcover format.

Finally, to my wife Eileen, my deepest appreciation for her patience, advise, support and encouragement.

About The Author

Born and raised in Manila, Philippines, Jules Delgallego was educated under the Benedictine and Dominican friars for sixteen years where he developed his love for history and the arts. Delgallego's personal history was his motivation for completing his novel. Both his grandfathers served in the Spanish colonial military forces and his wife's great granduncle, Jose Burgos was a martyred Filipino hero and priest. Numerous other family members and friends were descendants of the Luna brothers as well as some of the major characters in the book. Delgallego currently resides in San Diego, California with his wife.

Made in the USA
Charleston, SC
05 January 2014